Roanoke

Roanoke

MARGARET LAWRENCE

DELACORTE PRESS

ROANOKE

A Delacorte Press Book / February 2009

Published by Bantam Dell
A Division of Random House, Inc.
New York, New York

Book design by Diane Hobbing of Snap-Haus Graphics

Delacorte Press is a registered trademark of Random House, Inc., and the colophon is a trademark of Random House, Inc.

Library of Congress Cataloging-in-Publication Data

Lawrence, Margaret (Margaret K.)
Roanoke / Margaret Lawrence.
p. cm.
ISBN 978-0-385-34237-7 (hardcover)
1. Roanoke Colony—Fiction. 2. Roanoke Island (N.C.)—History—16th century—Fiction.
I. Title.
PS3562.A9133R63 2008
813'.54—dc22
2008019770

Printed in the United States of America
Published simultaneously in Canada

www.bantamdell.com

BVG   10 9 8 7 6 5 4 3 2 1

Roanoke

I

one

Blood and Pearls, *OR* How It Began

THE LAST DAY OF SHROVETIDE, A DAMP FEBRUARY IN THE YEAR 1585, great Elizabeth's twenty-seventh year upon the throne. A small rain falling. A tender rain, veiling London's scars.

The streets and lanes round St. Paul's throbbed with stiltwalkers and fire-swallowers and pancake sellers and herb women and ratcatchers, all frantic to snatch the last bit of pleasure and meat pie they'd get until Lent was over. A delirium of smells—roast goose, Shrove buns, early flowers brought in from the country, cinnamon and cloves in the spice merchants' barrels. Chimney smoke. Sour piss in the gutters. Sounds, too—damp silk banners flapping from diamond-paned casements, chickens gaggling, dogs barking, a bookseller beating a thief. Street cries, high and low, overlapping each other in a sharp staccato. "Pails! Any pails to mend?" "Buy new broom, buy new broom, sweep and clean!" "Today's broadsides, master! Penny each, latest Irish atrocities!" And music, of course. There was always music—fragile, rowdy, bawdy, tender. Lute players and flute players and little boys with tin whistles. Whores young and old. Beggars. Dwarves. Gypsies. Giants. Players in fusty wigs and cast-off velvets. Mummers in animal masks and bells on their shoes. In the middle of every-thing, a gang of apprentices pelting a huge wicker Jack o' Lent with squidgy handfuls of mud.

I scanned the revellers and the market stalls, but aside from a long-faced Puritan or two, nobody looked like an assassin. No-body ever does. A gingerbread seller dropped his tray with a curse and a clatter and I spun round, dagger drawn.

Gabriel's hand touched my arm. "Robbie? What?"

"Nothing." The Angel of Panic passing over my house.

"Bluddy holy war. 'Kill the heretic queen and earn a thousand extra years in bluddy heaven.' The pope's turned them all loose on us now."

In half a dozen cities of France, Catholic seminarians were trained in the latest Italian poisons and the best way to lay an un-detectable trail of gunpowder into a queen's bedchamber. Not counting the wax dolls with pins in them and the horoscopes with her birth hour smeared in blood, there had been, by my count, twenty-three serious attempts on Elizabeth's life since her excom-munication. Our master, Lord Secretary Burghley, had sent us out that day to prevent a twenty-fourth.

I filched a sugarplum from a sweet stall and popped it into my mouth. Felt the smothering tightness begin to ebb away from my throat. I wonder, does poison soothe before it kills? Does it taste sweet on the tongue?

"Our lady queen's past fifty," I told Gabriel. "An heir's out of the question, so the marriage game won't keep France and Spain at bay any longer. They want Mary of Scots on the throne and England back in their Catholic pockets. The rules have changed, that's all. It's a fear game now. A death game."

"So it's still about money."

"Idiot. Everything's about money. Including sex and religion."

We were fighting unofficial wars in half a dozen places and loy-alties at court changed every time there was a royal patent or a monopoly to grab for. Of every three English, one was either an informer or a spy for whoever would pay most. For those in need of money, you spied to help them snatch it. For those with the chinks in their pockets, you spied on the snatchers. For Burghley and the queen, you spied on everyone at once. Spiders, some called us. Intelligencers. Robert Mowbray is not my real name, as Gabriel North was not his, but they served us well enough.

"Christ, I hate games," he said softly, and his grey eyes flickered and went out.

W E THREADED OUR way deeper into the throng. The rain had stopped, and people climbed walls and scrambled onto slippery rooftops hoping to see better. A ragged man held out his hand to me for alms and tried to speak, but when his mouth opened, I could see that his tongue had been cut out. For a split second, I stared helplessly into the furious cave of his soul.

"Think he's dangerous?" I said, as he went off clutching half a penny.

"They took his tongue, old heart," Gabriel said quietly. "Not his balls."

We walked on. Music and laughter came from the doorway of a barber's shop. A maid emptied a chamber pot out a second-floor window and barely missed a pear-shaped old parson.

"Anything?"

"Hide an arsenal under that parson's gown, actually."

"Never. Old John Tydway. Rector of St. Onesimus these thirty years."

"The lute player, then? Don't like the look of him. Piggy eyes."

"Fool. He's one of ours."

"Bollocks."

A snot-nosed little boy stood tiptoe on the roof of a cookshop and shielded his eyes with his hand. Suddenly he began to flap his arms and crow like a rooster. "I can see her!" he shouted. "The queen! Long live the queen!"

The whole crowd was set in motion, swirling and turning like a flock of hysterical starlings, settling, then swirling off in another direction. "Rose!" cried a woman's shrill, frightened voice. "Where are you, child? Oh, Rosie!"

A fair-haired little girl of four or five clutching a bedraggled bunch of primroses came tearing past us. Wide blue eyes that turned green in the light. A bounce of coarse homespun petti-coats and a determined stamp of clumsy, eager little shoes. She owned the morning utterly, as only children can.

But she was poor and small and of little account to the grown-ups. Pushed aside by a hard-eyed woman with a servant in tow, she stumbled against a bookstall and wobbled for an instant, try-ing to right herself. Then down she went in a puddle of muck, her flowers scattered everywhere.

In the blink of an eye, the primroses were brown mush, trod-den by a dozen pairs of feet. The child turned her stubborn little face up and fixed Gabriel with a disapproving stare. What kind of grown-up was he, just standing there while the sky fell on her? Her chin began to tremble. One sob, then another. Then all the tears of the drowned. She sat there on the filthy cobbles, head bent, small body rocking back and forth.

"Ah now, my pet," Gabriel said, folding his long frame into a crouch above her, his cheek almost touching her fine hair. "Come on. Rosie? That your name, then?" He wiped her wet eyes with his sleeve. "Want a ride, my love? Come on, come on, come here."

Coom on. Coom on, coom 'ere. With me he spoke perfectly good London English, but with children, with most women, he often slipped into the country speech he'd grown up with—Yorkshire, Lancashire. I'd known him sixteen years and I had no idea where his home was, or even where he slept at night. He had no wife, but there were twin daughters somewhere called Judith and Sarah. He carried miniatures of them painted on the backs of playing cards.

"We can't stay standing here," I told him sharply. "The child can find her own way home." Friends we might be, but in the petty hierarchy of spies I was Gabriel's proctor; I gave him his orders and took his reports.

He shot me a withering look. "You're a heartless bugger, Rob. No wonder you're a dead loss with that French girl of yours. We can't just leave the poor mite to herself."

I couldn't budge him when he knew he was right—and he was, of course. In such crowds, stray children were often stolen and sold into service, or worse.

So Gabriel swooped down and picked Rosie up, lifted her high in the air where her mother might catch sight of her, swung her round, then lifted her up again and again, till she was squealing with delight. In a moment, a frightened young woman in a rain-soaked white cap came pushing through the press of people towards us. "There you are, you naughty baggage," she cried, taking her daughter in her arms. "Nay, it's all right, my lamb. It's all right."

A pale creature, the mother was, little more than a girl herself, with a look of permanent weariness round her careful mouth, a nasty black eye, and a bruise on her neck. *A wife, a dog, and a walnut tree,* so the old saying went. *The more you beat them, the better they'll be.*

"Them flowers was for the queen," she said uncertainly. There were bound to be gossips in the crowd, people who knew her. If she stayed talking too long, there'd be more bruises before morning.

For a moment she studied her daughter's rescuer, deciding how much deference he deserved—a tall, slender fellow of middle age, more unshaven than bearded, his sandy hair frizzled by the river damp and spangled with mist. A face that might have been made with a chisel—broad forehead, high cheekbones like the folded wings of a bird, nose a perfect narrow plane. Bootlaces undone, secondhand velvet breeches too big and balding at the seams, brown doublet flapping, shirt frills unfastened. Within the ratty costume of fabric and flesh, he waited out his private apocalypse.

The young mother settled for a nod of her head. "God bye you then."

"Don't go yet." He tickled Rosie under the chin and tossed a coin to a flower seller. "Mustn't have the blessed old queen disappointed, hey, pet?"

LET ME TELL YOU. There are fragments of living that slip beyond time and lodge themselves permanently in the present, that bring you suddenly out of hiding and drench you with a precious mortality. What comes next is such a moment.

Gabriel hands the little girl a nosegay of pansies. Heartsease, people call them. A simple act, deceptively casual. But then he does a thing I could never do. If I tried, it would become a clumsy ploy in a game of seduction, the sort of thing Annette's disapproving French Protestant eyes would condemn in an instant and for which her sleek body would punish me all night long.

In him, it is without motive. It is real. He lets his hand stray towards Rosie's girl-mother, his long fingers poised upon the air a quarter inch from her blackened, swollen eye, his broad palm so near he must feel the painful quaver of her lashes. He is learning her as he does every woman—farmer's wife, whore, lady's maid, duchess, little girl. When we use him in the dark work, it is for this secret communion with women, for the ways he can maneuver them to further our needs. Whilst I maneuver him.

But whatever I let my masters believe, this is beyond me, beyond my spider's control. It is how his blood thinks.

Watching him, a part of me is crippled with envy and love.

A ND THEN THE moment shatters and another begins, and another and another. The wild bells start to ring. Trumpets sound and the Queen's Guard appears with Captain Ralegh, dark and tall and splendid in his silver-chased armor and crimson sash, riding ahead of them. Four Yeomen run beside Elizabeth's great white horse and four ladies ride horseback behind her, all dressed in velvet gowns of sea-green and peach-color and lion-tawny.

The queen herself wears dove-grey velvet, the sleeves pinked with claret-colored satin and the skirt and bodice and stomacher sewn with hundreds of pearls. The lace partlet and the pale pink ruff are studded with smaller pearls, and the silver caul that catches her flame-colored wig under her riding hat is pricked with pearls. They are a magical armor. Behind it, she will never grow old.

She pulls up the horse, untangles her skirts from the sidesaddle, and slides down to the ground. Ralegh dismounts and sweeps her a gorgeous bow, and the queen laughs her famous wild laugh, courting the crowd. "Oh, he's a pretty fellow, don't you think? Pray God this rain does not rust him!"

"Long live Her Majesty!" cries a pieman, and a great cheer rises and rises, flowing like a joyous and dangerous tide. Elizabeth waves, laughs, waves again, making a face at the stiltwalker. Another cheer.

The hysteria is reaching its height. Her body sways in an invisible current, and Gabriel's eyes do not leave her face. Her elegant head turns slightly, the fine bones almost visible through the alum-and-eggshell cosmetic.

Then the light thickens. Time stops and the universe stumbles. Beneath the gaudy surface of the crowd, some new darkness gathers. People moving aside, people grumbling. Figures inching towards her. Shadows. Ghosts of shadows.

The hot-apple-pieman approaches, holding out some of his wares. "Come, sir," Elizabeth beckons him. "Queening—it is hungry work, you know."

He moves forward. My throat tightens and my eyes scan the square. No sign of the tongueless man. A cutpurse is hard at work now, and a young girl is foisting pockets. A one-eyed mountebank has been selling potions, a hundred tiny bottles swinging from cords on his jerkin, his shirtsleeves, his breeches. Inside his ragged cloak something else clatters. A dull, thick, implacable sound.

Elizabeth's eyes are like whips, flicking the crowd. She sees the potion-seller. Disregards him. When she sees Gabriel she looks away and then looks back again, intensely aware of him. A slender human scratch on the grey morning, older than the flexed curve of his body. Older than his unaccountable smile.

The dull sound comes again. The queen glances at the mountebank and her gloved hand lifts, one long, thin finger pointing him out. *That one, there.* The shape of death. The sound of it. Rattle of steel. Boots on the cobbles. *There.*

A ND THEN OUT of nowhere, children's high voices are singing. *Long may she reign, in majesty glorious, ever victorious, God save the queen.* They walk in procession, herded by the tubby, beaming old parson. Little boys with jenny wrens in gilt cages, and Shrove buns, and poems on scrolls tied with ribbons. Little girls. Little girls with bunches of flowers. And Rosie, her blue-green eyes shining. Rosie, with her bunch of heartsease.

Gabriel's head jerks round and his body pivots to face the potion-seller. Something gleams in the pewter light and then everything happens at once, a blink, a shard of time, quick, quick. Woven under the noise of the crowd, the fragile chiming of glass bottles as the mountebank throws back his cloak and raises a pistol, a petronel, to take aim at the painted oval of Elizabeth's face.

"*Miserere mei, Deus!* " he cries, crossing himself. *God have mercy on me.*

Gabriel lunges, long body sprawling, knocking down people like ninepins. Knocking down children. Rosie is somewhere in the midst of them, I can hear her wailing. The sound of a hundred tiny bottles all smashing together as the two men struggle. Then a flat thump, not much louder than the fistfuls of mud that hit the Jack o' Lent. The gun has been fired, the muffled sound of damp powder. But at so near a distance even a bungled shot can kill.

Someone's blood spatters Elizabeth and she crumples, only her stiffened farthingale and her five layers of skirts keep her out of the gutter. "Get her up, you fools, get her up!" Ralegh shouts, as though she is a bit of fallen plaster or a broken cup.

"God's death!" she screams at him. "God's deeeeeeaaaaaaath! The children!"

For an instant, Gabriel's fist poises itself like a hammer in the air, and then I lose sight of him completely. The mummer with the lion mask dives for the assassin's weapon, kicks it under the bookstall. The old parson snatches a little girl out of the way, then another and another. One boy's arm is broken, he is howling. Another has a bloody nose. Rosie's grey gown is smeared with blood, but she is not hurt, she still clutches her pansies. Her mother screams and screams and screams.

And what do I do? Why, nothing. I see the apple tart smashed on the ground at Elizabeth's feet. The grit of broken glass. The pieman staring down at his bloody arms where the pistol ball has passed through both of them. His blood on the flank of the white horse. The queen's pearls splashed with blood.

But I keep my distance. I am a watcher, it has always been my part in the dark work of spying. I observe. I remember. I hear confessions, but I do not extract them. I attend upon history's cock-ups. I wait and do nothing, even when waiting is the worst crime of all.

T HE WOULD-BE assassin lay dead, his skull smashed on the cobbles and his neck broken, his ecstatic eyes staring. Did he see at last the promised throne of God?

Well, frankly, I doubt it. Besides, I had other things on my mind.

Gabriel had vanished, but that was a habit of his. I found him where I expected—at the nearest river stairs, washing the dead man's blood off him with Thames water. He looked years older and when he spoke, his voice was brittle and raw. "Poor mad bugger," he said. "I'm no christly good at killing. Had to smash his fool head in."

"If he'd been taken alive, there'd be torture. Whatever they do to him now, he won't feel it. I'd say you did him a favor."

"Did you see?" he said, very softly. "Jesus. He was young."

There was a sound of jangling bells from the quayside above us. Then a pair of legs swung into view, wearing the motley costume of the mummer-lion. "God's balls, it's hot inside here," said the deep and unmistakable voice of our friend Nico Rands. He trotted gracefully down the stair, tore off the wicker mask and sailed it neatly out into the current, then did the same with the harness bells on his ankles and wrists.

He had gently curling black hair, skin the color of a creamy light ale, and the proud bearing of a lord. In truth, Nick was the son of a Thames wherryman and a Venetian dancing master's half-Moorish daughter; he was also the most skillful sifter and winnower of papers and reports in my lord Burghley's service.

"I suppose you know you're a damn fool." He laid a hand on Gabriel's shoulder. "Any holes in you need stitching up? The horse-groom at the Cardinal's Hat has some skill at it. Or your sister . . . ?"

I had no idea there was a sister. "God, no," Gabriel grumbled. "Sour old rhubarb. Kill me before she'd cure."

"Then shift your arse. The queen wants to see you. Both of you. I'm not to say where and when. You'll be fetched, so be ready." Nico spun on his heel and ran soundlessly up the stair again.

"What do they want?" I shouted after him. "What's it all about?"

"Roanoke." He shrugged and laughed. "Whatever the hell that may be."

two

What the Tapestries Saw: Elizabeth

Next morning, after Ash Wednesday chapel, Her Majesty of England swept down the long upper gallery of Hampton Court palace towards the Flemish Chamber, her sad-eyed monkey Pliny the Younger scuttling after her.

Elizabeth never moved slowly. An usher opened the heavy door and she dashed through, the little animal tangled in her skirts. Paying no attention to the men of the Queen's Council, who were bowing very low at her entrance, she moved round the tapestried room, bright amber-colored eyes searching each hanging, looking for worn spots.

Peepholes—that was what tapestries were good for. You hung them with the broken threads just on top of certain holes in the oak panelling of the wall underneath. Within the wall itself, there was a space just wide enough for a watcher to walk through. It honeycombed the palace so that, once inside it, we could move from one room to another, slipping in and out of chambers through invisible doors.

Elizabeth knew the spy-passage was there, of course she did. Her father had used it to spy on her mother. But if she ordered it blocked, we would only invent something new. Her life was an endless performance. We watched her even when she slept.

I was part of the audience that morning. I stood in the hidden passageway, peering through the bright-colored threads at the queen's face.

Her sharp, thin nose wrinkled and she sniffed, then sniffed again. *"God's neckbones!"* she shrieked. "Walsingham's been pissing in the hearth again." Another thrust. "And my lord of Leicester! Your boots stink of civet. Take them off and set them outside. You know scented leather makes me puke."

There were two more of our fraternity hidden in the spy-passage alongside me. One was a chubby overaged cupid called Rowland, with small pink perfumed hands that never stopped fluttering. A little askew and not really reliable, but the smart ones seldom are. The other man was called Harry. Thin-souled and emotionless—the kind of climber I once emulated. He would either acquire just enough power to make his stupidity a permanent public hazard, or else take one chance too many and get himself hanged.

Beyond the tapestry of David seducing Bathsheba, Lord Treasurer Burghley frowned and twisted the two halves of his beard. Sir Christopher Hatton looked like a mournful sheep, and the nerves in Sir Francis Walsingham's sallow face twitched. They had all been many years in Elizabeth's service and their day was almost done.

Burghley's crookbacked son, Robert Cecil, was here only to wait on his old father as yet, but already the queen had begun to depend on him. Intelligent, efficient, dedicated. He knew her moods from his boyhood and he worked harder than all the Council put together, so they said.

He moistened his careful lips and shuffled his ever-present papers. In governance as in spidering, timing is everything. The safety of the realm sometimes depended upon the order in which Elizabeth was shown—or not shown—her documents of state.

"Where is Ralegh now?" she demanded, as the Earl of Leicester padded stocking-footed back to his seat. "God's ears, can he not attend when he's bidden?"

Her face was swollen and her tooth ached terribly, the pain rising and ebbing visibly with each word she spoke. Awake or asleep, her nerves jangled and fought. There were reports of violent nightmares, of sleepwalking in the gardens. Sometimes her body swelled with dropsy, setting off silly rumors of miraculous pregnancy. Her hair came out in great handfuls, tried to grow back, then came out again. Lists of suspected spies reeled ceaselessly through her mind, murmured aloud in her sleep: *Resurrection Barrington, agent of my lord Burghley. Edward Breech, agent of the French king. The player Sam Pickle, agent of Sir Francis Walsingham. Johannes Klippmacher, agent of the Duke of Saxony. The scribbler Marlowe, agent of Sir Francis Walsingham. Simon Fernando, agent of—*

"Who is this Simon Fernando, gentlemen?" she snapped. "Not a Devon man by the sound of him, else I'd think him one of Ralegh's countless cousins."

"Master Fernando is an excellent open-sea pilot, Your Majesty," said Walsingham in his deep, expressionless voice. "Portuguese. He sailed with the earlier voyage of discovery to Virginia—as I am sure you recall. Now that we have agreed upon Roanoke Island as a location for military settlement—"

"*You* have agreed, sir. I've had half a score of boastful reports, but I've seen no proper map of the place, only piddling sketches."

"My lords of your Council have as yet authorized no map to be made, Majesty," Robert Cecil told her mildly. "Lest the Spanish lay hands on it."

By mischance, his nurse had dropped him as a baby and he had not grown properly, his spine damaged. He was forced to look up at everyone, constantly expecting a sneer. For the most part, he was not disappointed.

Cecil's father sighed. "Ma'am, we are already assisting the

Dutch and the Huguenot refugees in France, and we're obliged to maintain a large force in Ireland. We cannot afford to invest our scant capital on giddy schemes in the Americas."

"It's not at all giddy," said Leicester. "A rich colony there could bring us enough gold to fight Spain."

Elizabeth's eyes flashed. "I do not *mean* to fight Spain, sir, nor anyone else. I will have no wars!"

"There may be no help for it, my lady," Walsingham said. "Our intelligencers in Lisbon and Madrid report that King Philip is mounting a great crusade against us. The Inquisition threatens to invade—"

"Yes, yes." She drummed her thin fingers on the tabletop. "Priests will scheme, sir. Their threats move me no more than a fart."

It always pleased Leicester to hear her talk like a sailor. "An invasion fleet of two hundred ships, dearest madam," he said with an indulgent smile, "is a sizable fart."

"The *Spanish* prefer to call it the Grand Armada," said Walsingham drily.

"Galleons big enough to house Plymouth and half of Dover," Leicester said. "Three hundred men on every ship. Warhorses. Cannon and siege equipment. Whatever you call it, Spain means to wipe us from the map of Europe."

"But it's still only talk," said Hatton. "And they've been talking for a decade. Not one galleon lies in the Bay of Lisbon as yet. Such a force will take years to assemble."

Leicester's fist made the inkpots tremble. "We've all seen what they've done in France—three thousand Protestants murdered in Paris alone. Ten thousand more dead in the countryside." He turned to Elizabeth. "An open war of religion on English soil—it's unthinkable, madam."

"There are no wars of religion," said Walsingham. "It was a civil war in France. The Medici power was threatened."

"And do we not threaten it, too? If France joins with Spain, it will more than double the size of this Armada. We can muster, at best, fifty fighting ships." The Earl's temper always smouldered behind his dark eyes, but it was properly up now. "Philip has a great navy and thirty thousand troops in Holland, not five-and-twenty miles of open sea from Dover. Shall we delay until they set sail? I tell you, we must prepare for war at once."

Elizabeth smiled sweetly. "And pay for it with what, Robin? Your patent on wines and spirits? Ralegh's monopoly on playing cards?"

The door creaked again. The monkey chattered and turned a somersault on the tabletop. Captain Ralegh—*Sir* Walter now—slipped into the room and performed a low, graceful bow. (At least, I assumed he bowed low. From my peephole, I could see only as far down as his waist, but I could hear his jewelled laces rattle.) He took the place nearest the queen and leaned close to her, soft dark hair falling over his forehead. She stroked it back with a fingertip, and laughed. "Listening at the door again, Wat?"

"England's treasury is empty, my lady," he said. "It takes no ear at a keyhole to tell me that. Very well, let us fill the Tower vaults with wealth. I believe, as Hatton does, that we have time before we must meet Philip's forces. Let us use it to our best purpose."

Cecil winced. *Porpose* instead of *purpose*. *Oy* for *I* and *toime* instead of *time*. Leicester's dropped *h*'s were bad enough, but all the Londoners at court resented Walter Ralegh's uncompromising Devonshire twang. He was the son and grandson of farmers and sailors, and he made the capital error of being proud of it.

Still, resentment was better than being ignored, and it was hard to ignore Wat Ralegh. He was taller than almost any man in England. A poet, a scholar, and vain as a peacock. Bold in battle and in bed—not that he bothered with beds, as a rule. Two years ago, nobody at court had heard of him. At times he seemed entirely guileless, but arrogance often is.

"Virginia is English soil," he said. "We have claimed it in Your Majesty's name. Now let me mount a proper expedition to explore the place. Take men skilled in metals, plants, animals, gems. Best minds in England. If there's wealth to be found, we'll find it."

Old Burghley shook his head. "I tell you, Sir Walter, we have no more money for expeditions than we have for making war."

"I ask only a royal charter and a modest muster of troops to defend us in case of attack by the Spanish. The rest we'll manage with private investment—a sale of shares among gentlemen of interest."

Hatton glared. "You won't get a farthing of mine, sir."

"Why, what's the trouble, Kit?" Ralegh smiled, white teeth gleaming. "Bribes fallen off a bit, have they?"

"Tomcats," said Elizabeth. "I have a Council of tomcats. Go and lift your tails at each other elsewhere, or cleave to the matter at hand."

"We might build a real fort on the Roanoke, if it proves," Leicester said eagerly. "King Philip's treasure fleet returns to Spain through the Straits of Florida every autumn. That's an easy striking distance."

Ralegh seized the point. "If we break Philip's hold on his South American colonies, we break his power. Roanoke Island is naturally defensible. And the Secota—natives of the place—will give no trouble, they're kind-natured. Generous. And prosperous."

Elizabeth rose and began to pace; I could hear her skirts sweeping the lavender-strewn rushes on the floor. Ralegh spread his wings a bit further. "In fact, ma'am, we may not need to snatch Philip's gold. We have intelligence that the savages possess gold mines somewhere in the interior forests."

The sound of her footsteps stopped abruptly. "This intelligence—is it credible?"

"When Sir Walter sniffs out an adventure," grumbled Burghley, "I fear credibility and common sense may go hang."

"Common sense keeps timid huswives at home and puts their husbands to begging." Ralegh stood up, towering over Elizabeth's slight body. "Reason and the lessons of history endorse the possibility of American gold, my lady," he said, his deep voice grown suddenly tender. Ralegh the seducer of maidens. "During your father's reign, the Spanish plundered two great kingdoms to the south—"

Elizabeth was not to be coaxed. "Yes, Wat, I've read the accounts of the Inca conquest, and of the Aztecs, too. And a bitter, bloody business it all was."

"Philip's explorers say there are seven cities of gold somewhere to the west of the Roanoke country. The kingdom of Cibola, they name it. Some speak of an El Dorado, a city of pure gold. Men have *seen* it."

"Spinners of tall tales in the taverns of Lisbon, no doubt. My good Dr. Dee says he can breed gold by the action of the sun upon a dead dog, but I've yet to see a result of it that will buy pig's-foot pickle."

Burghley laughed. "Quite right, ma'am. If there were such a place as this so-called El Dorado, Spain would have found it by now."

"They have explored the Floridas on the strength of it and built Spanish towns there to secure the wealth," Ralegh insisted. "Surely it's not beyond reason to expect that if we penetrate the deep coastal forests where the Spanish have not yet ventured—"

His dark eyes danced and his cheeks had grown flushed with excitement. Elizabeth laughed. "Why, I do believe you'd like to be *king* of America, Wat."

He gulped. "I . . . ? By—by no means, my lady. But if the gold—"

"Oh, England needs treasure, I do not deny it. Only take care, sir. The Dragon Gold has a cruel will. He dazzles us with dreams. And then he devours us."

As a golden young man, King Henry VIII had dressed himself from head to foot in cloth-of-gold, caparisoned his horse in it, had his royal pavilions made of it. He all but bankrupted England. He ended mad. Pox-ridden. Spent.

But Ralegh's eyes were not hooded with madness. "Gold is not all, Your Majesty. Roanoke gives every promise of other riches. Farmland. Fishing grounds. Timber without limit. Products for our merchant trade. Their women wear many excellent pearls. And— And there is a certain bush that bears pure silk, and—of course there's the tobacco weed, and—"

"You may cease to astound me, Sir Walter. Draw your charter and I'll sign." She turned to face the others. "If Philip means to invade us, let him pay the cost of our defenses with his own gold. God knows England cannot pay them, and Wat's magic island may at least give Drake scope to strike at the treasure fleet."

Ralegh went down on one knee. "If I may, Your Majesty. We will need—"

"I'll give you one ship, three hundred common soldiers, fifty kegs of black powder. And one year to explore the place. That is all."

"But as to cannon, ma'am—"

"No, sir. If these Spanish find their way through our defenses, what shall I tell my conquered folk? 'One cannon more might have stopped them, but I sent it to America with Wat'?"

Elizabeth took his hand and raised him to stand very near her. When he bowed to kiss her ring, his dark hair brushed her breast where the cut of her gown bared it. Beside me, chubby pink Rowland stuffed his fist in his mouth to stifle a giggle. Leicester glared into the fireplace. Robert Cecil turned his head away.

WHAT ARE THEY thinking? Why, what they always think of her favorites. *Has he fucked her, plucked her, pumped her, humped her, wived her, swyved her? How many times? Was she any good? Did she squeal, did she moan, did she wriggle and bite, did her eyes pop and her lips turn bright blue? Is it true that her membrane is so tough no man's penis will pierce it? Or has she borne them all bastards? Is she with child now? Miracles happen. Shall we kill it? Will it topple us? Will it challenge the throne? Will it take away all our profits?*

She slips her arm through Ralegh's, taunting Leicester, scandalizing old Burghley, making Hatton's blood boil. "There is a savage woman on this island of yours, Sir Walter," she says quietly. "A queen, they tell me."

"She may be a queen one day, my lady. In that country, governance is passed down through the female line. But it's a complicated business and there are many obstacles—"

"When are there not?" Elizabeth's painted eyelids flutter. "She is young, this heir to the kingdom where silk grows on bushes? And handsome?"

"I am told so, madam. Of course, savage beauty is measured in—tenuous terms. I've not yet seen her."

In an instant, her practiced and melodious voice grows stern and cold. "Nor shall you. Send your experts to find my gold. But you shall be Moses and keep on this side of the Promised Land. Send this Portugee of Walsingham's, this Fernando, or some one of your thousand cousins. If I'm to fight Spain at sea, I'll want you by me."

"But, Majesty—"

"No discussion," she says, taking up the monkey's silver chain. Stepping aside, where my peephole cannot find her. "That will do, sirs. I am finished with you."

I TURNED AWAY FROM the moth hole in King David's purple robe, as the queen swirled out of the chamber and her Council followed. In a moment, a door in the panelling opened behind us and a clerk motioned us out into a small, dark, cold room. He made himself scarce and Rowland wheeled round to stare at me, his silly affectations suddenly edged with danger.

"Has Gabriel North been instructed? Will he behave himself?"

"I've told him to mind his manners when he meets the queen," I said.

"Don't be thick," Harry snapped at me. "We need information about the Roanoke country and North's been suggested as a way of obtaining it peaceably. War costs money, even war on savages. But if we're to get the wretched place firmly into our control without a fight, we need clear, verifiable facts."

The least informative sort of information, Lord Burghley often said. To know a fact and nothing more is like measuring a box on the outside and never lifting the lid.

Rowland fiddled with a candle stub. "It's said North can get a woman to do almost anything, in bed or out of it, and that's what we want of him. Though he certainly had no success when we sent him to Mary of Scots."

"Gabriel was sent to her kitchen maids. He brought back useful gossip. He's not a magician."

"But could he maneuver this savage woman they were speaking of just now?" asked Harry. "One of the native girls was of great use to Cortés during the Aztec conquest—all but led him to the front door of their treasure-house. Could North get the information out of this savage—princess, I suppose I must call her? Make her our collaborator? Under your control, of course."

"Very likely, but—must I go to America myself, then?"

"Naturally. As his proctor, you'll manage all his actions and he'll bring the information to you for assessment. A map to wherever their gold is mined and a guide to their pearl beds, anything else of profit. As to his methods—seduction's perfectly acceptable. A little boldness, perhaps, if she resists. But no obvious rape, or Captain Lane will hang him. Rafe Lane. He'll be in command. Veteran of the Irish campaign. Knows how to deal with the savage mind."

The name conjured horrors. During the last uprising, Rafe Lane had ordered the hangings and beheadings of more than a thousand Irish captives and their Spanish allies. "If you hope to avoid war," I said, "he's hardly a man to conciliate—"

Just then there came a faint sound from the spy passage, and Harry froze, listening. Servants, no doubt. Or rats. We heard nothing more and he turned back to me. "You and North will leave for Virginia in two months. Three at the most. Get yourselves ready."

"But the charter—"

"Oh, please. The charter's been drawn since October, it only needs signing. Ralegh's been recruiting investors for months. Walsingham's in it. Leicester. They're all risking their last pence."

"So Her Majesty . . . ?"

Rowland sniggered. "She's known all along, the clever cow. Played them like so many fish on a line, got them to spend their money and not hers."

Harry picked up a folio of papers from the secretary's table and plunked it down in front of me. "Details of climate, description of savages, topography, and so on. Read them, and then instruct North. No need to tell him too much. He doesn't look very bright."

I bit my lip to keep from laughing. I had first met Gabriel North at Cambridge, a pork butcher's son on a Queen's Scholarship. He knew Greek better than I did, and there was nothing he couldn't teach himself. Carpentry, French poetry, part-singing. When the Russians sent an ambassador to court, Gabriel disappeared for a month and came back speaking passable Russian.

The ambassador's wife, he said, had a good-hearted maid.

I FOUND HIM EXACTLY where I had left him, sitting on a low stool at the confluence of five echoing corridors. The flames of torches spat and flared. Shadows drifted, cast by nothing.

"Well? Did you see the queen?" I asked as we made our way out through the tangle of presence rooms and passageways. "What did she say?"

"Said I looked like a ragpicker."

"No news there. And?"

"Told her to take daisy root and dockweed boiled in olive oil for that tooth. Bring the swelling right down. Gave me this." He held out a tiny gold earring in the shape of a new moon—the queen's virgin symbol.

"Not bad," I said. "Don't give it away to some doxy. And?"

"Asked me why I was smiling. Yesterday, when I took that poor sod down? Seems I was smiling when I looked at her just before. 'You wore a smile.' That's what she said."

"Marvellous. She was about to be murdered and you were smiling. What did you tell her?"

An icy draught swirled past us and Gabriel shivered. "Told her I was squinting at the sun."

"Ass. It was raining. You should've said you were blinded by her dazzling beauty."

"Oh, bollocks. You need lessons, you do. Clever women hate trash like that." He stopped short and I almost ran against him.

"She asked me if it was her life or the child's I meant to save." He shook his head as if he could shake off confusion. "To this hour, I don't know, Robbie. I didn't choose. You don't, mostly."

"That's what you told her?"

" 'The little girl in the grey dress,' I said. 'How could I waste her? And you wore a grey gown, too. Your bright hair . . .' "

Around us the draughts of power sucked and billowed like a tide, and his voice trailed away. He was unlike anyone else I knew. He still believed that the heart is a connotative as well as a denotative organ. In fact, he doubted almost everything else.

three

WHAT THE TAPESTRIES HEARD: REPORTS
AND INTERCEPTIONS

*A Certain Conversation of King Philip of Spain with His
Under-Secretary, Overheard at the Escorial Palace, Madrid,
and Transmitted in the Cipher Known as Stella Sirius.
Transcribed at Whitehall by Robert Mowbray.*

YOU THERE, OUT IN THE CORRIDOR! YES, YOU. CLOSE THE DOOR,
por favor, and lock it from outside. I cannot sign the requisitions now, I must have a brief *siesta.* I AM PHILIP OF SPAIN, I SHALL
SLEEP OR NOT SLEEP WHEN I WANT TO!

My cold is much worse, and I have a *dolor del estómago.* I
haven't been able to pass anything in three days. And these piles of
papers and documents you bring are the worst of it, de Cuevas. I
start to sneeze every time you come in here. My knees are very
bad today, too. I prayed for only four hours, but I could hardly
stand up afterwards.

No, I do *not* wish to see the nuncio. I have already sent my orders to the pope, he knows the will of God. That is, he knows
what I want, and it's the same thing.

My what? *Siesta?* I have no time for *siestas*. How can you suggest it? Just look at those papers, I'll be reading papers and signing papers and dictating more papers ten years after I'm downstairs in my tomb. The clerks? What do they know? I am the king. *Yo, el Rey.* Christ had disciples, but He did the miracles Himself.

That's all now. You may go, de Cuevas.

No. Wait. What is the number of heretics in England at the last estimate? Are you sure? *Diós,* but they breed at a terrible rate! And how many priests have we sent on their martyrs' missions to achieve divine ecstasy by assassinating the English Whore and her minions? Only fifty-three? Double the number, see to the recruitment yourself.

Mark my word—what's your name again? De Cuevas? Are you sure? I thought— Well. Mark my word, de Cuevas, then. When our brave troops march into London, we will not be resisted. No, no. We will be welcomed with great joy and led as heroes through the streets to the cheers of the people, like Christ when He entered Jerusalem. We will be greeted as liberators. The bastard queen is not loved, she is not loved, she is . . .

I mean to have her burned on a slow fire at Smithfield, you know. Come closer. There are spies everywhere. I used to—*affect* her. When she was young. I was married to her sister but I lusted after her. Once I backed her up to a garden wall and thrust my hands into her bodice and squeezed her nipples. They were scarcely formed, as I remember. Quite lovely. It will be painful to think of her burning, but I owe God a penance. I destroy her for the sake of my soul.

Besides, I would see my own son burned, if he had betrayed the Holy Faith as she has. Though of course poor Don Carlos is dead now, and for that I am grateful to God, as otherwise we'd have had to hire even more keepers for him, and the expense was tremendous, not to speak of the nervous strain when he got loose.

Christ, my knees hurt. Help Thou also my immovable stool,

and if the piece of St. Ursula's finger be genuine, I promise to acquire it for Thy sake. That is, if the abbot's price is not too high. It will bring the collection of holy relics to seven thousand four hundred and twenty-two. Twelve entire bodies of saints, apostles, and martyrs. One hundred forty-four complete heads. Three hundred and six undamaged limbs. Indeed, God has blessed us with—

What? What's that damnable noise out there? A parrot? Who on earth would send me a parrot? Go out and wring its neck, de Cuevas. You know I'm afraid of birds.

No. Wait. Take a letter first. To my loyal servant de Falla, Count of Somewhere or Other. Please let me know what your agents make of this latest English venture being mounted for Virginia. Wherever they settle, we must find the location and destroy them. The South American treasure fleet must be protected, above all. We cannot spare even a single emerald or a flake of gold. We must give all to the Armada in the service of God. Have we enough spies in London and Plymouth? Have you alerted our governors in Florida and the islands? Take captives at random. Put them to torture. Write me a letter. If I remember anything I have not put into this letter, I will write you another letter. It is best to write everything down, but the papers have grown again. They double in number every time I'm not looking.

En el nombre de Jesucristo, y para el honor de España. Felipe, el Segundo. I, the King.

De Cuevas? Go and strangle that filthy goddamned parrot now.

four

The Unsatisfied Lover, OR
the Spy and the French Girl

I T WAS NEARING THE END OF MARCH, AND I HAD BEEN KEPT BUSY
for many days transcribing coded dispatches from abroad
concerning the Roanoke venture. Naturally the Spanish were
livid, but the French seemed to be having a good laugh at the
idea.

To me, the voyage was certainly no joke. I'd never been on the
broad sea before and I began to dream of drowning, and of some
deeper darkness I could not identify. Spiders' nerves, I told myself. Fear's healthy, it sharpens the wits.

"I don't want you to go away, Robbie," Annette said.

The pale skin along her thigh gleamed in the candlelight like
French satin, but her straight black hair veiled her face from me. I
reached out to brush it back and felt an almost imperceptible
shudder.

"Are you cold, dearest?" I whispered. "The fire's almost burnt
out. Shall I draw the curtains?"

"Forget bed curtains."

She liked the light to find us. She drew me onto the fine
needleworked linen that covered the featherbed. The candles

flickering beyond us, perhaps a dozen of them, on cleverly wrought iron racks. Her husband had money. The expensive fragrance of spiced oranges and partridge baked in almond milk, the food we had just finished. The soft hiss of the dying fire.

I kissed the hollow of her throat. "Do you still fear the dark, my love? Or is it me?"

"Don't be foolish."

She eased herself open and let her hands lead me almost inside her. Her cool fingers urging me, stroking my thigh. Then within her at last, swimming deeper, watching her small mouth relax. Hoping for the rare, half-smothered cry of release where her pleasure lived.

"Hush," she said. "Ah, Robin. Let me. Ah, please."

"I don't want to leave you with child, sweet."

"You won't. Hush."

But I could feel, even as she held me, another kind of fear— that I was too near the edge, too near to dissolving completely the careful boundary between us. The safety of the illicit. Her fear of un-light. My thousands of lies.

An instant before that last dangerous wall came tumbling down, I heard a creaking sound. My breath stopped. Everything stopped. Men have been murdered in bed.

"What was that? The chamber door?"

"No, no. The bed ropes. Hush. Don't stop."

It was no use. Crash. Rattle. CRASH. It sounded like the house was collapsing under a slide of rocks. Naked and defenseless, I fell away from Annette and rolled over, fists clenched.

She laughed. "Don't be silly. It's only the servant."

The last of the bucket of coals clattered into the box by the hearth and the maidservant's coarse shoes clumped to the door. It banged shut behind her.

I was shaking, my whole body convulsed with fury and shame and confusion. "Christ. It's hopeless. I'm sorry. I'm sorry."

Annette reached for me and held me, my face on her shoulder. "It doesn't matter. It was lovely for a while, *ami*."

Ami, she always called me. *Friend,* it meant. That was all.

I sat up on the edge of the bed. "Damn the bitch, I ought to break her head."

"Esther only brought some coals. It's her duty."

"Not while I'm fucking her mistress, it's not."

"Shame. Naughty boys with the pox do fucking, not gentlemen."

"I'm sorry. Sorry. But you're too trusting. She's not blind, you know, that servant. She's not a piece of furniture."

Her dark eyes closed. "Believe me, she wants to be. The Spanish chest doesn't have to empty our pisspot."

"The Spanish chest won't tell your husband, either."

"Gerard doesn't listen to servants. Besides, he doesn't care what I do."

But he might care who she did it *with*. He was a wealthy man, a wine merchant. Wealthy men knew other wealthy men, and servants sold what they knew. And if ever they learned of the dark work I did—

In that respect at least, I was safe. Annette knew nothing at all about my spying, and please God she never would. She knew I was going to Virginia, but she didn't know who had sent me, or why.

She pulled the velvet cord that closed the bed curtains, then knelt for a moment behind me in the sheer cave made by the painted Venetian silk. Her cool fingers drifted downward to the hollow of my hip. Then, practical as always, she left me and went to pour some wine into two silver wine cups. It was vintage Bordeaux, one of Gerard's best.

He'd given her a life I could never have dreamed of, but for the most part, occupied with his business abroad, he treated her like one of his treasures. The table rug was from Persia. The colors of the Arras tapestries, less faded than those at Hampton Court, danced and sparkled in the candlelight. He had bought her a lovely old manor farm called Staple Oaks at the foot of the Chiltern Hills near Oxford, for escaping the plague when it ravaged the city. The London house where I did my best to cuckold him at least twice a week was a spacious and dignified stone residence in the Crutched Friars district, the rooms panelled in deeply carved and blackened oak, scented underfoot with cinnamon and lavender and sweet cicely.

Music seemed to come from everywhere in that house—from the virginals Annette played with such delicacy to the lutes and recorders and viols that lay on every window seat and crewel-worked cushion. From somewhere in the maze of passages, even at this late hour, I could hear the notes of a lute and a song. *For the wind is in the west, and the cuckoo's in his nest, and you won't have a lodging here.*

Annette's naked body swayed gently to the tune, small breasts curving slightly downward, nipples half-risen in the damp chill from the garden. She was a Huguenot, a French Protestant refugee, but if she still believed in a god, he was nameless and absent. As a child, she had been through the massacre at Paris and fled with her father. They had been rich, then poor and half-starved. Now she was rich again. At fourteen, ten years ago, she had married Gerard. He was nearing sixty. They had no children.

"Tell me again about this Roanoke," she said. "Will you write a play about naked savages?"

I scribbled silly potboilers for the theatres now and then, and I had once appeared on the stage of The Curtain as Third Servant to the Duke of Braggadoccio. It was all she knew of my life apart from her.

"Who needs naked savages," I teased, "when I have you? I just want to see the place, that's all. An adventure. I'm getting old."

I slipped out of the bed and stood beside her, and she turned and quite suddenly put her arms round me. She felt very small, almost a child. She had seen her mother murdered, and two brothers. Wherever innocence had lived in her, there was still a scrap of it left in that half-frightened embrace.

"A whole year," she said. "Oh, don't go."

"I must, sweet. My passage is paid." I let my fingers drift through her hair. "May I at least dream of you while I'm gone?"

"Write me a poem. Then I will think of you. Perhaps."

"But will you wait for me?"

"Would you," she said, "if I went from you for a year?"

I took her to bed again and as always when I'd failed her, she was tender and full of comfort, as though I were wounded or sick. We made love with a tenuous solicitude, almost at a distance, achieving nothing much.

Afterwards she slept and I lay propped on my elbow, watching her. The sky was growing light outside, the wheels of bakers' and butchers' carts already beginning to rumble past. On the windowsill, Gerard's silvery carrier pigeons cooed and flapped and pecked at crumbs.

In the soft golden-grey light, I crept silently out of the bed, dressed, and sat down to leave the poem Annette had asked for. When I'd finished, I signed it with a flourish and left it on the pillow-bier, tangled in her dark hair.

It wasn't my own, of course. I can fracture a blank verse, but I couldn't write a sonnet to save myself. It was one of Kit Marlowe's. If there's one thing I do well, it is lie.

I⟶T WAS ALMOST a day's ride to Staple Oaks, Gerard's country house. I used it sometimes when the wronged husband was safely out of the country and I needed a quiet spot to study dispatches or work out the cipher codes. I had left Gabriel there a week ago with Harry's folio of Roanoke information, but to be honest, I went because I loved the place, and because it is safer to love places than people.

The roads were muddy and crowded with beggars, whole families put out of their cottages and trudging along in the dirt. "Here, master! Penny for the baby?" A worn fellow ran up and caught hold of my stirrup. "Come on, sir, you can spare us a penny. Or a ha'penny, buy bread and beer for the little-uns?"

The baby on his arm was much too thin, its belly swollen with hunger. I tossed a coin to the fellow, but when the other beggar-folk noticed, they came charging at him. To keep from dropping the babe, he loosed his fist and the penny fell into the rutted road and was snatched up. Too proud to beg a second time, he turned away.

"Here," I called out to him. "Have you no wife, friend?"

"Died when this-un come. We was already put out on the road by then."

"Could you not pay your rents?"

"There's few as can, sir. Money don't buy much nowadays."

"How many little-uns have you, then?"

"Had five. Three left. 'Prenticed the eldest lad. Sold the girl-child."

He looked up at me, his eyes narrowed. He meant he had sold her to a bawd. There was a rage buried deep in those eyes, and in his voice, and in the heaviness of his step.

"We do what we must," I said, and threw him another coin.

B Y THE TIME I reached the manor, I had nothing much left in my purse. "Nasty shiftless creatures," muttered Mrs. Trott, the housekeeper, setting a plate of roast venison before me. "Ought to be put in the stocks, that's what Trott says. Poaching the master's deer and partridges and rabbits, and them sluttish womenfolk coming into the very orchard, the bold hussies, looking out for last year's apples that's still a-hanging on." She tugged the strings of her prim cap a bit tighter. "Now, sir, just you eat that up and I've a nice bit of anise cake to finish."

"And where is Master North?"

"Oh, him? Blessed if I know. He's here and he's there and then he's here again. Some men can't abide to stay long within four walls."

I FOUND GABRIEL OUT in the orchard, climbing a tree. The spring grass was lush and still uncut, the apple and pear trees just coming into fragrant bloom. White petals fell like rain as he worked his way up to one branch in particular, where three withered apples from last autumn still hung on. Beneath the tree stood a basket half full of wrinkled orange pippins.

"Not so bad," he said, snaffling the fruit in one big hand and swinging down to earth. "Winter wasn't too cold. I've eaten worse."

"For the beggars, I suppose."

He grinned. "Already foisted a cheese and three nice loaves from old Trott's pantry." He began to poke about among the herb beds, still grown into their autumn tangle of rosemary, dockweed, parsley, lavender, and nettles. "You can make soup out of nettles. Strengthens the blood, they say."

He wrapped his hand in his shirttail to keep from being burnt by the caustic leaves and proceeded to pull as many as he could, stuffing them into a piece of sacking. The sun was lowering, the apple boughs frosted with golden light.

Suddenly there was a sound of wings cutting the air and Gabriel looked up. One of Gerard's pigeons—the one Annette called Sultan, a plump silver-grey male with a rose and green breast—came flapping down to strut round the old-fashioned thatched dovecote in the garden. Four or five other birds cooed their gentle notes from behind a small iron-barred door.

"Have you studied the information I left you?" I asked Gabriel.

"What for? Three-fourths of it's bound to be wrong anyway. Just give me the two best maps and tell me how cold it gets in the winter. Besides, there's nothing much about *her* in those finicking notes of yours."

"Who? Oh. You mean the savage woman?"

His eyes were clear glass in the late light. "Which one's the insult? Woman or savage?"

"Don't preach. Just do the job you've been given. Sleep with her, but for God's sake don't get involved with her."

"You sound exactly like Toady and Ratsbane, do you know that?"

He meant Rowland and Harry, and he couldn't stand them. Still, he was more worried than angry. Beyond this place, there be dragons.

"We leave for Plymouth in the morning," I reminded him. "Have you said your farewells? And your prayers?"

He gave no reply. Instead, he strode away through the deep, sweet-smelling grass to pick up Sultan, his fingertips stroking and stroking the bird's pearly breast. "Grey wings. Grey breast. It's all colors, actually, grey is. See there? Blue-green, sea-green, silver, rose, purple. Even a bit of gold." He brushed his face against Sultan's bird's frail wing. "Come on, Rob, come and touch him."

"The dead are grey," I said. "Their faces."

I suddenly wanted nothing to do with the Roanoke. I wanted Annette's small arms, Annette's shape against me. Annette's bad dreams joined with mine in the dark.

The bird flicked its wings, eager to fly. "Gerard's trained him to carry messages," I said dully. "Better lock him up safe. He's used to it. He'll be frightened, otherwise."

"Bollocks. He'll be free." Gabriel jiggled a loose stone in the wall of the dovecote. "Can't stand christly cages, me. Look there. Whole thing's falling apart round them and still they keep inside it. All but him. Let the poor bugger go, eh? Let him fly."

He thrust his long arms upward and the bird's wings beat the air. It is how I always think of him—a dark, slender shadow in the last light of a spring evening, with the queen's gold earring gleaming bright in his ear. I never saw him wear it again.

five

THE SAVAGE WOMAN AND WHO SHE WAS

*S*HE WAS CALLED NAIA. I CANNOT TELL YOU HER AGE. Among her people there was no age as we understand it, for there were no numbered years, no days of the week, no hours, minutes, seconds. There was only the rooting and falling of trees. The rising and setting of sun, moon, and tide. Memory, undimmed by the written word, carried the past like a cupful of pebbles.

In European years, she was perhaps five-and-twenty on the last day of June, 1585, when our seven English ships finally weathered the Cape of Feare and crept up the coast of the Floridas to the long chain of sandbanks that sheltered Virginia. I did not really see her that day. True to my duty, I watched her from the first moment and all through that alien year, but I do not think I ever *saw* her at all.

What I say of her comes from Gabriel. From our long nights of talk in the stifling heat and then the damp winter cold of the newly built barracks. And later, elsewhere, from the hoarse ache of his voice as I dragged her secrets from him. A voice of dreams and of memories. Of truth, when there was truth to be had.

N<small>A'IYA—SO THE</small> Secota tribesmen spoke her name, with a slight stop of the throat, as though she took their breath away. A quiet woman, orphaned in childhood, raised by her uncle and the old village priest. Widowed for almost two years when we met her. She was small in stature, slender of face but strong-muscled, with an elegant economy of movement that seemed to be bred in her. She could walk many miles in a day, and run long distances with a heavy pack on her shoulders if need be. Her waist was narrow, her bare breasts naturally small but swollen with milk for the child she was still nursing when we arrived—a girl born some months after the father's death. There was a son, too, a sturdy little boy who looked just like his mother—determined, curious, oddly dignified.

But Naia was quite alone when we caught our first glimpse of her. She might almost have been waiting for us. Perfected, opaque as a shell.

T<small>O ARRIVE AT</small> Roanoke Island, our ships had to pass into the sound through a breach in the long chain of outer sandbanks that fronted the Atlantic. It was a narrow passage and the current flowed very fast through it at high tide. When the tide was low, it was safe enough for small boats like the two transport pinnaces we towed, but too shallow for our great ships—the *Tyger*, the *Red Lyon*, the *Roebuck*, the *Elizabeth*, and the *Dorothy*—to sail through without running aground. The captains and our admiral, Ralegh's cousin Sir Richard Grenville, met on *Tyger*'s deck to consider matters.

Simon Fernando lounged against the cookhouse bulkhead

watching like a proper spy as our soon-to-be-governor Rafe Lane, red-faced and fuming and carrying his long-barrelled pistol, elbowed his way into the assembly.

"Why was I not informed of this council?" Lane demanded.

Grenville ignored him and turned to the others. "If we lighten the tunnage and empty the holds, we *may* pass the breach safely."

"Lighten her you may, sir," said the gruff old captain of *Roebuck*. "But high tide in them narrows, even running empty? Fool's venture, I'd say."

The others nodded agreement and Grenville seemed relieved. "Let us ferry the men and supplies at half-tide, then," he said, "and leave the great ships moored offshore."

"Where the Spanish may spy them?" Lane stamped his foot. "Nay, sir, the queen has need of the savage gold. Take the tide and go now!"

He never backed down or took advice, and no one on that deck seriously believed he wanted the gold for Elizabeth. As a commander in the Irish wars, he had hanged and beheaded civilians by the dozens for no serious reason. Then he seized their lands and grew rich on the spoils.

Still, Rafe Lane was neither better nor worse than a dozen other commanders, and *they* did not send a cold spasm down my spine. It was the ravelled panic at the shrill verge of his voice. The blank incomprehension of his ice-blue eyes.

"Where's the goddamn pilot?" he demanded. "Pilotpilotpilotpilot."

Nothing was ever done quickly enough. No one ever told him the truth. His orders were never carried out properly, or if they were, he changed them.

"Motherfuckingwhoremongeringportugeesonuvabitch PILOT!"

Simon Fernando's face betrayed no emotion. Too vain, I thought, to make a good invisible spy. Even in the oppressive summer heat he wore the flamboyant striped stockings that were just then the fashion in London—crimson and black, and cross-gartered with black satin ribbons.

But whatever his taste in stockings, you didn't make an enemy of a pirate. The rigging was full of his men. "Can you take *Tyger* safe through the breach here, sir?" Grenville asked him politely.

"Never make land at all with such a milksop wretch in charge of the helm," sneered Lane.

At last Fernando had had enough. He stalked angrily away and disappeared down the hatchway to the whipstaff that controlled the great rudder. The other captains returned to their ships. In ominous silence, the sailors manned the lines and *Tyger* nosed into the breach.

The leadsman began to take soundings: "Six fathom. Six and half. Seven."

I F IT FALLS to five fathoms—thirty feet of water beneath us—or if there is a shoal directly under the hull where the lead fathom cannot find it, we will founder. *Tyger* is still loaded with the precious cannon Ralegh's last farthing has paid for, a quarter of the powder and shot, more than a hundred men, two of our eight horses, and a half-year's provision of meal, pickled mutton, and dried pease.

Men line the decks of all seven ships—six hundred men, scarcely breathing. Merchant-traders of furs and lumber, land speculators, younger sons in search of the fortunes they cannot inherit, bankrupts hoping to reclaim their losses with Secota gold. Lapidaries, weavers, mapmakers, daredevil explorers. Ruined men and lost men and men who were merely unlucky enough to be snatched by Ralegh's press gangs.

Gabriel stands at the root of *Tyger*'s mainmast, his arms full of coiled ropes. I see him clearly one moment, and the next he is gone.

"Six and quarter. Five and three-quarter. Six."

There is a deafening crash as we strike the shoal full-on, and men topple like ninepins. Cries of "Hard a-port," and "God save us!" *Tyger* shivers where she stands, stuck fast on a submerged bar of gravel. "Float her off, man!" shouts Lane. "Don't be a fool!"

The sea has grown wilder, the tide at its height and the waves through the narrow passage crashing against the side of the helpless ship. She gives a huge groan, then lists over dangerously. From belowdecks, horses scream in terror. I feel something like an earthquake as Ralegh's cannon breaks loose and slides across the hold, to crash into the hull.

"She's stove! Taking water!"

Behind us the other ships strike aground as though they are chained together. We grasp at rails and riggings and lines, and some jump overboard hoping to swim ashore. *Tyger* lies at a dangerous slant, taking hit after hit from the waves, water pouring into the hold.

Lane's command barely reaches us. "Fight, damn you! I'll shoot the next bastard that goes over the side!"

Then the water swirls round his own legs and he is washed down the madly sloping deck to the rail. He catches a tenuous hold and begins to fire, aiming at those in the sea. Missing them. Shooting the waves.

A spar cracks and falls, breaking the arm of a little fair-haired serving boy who sometimes plays the lute when Lane needs calming. "Jem!" I hear myself gasp. But I do nothing else. I take no risks. I watch as the body of the lute boy rides the flooded deck and slips into the sea.

Gabriel and some others are throwing rope-lines down the afterhatch now, pulling up one half-drowned man after another. A huge crest of wave knocks me over and I start to slide helplessly down the terrible precipice of the deck. "Catch hold," Gabriel shouts, and I grab the line he throws and drag myself to my feet. "Don't be a fool," I scream at him. "Come away!"

But he and the rest are back at their work. The ship lists again and heels over, and I jump from the rail.

I have to swim only a few yards before a brawny Dutchman from the *Dorothy* grabs me and flings me ashore. I lie still, dragging my mind back from the waters. Watching the drowned rise and fall on the waves.

A T LAST THE order is given to abandon *Tyger* to her fate. Only Fernando, Lane, Grenville, and a few of their officers remain aboard, still trying to float her off the shoal.

Gabriel is safely ashore, too, now, busily pummelling the salt water out of a half-drowned Thomas Hariot—Ralegh's jack-of-all-trades genius. The mapmaker and artist John White still clutches his oilskin drawing case. The old Jew Joachim Ganz, alchemist and expert in precious metals, sputters Polish curses. I see botanists and husbandmen I know, and bricklayers and soldiers. But some I do not see at all.

Duties finally done, Gabriel lowers himself wearily onto the sand beside me. "How many dead?" I ask him.

"Five men. And two boys. Little Peter, the cook's scullion. Jacky Bean, the swabby." He frowns at the sun. To speak of such things in the broad afternoon makes them harsher, it hones the edge of waste. His voice slashes at me. "'Seven human widgets and a bag of barleycorn, total price three shillings and ninepence. Replacements requested.' That how your report'll read?"

"Eight," I say dully. "Eight widgets. Jemmy's dead."

"The lute boy?" he whispers. "I didn't know."

We fall silent then, glad to lie side by side on the warm and healing sand, listening as *Tyger* fights for her life. Perhaps she will sail away home after all. It is dangerously easy to believe in the fabulous here, in golden treasure and life everlasting. The precious cleanness of the beach is real, but it seems to have been created, at most, a few hours before. No stinking fish guts and no rusty anchor chains. Only the bitter-sour-sweet of sea salt, with a strange edge of ripening fruit from somewhere in the dark, mysterious ocean of trees to the west. Only the colors that paint the air and wash the flat beach, blending sea, land, and sky. Apricot, rose, pale amethyst, topaz, silver. And gold.

T HE OTHER SHIPS finally managed to work themselves free and find deep water again, but *Tyger* could not. There was a terrible grating noise and we looked round, expecting to see her go under. In fact, the tide had reached its height and lifted what was left of her off the shoal at last. At the mercy of the current, she heaved sideways, struck the shore of the sand island, and couldn't be budged.

From somewhere aboard, we could hear Lane and Fernando screaming at each other.

"Get himself topped, the damn fool Portugee," Gabriel muttered. "Lane's mad as an owl."

"But Fernando's Walsingham's man. I fancy he's safe enough."

"A spider at the helm? Christ, no wonder he ran her aground."

The afternoon lengthened and the waves stilled. From beyond the breach, in the marsh at the edge of the sound, a flock of swans rose up, and moments later a small boat came bobbing down the shoreline.

There had been rough sketches of the savages' boats in Harry's folio, but this was nothing like them. It was more like the coracles the Welsh used, fragile willow frames woven with vines and tree roots and covered with oiled skins, made to manage the shallows. A Moses boat.

"Only one oarsman," I said, peering into the clear afternoon light.

"That's no oarsman." Gabriel shaded his eyes with his hand. "That's a woman. That's *her*."

"Fool. You can't know that."

Look at her, he said. *Look at how proud she is. Look at the pearls.*

Lady Naia caught sight of our ships. She lifted her oar and paused for a moment, then spun the little boat skillfully into the current of the sound and rowed away, out of sight.

It was just before sunset when she returned. A shout went up from Lane's shore guard and six dugout canoes appeared, moving like swift shadows towards the breach. As they drew near, we could see that they were rowed by warriors with half-shaven heads. Some of the faces were terrifying—painted black and white, their eyes circled with bloodred. Other men bore complex designs of some sort on their chests and arms, and all of them wore neckbands that gleamed like gold in the twilight. Bright metal shone from the slivers of bone that pierced their ears, and snakes' rattles, birds' beaks, bears' claws, dangled from them proudly.

"Mary and Joseph," breathed the big Dutchman, taking up a hayfork for a weapon. Others snatched shovels, wooden rakes, knives, iron kettles. Most of us were unarmed and half naked, trying to dry ourselves at smoky little driftwood fires.

The dugouts drew near and the last crimson shafts of the sun struck the oarsmen. "That's gold round their necks," said an awestruck voice. "See there, how it glitters?"

Gold.

Rafe Lane heard the word and was on his feet in an instant. "Form a line!" he roared. "Load your weapons, damn you!"

"The water, sir," said his nervous orderly. "The guns won't fire."

Lane's fist shot out and broke the fellow's nose.

"Put up those weapons!" commanded Grenville as the Secota calmly beached their boats. He turned to Master Hariot. "Go and greet them, Thomas. Try to explain matters."

The expedition of discovery had brought back two natives to London the previous year, and with their help Ralegh had set Thomas Hariot to learn the language and compile a Secota grammar. Meat and drink to Gabriel, of course. He'd been studying all the way from Portsmouth.

"Sounds like gibberish," I complained.

"It's perfectly simple, you poor clot. Well, not *that* simple. But I think they've only come to welcome us." Suddenly he snatched at my arm. "Jesu, Rob. *She's* come with them. Look."

Five women climbed out of the boats. Two young girls, giggling and staring. Two nervous matrons of thirty or forty, chattering and pointing at us. And Lady Naia, walking calmly behind.

It could have been no one else. She clapped her hands twice and the giggling stopped abruptly. Her women stepped aside and as she passed, they bent their heads slightly and their features became decorous masks. Gabriel's voice was an indelible whisper.

Where'd she get that wavy hair from, Robbie? Little soft fringe over her forehead. Darkest eyes I ever saw. And her skin. Throat the color of new honey. Shoulders like pale brown silk.

She was still some distance from us, the crest of bright metal and pearls in her hair a soft glow in the twilight. She wore a soft doeskin apron tied round her waist, and long ropes of freshwater pearls—many shades of white, cream, purple, pink, silver-grey, black—looped themselves across her bare breasts. Her buttocks needed no adornment. They were, as I remember, the color of nutmeg cakes. When she walked away from you, she could make your heart stop.

What? Nutmeg cakes? Randy old stoat you are, Rob.

"What're those marks on her forehead and her arms?"

Tattoos. Like narrow pale-blue diadems, pale as colored ice on her brow. Painted necklaces, too—red, green, blue, patterns weaving like threads, and her body the tapestry. Christ.

I had to drag him back to me. "What's that other mark? See there, just between her shoulders? They all have them, the men, too."

"Her lineage. Her clan mark. Two wavy lines—that's the sea."

All his weeks and months of study came together and attached themselves to her—and what else, after all, had I wanted? But it was happening much too fast. I had almost to shove him aside as she began to move towards Grenville and Lane. Her women followed, carrying clay jars and handsome reed baskets, and her men were unloading more from their boats.

Grenville made her his best court bow. "Ask what she would have of us," he told Hariot. "Tell her we bring greetings from our queen."

IN THIS PLACE, the words of English courtship seem adolescent and full of themselves. There is a lag, a displacement in time between these native people and ourselves; they are subtler, older, more civilized. Perhaps that is what savagery means.

Naia listens politely, her soft hair blowing round her face, and when she speaks Hariot translates: "In ceremony, there is comfort. In feasting, there is peace. Within this circle, it is the duty of women to offer hospitality."

The two maidens spread a painted skin on the ground and begin to set out the baskets and jars. There are bowls of tiny wild strawberries. New beans cooked with several kinds of shellfish. Baskets of corncakes. Many jars of fish and venison stew. Dried-cherry cakes sweetened with precious wild honey. After months of weevily porridge and bad beer, it looks to us like a Twelfth Night feast.

But the soldiers' eyes are huge with a hunger for more than food. For months we have been all men on the ships, over-crowded in wretched quarters. Night after night, in heat and tropical storms as we travelled along the African coast and then turned west towards the Indies, we have heard men pleasuring themselves or one another, or praying to keep themselves from it. And now these fragrant women. This food.

Desperate to cover his swollen appetite, one boyish soldier breaks ranks and snatches up a pair of worn breeches. Lane glares at him; the silly boy will pay dearly for his lust.

Quietly, Hariot tries to return to his translating. "She says her mother's brother who rules them is away to the north. In his stead, she would bring ten of us back to her village for feasting and dancing. I have heard of this. It is ever their custom when strangers arrive. The lady would know which men are the heads of our clans."

"Lady?" Rafe Lane plants himself squarely in front of her. "Don't palter, man, she's only a female and a savage."

Scorn needs no translation. Naia steps neatly past Lane and begins to walk again, studying our faces cautiously. "Never thought their women would be so clean," I hear somebody say as she passes. "Just look at the gold on her," says a one-eyed man. "Our fortune's made."

LANE WILL GO to the feast as governor, along with Grenville and three of the gentlemen who hold shares in the venture, with

Hariot to translate. The chaplain and the artist John White both step forward. "She will choose two others from among the commons," Hariot tells us.

She stops first before the old Jew, Ganz. Takes his hand and bows her head over it. Age is to be respected. He joins the others waiting by the boats.

There is still one guest to choose and for a split second I think it will be me. Naia smiles at me—oh, a dazzling smile. But when I look straight into her eyes, her smile disappears and I hear Gabriel's breath catch as she turns to him.

In the shadows, his hair and beard and his forearms still glisten with a hoarfrost of sea salt. Naia laughs her soft, private laugh and begins to chafe his arm with her palms, the salt falling in a glittering shower.

I can see his grey eyes in the darkness. Face turned a little aside from her and head bent. Already ashamed not to be what he seems. Already in debt to her. Ruin in those eyes.

It will not be easy, after tonight, to keep him to his task. The spying. The gold mines. The pearl beds. The silk that grows on bushes.

Her hands lie motionless upon his arm for another long moment, considering him from under the fringe of her lashes. Then she claps her hands twice and is gone.

"You must've done something wrong," I fuss at him. "You've put her off you now."

"Ah, bugger it," he growls, and disappears among the rest.

The final guest is chosen. The Secota men light cattail torches and their canoes pull away, the smoky torchlight carving the darkness over Roanoke Sound. I go looking for Gabriel and find him on the crest of a high dune, watching the boats disappear.

"You might've tried harder. You're not just here for the grand tour, you know."

He turns on me, hands balled into fists. "What did you expect me to do? Take her behind a sand dune and plant the English flag in her?"

"Just get her to trust you and then ask the right questions."

"Toady and Ratsbane give you a list, did they? *The Intelligencer's Book of Dirty Tricks*? Or do you make it up as you go?"

"Don't fight me. I may be your friend, but I'm also your—"

"Master?"

"It's how the world wags. I have masters, we all have. What did you come for, if not to follow orders?"

"Oh," he says, his voice so soft and inward I can barely hear him. "*You'll* never know what I've come for. Never in this world."

Next morning we buried Jem and four others whose bodies washed ashore. With some amazing helmsmanship, Fernando at last got the six undamaged ships through the breach and up the sound, to drop anchor at Roanoke, where our men set to work unloading cargo. Their mood was high and hopeful— long lines of men laughing and joking, planning how they would squander their shares of the Secota gold. They handed off bags and crates and kegs of supplies, and lutes and flageolets, and featherbeds stinking of bilgewater. Lane's bulldog and somebody's pet ferret. Goats and pigs, and laying hens that had already ceased to lay.

I found Gabriel with Master Williams, the Welsh house carpenter we called Taff, marking spaces in the sand where our cottages would be built. Taff drove in a holly stake for good luck at the corner of one house and stood up to straighten his back, grinning his toothless grin. "Need a bit of luck under this roof, eh? Old Captain Rant-and-Rave's cottage, this is."

"Barracks over there?" I asked Gabriel.

Gabriel was concentrating. He liked building things. Then at last he seemed to realize that I was beside him. "Ganz's metalworks about here," he said, scraping his toe in the sand. "Lot of heat in that smelting furnace he wants. What do you think, Taff—maybe a bigger door? Catch the breezes?"

"There's sense in that." The stubby little Welshman scratched his head. "Only we can't, see. No open doors by day or night, and shutters on the windows. Captain's orders." Suddenly his bushy eyebrows shot up. "Orders! Oh, the devil! There's a flogging in an hour and I must set up a whipping post. Come on, Gabe, lend us a hand, eh?"

MY FRIEND HATED public entertainments. He was gone before Taff turned his back and I was hardly surprised that he did not reappear when the drummer sounded assembly. The bagpipes wheezed and the drum rose to a deafening rattle as Rafe Lane, trailed by his swollen-nosed orderly, arrived in full armor and gave the command for the offender to be tied to the crossbars. It was the poor young fool from last night, the one who had broken ranks to snatch up his breeches. Seventeen, at the most. The pale skin of his bared back still perfect as a child's.

The serjeant used a double lash, able to cut to the bone. The sound of it came steady and cold, broken only by the low voices of those who took wagers on whether the boy would cry out, and how many times.

He made no noise, really, just a faint, involuntary grunt when the cords struck home. Widgets are granted little else in this world. But they can be iron-proud.

six

CRIME AND PUNISHMENT, *OR* THE FINE RULES WITH WHICH THEY BEGAN

First, That no man shall violate or lay hands upon any woman of the savages. To this crime, the punishment, Death.

Second, That none do take any man's goods forcibly from him. To this, a restitution of double what was taken, or a year in the prison, the whip, and banishment to the forests upon release.

Third, That no Indian shall be forced to labour unwillingly. To this, three months in the prison.

Fourth, That no man shall defraud Her Majesty of her fifth share of profit. To this, Death or condemnation for life to slave labour.

Fifth, That no man desert from his company without leave of the captain. To this, Death or seven years at slave labour.

Sixth, That none shall strike or misuse any Indian. To this, twenty blows of the cudgel in the presence of the one struck.

Seventh, That none shall enter any Indian's house without his leave. To this, seven months at slave labour.

Eighth, That none shall strike another within the fort nor fight within a mile of it. To this, loss of a hand.

Ninth, That none attempt to draw any weapon against any official or officer. To this, Death.

Tenth, That none sleep at sentinal nor abandon his guard. To this, Death.

seven

WHAT THE SPY SAW IN THE FOREST

A WEEK PASSES, THEN ANOTHER AND ANOTHER. LANE HAS A NEW lute boy, a pimply stripling of fifteen who only knows how to play "Green Garters."

The puny fort on the headland is laid out in the shape of a star, with pointed ramparts in all directions—a place to set guards, but of no use for protection. Hariot salvages the cannon and it is planted with its black barrel, an erect and syphilitic member, aimed in the direction from which the Spanish are most likely to come.

Our depleted supplies soon begin to be rationed. A portion of barley bread the size of my palm. A quarter pound of cheese. A half-blackjack of sour beer. We are deep in a drought and there are no deer to hunt; even the fish seem to have found better feeding grounds. We slaughter a lame horse. The cook finds weevils in the barley. A fox helps himself to the hens, and the pigs run away to the woods.

For the first fortnight, a messenger from Naia's village arrives each morning with a gift of food—fish, corn, beans. Our cooks begin to rely on it, but gradually the gifts decrease in size, then stop altogether. Lane's command is terse:

"Send Hariot to trade for food. Whatever the pissing bitch has got."

"If she won't trade?"

"Then take it, you arsehole."

But he miscalculates. Naia's uncle, the savage king Wingina, has returned from his mainland towns, where he has been collecting taxes. They are paid in corn, dried meat, furs and skins, pearls. And perhaps in gold—or so the rumor goes.

Again and again, Wingina turns Lane's scavengers away; instead he sends his own men to instruct our hunters in the Secota way of taking down a deer. They flush out game with smoking torches and shoot it with many shell-tipped arrows. Once the animal is down, they club it to death. The chaplain forbids this unseemly procedure. Instead we use guns, which blow the game to inedible bits.

The mosquitoes and the sand flies devour us. The bites fester and some men fall sick. Lane beats the pimply lute boy relentlessly and sometimes wakes us in the night, stalking the camp as he tells his covetous rosary. *Goldgoldgoldgoldgoldgoldgold.*

B Y THE FIRST week of August, our piddling little cottages and the long narrow barracks have begun to rise on foundations of clay bricks. A frame of timbers, its walls filled in with mud and plaster daub as at home. Then a narrow brick chimney, and finally a roof thatched with marsh reeds.

Another week. *Tyger* is relaunched, her hull repaired and her seams and decking newly caulked. Grenville sails her down the coast to explore the mainland villages and Lane goes with him, taking a contingent of troops. In less than a month the great ships will be ready to sail back to England. No more than fifty soldiers and a hundred and thirty civilians will stay out the year.

Time drips like Spanish moss from the swamp oaks. I am spying again.

E VERY DAY GABRIEL goes out alone—or thinks he does. Marking saplings for the palisade we will build around our village; gathering botanical samples for Hariot; recording varieties of fish, of birds, of wild animals, of edible fruits. Placing himself always within Naia's compass.

Sometimes she does not appear and he cannot sleep that night, he tosses on his pallet or volunteers for night guard. Sometimes she puts in an appearance but remains aloof, far too busy gathering wild raspberries or picking sassafras leaves. Whatever she does, Gabriel smiles and greets her in her own language; sometimes she allows him to teach her a few English words.

It is a slow and delicate dance, and for weeks he lets her lead him. Then one day in late August the steps suddenly change.

As usual, Naia arrives with her maidens—this time to pick the last of the wild plums in a small meadow between two groves of tulip poplars. Gabriel is stripping the branches from a cut sapling and at first she pretends to ignore him, slowly inching nearer until he finally looks up at her and smiles.

Behind my tapestry of yaupon and sassafras bushes I move, soft-foot, until I am near enough to hear them both breathe.

The maidens flutter and giggle, hiding their faces in their hands and peeping out at Gabriel between their fingers. It is very hot and he is shirtless.

"What are they laughing at?" he says.

Naia claps and the girls fall silent. "Your skin is white," she tells him. "Naturally they laugh at this."

"Why naturally? There are white flowers in the woods. And your pearls are white, some of them."

Today the long strands are wrapped around her arms, reaching from wrist to elbow. "What do they mean?" he asks her, one fingertip hovering over a silver-grey pearl.

Not *where are the pearl beds*. Not *draw me a map*. Not *is the bright metal gold*.

"Spirit," she says. "They are spirit-pearls."

"And you believe in spirits?"

"I do not believe in the swamp witches. Pfu."

"Is your husband a good spirit? Or a bad one?"

She grows distant, very quiet. "When I sleep on his grave, he is with me. When I need his counsel, he knows." Looking up at Gabriel then. Fingering her earring. "Pearls are not only spirit. They mean—what word is this of yours? Tooth?"

"Oh. Truth. Honesty."

"Are you this word? Are you honest?"

Tell her yes, damn you, I almost shout. *Tell her yes, of course I am.*

Every muscle in his face is concentrated on her. "I'm honest with *you*," he says. "God's own truth. Always, with you."

H E HAS WORKED like a madman to learn more of her language, staying up long after curfew, making lists of words on an old hornbook, saying them over and over, turning me into his schoolmaster until even I learn a few words. There are still huge gaps, like glacial fissures, between himself and Naia, but he forces his mind and his agile tongue over them, eyes closed and heart pounding. Risking everything to catch up, while she waits calmly on the opposite side.

I venture dangerously near them now—the *voyeur par excel-*

lence. With or without words, my mind invades them both. I am achieving the omniscience of the perfect spy.

Lane has ordered us all to keep clear of the Secota village, but one day Gabriel goes to gather wild roses for our apothecary very near to the rickety old palisade. Whole sections of it are in disrepair; there can have been no real war here for years.

From my hiding place in the woods, I count nine dwelling houses that look like loaves of English bread. They are framed with hooped cedar poles, then layer after layer of reed matting draped over them and neatly fastened, able to be rolled up in hot weather. There is a spirit circle for dancing-in the harvest and for praying and smoking tobacco, the whole village set in a lovely grove of dogwood and sycamore and pine, with a meadow where children and dogs play and run races. There is a large storehouse and deep pits to winter-over the root crops and the dried venison and fish. The temple where the aged priest Airstalker lives and tends the cattail lamp before the black statue of God. And of course the Great House where Naia lives with her uncle and her children.

So close to her own village, she does not come out to meet Gabriel. Shy, perhaps, or fearful of gossip. Two days go by, then three. He tries setting snares for rabbits. He tries cutting more saplings. He takes to singing, just to let her know he is near. On the fifth day, as he loads sand from the nearby cove into a barrow for more chimney bricks, his voice fairly roars through the woods.

> *Let the queen's health go round and round,*
> *And may her praises loud resound,*
> *And he who would not have it so,*
> *May he be cursed with a gouty toe.*

"What is this—gouty?"

Naia materializes out of the shadows, alone this time. No maidens. No children. Not even a dog.

He grins at her. "Gout? It's like—toothache. Only in your toe. Rich men get it. Too much sitting about giving orders." He begins to dust himself down. "I've been wanting to ask you," he says, and for a moment I think he will do his duty and get to the gold. I might've known better.

"Tell me about this famous boat of yours," he asks her instead. "The one you were using that first time we saw you."

"There is no telling. A boat is a boat." She hesitates, a little afraid of her new boldness. "Ena made it for me. My husband, who is dead."

"Ah. So it was a love gift, actually, was it? Bedtime gift? 'Here you are, sweeting, I had nothing to do after supper so I built you a boat'?"

"What word is this? Sweet—Ning?"

"Ing. Sweet-ing," he says. "Sweeting. Term of endearment. Love words."

"Pfu. *Love* words? Ena was my husband, we made children together. He did not call me foolish names anymore."

"He did once, though?"

"Men are all idiots when they are courting."

"But you married him anyway."

Her smile is generous, secret, and rare. "Others came courting, but I wanted only Ena and he would not come. I waited and waited, so long the old grannies put shame on me. Then at last he dropped the stick before me."

"Stick?"

"Yes, *stick*. Why not stick? If the man drops it and you pick it up, you will marry. If you leave it or kick it aside, it means 'I don't like you, go bother some other woman.' I picked up the stick from Ena. That night we were the first time lovers."

"Could you still have sent him away then?" he asks her very quietly. "If he turned out to be a filthy fraud, you know. A liar. Not at all what he seemed."

Gabriel's dirty hands lift towards her, then retreat. Some crucial bone in him long ago broken. The spirit, too, has bones. Her voice softens, tending this invisible damage.

"Ena was the same always. He *could* have deceived me, if he had wished to." Then she laughs, teasing. "He was much more clever than you."

"Old heart, there's a small continent of people more clever than me. And of course he built boats and everything. Sink like a stone if I tried that. Like to see it up close sometime, how he made it."

She allows herself to be pleased by this. "Of course I will show you. Ena knew how I like to go off by myself. He was thinkful of me."

"Thoughtful."

"You should not always fix my speaking! Thinkful is good enough. Even when you said you had a fish in your ear the other day, *I* said nothing."

"Laughed, though, didn't you? Just let *me* make a mistake in Secota and it's giggles all over the shop, you and those two girlies who trail after you."

"Amagaya and Manina. They can be very silly, but I will be queen so I must have maidens whether I like them or not."

"Not today, though. No maidens this morning. Does that mean you trust me?"

The long eyelashes flicker like birds' wings. "It means I am not afraid of you. That is not trusting. But it was not kind of us to laugh at your fish-ears. I owe you a sorry gift."

"What's that?"

"When you do wrong, you must give a gift to show you did not mean badness. Otherwise the wronged one can be feuding, his clan with your clan. Wars can come." She considers. "I will give you some hazelnut oil to rub yourself. It will make you smell better."

His huge laugh explodes. "Wonderful! I hope you have a lot of it."

Naia stands watching, trying to settle her mind to him. "I can also ask you things, Mr. Fish-Ears?"

"Fire away."

"There are only men in your camp. Don't you have any women?"

"Who, me? Personally? A woman?"

Gabriel looks, then, straight at where I am hidden. I have not fooled him for a single minute. It is the other way round. I feel cramped and crooked and degenerate. I will not do this again. I will find other ways.

"No woman," Gabriel tells Naia in a voice that is distant and sorry. "Don't have a one."

"So. Not one, but many. And perhaps many children?"

"God, you're suspicious." He deflects the question. "You have children. Think I've seen them. Boy and a girl?"

Her sandy voice grows warm and strong. "Masu is— One. Two. Three." She counts on her fingers as Gabriel has taught her. "Five?"

"That's right. Five years old."

"No, no. Winters. Years are foolish. Five—years?" He nods and so does she. "Tanokia is not two—years. She eats. She cries. She sleeps."

"Do they like to play bears? Can I take them swimming? Do they look like you, or like Ena?"

"They both look like him. It means he is still with us. So."

Naia falls silent again, staring out at the sound that sparkles silver-blue beyond the trees. But Gabriel cannot yet bear her sudden distances. He has to tease her back to him.

"What was your husband like? Was he tall? Short? Did he make your heart thump? Was he handsome?"

"How he looked does not matter."

"Ah. Broken nose and warts, then."

Her dark eyes remember how to dance. "If you must know this, Ena was very handsome before his sickness. Much more handsome than *you*. Your nose is too long and thin. Like a fish-hook."

Gently. Slowly. "I'm glad you loved him. I'm glad he was kind." Then more teasing. "Or did he beat you on a regular and beneficial basis? Did he sing dirty songs? Did he rattle the walls when he snored?"

"When I was pregnant with Masu and sick every morning, Ena would bring cool water and wash my face with his two hands." She looks up then, a glance like a surgeon's knife. "I think *you* would not do so much, Mr. Fish-Ears. For these hundreds of women of yours."

eight

HOW THE SAVAGES WERE
TAUGHT THEIR PLACE

"WHAT ABOUT THE PEARL BEDS?" I ASK GABRIEL. THE LATE SUMmer continues scorching hot and rainless and we are all at one another's throat. "Has she at least told you where the fisheries are?"

"They're mussel pearls, freshwater. Best ones are inland somewhere, one of the rivers. I need a christly map, and I can't just—"

"And the black pearls? They're rare, you know, of great value in the pearl markets."

"These are only black because the women throw the mussels in the pot to boil before they open them. Black, grey, brown, purple—it's boiling that does it. Pink and white ones are fine, but the rest aren't worth spit."

"All right, never mind black pearls. What about the gold?"

"I told you. I can't push her."

"Have you slept with her yet?"

"You mean have I screwed her."

"Well? Have you?"

"Three times. No, four. Or was it eight? Want the details? Maybe I could get White to draw you pictures."

"You haven't touched her, have you?"

"No. Yes. No."

"Will you tell me when you do?"

"Bollocks," he groans, and storms off into the woods.

AUTUMN BEGINS, BUT the heat is relentless. The leaves of the trees droop and the trailing moss hangs crisped and brown from the swamp oaks. Our mouths are dry and our skin cracks and bleeds. Lane orders a grove of black oaks felled and there is no shade in our village. The Secota women carry water every day to their cornfields and we hear them weeping for the spirits of the lost trees.

By September our great ships have all gone, taking most of our men with them. For boats, we have only a pinnace, a tiltboat with a canvas roof, and two Thames wherries—none of them any use on the open sea. Our rations are cut again. A cup of rice gruel. Half a salt codfish. One dipper of tepid water.

Even when the weather begins to cool, we all sleep badly, our nerves frayed by whispered stories of Lane's inland exploring. An old Weapeme wise man killed for refusing to hand over his gold. A woman raped and her pearls stolen.

At last the heat breaks, but there is still no rain as September passes into October. Rafe Lane's orders keep coming. Build a gallows. Build a prison. Dig a hole. Not a round hole, a square one. Don't speak at table. No laughing out loud. A soldier has his tongue slit for singing after sunset. Another is flogged two hundred strokes for walking too fast.

We all know something is waiting its chance at us, but we cannot prevent it. We cannot even run away from it. A ship will be sent for us from England, but not for eight months, or perhaps nine. Or perhaps never, if Elizabeth cannot keep the Armada at bay.

We wait for calamity to bare its claw.

✦

IT COMES FROM a direction we have not expected. On a clear autumn morning Naia comes running, running through the woods to find Gabriel, nobody with her, not even wearing her pearls. It is not yet midmorning, an edge of winter in the October air. He is gathering walnuts, cracking them open with his bootheel.

"Please please please," she cries, clinging onto his sleeve. "Oh please!"

Shaking all over, Robbie. Wrapped in the painted skin cloak, holding it tight around her, suddenly afraid of her own body. I could see her throat tremble when the breath fought its way out of her.

"Maaaasuuuuuu," she groans. A wail that might go on forever. Her voice cracking, shivering with fear. "Soldiers toook hiiim . . ."

"Your boy? Why, for God's sake?"

"I don't know! If I knew, would I let them? I was out in the marsh with the women and children, digging swamp lily roots for the winter. Somebody screamed. A soldier had Masu, and he was kicking and crying. Oh please, my boy never cries. Oh please please, don't let them hurt hiimm . . ."

She slides down to Gabriel's boots, clinging onto them. If he lets her, she might stay down for good, and he cannot allow that. He catches her by her wrists and hauls her up, forces her to stand again. The first time he has dared to touch her flesh.

"Walk with me now. Come on. That's right. That's right." Her people believe in the saving virtue of circles, so he takes her around and around the tree stumps, half-embracing her to keep her from falling. He can feel the sweet oil she rubs into her skin. The slight weight when she leans against him, and the warmth of her. "Where's the baby?" he says. "Where's Kia? Are there soldiers in your village? Is there fighting?"

"The young men are away hunting deer. I don't think there are soldiers. How do I know? I am here, I am not there!"

"Come on, then. I'll take you home."

But Naia has found herself and she pushes free of him. "No. It would not be proper. I must go by myself."

She dares not be seen alone with him; he is English. He lets her go, but he skirts through the woods, keeping her constantly in sight till she reaches her village.

It looks quiet enough. Children playing, heaping piles of leaves on each other and burrowing out again, laughing, their dogs barking joyfully. One woman pounding corn into meal with a heavy wooden maul. Another cooking stew in a red clay jar over a firepit—the fragrance of venison, wild mustard, oysters, walnuts, dried cherries. The spirit circle where the men smoke and dance is empty and silent, drifted with big sugary leaves from the syca-more trees and smaller ones from the dogwoods.

The priest's house and temple stand open for worship as usual, the reed matting rolled up and the cattail lamp burning before the polished black statue of God, inscrutable and vaguely amused. It is hung with offerings of white coral and shells, greeny-bronze swamp oak leaves, and pearls of many shapes and colors.

Naia crosses the meadow and enters the Great House. At al-most the same moment, Gabriel hears the sound of a canoe bumping onto the beach at the foot of the slope and the shrill keening of women. The other lily root gatherers have returned from the marsh, the old grannies wailing, the young women run-ning, shooing their own children before them.

He hears Kia begin to cry and then Naia appears in the door-way, giving the baby her breast. The women cluster around them, stroking Naia's hair and patting her arms. Their voices bring the priest Airstalker from the temple-house, wearing his owl-feather cloak. Naia's uncle is with him—Wingina, the king.

It is a foolish word for him, insufficient. He is taller than most

Secota men, broad-shouldered and deep-chested. He wears a gorget of golden metal around his neck, gleaming rings on several of his fingers, and heavy arm bracelets and earrings of bright metal and spirit-pearls. He has many intricate tattoos, and his throat and chest and arms and legs have been painted with delicate tracings of red and blue. The paint follows old scars, zigzagging in jagged tracks across his body. His black hair is beginning to grey and he wears it in the fashion of their warriors—half his scalp shaved clean and oiled, the hair on the other half grown long and drawn sideways, oiled, then braided just behind the ear and fastened with the claw of a bear. He might be Egyptian, Minoan, Babylonian, Tartar, Greek.

"Ayyiieeeeeeeee," the women cry. "Ayyiiiieeeeeeeee-yaaaah!" They flutter like a flock of birds, rising together, running in a cluster with small, frightened steps. Naia walks among them slowly, the little girl still at her nipple, and as she goes they make way.

GABRIEL WATCHES HER one moment longer. Then he turns and runs, full out, careless of everything—soldiers, returning warriors, mad captains. He finds me sitting inside the open door of one of the cottages, watching old Joachim Ganz, across the muddy lane in his alchemical workshop, testing gravel from the streambed for traces of gold. The little boy, Masumeo, is screaming and screaming, you can hear him all over the camp.

"What the hell's going on, Rob? What've they taken her boy for?"

"Captain Lane ordered it. Wanted a hostage."

"God's sweet eyes, man, he's only five years old!"

"The theory is, he'll get us what we want. Food for the winter. Enough pearls to impress London. Directions to their gold. *You've* been no use and Lane wants to mount an expedition to claim it."

"Damn your soul." Gabriel grabs my arm and jerks me to my feet. "The Secota have been feeding us these two months already, they can't go on forever. In case nobody's noticed, there's a drought and their crops are no good. Anyway, what if the damn gold doesn't exist? What happens to the boy then? What happens to *her?*"

He doesn't wait for the answer. Masu's screams are growing hoarse and tight now. So strangled they make you wince just to hear them.

The little jail is rickety and not meant to hold more than two people at once. There are no bars, no windows. When the door is shut, it is black and airless inside, except for the unchinked cracks in the upright log walls where thin shafts of daylight sift in. A coffin, not a cage.

The camp physician is talking to the soldier on duty. "Can't you bleed him or give him a cordial or something?" says the soldier. His face is pale and his eyes bulge. "Jesus, can't you stop him screaming?"

Gabriel walks up to them. Lays a hand on the soldier's tensed arm. He has a knack for touching, some subtle calm that his grubby fingertips restore. "Got the key have you, Ned? Right, then. Just unlock the door and let me in."

The soldier shakes his head. "Lane'll flay the skin off me. It's orders."

"Screw orders. That's a baby inside there. Let me quiet him down a bit. You can lock me in with him, only keep your mouth shut and nobody'll know. Coom on, old heart."

The child's screams are very hoarse now, almost voiceless. "Go ahead," says the physician. He is middle-aged, Dutch. An army surgeon who's seen hell fighting the Spanish in Holland, fled to England, and then gone through another hell in Ireland. He knows Rafe Lane, what he is capable of. "If you're caught out," he says, "tell them I ordered it."

THE GROWN-UP leg irons are too big, so they have locked a chain to the bolts in the wall and wrapped it twice round Masu's small, bare waist. As he screams, he runs forward, then is jerked back by the limit of the chain. The soft brown skin of his belly is oozing blood from a dozen dimpled gouges halfway round to his back. When the door opens, he stops straining and stares up at the men, and his baby hands make themselves into kitten-claws.

"Water, Ned," Gabriel orders quietly. "He's shat himself and he's bleeding. Jesus holy Christ."

They snatch up a bucket and set it inside, and then the door closes and the lock rattles.

Come on now, my boy. Shhshhshh. No, no, you're not a cat. Ouch! Jesus. Come on, drink some water. That's right. Good. Get you out of this damn fool mess now. Masu? Masumeo? I won't hurt you, you know me. Your mama sent me. Nama, that's right. Nama says to be a good boy and let me wash you. That's right. Hush, my good boy. Come on come on come on. Ah, come here.

H E NEVER KNEW who opened the door that night, nor at what hour. The moonlight roused him, he said, and the small cool wind, and the breathing of the tide. His own face raked with little cat-scratches, he lay holding the exhausted child, warm and clean and wrapped in the tattered brown doublet, the small milk-brown arms clinging tight.

I had not been able to sleep and sat watching—alone as usual. Listening to the occasional grunts and soft cries of the men in the barracks. Thinking of Staple Oaks. Of the proud beggar on the roadway. Of Annette.

Then I heard the heavy rattle of the key in the lock of the prison house and the unmistakable flat-footed lope of Gabriel's feet on the sandy path.

"Let me take the boy," I said, catching up with him. "You're spent."

I have never been much at ease with small children. I have no sons. That night, though, for some reason, I needed to feel the intense baby-warmth of the little boy's body, of his breath on my arm. But Gabriel could not seem to let him go.

There was lute music from Lane's quarters. Then the noise of smashing wood, the discord of snapped strings, and the yowl of the pimply lute boy. A candle passed back and forth from one window to another, a dim stumbling flare behind the cracked shutters. Lane's deep, harsh voice. *Goddamnfuckingshitholewildernessbarearselying-savagecuntgoldhopelesskillkillkillkillkillgodkillgodkillgod. Bastard! You! Fucking! Bastard!*

"Saying his prayers," I muttered.

"Mad as crackers."

"Ambitious."

"Same thing. Will it come to a real battle?"

"Maybe. Get the boy safe home now." I let my hand rest on Masu's shaven head. "If there's war, it won't happen tonight."

nine

DISPLACED PERSONS

IT IS ALREADY DAYLIGHT WHEN HE REACHES NAIA'S VILLAGE WITH the little boy in his arms. There is a woman stirring the embers of a fire in the cooking pit. A handsome, sullen-faced young man of about Naia's age sits cross-legged in front of the Great House with his bow near at hand. In the shadowy interiors of the smaller houses, human shapes move, secretly keeping watch.

Masu wakes and wriggles free. "Go and find Nama," Gabriel says, but the boy is already halfway across the meadow. The guard gives a shout and Naia appears at the door of the temple.

What a sight she was, Rob. The secret calm that lives so deep in her bones that only the worst fear can rouse it—it was in her face then. Ready to die for her boy if she had to. Wearing all her finery at once, strand after strand of spirit-pearls, long ropes falling almost to her ankles and wound around her throat and covering her breasts and her arms. Heron feathers in her hair, and the twisted wire that gleams red in the sun. I never quite realized till I saw her then. Never understood what a queen is. The past and the future. It's the present that goes missing, the here and the now.

Naia. Na'iya.

She stops a few feet from Masu and opens her arms to him. Whispers something that makes him laugh and squirm. She laughs, too, and lets him go. Gabriel slips back again, into the shadowy woods.

B Y THE TIME her uncle sends for her, she has taken off all the fancy trappings. She lives every day in the Great House, but it seems strangely forbidding as she walks behind Osawi the Herald, Wingina's fastest runner, to the formal Council Room at the far end. It is separated from the living quarters by a handsome quill-worked story-curtain of her own design, the quills dyed peach and blue and willow and rose. There is no fire in the pit under the smokehole. Bear-tallow lamps drift in the dim, airy space, hung from fragrant cedarwood roof poles. The pounded dirt floor has been carefully swept and strewn with wild mint and sweet-smelling dry sycamore leaves that crackle underfoot.

Airstalker is there, and Wingina sits on a raised platform built against the back wall and covered with furs. He goes to Naia and lays his warm, hard hand on her shoulder. "How's the boy?"

She laughs. "Oh, he's now completely delighted with himself. Bragging about his adventures. I gave him mulberry tea to make him sleep."

Wingina studies her soberly. "This tall Englishman, my dear, the one who brought the child home?"

"So you've seen him, then." She smiles, her feelings wide open to them. "I knew he'd help if I asked him."

"You mustn't ask him again. He was spotted and the guard wanted to chase him down and kill him. You know Tesik—hot-tempered, always was."

More ambition than hot temper. He had wanted to marry her once, before Ena. Now, having failed to marry a royal future, Tesik talks war in every council. In a war, power is easily seized.

People get used to taking orders without question, and once things calm down they just keep on doing it. They begin to elect their own ruin.

Wingina seems to read her thoughts. "If that one had his way, we'd be at war with the English now. Maybe we ought to be, I don't know. In any case, you're not to see this Englishman anymore."

She draws a painful, ragged breath. Then she bends her head again, regaining control, and the sunlight, filtering through the crimsons and blues and greens of the painted reed mats that form the house walls, falls across her face. Light is courage. The two old men have raised her to speak her mind and she does not fail them now.

"He's not to blame," she says. "He can't help being a European and foolish. I haven't been quick to trust him. But I believe he understands us. At least he tries."

"So much the worse for him. They'll make him pay for it."

"You don't know that, Uncle."

He laughs—a hard, sudden noise—and she feels as though he has bitten her. "What is there to know? He disobeyed orders. He took our side against theirs. To them, he's a traitor. You know what that means. Besides, these Europeans are savages. You've heard what they did to that Weapeme woman."

"*He* would never do such a thing. Never!"

Airstalker's cagey old face is blank and sad and his shoulders stoop more than usual as he puts his arm around her. "The truth now, my dear. The old women are talking. Have you had the Englishman in bed?"

"No, of course not. What do you take me for?"

"But you've been alone with him. You should've taken your maidens, you know. Only proper."

"Do you think I lie down for any man who comes near me? Of course if his people call him a traitor, I suppose you say the same of me, so I won't see him anymore. But we owe him a debt of honor for the sake of Masu, and he must be thanked. If I could just go and tell him—"

Wingina's voice is hard now, and angry. "I said no, Naia! Let him be. Don't go near the English from now on."

CAPTAIN LANE RAGED for weeks at the loss of his little captive, roaring his plans for marching on the village and taking the old priest hostage in place of the boy, demanding a bushel of pearls and the map to the gold as a ransom. Planning an expedition here, another one there, blind to hunger and the coming of winter. Determined to find his golden hoard and take it back to London.

Wingina refused to see all our messengers, leaving them to a sullen-eyed and wordless Tesik. Again our rations were cut. The salt cod turned mouldy. The last English horse was slaughtered and butchered, the meat gobbled up in two days.

The old Jew Ganz was kept at his smelter and his mallets and vials day and night, testing sample after sample of ore. Some was yellow-white in color, able to be polished to a fine gleaming shine, and very soft.

"What do you think, Joachim?" I said, venturing into his sweltering little Hades. "Is it gold?"

He took off his thick, leather-rimmed spectacles and mopped his face. "Pfui! Do I look like that great wizard John Dee who collects turds from different colors of horses and makes from them the Juice of Eternal Youth? I tell you, I've seen nothing in these ores but copper. There are many kinds and qualities, and some has this pale brightness. When it's correctly polished, it looks something like gold. Several metals do. Pyrites. Other things. But you see here?"

"The greenish stuff?"

"This you do not get with gold, Robert. Never. Does true gold leave a green ring on your finger? Pfui."

"Have you told Lane?"

"Ha. Who can tell him anything? I say it's copper. He says I'm a lying old Jew, I ought to be hanged. Do I want to hang? No. My back aches, my belly wants a nice bowl of chicken and *nudeln*. I tell you. The first Jew in America just wants to go home."

A T THE END of October, Naia's uncle called his Council to-gether—the head men and women of all the clans, the war chiefs and the chief of the hunting parties, Tesik who captained the King's Guard, Osawi the Herald, and Nasimi, who had charge of building and repairing the houses.

They talked far into the night and next day Osawi brought round the word. "The Council has spoken this. We will leave this village and build a new village on the mainland. With the water and the marshes between ourselves and these English, they'll find it harder to snatch up our children and come begging for our food and making threats when they don't get it."

"Leave our island?" one of the hunters said. "But we've always lived on Roanoke, it's our home. It's crazy to leave just because of those beggars! My father's father hunted here, and his father before him. I know all the best coverts."

"He's right," said a fisherman. "The Spanish came years ago. They strutted around and scared the fish with their shouting, and then they went away again. These will go home, too, if we just wait them out."

Tesik made a noise like a growling dog. "They'll pick us clean before they leave, no matter where we go. I say we beat them to it. Attack them before they attack us. Fight them on their own ground instead of ours."

"War of our own making?" said Asa'ni, the hunter's wife, with a shudder. She was pregnant, as usual.

Her husband frowned. "If there's war, you won't find a deer or a rabbit in two days' travelling, I can promise you that. We haven't got much food, and it's coming on winter."

It was never a wise thing to make war in the winter. But to be forced from their own island . . .

"Well," said the hunter's wife. "It might not be so bad on the mainland. There are good lily roots and wild onions in those marshes, and plenty of turtles. And once the English are gone, we can always come back."

L EAVING AN ISLAND forever is like dying. It is the surrender of a personal kingdom. Of self-reliance, solitude, ritual, magic. The safe hiding place of the soul.

In their secret hearts, they all know they will never return. The move takes a little over two weeks and they go secretly, working at night, the women weeping quietly as they fill the big war canoes with cooking pots, fishnets and spears, baskets of corn and beans from the storehouse, strings of dried pumpkin, family heirlooms, furs and heavy robes from the bedplaces. When their torches are seen by the English soldiers, they pretend to be night-fishing.

On the last night, they take the reed mats from the cedar house poles and the men knock down the poles to be ferried over and set up on the mainland. Last of all, under a guard of four with Tesik in command, goes the stolid black statue of God.

Airstalker enters one of his famous trances, hoping for a vision. The night is cold, but Naia and her children sleep on Ena's grave under the big yellow pine at the rim of the cove, in the hope that his spirit will come and wake them with a blessing.

It is their last chance. The dead cannot cross over water.

G ABRIEL, TOO, SPENT that night watching. I remember how fragile he looked the next morning, brittle as paper. If he had known of the move in advance, he'd said nothing. He still kept an eye on her, put himself where she could glimpse him. I assumed—wrongly—that they had finally become lovers, and I should've asked again about the pearl beds and the gold. I should've maneuvered him, teased, baited, flattered, built him up, knocked him down.

I didn't. It was too late for all that.

Smoke hung in a dank curtain over the woods and the marshes. Lane was raging again. The Secota could not have been away more than a few hours when he sent some men to the old village to demand food. They found the place gone, of course—cornmeal, smoked fish, pearls, reed houses, cooking jars, everything.

"Burn it!" he screamed. "Burn it all!"

"Nothing to burn, sir. Dry squash vines and cornstalks, is all."

"Burn the trees, then, you arseholes! Burn them all, or I'll cut off your heads!"

So they did the best they could. They set fire to Ena's yellow pine. It rose like a torch, catching other trees alight—dogwoods and cedars and sycamores. *Burnthetreesburnthefuckingwaterburnthegoddamnsonuvabitchbirdsburntheskyburntheghostsburnjesusburnthemotherfuckingqueen.*

A ALL THAT DAY, smoke hung in a dank curtain over the woods and the marshes. Hoping to stay out of Lane's way, Gabriel and I took a leaky rowboat on the pretext of fishing and went across the sound to the nearest of the Outer Banks, the barrier islands. Dunes heaped up by centuries of wind and sea, and behind them the dense maritime forest, a patchwork of russet, bitter green, bronze, glittering that early morning with the winter's first frost. We stalked the beach like a pair of shipwrecked sailors, barefoot in spite of the cold.

"I waited for her all night," he said. "Thought she'd be sure to come here, to her parrot tree. Brought me once to show me the little birds. Gathering the red and green and blue feathers and sticking them in her hair. Not as long as your finger, those little parrots, but hundreds of them, all in the same huge old tree—a white elm, must've been growing there when Edward the Confessor was king. Have you seen it?"

"No."

"You don't look. You never see things. You watch everything, but you never see. You don't even see yourself. Why don't you open your christly eyes for a change?"

He would never be a spider again. His gaze was already fixed on that dangerous spot in the inner distance, the one that means you've caught sight of something greater than the game. Gabriel no longer cared what Burghley wanted or what the Council expected or whether Europe went up in a puff of overbred smoke.

If she'd come to meet me last night, what would I have said? I love the little bead of moisture beneath your bottom lip. I love the sand in your voice and the tiny mole in the hollow of your throat. So strange, it is, so strange that I don't really think much of sex when I'm with you. Not yet. Not now. Because for the first time in my life I understand that there's an order in these things, and if we break it, everything's ruined. And you have taught me that. You have taught me how to be proper. At last.

ten

REPORT, WINTER AND SPRING, 1585–86: THE GOLD HUNTERS, *OR* WHAT THE SPY OVERHEARD IN THE VILLAGE

Marmaduke Constable, Lieutenant to Rafe Lane

I'M A YOUNGER SON, DON'T YOU KNOW, SO PA WILL LEAVE ALL THE best manors and most of the chinks to old Radford, my idiot brother. Well, when I saw the chance to come out here with the great Rafe Lane and stake myself for gold and glory, I took it. He's famous for taming these wild countries and his reputation rubs off. I mean, look what it's done for Wat Ralegh. Served with Lane in Ireland, hanged a few hundred. Now he's *Sir* Walter and the queen's tickling his pecker.

You see, it's all about who you know and who knows you and what you've got to hold over him and whether you can sell it and for how much. The chief skill of government is knowing who to use and who to throw away. If Lane goes back to England with a boatful of gold, he'll be in Ralegh's place next year, and his friends will rise with him. So I mean to be one of his friends. Then, once I'm greater than he is, I shall throw *him* away. Parliament after that—fine place for good bribes and the odd royal patent or two. Then a knighthood. Seat on the Council, whatever falls vacant.

Sets the brain humming, don't it? No end to a man's chances over here.

Ned Kettle, Common Soldier

I had no wish to come here, only I were took by a press gang on the road to Exeter, see. In all my life afore, I never had so much as a cheese rind without paying, in money or in toil. That were my pride and my worth, but I'm a thief now, right enough, and they did make me so—Lane and them he serves. And the queen, too, for what we do in her name, she does her own self.

Once the winter come and the frosts drove the geese southwards, we soon ran out of food, nor would the savage king give us none, for he said they could spare naught, the harvests being scant. A poor Christmas it were, though the men brought back holly from the woods and Taff sang *Isaiah the Prophet*. But we had not meat nor bread, nor corn to make bread, nor any ale, nor beans, nor fish. So in the New Year, Lane sent us by night across the sound to the savages' new town, to break open their storehouses and take what was theirs. And we took many jars of venison and dried fish and corn, not caring if them people starved, so long as *we* did not.

Now the spring is come, and soon we shall go inland to find their gold and steal that, too, if we can, for Lane says he will have us all shot if it be not found and taken. As for me, God send I may die in the forests, for my worth is all gone and my pride, too. I am more savage than Christian now, and I care not what harms I may wreke.

Joachim Ganz, Alchemist and Metallurgist

As a boy in Prague, I once knew a madman. A rich merchant, but when I met him a simple and kindly creature who had given away all his riches. A man touched by Heaven.

Believe me, no heaven has touched Rafe Lane. The Devil dances in those eyes of his. He cares nothing for England. He wants to rule the world—the shellfish, the sparrows, the dogs, the trees. All of it. He has no special liking for gold—what can such a man possibly care for? The world is his whore. Since gold just now eludes him, naturally he has to get it under his thumb. But it is the thumb that matters, not the gold.

The worst of it is, Lane will waste good men with this madness. The Welshman, Taff—not educated, but a thinking man, a clear spirit. And that poor fellow North who tries to love his way to the mind of God. There is no guilt in them, but there is no power, either.

In the end, there comes for the innocent and the guilty alike a great reckoning, an hour when a choice must be made. Orders or justice. A stain on the soul or a head on the executioner's block.

I made my choice. I took out a bucket of useless rocks veined with white copper. "You were right all along, sir," I told Lane. "It's most certainly gold."

So they go inland to find what isn't there. Am I responsible? Perhaps. But God is merciful. He washes a stained soul. And you can't sew a Jew's head back on.

Thomas Fox, Goldsmith

In the first days of March, when the great mainland forest was spotted white with dogwood blossom, we crossed the sound and took our boats up the largest of the inland rivers to discover the source of the Indian gold.

Lane shattered every rule he had set us. At one place, we fell upon a village by night and when we found no gold, he ordered the place burned and the people slain. No count was made of their numbers, being savages. I believe there were seventeen men. Of women and children, perhaps twelve.

At another village deeper inland, we took captive an old crippled chief and Lane demanded a ransom of gold. But the old man was no fool. He told us we must fetch the gold ourselves, as he was a cripple, and his directions led us in circles, always deeper into the forests and swamps. The trees grew so dense that we could see no light and had no notion whether it was day or night. Our food was consumed in those wanderings and we boiled our jerkins and ate them, and at last we had only the flesh of Lane's bulldog. Men took fever and their bowels would not hold. Our bodies swelled and grew loathsome. We saw visions, and voices called out to us—ghosts, some men said, and others said witches. I saw my dear wife come towards me through the trees, and when I tried to go to her, she faded away. We got lost in a thick marsh of reeds and the boats were mired in mud. Then the savages began to rain arrows upon us; they were men of a strange inland tribe, and very fierce. We fired back, they drew away, and so it went for many dark hours, by my calculations almost six days before at last we were able to free the boats and turn back for the coast and the island. Men died and we pushed them into the swamp and went on. We were all fevered, all raving and starved.

I came here for money, for patronage back in London, for a way to end my debts and buy a little shop in Cheapside. But there is a curse on this place. Grace has abandoned us here. We found no trace of gold, but Lane still insists he must have it. And whatever he tells us to do next, I fear he will be blindly obeyed.

eleven

THE RECKONING

A T LAST THE STARVING WINTER AND THE GOLD-MAD SPRING WERE ended and the air grew rich with the fragrance of wild fruit. Heartberry Moon, Naia's people called the month of June. It was their word for strawberries.

One soft night, loud with the croaking of frogs and alive with birds and spirits, she sat with her uncle outside the Great House in the long summer twilight. For almost the first time since Lane's boats returned from their useless gold-hunting upriver, it was quiet across the water on Roanoke.

There'd been shouting and marching and small boats sent across with angry messages to the Secota demanding food, demanding they become Christians, demanding a bushel of pearls, demanding a map to their gold mines. It had gone on for weeks, and often there were accusations. The Secota had stolen the captain's velvet nightgown or his gilt salt cellar or his silver wine cup. If it was not returned he would take revenge on those goddamn-motherfuckingbarearsedcattle. The cannon on the ramparts of the star-shaped fort was fired over and over again, out across the empty sea, aimed at nothing.

"They're starving and it makes them crazy," Naia's uncle said, refilling his pipe. "All this ripe fruit and the wild asparagus coming on so well this year, and still they starve."

He and Tesik had turned away another English trading party that day, half a dozen men with the huge, frightened eyes of hunger. None of them was Gabriel North; he had not been seen by the Secota since the previous autumn. Sometimes when she was out with the children, Naia was almost certain he was somewhere close by. But the village seethed with anger at the English, and she dared not risk calling out to him. For all she knew, he was dead.

"Poor things," she murmured. "They need help. One of them told Chako they're waiting for an English ship to come and rescue them."

Wingina drew at his pipe for a few moments in silence. "I don't understand them," he said at last, with a deep sadness in his voice. "Maybe I'm too old or too stupid. But I can't make any sense of their thinking. When they first came, Sikwo helped them build a fishing weir and showed them how to use the nets and the spears. But they don't bother, they sit in their boats with a piece of string and catch one fish in two days and wonder why they can't feed two hundred men with it. You can't buy a life or steal it, it has to be made, worked for. If they hunt, they don't hunt deer, they go looking for gold and pearls. Can they eat gold and pearls? Will gold and pearls kneel by their deathbeds and sing for them? They live in a terrible dream."

He finished his pipe and went inside to his bed, but Naia sat watching the children chase fireflies in the meadow, Masu running in widening circles and Kia toddling behind him, laughing, tumbling into the grass, then laughing again. As the boy ran, he seemed almost to float through the gathering darkness. *Like a boat*, she thought. *Ena's little boat.*

She felt ungrateful that she hadn't used the reed boat for

months. The willow frame would be sound, but the cedar roots and skins would have dried out a bit over the winter. A good soaking in the marsh would help. Here on the mainland there were streams she could explore with the children. And no simpering maidens trailing after her, that was the best part. In such a small boat, there wouldn't be room.

So before she put Masu to bed, she let him help her drag it down to the marsh and push it into the water. He jumped up and down, setting off a panic among the frogs. "It's not sinking, Nama, it's not sinking!"

"Of course not." She fastened the boat to the branch of a half-submerged live oak, where it bobbed hopefully. "Your father knew all about boats. He was wise."

THE REED MATS of the Great House are rolled up to let in the summer breeze, and a young couple are courting, the boy playing a flute in the grove of pines beyond the meadow. But Naia finds it impossible to sleep.

Images assail her—Ena combing her hair at night with a comb of carved shell, Gabriel bounding across the sand on all fours with Kia riding on his back. Even when the flute music ends and the lovers go hand in hand into the pine grove, she drifts in these memories.

Then she hears something, an odd noise out in the meadow. Holds her breath, listening, but hears nothing more. She reaches out for Kia, but the baby is sleeping peacefully, thumb in mouth, nuzzling against her. Fool, she thinks. Nothing's wrong. What did you think you heard?

Then it comes again, a mechanical rattle in a dull, even rhythm, coming closer, growing louder. *The feet of many men, marching. Our men don't march.* The sound again—metal on metal when the steel armor shifts, the rattle of swords and pikes, the slide and click of the hackbuts and petronels being primed and loaded.

She snatches up Tanokia and runs to peer out. Her heart slams against the wall of her chest, crashes there, recoils, slams again. English, their gleaming steel breastplates and helmets moving as though of their own accord through the darkness, empty of human bodies, moving like an army of bad ghosts. The crazy captain marches at the head of them, she can see his wild shape in the dark.

"Nama, what's the matter?" Masu is awake.

"Cover yourself," she says. "Put something on your feet. Help your sister."

"For Christ and St. George!" screams the captain, his sword raised. An old man—Grey Owl—comes out of his house at the far edge of the village, and she sees the blade crash down on him. In one gleaming stroke, the sword cuts off his head.

There is a death-scream, then another and another. The English are going from house to house, pushing the men outside where the swords and the guns can find them. They tear the matting from the walls, pull apart the bedding, break open the cooking jars. When they fail to find what they want, they set the houses on fire with their torches.

Naia dresses herself quickly. The moccasins. The painted doeskin apron. The spirit-pearls. Death must be met in the proper way.

The guns begin to fire in unison, a dull thump against the damp air of the marsh. Women screaming, bodies falling. "Tesik!" she calls out for the guard, but she catches sight of him trying to run to the house of his brother. It is burning, all the reed mats on fire, children screaming inside. One of the soldiers blocks his way with a drawn sword and Tesik roars at him in Secota, a curse too wild to be understood. He has only his war club carved with a ghost face, but he is expert with it, swinging it round and round with a heavy sound like thunder, his body twisting in a frantic dance. The war club splits open one soldier's skull, but the rest hack at Tesik and blood streams from his face and arms.

Airstalker stands in the swirling smoke of the burning houses, weaponless, his face blackened like the statue of God. He begins the death song to give courage, beating his small drum. Sometimes the priest's song is smothered by the noise of the guns and the screams of the dying, but each time it rises again, slow and deliberate.

"For Christ's sake!" Lane shouts. "Shut the old heathen up!"

A soldier raises his long gun and aims it. Fires. The old man disappears and Naia thinks he is dead. But in a moment she hears his voice again, singing from some invisible place. She sees Osawi fall, the king's herald, the great runner.

By now the killing has become a bizarre routine. Men and boys first, dragged out of the houses, then shot or hacked to death. The rattle and clash of swords, of knives. The war cries of the Secota men and the wild high wails of the old women. Children screaming, babies howling. Young girls with their long hair on fire, running for the woods, for the marsh, screaming prayers as they run. Swords slashing the darkness, fire belching from long guns, from short guns. The tin suits and hats of the English gleaming cruelly. Is there a cannon? The noise is immense, like the roar of a hurricane.

Naia's uncle is praying, she can just hear his voice from the shadows at the far end of the Great House. "Come away, dear!" she cries. But he gives her no answer and goes on with his prayers.

She dares wait no longer. She snatches up an old deerskin cloak and puts terrified little Kia into it, tying it on like a sling. "Masu," she says. "Give me your hand and whatever you do, don't let go."

But outside in the smoke, and the dark that is no longer dark, and the tangle of fighting and dying, she stands there unable to move. She is dazed and she has lost her sense of direction. Which way is the path to the woods and where is the marsh?

Slowly, with a horrible clarity, she realizes that the English aren't killing the women and children. She and Masumeo and Kia will be captured and sold, that is always the way of war. Her legs give way and she staggers back against the house poles. "God let them kill me!" she screams. "Don't let me be taken and sold!"

A shape appears out of nowhere. Huge, it seems, tall as a tree. It comes between her and the smoke and a hand grabs her arm so hard it hurts her. She screams again, "God let me die!"

"Hell you will." Gabriel's shirt is charred black and his chest is burned. Blood trickles down one arm, but he scoops up Masu with the other. "Thought I'd lost you. Thank God you screamed." The words come out in jerks, half-sobbed. "Come on now. Oh, come here."

He pulls her against his body and lets his mouth brush her forehead. Feels her fingers grip onto his waist, sending her life through him.

She is shaking so badly he cannot get her feet to move at first, and he has to drag her a few steps, urging, seducing, cajoling. He, too, has a kind of war club for a weapon—the heavy tree bole he uses for a hammer when he is building the houses.

"Listen, old heart." The words give her back to herself. *Old heart.* "When we run, you have to go first, but for God's sake don't fall. If we pile up, I can't carry all three of you."

She gives a sober nod and begins to fasten the baby's sling tighter, when suddenly a soldier crashes out of the smoke no more than a foot from them. Gabriel will surely hang if he is seen and reported. He smashes the heavy club into the backs of the man's knees.

"Run!" he cries, but Naia needs no command. They zigzag through the worst of the smoke, splash across a space of marshy ground, then enter the relative quiet of a small grove of black oaks densely undergrown with sassafras and brambles.

The burns on Gabriel's chest scream, but somehow he manages to shove the pain into another dimension. He breaks out a hiding place in a thicket, makes sure no one is hurt.

Behind them, the killing goes on.

H E GAVE THEM what little sanity he had left, he said. Held the baby while Naia hid herself and Masu. *Didn't cry, Robbie. Good little sprouts.*

While Gabriel made his report, I was dressing his burns with some ointment the Dutch surgeon had given me. We were on the tiltboat going back to the island, the air still bitter with smoke and death. The men were silent and shamefaced, the battle-drunk craziness beginning to wear off at last. We knew what we had done, even though nobody said it. That night was our bequest to anyone who came after us. We left them madness and death.

"What about Naia?" I said. "How did she take it?"

Burghley would demand to be told in detail and I was anxious to write my report. But Gabriel's mind did not seem to focus on my questions and his words came slowly, as though they were ex-tracted from him with thumbscrews. He was still with her.

"She had to do it properly," he said. "We were still within sight of her uncle's house and she kept watching, waiting for the worst of it. Wouldn't do herself the dishonor of looking away."

I gave him a blackjack of Dutch gin and he hunched over it like a freezing man over a fire. "Other women were hiding in the thickets around us. Now and then you could hear their voices, and the children with them. Lane's men had set light to the Great House, and to the temple. We could see smaller fires down by the shore."

I smeared on more of the ointment. "Yes. He ordered us to burn their canoes."

Gabriel braced his hands on the edge of the boat for a moment. Then the end of the story spilled out of him, as though the fiery liquor had cleaned a festered wound.

"Finally Wingina came outside. Just stood there with the house burning behind him. Our men had broken open the storehouse, but he had hidden his treasure and it made them wild not to find it. One of them turned and saw him standing there, not moving at all. My God. He was brave.

"They fired at him and he finally made a run for the woods. Second shot took him in the back and he fell. The English came on, priming their guns as they ran, ramming the lead home. Suddenly he was up again, running again, blood streaming from his shoulder. Christ. The next shot caught him in the buttock, but he ran on into the woods with the English close behind him."

I should have known then. Gabriel was exiled already. *The English.* Not *us.* Not *our men.* I said nothing and let him go on.

"She didn't even cry out when they shot him. Didn't move at all. Now and then she'd lift her face to the smoke as though she saw something in it. Her spirits—husband, mother, sister. What you do in a mess like that. Tell yourself life isn't finite. Nothing really dies.

"We waited—two minutes, three. Lane's orderly came running out of the woods, yelling and waving his sword in the air, blood all over him. In his other hand, he was holding her uncle's head by the hair, swinging it back and forth."

I put my hand on her then. Go away, she said. I'm theirs now. I'm dead.

twelve

THE QUEEN OF AMERICA

THE SECOTA MOURNED FOR THREE DAYS AND NIGHTS, WHILE THE spirits of the lost remained near them.

Tesik survived, raging and talking revenge, gathering around him the few young men who were left. Old Airstalker, too, was living, hollow-eyed and silent, poking about in the blackened ruins of his temple.

For the first time, Naia sat as their queen in her Council circle. She was shy and vulnerable around men now, even more than usual. She had seen the death they caused. Body parts scattered, brains spilling out of smashed skulls. She had picked up someone's arm and carried it from family to family, trying to find what torso it had come from. With a sharpened shell, she had cut off most of her hair to show grief, leaving jagged sexless tufts. When she gave her breast to Kia, she stared at the milk that still flowed from her as though it came from some other woman's body.

"What are we good for if we don't go after these bastards?" cried Tesik.

"How many fighting men are left?" she said dully.

The fisherman Sa'anso frowned, reckoning the faces. He scratched with a stick in the ashes the tiny figures of men. "If you leave out the old grandfathers and the little ones," he said, "that's what is left of us."

They all started down at the few uncertain figures in the ashes. There were not enough to count on the fingers of four hands.

Naia shook her head. "They still have more than a hundred. It's out of the question."

"We could raise men from the other villages along the coast," Tesik insisted. "We could hire Powhatan mercenaries."

"We have nothing to pay with. Would you sell them our children?"

He stared at her, furious. They had grown up together and she felt something for him. Not love. She was finished with love. But something. It was a miracle he was alive at all, and he looked terrible, ruinous. There were long cuts on his chest and both his arms that had not healed yet. Some were from the swords and some he had made himself, grieving. His brother and two nephews had been killed.

Then Airstalker spoke. "It would be suicide to make war on the English. Besides, it won't be necessary. There's a great ship coming up the coast from the Floridas. It will take them away."

"Have you seen this ship? Is it English or Spanish? Has it reached the sand islands?"

The old man was imperturbable. "I have seen it in my vision."

Tesik scoffed. He was not a man of faith.

"Go and look," said the priest. "You will see it. Coming up from the south."

"Send scouts," Naia said. "You go, Sa'anso, and take Memiak with you."

"I'll go myself." Tesik would not be denied.

"No," she told him gently. "You're exhausted."

"I tell you, I want to go. I have to kill that bastard of a captain before he gets away."

Naia spoke in the calm, sensible voice to which almost nobody listened. She had not yet learned how to roar. "Tesik," she said. "Will it serve your people well to start more trouble? If you strike back at the English, they will only come and kill more of us."

He was still too fond of her to argue in public, but out of her sight he would do what he pleased.

Indeed, he did disobey her and go himself to spy on the English. He made no war on them, but when the ship sailed off with all but fifteen terrified soldiers on board, Tesik and his best squad of fighters claimed the credit. They painted their chests and danced the hero-dance in the spirit circle that night, while the women beat the skin drums and the old men smoked tobacco and told stories.

Tesik shook his spear and threw back his head and rattled the bears' claws tied to his ankles, and the firelight glistened upon his hollow eyes and his grief-scars. Naia's heart ached, but it was only the scars she ached for. When the dance ended, he threw down his spear at her feet. She did not pick it up.

WHILE OLD AIRSTALKER prays and dozes and dozes and prays, the men linger in the spirit circle, talking and smoking the strongest tobacco, the kind that brings visions. Naia puts her children to bed and lies down in the makeshift shelter where her uncle's Great House had been. It still smells of the fire, everything charred and black around her, a whole world become ashes.

She weeps for a little while, quietly and simply, as you might wash your hands and face before sleep. Then in the darkness she feels someone touch her. Before she opens her eyes, she knows whose touch it is.

"Tesik? What's wrong?"

"Let me be with you, Naia. I know you love me. I've known all along."

The love part isn't true, but she does not contradict him. He is so sad. What does it matter to her if he takes this strange, numbed woman she has become? Gabriel was a kindly dream, nothing more, like one of Airstalker's visions. Besides, he has gone on the ship with the rest.

Tonight she needs what is living and real. She lights the little bear-grease lamp that still swings crazily from one of the charred house poles, but Tesik does not offer to hold her or even touch her. He strips and lies down to wait, and the sight of him in that place almost dissuades her. It is not proper, not real or living. It is cold and heedless and dead. He is not the man who should be there.

But it will only be the one time, this one night. Nothing matters. Such a small, foolish business, over so quickly. She walks the closed circle against bad ghosts around Kia, half-hoping for an excuse to tend her. But the baby doesn't make a sound, and Masu, exhausted from watching the dancing, lies with his mouth open, his warm breath coming out with little soft puffing sounds as he sleeps.

"How soon shall we marry?" Tesik says all of a sudden, and her mouth goes dry. How long has he planned this? His trap is closing on her life.

Most of her jars of medicines and oils are burnt or broken, but she finds one that will do. She sits down at the edge of the bed-place and begins to rub his scarred chest and arms gently with healing herb-scented oil, her fingers barely touching him. Thinking. Trying to think. His clan has great power. If he rouses his cousins in the other towns along the coast against her, a clan feud will start, or worse.

"Why hurry into a marriage?" she says carefully. "We've been through so much. I need time."

He smiles. "You know it ought to have been you and me in the first place. When you married Ena, I never understood it." She can feel his body shiver with anticipation. He is always at war.

"Whoever else there's been," he whispers, "it's all in the past now. If you erase the past, you own the future. Let me prove myself to you, Naia. I'll kill all the English they've left here, I swear it. I'll leave their bones for the wolves."

THE NEXT MORNING, without asking permission, Tesik moves his bedding into the ruins of the Great House. The maidens whisper behind their hands and the old women smirk. They all approve of it—at least he's Secota, and he's handsome. Airstalker says nothing, but Naia knows what the old priest thinks.

She, too, thinks it more and more as the grief in her dulls and the wretched summer ends. She doesn't want Tesik. How has this come upon her? Whom has she betrayed?

"There's a beautiful moon," she says one night when the wild geese are just beginning their autumn flights. "Put out the lamp, why don't you?"

"No," Tesik says. His voice has a cold distance in it; she is being punished for something. "Leave it burning."

"Why? What's the matter?"

"I've told you a dozen times. I want you to make me your war chief. Will you do it?"

She fears giving him more power than he already has. As war chief, he would be almost her equal in the councils. But with so few fighting men left to them, there is really nobody else. "Yes," she says. "All right. Let's put out the lamp now, before the children wake."

"No. I said leave it."

He begins before she is ready, and it hurts her. But that happens sometimes; even Ena's timing wasn't always perfect. She bites her lip and keeps silent, waiting for the brief release of her body, hoping his voice will warm and draw him near to her. As a boy,

Tesik was high-hearted, full of laughter and jokes. For the sake of that vanished boy, she forgives him.

Separate, but still arched over her in the lamplight, he stares blindly down into her face. "It was a good day for hunting," he says. "Two more dead English soldiers. That only leaves eight."

She says nothing, but he will not be put off.

"Doesn't it please you? That they're dead? That we're winning?"

Arms. Legs. Smashed skulls. How can it please her? Women give life. Men take it and call it a victory. Then they want your praise. But she is too afraid of him to resist. Something in him has gone wrong. He is a dark flower, sprung up from envy and pain.

"You please me," she says, and kisses his shoulder. It has a bitter taste.

He turns her the way he wants her. "Naia, why do you take that silly little boat to the sand island so often? You've been there every day this week. Are you waiting for someone?"

She fights hard not to lash out and curse him. He must be following her, spying on her, or having his friends do it. Young men from the other villages come seeking him out now, to practice their war skills or to sit talking vengeance and hate.

"I like being alone sometimes," she says instead. "Remember when we were little and I used to hide in that black oak by the cattail marsh?"

"Did you sleep with the Englishman?" The words crack the darkness. "Is that who you're waiting for out there? Did he tell you he'd come back?"

"What?" she whispers. "What did you say?"

"You heard me. Did you sleep with the Englishman? The one who brought Masu home. Did he fuck you?"

It is the cut of a dirty knife, that word. She tries to move, but she cannot escape him.

"Answer me! Did the Englishman fuck you?"

"No, of course not."

"Liar!"

"If you didn't intend to believe me, why bother to ask?"

Tesik's body is a great weight pressing down on her. "All right. Now say you love *me*, Naia. Say it now. I want to watch you say it."

He holds the lamp so close to her that the flame almost burns her face. His own features in the light are scraped with a terrible fear. Of smallness. Of failure. Of being ignored.

"I love you," she lies. Her children are sleeping in the next room. The lie tastes sour, it leaves grit in her mouth. "Of course I do."

"And you've never loved anyone else. Say it. Not even Ena. Say 'I never loved Ena.' "

She loved her husband so much that she almost ceased to exist in his dying. Even now, she can see his worn, steady hands in the darkness, and the little blue vein on the inside of his elbow she always kissed before he slept.

The lamp flame licks at her cheek and her voice is the groan of a branch in the wind. "I never. Loved. Ena."

Tesik quenches the lamp. He slips his hands under her and lifts her up to meet him and even her body betrays her, betrays Ena. And Gabriel. Is he there, too, is his spirit watching? Great shudders pass over her, a deep warmth spreading up through her thighs to the pit of her belly. Tesik moves within her, changing his position slightly now and then, not wanting it to end. His seed pours into her, spills onto her belly and the robe where she lies. When it is finally over, he cradles her, both of them spent.

"Now I believe you," he says, kissing her forehead. "If they send more English ships and more men, I'll kill them all for your sake."

She feels broken and old, the dry shell of a locust. He takes her nipple in his mouth, kisses it, bites it playfully. He likes to leave tracks on her: tooth marks, slight bruises, meaningless scratches.

"Whoever comes," he whispers, "we'll kill them before they get a chance at us. Attack them in their sleep, that's the answer. Strike the first blow."

Preemptively, he parts her legs again with hard, competent movements. He has his fingers inside her, and they seem to be making a fist.

thirteen

THE SECOND BEGINNING

Let me tell you. A story isn't a birth or a death. You never know where it ends. Sometimes it begins over and over and over again.

It began for the second time when we got back to England, in late summer of 1586.

There was still no sign of the Spanish, no Armada floating up the Thames and no Inquisition roasting the Queen's Council at Smithfield. To tell you the truth, I was too sick to care. I had that most noisome of complaints, the bloody flux, and Gabriel had a low fever that wouldn't let go of him. As soon as we touched solid ground, he quietly disappeared. I had no idea where he'd gone or with whom, but I knew he would find me when the time came. We had reports to write for Lord Burghley, and questions to answer.

I was better when I finally reached London, but still so weak I barely managed to find myself lodgings. I settled for a second-floor room above a ruinous wigmaker's shop in one of the lanes between Fleet Street and Whitechapel, run by a fearsome old bell-wether called Dame Phoebe Netley—the wigmaker's widow.

She wore a crimped wig of an odd shade of greenish-orange,

and a remarkable old crimson busk strained to bursting by a pair of bosoms that would have floated her safely to Calais without the use of a boat. "Twopence a day or shilling a week," she said, poking at the spreading evidence of rising damp in the outer wall.

"Nonsense. There's no furniture in it, not even a bed."

"Bed's extra. Sixpence for the bed. Pisspot provided. Empty your own out the window, else it's another sixpence a week for the servant."

"I'll give you one and six. Bed, chair, table. Pisspot emptied. A coal brazier for the winter. And a key to the door."

"You'll be needing a mattress on that bed, then. Straw, not feathers. Feathers is consumptive. Won't have 'em in the house."

"How much?"

"Sixpence. I've got a nephew."

"Clean straw, no horse dung."

"Done."

She spat on the palm of her hand, slapped mine, and turned to go down the stairs. "No doxies, mind," she called over her shoulder. "This ain't the stews, it's a respectable widow's house. And no loud drinking bouts, neither! I won't have the neighbors calling out the Watch."

She stumped off downstairs through a cloud of the orange powder they used to dye wigs, and I stood on the landing, feeling completely wrecked. Another minute's haggling and I'd have keeled over. If I ate a meal, I shit blood a half-hour after, so I had simply stopped eating. I'd begun to manage a bit of bread now and then, and rice porridge when I could get it. But it was weeks since I'd had a decent meal and my strength didn't last me.

I wavered there, clinging onto the worm-eaten railing, working up the nerve to make my way inside my new lodgings. Someone seemed to have left a canvas bag on the upper landing. I nudged it and it heaved, expanded, sprouted feet, and sat up.

"Oooh, sir, you paid her a deal too much, the old clap-dragon," said my neighbor. "I give a groat a week for this landing of mine, and that's highway robbery."

He untangled himself from the bag and pulled himself awkwardly to his feet. He was around fifty, a small fellow with bright brown eyes and straggly grey hair. He wore a shoemaker's apron, with awls and bits of leather dangling from half a dozen pockets.

"Peachum's my name, sir," he said. "Peach, for short. Had a proper baptized name once, but I've long since forgot it."

"Robert Mowbray. Robin." I tried to take a step towards him and my knees misgave me.

"Ooh, sir! You're badly. Fetch the apothecary, shall I?"

"No, no. Just help me inside, if you please."

"You're that pale, though. And thin as a rake. You need food in you. I've some brown bread and a nice bit of cheese in my squirrel's hole."

"Your what?"

"Safe hiding place, sir. There's a loose floorboard in my landing, and I keep my goods there, if so be I've got 'em. Sticky fingers, the Dragon has, sir, so best be warned. There's the mice and the bugs, too— You'll find there's more mice than Christians in this house, though the rats don't come up the stairs much, so that's a blessing. And a good smoking with a bit of gunpowder in the cracks of the floor will soon shift the bedbugs and fleas."

He dragged my sea chest inside, then helped me down onto a kind of window seat for which Dame Netley had forgotten to charge extra. He walked with a limp, but he didn't move slowly, nor did he spare himself. He went out again and I heard the creak of an old nail letting go of the landing floorboard. In a moment he returned with the food. Humming under his breath as he worked, he set the cheese on a bit of leather he pulled from his apron, then broke the bread and handed me half.

I picked at it carefully. "A cobbler with a limp must find it hard to earn his living. How did you come by it?"

"I used to travel outside London a fairish bit, and I froze off two toes on the Nottingham road one January. 'Seventy-eight, that was. But I hobble on as best I may. And I've got my little home now, which is ever so cozy."

"What? The landing, you mean?"

"Ah, I reckon you're used to better, sir. I can see you've got gentleman writ all over you. But compared to the pissing alley back of the Cock and Feather, it's a palace. Besides, there's a deal to be seen, with folk coming and going downstairs to be fitted. And the wig dye don't trouble my lungs overmuch, for I'm out with my last and my leathers most all day, you know. There's a satisfaction in all things, if you just seek it out."

"You're a philosopher, Peach," I said. "As a matter of fact, I travel a good bit myself." I gave him the story I had given Annette—a gentleman poet and writer of theatre-plays, with good blood but little money. A sometime actor who travelled with a company of players to perform at the lordships' estates. "When I'm abroad in the country, you might stay here in my room. Sleep in a bed for a change. Keep Dame Dragon from nosing through my clobber."

"Oooh, she'll be in there, and no mistake. If she's got one key to that room of yours, she's got seven. But I don't know, Master Robin. Haven't slept in a bed since 'seventy-eight. Don't know but it might not prove distressful."

"Penny a day. And a cookshop dinner, when occasion serves."

His small pink tongue ran round his lips. "You're a temptation, sir, that you are. Right. I'm your man, then. When would we start?"

"Tonight, Peach," I said, pulling myself up from the window seat. "We start now."

I COULDN'T BEAR TO be so near to Annette after a whole year and not at least try to see her, but I had only an hour before the

Night Watch went round crying "Remember the clocks and look well to your locks." After that, the streets became the kingdom of footpads and thieves.

Still, I risked it. I could think of nothing but her sweet body.

I wasn't fit to walk all the way to Crutched Friars, but a chandler's cart was going past with crates of candles, bound for St. Paul's and St. Mary Colechurch. I hailed the driver and bought myself a ride.

Gerard's house looked just the same. There were heavy damask curtains, but I could hear the music of Annette's virginals—a galliard called "My Lady's Goodnight. "And a lute. She was not alone.

I knocked at the street door. Knocked again. Clumping footsteps approached and the latch clattered open. It was the servant, the dreaded She-of-the-Coals.

"Oh," she said, wiping dirty hands on a dirtier apron. "You? Holy Mother, you're thin. Had the French clap, eh?" The music stopped. There was laughter. Male laughter. "Yes, that's right. She's got a *real* gentleman to supper. Far grander than you, so you best take yourself back where you come from."

She was about to slam the door in my face, but I caught it and handed her a shilling. "Tell your mistress Fleet Street at Cross Lane. Sign of the Wig and Hat."

She bit the coin to be sure it was real. Then she gave a quick nod and turned back inside with a whoosh of her skirts. The door crashed shut and the latch was thrown home.

The music began again and I paused for one last moment to listen. The song was "Gentle Robin, Bide Not Here."

I REACHED DAME PHOEBE's safely, lay down on the bare floor, and slept—oblivious of bugs and atheistical mice—for what must've been at least nineteen hours. When I woke, the bell of St. Bride's was ringing Vespers and Peach was knocking on my door.

"Sir? You yet living? Master Robin, sir?"

I stumbled to unfasten the latch before he sent for the Dead Cart to haul me away.

"Ooh, I fair thought you was a goner. You've give not a whimper all this while. Sleep's done well by you, though. You don't wobble so bad as you did."

A blowsy servant girl reeking of cheap civet perfume pushed past him, carrying a washing-basin and a pitcher of water. She set them down and fussed over them, taking her time to look me up and down. "Your *bed*'s downstairs," she said, lingering over the word. "I'd quite fancy sleeping in a real bed. Help you warm it, eh? Auntie talks righteous, but she won't mind."

Ah. Dame Phoebe had a niece, then, as well as a nephew with a mattress concession.

"Arabelle's my name." She bent over to show me the family resemblance. Bosoms. "Penny an hour, shilling for all night. Better'n the stews. What you say, darling?"

"A whole shilling? On your way, you little strumpet!" cried Peachum, shooing her out. "You may laugh, sir," he said once she'd gone, "but Arabelle listens at keyholes and what she don't hear, she makes up."

And, I thought, sells. With most people spent down to their last farthing and the law courts paying informers half of any fine that was collected, there were listeners everywhere.

"Ooh, I near forgot," said the cobbler. "You had company while you was sleeping."

My breath snagged. "A lady? French lady? Dark?"

"No, sir. Tall fellow with shaggy hair. Nice chap. Give me half his pork pie, he did. Said to hand you this."

I unfolded the letter. It was Gabriel's handwriting—clear and painstaking.

Meet me at Whitehall, he had written. *I want to go back.*

✣

"I knew what was coming," he said. "At least I knew something was bound to. I mean, Christ, what a fool! How could I not have warned her?"

He was hollowed out from lack of sleep and from the fever that had not left him. We sat in a small, coffin-shaped room, the huge door bolted shut from the outside and guarded by two of Elizabeth's men in their playing-card livery. The worktable spilled over with reports and maps, as well as some of White's watercolor paintings of the Secota village, of the people. One was of Naia, with her little girl Kia clinging onto the tatty trade-goods doll Gabriel had given her.

He let his fingertips lie on the painting as he went on. "Coward, that's what I was. Should've marched myself into her village and the hell with her maidens and her uncle and the hell with Rafe Lane."

There were no windows and only the one locked door to our room, but papers fluttered unaccountably in a draught. On long racks overhead, hung by their spines from wooden poles, were thirty years' worth of bound transcripts of interrogations and torture sessions, reports, commission hearings, executions, findings of experts, depositions of our spies, their spies, spies nobody claimed. A chicken-scratch history of the reign of Elizabeth.

"Don't be stupid," I said. "You did your best. Lane was in command. You just followed orders."

"So did Pontius Pilate, Robbie. It's no damn excuse."

"Did you even ask her about the gold mines? Straight out, I mean? Did you try to enlist her help, get her to collaborate?"

"There's no gold, and you know it. Ask the old Jew."

"Surely you at least got her to tell you where the pearls come from?"

"Pearl vines. Pearl bushes. Bluddy pearl trees. Hell do I know?"

He fell silent, becalmed in those strange draughts from the deserts of God, and at last I saw clearly the determined and underestimated man who hid behind the half-dozen others inside him. To use Naia and throw her away, to smear her with the poison of collaboration—that man had never intended it for a moment, not even at the beginning.

"Help me, Rob," he said at last, so quietly I almost did not hear him. "Speak to Burghley. Talk to Toady and Ratsbane."

"For God's sake, we're in Whitehall! They might be listening!"

"Screw 'em. Get them to find a use for me. Stand for my passage. I want a place in the new colony."

"New colony? You're joking. After what's in these reports?"

"Ralegh won't read 'em. If they don't say what he wants, he'll just burn them or bury them somewhere. He started subscribing investors for a new colony last year, while we were still over there starving. He can't back down now. Look a fool to the others. And to the queen."

"Another military expedition?"

He shook his head. "Settlers this time. Women. Children."

"Jesus."

"Will you do it? Get me a place. I don't care what. I have to find Naia. I have to, Robbie. I can't live in England anymore. I have to go back."

fourteen

BROADSIDE:
A BILL OF PLANTATION

HIS WORSHIPFUL LORDSHIP SIR WALTER RALEGH DOTH SOLICIT
IN THE NAME
OF HER MAJESTY QUEEN ELIZABETH,
SETTLERS
FOR THE PLANTATION OF THE COLONY OF VIRGINIA,
TO DEPART FROM PORTSMOUTH AND PLYMOUTH WITH THE
SPRING TIDES WESTWARD
TO BUILD THERE
THE CITTIE OF RALEGH

Fair prospects. Fruit, Fish, Game. Good Timber for Building, Lime for the Making of Brick and Tile. Rich Tillage, bringing forth Corn, Melons, Wheat, Pompions, Tabacco, and Other Such in Abundance. Veins of Copper, Silver, Gold, Tin, and Lead. Fair Pearls and Other Jewels. Plants Bearing Silke. The Native Citizens Frugal, Well-Disposed, Generous, and Kindly. The Winters Short and the Climate Sweet and Equable.

(If Any Have Heard some Weak and Slothful Fellows Returned from Thence Who Do Speak the Place Ill and Call it a Desert, Pray Discount them, for Sweet Grapes be ever Sour to the Fox that Cannot Compass them.)

I. Capital Shares in the Venture Are Yet to Offer in London, Portsmouth, and Plymouth, at rates of five hundred, one thousand, five thousand, and ten thousand pound. The Investors, All Gentlemen of Title and Bearers of Arms from Her Majesty, Thus Far Named,

SIR WALTER RALEGH, THOMAS SMITH, WILLIAM SANDERSON, WALTER BAYLY, WILLIAM GAMAGE, EDMUND NEVIL, THOMAS HARDING, WALTER MARLER, THOMAS MARTIN, GABRIEL HARRIS, WILLIAM GEORGE, WILLIAM STONE, HENRY FLEETEWOOD, JOHN GERRARD, ROBERT MACKLYN, RICHARD HAKLUYT, THOMAS HOODE, THOMAS WADE, RICHARD WRIGHT, EDMUND WALDEN.

II. Lesser Shares Are to Offer at one hundred, two hundred, three hundred, and four hundred pound, such Investors to be Nominated as Assistants to the Governor, and Each to Receive the Title of Gentleman and a Coat of Arms from the College of Heralds.

JOHN WHITE, SIMON FERNANDO, JOHN NICHOLS, JAMES PLAT, HUMFREY DIMMOCKE, ROGER BAILIE, ANANIAS DARE, CHRISTOPHER COOPER, THOMAS STEVENS, DYONIS HARVIE, ROGER PRAT.

III. Each Man who Sails with a Paid Passage of Fifty Pound to Receive the Return of Five Hundred Acres Good Farm Land. In token that he bring his wedded Wife to the Voyage, her Husband to Receive a Further Two Hundred Acres. For each Male Child, carried Thence by His Parent or Born in Virginia, Fifty Acres Further. For each Maid, Ten.

II. If Fifty Pound be Not Paid, Men and Women of Needful Skill Who Provide Victualing Sufficient for the Voyage and agree to Remain Five Years at Their Trade in Her Majesty's Colony shall Be Carried Thence at the Investors' Expense, and Shall Receive Each Man Fifteen Acres and Seed for the First Harvest.

III. If Man or Maid Possess no Needful Skill but Be Carried in the Service of Lawful Masters to Venture Their Person and Body to the Plantation's Labor for one Year, they Shall Receive Two Acres and Victualing for One Winter Season.

Contracts to Be Signed and Assured and Passage to Be Paid by the Thirtieth Day of March, the Year 1587, and all Victuals and Baggage Stowed within the Fortnight Following, to Clear Passage from Portsmouth, Cowes, or Plymouth as soon as may be in April.

SKILLS AND ARTS NEEDFUL FOR THE FOUNDING AND PLANTATION OF THE CITTIE OF RALEGH

Masons, Thatchers, Shipwrights. Burners of Charcoal, Woodwards, Bowyers, Fletchers, Armorers. Warreners to Breed Coneys, Fishermen, Huntsmen, Shepherds, Husbandmen and Such as Labour at Tillage. Quarrymen and Miners, Goldsmiths, Lapidaries. Watermen and Wherrymen. Tanners and Glovers, Cobblers, Coopers, Tallowchandlers, Dowsers to find Sweet Wells, Blacksmiths, Bottlemakers, Weavers, Tailors, Spinsters, Starching-Women, Laundresses, Cooks, Dairymaids. Potters, Tinkers, Brewsters, Bakers, Innkeepers, Apothocaries, Physicians, Barber-Surgeons, Midwives. Parsons and Schoolmasters. Men of Law, as Sheriffs, Constables, Lawyers. Labourers and Serving Men and Women lawfully Contracted to Masters. Soldiers, Sailors, House Carpenters, Joiners, Lathmakers, Lymemakers and Plasterers, Glaziers, Tilers and Brickmakers. Merchants and Others Acquainted with Trade.

fifteen

THE LAST MERRY CHRISTMAS

THE BLACK-LETTER BROADSIDES FOR RALEGH'S LATEST ADVENTURE were on every signboard in London by Accession Day in November, and had spread all over the shires by post-riders before St. Lucy's Day. London was grey and wet and gritty and bone-cold, and as December unwound, I began to long for a real English Christmas, the sort I remembered as a boy. My uncle was still living on the family manor in Hereford, near the Welsh border, where there was always a crusting of snow and a huge Yule log dragged in from the woods. The holly always had plenty of berries, the ivy trailed lush and green over the chimneypiece and the stair rails, and the servants were old friends who never told tales.

At least, I hoped they didn't. The country was wild with rumors about Mary of Scots and the Spanish invasion, the roads full of starving, shivering wretches with no work to be found. Even the rich were secretly poor, and everyone was frightened. In London, there was torture in unknown houses and cellars, for private gain and public good—or so we were told. The queen had weathered three more attempts on her life, and Walsingham's men had begun to raid neighbourhoods at random, looking for assassins. Boots marched in the cold London midnights and halberds struck sparks from the frosty cobbles. Richard Topcliffe, the Royal Torturer, worked night and day.

No wonder, then, that I wanted the familiar laughter of uncles and cousins, and the warm breath of hounds, and coasting on the snowy hills and then thawing my frozen arse by the kitchen fire. I wanted the world as it used to be, as I thought it had been.

But I was not as I used to be. I was a spy.

Which is why I took Gabriel with me to Hereford. I needed someone to talk to, someone who knew what I was.

M Y COUSIN JULIANA, newly betrothed, was radiant. "Come, let's have dancing!" she cried after Christmas dinner. "Ladies to the left, gentlemen to the right, if you please. Shall it be a galliard or a coranto?"

My uncle made a sign to the musicians and they struck up a galliard. I pleaded too much roast goose and figgy pudding, but Gabriel was pressed to partner a pale, ungainly female. He'd spruced himself up for the occasion in a dark-blue woollen doublet clasped with polished brass, a shirt of fine Holland linen, and russet-colored velvet breeches. It was all secondhand, of course, but he was calm and graceful in the dance, never missing even one of the intricate little running steps and leaps, lifting his awkward partner so lightly she looked almost pretty in the glow of candles and firelight.

"I'd hardly have known you just now," I said when the dance ended. "Who the hell are you, anyway?"

"Never been quite certain, old heart. Father thought I'd make a pork butcher. Schoolmaster thought I'd make a scholar. Twins' mother thought I'd make a husband. All been wrong, so far."

"What's this?" I tweaked the tiny ring in his ear. A gold hoop—

even the cheap gilt ones that made your ear swell up in a few weeks—was a charm against drowning. "Still not wearing the queen's crescent moon? Lost it in somebody's bed, have you?"

"Rainy day, old heart. All tucked away safe." He smiled. "Safe as pigeons' eggs."

B ETWEEN DANCES THERE were carols and catches, and some of my uncle's best French brandy, and telling fortunes to see who'd be wed next. Then came the gifts of oranges and figs and pomanders of clove, and ribbon fancies and jugs of last autumn's cider, and embroidered pincushions and velvet nightcaps.

It was all very lovely and innocent and tiring. Nerves I hadn't realized were in knots began to untie themselves slowly. A game of chess was begun, and another of backgammon. In the hall, the young men took to fencing with some of Uncle's walking sticks. The light grew late and the expensive beeswax candles were replaced with everyday tallow. I dozed for a while and when I woke, Gabriel and the plain girl he had danced with were both missing.

"You old dog," I teased when he came down to breakfast next morning.

"Don't start. She's respectable."

"If she *will* play with sharp-edged tools, she must take her forfeit."

"Lout. We talked, that's all."

"Dear, dear. Too much brandy, had you? Or not enough?"

But he knew how to silence me. "Tell me, has your French beauty sent for you yet? Or are you still haunting Crutched Friars waiting for a tongue of flame to descend?"

I winced and pushed back my joint stool from the table. "*Touché*. A palpable hit. Well, shift yourself. I've got something to show you."

Wrapped in heavy cloaks, we set off through the snow-spangled wood. Beyond it lay a range of low hills that fanned out towards the Welsh border. We followed a narrow track above one particular valley dotted with clusters of cottages surrounded by carefully laid-out farm fields, till at last we stood on a hilltop overlooking one hamlet in particular.

"There," I said. "Down there, the cottage with the well-sweep. See the woman just coming outside?"

She was perhaps forty years old, a little thickened in body and feature from hard work. She wore no cloak against the cold, only a gown of plain grey-brown homespun. In one practiced motion, she grasped the end of the long pole, lowered the wooden pail into the well, then pulled it up again, slivers of ice floating on top.

I could feel Gabriel's concentration upon her. "Name?" he said.

"Rose Payne."

A man came out of the cottage. Strong shoulders and back—the kind of man who would still be strong-muscled in his coffin. He picked up an ax and a froe and began to split a heavy log that lay in the dooryard.

"Husband. Name of Henry. Farmer. Shepherd. Bankrupt, or nearly. They'll be going to the Roanoke in the spring."

I handed him a fold of paper—a list of those who had already bespoken their interest. "I had a word with Burghley's clerk. My lord's willing to venture your passage. On certain conditions. You're to sail in the first week of April. Three ships—a carrack, a Dutch flyboat, and a pinnace."

"What's the task? Surely not the damned gold mines again, and the bluddy pearls?"

"Of course the damned gold mines again. What with the Spanish about to invade us, the Council can't afford to give up the possibility of a profitable colony."

"Or a place to run to, if the Spanish should win."

"They've given you a second chance, you dunce. Don't waste it. Do your job."

He paid no attention. His eyes scanned the passenger list. "Seventeen women. How many children?"

"Forget them. Don't go getting involved with any of them. If you think of them one at a time, you'll accomplish nothing. They're a part of the whole, that's all. History needs mice as well as lions."

"Bollocks. They're not bluddy beans in a jar."

He went through life unarmed. It was useless telling him to keep his distance. Helter-skelter, he gave himself away.

"Just watch yourself," I said. "The voyage is bound to be thick with spiders. Simon Fernando will be admiral this time. In full command at sea."

"Christ almighty, these people. Kiss the right arse once and your fortune's made. What if he runs us aground again? Or does anybody care?"

"Not much. They'd have to send out another colony, that's all. The roads are full of widgets."

Someday I'd be flippant once too often and lose him entirely. His grey eyes held anger now, and so did his voice. "Who's in command once we arrive? Who's to be bluddy governor?"

"I don't know yet. But don't worry. It's not Rafe Lane. The queen wants him in England to help fight the Spanish. She's appointed him to the Royal Camp at Tilbury, under Leicester. Ralegh recommended him. 'A soldier of great skill and devotion.'"

"Sweet Jesus." He looked again at the list of names. "The mad lead the blind, the nobility's dazzled. Everybody's hand is in somebody's pocket. And God help the mice."

sixteen

What the Informers Reported, *or* History's Mice and Who They Were

Henry Payne, Reddling, Herefordshire. Farmer and Shepherd. Age 41

I RENT OUR TWO ACRE AND OUR COTTAGE FROM MASTER GEOFFREY Tillots, who holds the manor of Marcham, by Reddling Wood. We've no sons to help, and I won't have Rose at the field work. A woman good enough to be my wife is too good to be my servant, that's what I say.

I do labor by night and by day, and Rose cures up hams and bacon to sell. But workingfolk cannot survive now, not in England. Prices is great and money is shallow, and they speak of a new tax to pay for the Spanish war that'll cost us a third of our income. They say the rich must pay the same, but two-thirds left of great wealth is still riches and two-thirds left of a shilling's but eight pence, and sugar's twenty shilling a pound.

I can't pay the share-price to go to the Roanoke, but we'll stay five year at indenture to the company, and then we shall have fifteen acres freehold. In five years, men will be clamoring for land over there, and we may sell at a profit and come back to walk the green fields with our heads held high, as my father did, and Rose's father, too.

Joan Warren. Plymouth, Devon. Servant of Jane Mannering. Age 26.

They call me Fat Joan, and Greasy Joan, and Joan Wheyface, and sometimes Mad Joan. I was born on a roadside in a thicket of whitethorn, and when I was found they tied a sign round my neck that said "No Man Will Marry Her, Put Her to Work."

My father was a dog fox, and I was nursed on barley bread and put out to labour at six months old, and grew fat on the beatings. I cry, God save the poor with good porridge, though I daresay He will not. He will send them to America, rather. They say He would pardon the rich, if they asked it. But they would sooner have gold.

Hey-day, hey-day! The moon's been in the madhouse with Wheyface Joan. I have been locked up a space and survived it, but you must pay for a place among the mad and I was sold off to service. I will not hold my tongue though they beat me, and I care not a fart if they like of me or no. When you dwell in a mad world, you must needs feign a madness, else no one will feed you.

I am not such a fool as I seem.

Jane Mannering, called Janet. Plymouth. Widow. Age 29.

I did not think I would ever wed, for I am not handsome and I have no great fortune. When my husband began to pay court to me, he was three-and-sixty and no other woman would have him. His breath stank, it is true. But he came from a more guileless and honorable time, and I saw a deep kindness within him I thought I might live upon.

Now he's dead and the fear of the Spanish overwhelms me. We must black out our windows before we light fires and candles, and there are wild voices everywhere—*Will they strike us soon? Will they come before summer? Will there be torture? Will they come walking on the water or riding the air on the wing of a gull?*

Besides, I've no means to live here. My husband died on the same day the Queen of Scots was beheaded, the eighth day of February in this year 1587. My uncle John Tydway is the parson of St. Onesimus in London and he says he'll go to the Roanoke to look if he can find the God he's lost here in England. And I shall go with him, for good or for ill, and cook his meals and keep his house clean.

At least there will be peace in such a new place. England is a cabinet of terrors. Like the poor queen, I wake in the night and search my body for wounds.

seventeen

WHAT THE TAPESTRIES SAW: ELIZABETH

THIS TIME IT IS NOT IN THE COUNCIL ROOM THAT WE WATCH THE QUEEN. It is her private chamber. She has left it only two or three times since Mary of Scots was beheaded.

That was in February and it is late April now. Gabriel is gone. The ships should have left Plymouth for the Roanoke three weeks ago. Nico Rands—dark, graceful, handsome as always—is with me in the secret spy-holes of Hampton Court.

"She's aged twenty years since the winter," he whispers.

There are footsteps outside, in the dark narrow passage from the presence chamber. As usual, people are waiting for her. Ambassadors, gentlemen seeking monopolies and special privileges. Soldiers and sailors wanting command orders for the Spanish war. Francis Drake is among them, and Leicester's stepson, young Essex.

Hampton Court has eighteen hundred rooms with locks to them and eight hundred court gentlemen have apartments there, bringing with them their wives, servants, horses, hawks, hounds. Sometimes even the servants bring servants, and they all want something. They stay from autumn to spring, and until they depart for the country or follow the queen to yet another palace, the place cannot be cleaned. The court should have moved back to Whitehall two months ago, but Elizabeth cannot bring herself to give even so modest an order.

This is not merely the calculated indecision she often uses as a weapon against Walsingham's prophesies of doom and Cecil's urgently shuffled papers. Something in her seems to have gone with Mary—her native resilience, her ability to resist the mundane brutalities and betrayals of her life. Her capacity, perhaps, to give a damn.

There is a soft knock at the door. Elizabeth doesn't look up. She sits motionless on a low upholstered stool at the foot of her huge golden bed. It is carved with gryphons and lions and dragons, the heavy corner posts topped with purple and crimson ostrich plumes that drift in the currents of draught as the door creaks open.

The roar from the presence chamber invades for a moment, then recedes. One of the court ladies comes quietly in, black skirts sweeping aside the stinking, trampled rushes that cover the floor. She takes a small brazier from a niche beside the hearth, puts some glowing coals into it, and sprinkles dried rosemary on them to sweeten the smell.

"Majesty," she says, bobbing a curtsy. "What gown will you wear?"

"Get you gone. I will do as I am."

Over her white silk shift Elizabeth wears a black bedgown, some sheer stuff trimmed with silver passemayne and pearls. It falls open to show most of one breast—fainty freckled at the cleft, the skin still creamy. The nipple rose-brown, like a girl's.

Does she know I am watching? Suddenly, for no reason, she pulls the gown close. Ashamed, I take my eye from the peephole.

"My lady," the woman says, "I fear you must choose something. The fellows Sir Francis Walsingham sent are waiting to examine your garments for any traces of poison."

Finally a welcome spark ignites. "Fool! They'd have their noses up my royal hole if I let them. Send them away."

"But, madam, the Italian poisons are subtle. And they haven't looked under your bed in case there's gunpowder. And— Crave pardon, ma'am, but my lords of your Council are in the presence chamber."

"Fig for 'em. Tell them the hag's asleep."

Her days run backwards. No one leaves her alone in the daylight, so she works all night, reading reports, signing orders, studying maps and sea-charts of where the Spanish are, how many ships have come up to Calais, how many horses have been brought into France to prepare for the invasion, which informants have been tortured and what they revealed. In the early morning mist, she walks alone in the gardens, has a breakfast of dark bread and beer, and then sleeps until just before midday—no more than four or five hours. She should be asleep now, but here they are, the eternal demanders. At her again.

"I don't like this," mutters Nico. "Watching her like this. She collapsed on her way to chapel two days ago, did you know that? Can't they let her alone?" Nick searches houses, trunks, heaps of papers. Not souls.

The Council members will wait no longer. The door opens and they file in, looking like a delegation of crows. Burghley's back is troublesome and he leans on the arm of his son. Robert Cecil is as pale as the stack of papers he shuffles, but Leicester's swollen face is more flushed than ever. The gossips say his wife's latest lover is poisoning him. Walsingham has been suffering from a kidney stone and looks even more somber than usual. Hatton steps forward and kisses Elizabeth's hand, and there are real tears in his eyes.

Ralegh—still not a member of the Council—comes in last, closes the door behind them, and sweeps Elizabeth one of his famous bows. She has forced them all to wear mourning for Mary of Scots, but black garments set off Wat's beauty. Black velvet doublet and breeches, the black threaded with gold. A short cloak over one shoulder, the border heavily embroidered with seed pearls and gold.

"Well?" she says drily. "Since you're all here, what news?"

Burghley clears his throat. "A sound majority of the Commons applaud your decision in regard to the—er—Scots queen, ma'am. Parliament—"

"Don't try to diddle me. Parliament are not sitting. They only sit if I ask them, and I never ask. You invented this majority."

"Dearest madam—"

"You tricked me into sending my cousin of Scots to the block. You've all wanted this war with Spain for the best part of thirty years, and now her death will assure it. Now it's a matter of honor. And Philip will certainly come."

"Your Grace," says the old man. "It had to be done. The countryside was wild with rumor, the people—"

"Rumor, you call it? Your spiders have been hard at work among the broadside sellers for more than a year, planting misinformation. At Epiphany, I was said to be poisoned and dying. By St. Paul's day, a Spanish army of sixty thousand men was marching with six hundred cannon from Wales towards London. Or was it nine hundred cannon and ninety thousand men? These rumors were sown, cultivated, and reaped by this Council. By *you*, sirs! Oh, I have read Signior Machiavelli: 'The best way to keep an unruly people in tight rein is to keep them afraid. If no genuine cause of panic is at hand, then invent one. Power and fear are two riders on the same horse.'"

Lethargy suddenly fallen from her like a shabby cloak, Elizabeth tears back and forth in the room. Her words are as quick and sharp as her footfalls.

"The Spanish will avenge the Scots bitch, and the French will join with them. You'll have your war in spades, and if England should chance to survive it, all your threadbare pockets will be warmly lined with the spoils."

"The Queen of Scots was caught in a Jesuitical treason, my lady," replies Walsingham. "She plotted your overthrow and your death. The law called for her execution."

"Because Hatton wrote a law vague enough to prove anyone a traitor! And then you persuaded me to sign it. Young Cecil shuffled his eternal papers, Burghley looked grave as a sorcerer's owl, Walsingham thundered. And I signed. I lapsed into womanhood—God knows where I still found it. I was sad. I was tired. My tooth ached me. And I signed. You laid snares for me and I tripped them like a rabbit. Do you expect me to reward you for it now?"

"Ma'am, there were plots set plainly before you. We could not ignore Mary's continual—"

"She was old and fat and lonely. She was captive and bored with embroidery and prayers, so she plotted and planned and dreamed and grew ruthless, and I would have done no less in her place! Oh, I know what it is to be sold like a groat's-worth of cheese."

"If I have offended, madam," says Walsingham angrily, "it was from a too-great care of England's safety, and of yours. I think you know I have never sought my own profit in your service, nor shall I."

He kneels—clearly in pain—and she stares down at him for a

moment. Looking for the heart of him. Finding something heart-like. But not quite a heart.

Elizabeth races on, through the fragrant smoke of the burning herbs, past the glass-cased virginals and the close stool covered with purple velvet. Past the gold-inlaid table piled high with official papers.

"According to the dispatches," she says, "the Spanish have three thousand horses and armor at Calais, and more arrive every day. The invasion may come at any time. Drake will be massing his ships at the Lizard, off Cornwall, and early this morning I ordered the Channel ports sealed. I suppose that is the reason for Sir Walter's gorgeous presence among us. Eh, sir?"

Ralegh bows again. "My lady, the ships bound for the Roanoke have not yet so much as left Portsmouth. If the Channel is sealed at such an early date—"

I cannot believe my ears. "Not yet *sailed*?"

Nico, too, is surprised. "They ought to be halfway down to Africa by now."

Elizabeth turns on Ralegh. "What fiddling is this, sir? Another game of Queen or Fool? Those ships were to sail a month since. They were to be safe beyond the Spanish ports at Lisbon."

"The winds have been most unfavorable, ma'am. Our ships are small and heavy-laden and it was feared—"

"Never mind all that. What of their provisions? Who is your admiral?"

She knows perfectly well, and he knows she knows. But he plays by the rules. "Simon Fernando is in command, Majesty. An excellent pilot. He—"

"Oh yes, I know of him. The vain rascal with the striped hose, the one who pranks about London like a mummer at a country fair. And I know well enough what he's done to recommend himself.

Walsingham pulled him from the gallows and put him to spider-ing."

"Broad-sea pilots are not easily come by, ma'am. Fernando knows the ocean currents as well as the coastal waters in that part of the world, and he knows what sea-lanes the Spanish ships ply."

"So he should. He's pirated enough of them, and not for England's profit, neither. No, sir. The Channel ports are closed."

Leicester and Walsingham have declined any investment in the second colony, but Ralegh still owes them money from the last one. He has sunk everything he has into the venture. If it doesn't sail, they may all go down together.

But it is the little hunchback, Robert Cecil, who speaks.

"I beg Your Majesty to reconsider the time somewhat. You are zealous in defense of your people, but it is perhaps too soon to close the ports. Drake sets his shore boats to watch the Channel and will warn us in due time. After all, your merchants must earn money if they are to pay the war tax, and they can earn little if their trading vessels cannot leave port. Besides, many of your loving people, you know, have sold all their goods and posses-sions to sail with the Roanoke venture. They also trust to your goodwill."

"The more reason to keep them safe from pirates and savages. Return their passage money. Bid them go home."

She knows the money is already spent and twice the amount in debts incurred. Ralegh cannot possibly get enough from his in-vestors to repay anyone's passage. His dark eyes look to Cecil with more than a little panic in them. Elizabeth circles, eyeing Robert Cecil narrowly.

"I perceive you have money of your own in this venture, little man," she says in a voice of surprising gentleness. "Else why do you plead Ralegh's cause for him?"

Poor crookbacked Cecil attempts a bow, his hand braced on the table. His voice is calm and natural, almost warm as he addresses her.

"Your Majesty knows I must hoard my pennies and have not wealth enough for speculation. If I plead, it is for the colonists, who are not rich folk themselves. Some have next to nothing and work their passages. They venture their lives and their toil in that new land. What are they to live on here at home if the ships don't sail?"

Leicester snorts. "If they don't sail, there'll be a hundred and seventeen more sturdy beggars on the roads, that's all. Those ports must be sealed."

Elizabeth stops her pacing and returns again to the seat at the foot of her bed. For a long while she says nothing, and Ralegh kneels beside her with his handsome head bowed. Suddenly she takes him sharply by the beard. "Shall I trust you in this Roanoke business, Wat? Or will you make me your cat's-paw?"

"Your Majesty, I—"

"No courtship. The truth. Will these simple folk thrive in that place? Will they live decent lives? Or will they die for your great adventure?"

"God alone knows, ma'am. I dare not to read His mind."

"Yet you would think to read mine."

"I wish only to read your heart, my lady."

"What, that old rag? I have thrown it away."

Her eyes close and she falls into a silence so deep none of them dares try to follow her. It goes on and on, for five minutes, eight, ten. A jewelled lady with a golden sword comes out a tiny door in the gold filigree clock on the writing table, strikes the hour, and goes in again. At last Elizabeth looks up.

"Very well. It may be folly, but we must in some wise trust those who call themselves our friends. You have special license, Master Ralegh. A fortnight's grace to set your ships at sea."

When she speaks next, her voice sounds young and defenseless. The voice, perhaps, of the girl who once scratched on the wall of her cell in the Tower *Elizabetha Cautiva.* The prisoner Elizabeth.

"Go away now," she tells them. "I don't want you. I'm tired. I'm busy. I'm cold."

eighteen

THE INFINITE VARIETIES OF FEAR, *OR,* HOW HER MAJESTY'S RULE WAS SECURED

*T*hough we abhor torture and the rank methods of Spaniards and savages, and are a nation of law and consensus, we cannot but protect ourselves from the plots and dark schemes of our evil enemies, who would otherwise descend upon us and destroy us. To that end, in our own defense, we must strike as we are struck, and have devised the following methods for arriving at truth and uncovering the plots of the Evil One against God's Anointed Queen, Gloriana Regina, and her Own Loving People.

—THE REV. RICHARD WILDYE,
MASTER OF ARTS, OXFORD,
from *England's Paragon, London, 1584*

The Pit

This be a great hole in the ground, very deep, and so narrow a man cannot lie down, nor sit down, but must stand upright or lean upon the walls. The river washing up against the Tower seepeth within it, and there be always water at the bottom, so that when food be thrown down to him, he must fish for it and fight off the rodents, i.e. rats, &tc., who await it for their own sustaining. When the rope has been pulled up, a heavy wooden lid be closed down upon the prisoner, so that no crack of daylight may discover him, nor any sound find him out for his comfort.

The Little Ease

This be a cave of earth dug too shallow for a man to stand upright and too scant of height to lie down in, or to sit without bending of the head and the shoulders, but he must crawl on all fours and hunch like a very ape. After a few days, the tendons, muscles, &tc., do grow foreshortened, and if it hap that he be kept in the space of a fortnight or a month, they grow firm into their places, and if he be let out at last into daylight, he will ever be used to cripple and crawl.

The Rack

The rack be a great wooden frame by which rollers strapped to the wrists and the ankles do stretch a man's body to pull forth the truth from dissemblers. It hath been, howsomever, most foully maligned, for it breaketh few bones, only pulleth, in the worst and stubbornest of traitors, four or five ligaments now and then to snap apart and let the bones hang loose and rattle.

The Scavenger's Daughter

A band of iron doth capture the head and feet of the prisoner and press them into a circle, with iron gauntlets screwed down to crush his hands and many chains fettered onto his elbows and knees and ankles, and wound tighter and tighter until his body be smashed.

More Conformable Means by Which Traitors May Be Persuaded

Floggings with whips of three, six, nine, and twelve leathers.
Beatings, scaldings, and burnings of the feet and hands.
Hanging by the feet and hands and privates.
Pulling out or singeing of hair and beards.
Gouging of eyes.
Cutting off of ears, breasts, lips, noses, and privates.
Flaying of skin from the belly, back, and buttocks.
Knocking out or pulling of teeth.
Pulling out with pincers the nails of fingers and toes.

nineteen

MAY-GAMES

 At last word came up from Portsmouth. The three ships of the Roanoke venture had finally left harbor and sailed across to the Isle of Wight, where they harbored at Cowes. Another week passed and it was May Day. No word of the final departure from Plymouth.

"What's that rogue Fernando up to?" I grumbled as I deciphered the message Nico had brought me. "Cowes? What the devil are they doing there? The queen should never have permitted this. I don't like it, not one bit."

"Read on. You haven't come to the best part."

We walked at a snail's pace through the May Day crowds as I struggled with Dr. Dee's latest code. They got more abstruse by the hour. " 'A— A governor has been'— What's that?"

" 'Named.' "

" 'Named for the colony. Master John' "— I couldn't believe it. "John White? The artist? He makes a decent enough map. But— governor? Never. He's afraid of his shadow. And pompous, to boot."

Nico laughed. "Sounds to me like the perfect governor."

He stopped to buy a cannikin of jellied eels and a nosegay of violets. The mummers had been out before sunrise to bring home the summer with the Hal-and-Tow. Young girls hurried past us in pale gowns streaming with ribbons, off with their sweethearts to the woods beyond Hampstead to pick laurel and May-rose and gillyflowers and hawthorn blossoms. In spite of her mourning for the Bitch of Scots, the queen had finally come to Whitehall for the May-games and the jousting. For one day, the Spanish could do as they might.

> *Now welcome in the summer,*
> *Now welcome in the May-o,*
> *For Summer is a-comin' in*
> *And Winter's gone away-o.*

The Green Man finished his song and shook his leafy arms at me and I tossed him a penny. "I still don't like it," I told Nico. "It's going sour, this Roanoke business. Something's wrong, and Gabriel's in the midst of it."

"You've had too many eels already, my friend. Bad case of the black bile, face like a disappointed nun."

"It's not funny, Nick. Why all these delays at the port? You heard Her Majesty—Fernando's a right villain. I looked up the court record. Seven passengers robbed and thrown overboard, and Walsingham got the charges quashed to make a spider of him. So why does Ralegh trust him? There's sharp practice somewhere."

"My friend, there's sharp practice everywhere. That mummer who wanted a penny for his song? There's more pence in that bag of his than you and I make in two months. The alderman took a bribe from the eel-seller to allow him to set up his stall here. The eel-seller got the money for the bribe by demanding a bribe from the fisherman who brings him the eels. I don't know who the eels bribed, but I warrant there's coin in it somewhere."

"Yes, yes. But somebody must've talked Ralegh into appointing John White. I tell you—"

Nico did a deft little spin of frustration. "Ye gods, Rob, you're worse than my father. Look, you didn't want Rafe Lane in command again. White's not vicious, is he? Not likely to go out burning villages?"

"No, but—"

"He's Ralegh's friend—at least that's what Kit Marlowe says, and he should know, he spends enough time at Ralegh's house spouting poems and blaspheming. Anyway, you know what these great people are—never pay a professional when you can scratch the back of a friend. So stop looking for hugger-mugger. It's May Day."

"Gabriel's to board at Plymouth. I've got half a mind to go down there and pull him off that ship."

"You can't stop him, he's stubborn as a pig. And you're a watcher, not a bloody saviour."

He was right, and I knew it. But the sense of foreboding didn't leave me. "If you hear anything," I said, "come and tell me. Don't delay, come as soon as you can." He nodded, sniffing his violets with what looked like tender fancies. The big brown eyes were as soft as a girl's. I managed a smile. "And who, pray, are those for? A new mistress?"

"New?" he said with a grin. "Ah, ha. No. Never you mind."

I BOUGHT NO VIOLETS for Annette. What use was it? She was finished with me, that was obvious enough. No invitation had come to Dame Phoebe's to find me, not even a hasty hello. Besides, I couldn't get those ships out of my mind, and the people on them. The names of the womenfolk trailed through my head all that day. *Margery Harvie. Alis Chapman. Margaret Lawrence. Audrey Tappan. Agnes Wood.*

I spent the afternoon at Whitehall, trying to learn the new ciphers, but Dee had a fondness for sprinkling the simple substitution codes I was used to with astrological and mathematical symbols. You had to be a bloody alchemist to untangle them. *Elizabeth Viccars. Joyce Archard. Elinor Dare. Winnie Powell. Jane Jones. Emma Merrimoth.*

Now and then the cheers and the blaring of trumpets reached me from the tilting yard. Bloated old Leicester disguised as Hercules and Ralegh dressed as Neptune, complete with trident and jeweled diadem. What a farce. Great lords of the Council with their hair crimped and dyed and perfumed, and their cheeks rouged, and their bellies strapped in by corsets. *Elizabeth Glane. Susanna Colman. Rose Payne. Janet Mannering.*

I had a folio of notes in Gabriel's careful handwriting. In his workmanlike way, he tried to learn whatever he could about his assignment beforehand, to think like the people involved with him, to see through their eyes. There were no coded messages—he wouldn't have bothered. Besides, it was knowledge, not secrets. He gave us more than mere facts, that had always been part of his value. I looked down at the first page and as usual his voice leaped out at me through his words.

Margery's miscarried three times. Safely pregnant this time, but God knows what the voyage may cost her. Gentle creature, very soft-spoken. Papist family, don't know what she is now. Prays too much, though, can't be good for her . . .

George Howe sailed with Drake. Lost a leg fighting with pirates off the Azores. Keeps a shipyard now, lives in a beached ship like Drake used to. Boy going with him. Georgie. Hair like copper wire and eyes like the sea.

I tossed the folio aside, made my way through the maze of the palace to the river stairs, and caught a wherry for Bermondsey. At least there, nobody would be jousting. I found a tavern and drank as many blackjacks of the ale they called Hollow Leg as I could pay for.

Sometime around the fourth one—bitter, it was, and heavy with spice, like a shovelful of coals in the throat—a green-eyed whore passed my table, displaying her wares. I reached out and laid my hand gently on the comforting reality of her bum and she came to stand behind me, rubbing her warm breasts against my back.

She was very young—fourteen, fifteen. Her touch sweet, hopeful, not yet practiced and lewd. If I risked tenderness with her, she would not use it against me. I nodded to her and she went upstairs to wait.

With whores, I almost always succeed.

I HARDLY REMEMBER HOW I got back to Fleet Street. I was still half-drunk on the ale and the girl, but I remember a wherry. I remember a shooting under Tower Bridge and almost being caught in the backwash round the pilings. I stumbled ashore at last at Blackfriars' Stairs and made my way through the muddle of houses and shops and silent churches towards Dame Phoebe's unsavory huddle.

I lugged myself upstairs, feet gritting on the film of wig dye, and found Peachum at his post. He was worse than a maiden aunt; he never slept till I got safely home.

"Anything, Peach?"

"Friend of yours come up, round about Vesper bell. Your height, sir, and add, say, two inches. Hair and beard dark. Color of skin—tawny, I'd call it. A Turk, maybe. Maybe part Moor. Perishing handsome. Said he had a message, but he wouldn't tell it to me."

"Nico Rands. That's all right. I can find him in the morning."

He sucked his breath through the gap in his front teeth. "Wouldn't put a shilling on that, sir. Two men met him as he was going down the stair, and off they goes with him. And unless my eyes misgive me, the one of 'em had a dagger to his back."

"Christ. Where'd they take him? Did you see which way they went?"

"I did not. Only I do believe they had horses waiting. Heard a horse outside somewhere. Might ask old Tom Webley. Hostler and coffin-maker, two doors down? He don't miss much, when—"

THERE SANITY BREAKS off. A deep scream tears a piece from the midnight, leaves it bleeding. Another then, and another. A huge howl that only stops when the rich darkness of the voice cracks to pieces and shatters.

I know that voice as well as my own. "God, Nick," I say to nobody. If Peach is still there, I do not see him or hear him or feel him. "God, Nico."

I turn and tear down the stairs. My boots slide on the wig dye and my feet go from under me and I fall, bumping down the last few steps. Drag myself up by the stairpost and crash out into the street.

"Nico! Nick?"

Then I see. They have thrown him into the gutter at Dame Phoebe's door, his naked body crumpled onto itself. His eyes are wide open, his handsome face bleeding. Have they dragged him on the sharp cobblestones? No. Much worse. I cradle his head in my arms and it flops crazily. "God, Nick. God."

I don't care who has done it. I can think of nothing except to get him out of the stinking gutter. It is overflowing with a long day of piss and half-rotten food and smashed flowers and horse-shit.

I try to lift him in my arms and his huge voice explodes in my eardrums, the howls even worse than before. Dame Phoebe comes waddling outside. "Here, now, you keep your drunken friends from my door! Shameless! This is a respectable house! Get him away!"

With some vague intention of murdering her, I lay Nico back on the cobbles again. His body feels like a handful of loose, dry, screaming bones. I take his hand in my own and hold on to it, more for myself than for him.

Then Peach's voice. "Best give him something to shove in his mouth, sir. Dragon's right. Night Watch won't like this." He hands me one of his bits of leather and I put it into Nick's mouth. When the next scream comes, his jaws clamp hard. It stifles the noise, but it doesn't help him.

"We have to get him away, but when I lift him, he suffers so. Can you find something to carry him on? A door? Pull one off if you have to."

Peach goes limping away and in a minute he is back. "This'll do. One of Tom's seconds."

It is a coffin lid. We slide Nico's body carefully onto it. He doesn't scream when we move him, but he is trying to tell me something and I bend near him.

"What's he say?" asks Peachum.

"Kill me. He says Kill me."

A hiss through Peach's front teeth. "I best rattle up a surgeon."

Alone again, I crouch beside Nico. I can feel myself crumbling. I want something to batter, something to kick. It seems hours until Peachum returns, carrying a torch and accompanied by a blustering middle-aged surgeon, still wearing his nightcap.

"Why, it's a bold blackamoor drunk in the gutter, no more.

And you call out an honest fellow from his rest? I'll have the law on you, sir!"

I stand up to face the fool. Somehow I feel intensely powerful, able to overwhelm him with guile. "If you don't look to him, I'll have your license, and don't think I can't do it. The queen's personal physician is a close friend of the—bastard son of—my wife's cousin. Now do as you're told. And your best, mind. Unless you're not up to it."

He stares at me. "The queen's personal— Oh, never fear, sir. I am fully licensed and certified. The queen's . . . Oh, in that case."

At the first probing touch, Nick gives another stifled cry. The surgeon ignores it and goes on with his examination, lifting Nico's arms, moving his shoulders. By the torchlight I can see pockets of dark blood, like great bruises, under the tawny skin of the belly, the chest, the legs. Two black smears, one beneath each eye. Huge, cruel pools of unshed blood round the joints of the shoulders and hips.

I have seen this before, and so has the surgeon. He wets his lips. Then he suddenly stands up and backs away. "He's been racked," he says in what is almost a whisper. "Tortured. I'll have nothing to do with this. Let me go. For the love of God, let me go."

I beg him. "Something for his pain, at least. Mandrake. Poppy. Something strong."

"No. My license forbids me to prescribe. Find an apothecary."

He turns and runs, leaving the torch spitting on the cobbles. "Mad Rosalinda," says Peach under his breath, and goes limping away again without more explanation, to disappear into a tumbledown house across the lane.

Again I wait and in another interminable moment, he returns with a bottle of syrupy stuff. "Poppy juice," he says. "Mustn't use it all up. She can't live without it."

Laudanum. A dark, bitter world opening, in which not even

pain needs to matter. I lift Nico's head and he drinks too eagerly. I pull the bottle away.

"Peach?"

"Sir?"

"You heard what the physician said?"

"The rack, you mean?"

"I promise you, Nick's no criminal. I don't know who's done this, nor why. But you need take no more part in it. Go to your bed now."

The cobbler is silent. The torch crackles and hisses in the gutter. He looks into my face, then Nico's. "Think I know where I can borrow us a cart, sir," he says quietly. "If he's to die, best to do it at home."

IT IS ONLY a handcart. We lift Nico into it on his coffin lid and walk, lightless, taking turns with the pulling, all the way to Bishopsgate, where his father lives—the wherryman Matthias Rands. Peachum's limp is profound by the time we arrive, and my hands are blistered from the cartshaft. I pound on the street door and somebody with a voice as deep as Nico's shouts a curse from inside. I pound again.

"Matthias, let us in! Nico's hurt. Your son's hurt. Do you hear me? If you don't let us in, I'll kick the damn door down!"

It opens. A lean, muscular man in his late forties stands there in nothing but his shirt. Matthias doesn't like me. He hawks and spits on the doorstep. "You! Up to more of your trash and tricks? I told Nico—"

Then he recognizes his son's shape in the cart. Knocks me aside. Begins to run, barefoot on the cobbles. "Ah, Christ. Ah, the bastards!" He looks up at me. "I knew it'd come to this. You and your spiders and your secrets. It's you done this to him! Jesus. Jesus Christ."

"Pray later, old man. Help us get him inside now."

"Well, do it then, goddamn you. Hide him away to die and salve your conscience. And when you've done, you best get out of my sight or I swear to Christ, I'll murder you. 'Old man'? I'll split your head like a gourd."

"Shut up and lift. Gently, gently. Don't move so fast, he can't take it."

"I'm his father, you bastard, I know what my son can take and what he bloody can't!"

We carry Nick into the narrow little house. Cold even in spring. A fire barely burning in the hearth and a single guttered candle on the table. One bed built into the wall, with doors like a cupboard, and a rope bed against the farther wall, narrow and straw-mattressed, not quite enough for Nico's length.

Peach fusses "His feet mustn't hang like that. Roll up that blanket under 'em. That's the way of it, sir."

He takes the bit of leather from Nico's mouth and the mouth moves. The cobbler bends over him, listening. Peach glances up at me. Shakes his head.

Matthias stands with his fists clenched, glaring at me. "Tell me why. Damn your soul. Tell me why."

"I can't. I don't know."

"Liar." His body doubles over with a pain that is not physical. "Was it— His mother was Catholic. She raised him Catholic. Is that why?"

"I don't know. I don't think so."

"Get out, then. Get out and don't ever come back. Hear me? If you try to come back, I'll slit your lying throat."

The door slams. The street is quiet again. And then from inside the narrow house there comes a huge howl, so deep, so razor-edged, I feel it tear at my skin. It is rage, fed with lies. It is pain, robbed of words.

It is Matthias Rands.

✦

PEACHUM COULD WALK no more and I hauled him on the cart to a haberdasher's shop in whose doorway he sometimes mended shoes. He settled himself with a grunt and looked up at me. "What the gentleman said—is it true, Master Robin?"

"That Nick and I are spies? Yes, it's true."

"Queen's men, though? Not Spanish?"

"We work for Lord Burghley. He's her loyal servant."

It was, like most facts, equivocal. Even Burghley had schemes and plans of his own, and we never quite knew whose purposes we served.

But Peach was relieved. "I'll tell nobody, sir. Only you mind yourself. Don't want you pitched in some gutter, do we, and talking of angels."

"What's that? Angels?"

"Poor chap was out of his head. When I bent to him, there on the bed, he was a-talking of the angel Gabriel. 'Fetch Gabriel,' he said. Still craving his own death, I reckon. Said it twice over, so he did. 'Fetch Gabriel back.' "

I KNEW I MUST leave for Plymouth as soon as I could manage it. I must go and warn Gabriel, and keep him in England whether he liked it or not.

But I was exhausted and not even half in control of myself. Leaving the cart with Peach, I walked aimlessly, my mind drowning in questions. How did I come to Crutched Friars, to the peaceful street of old stone houses where Annette would be sleeping? Silence took me there. Need took me. I didn't care what her husband saw. I had spent all my caution and my shame.

There was an ancient well in the midst of the street and I sat down on the cobbles with my back against the damp stones of the well-curb. Did I sleep a few minutes? If so, I did not sleep deeply. From one of the gardens, an owl gave its soft, secret call. A dog barked.

When I opened my eyes, she was there. Annette. Her dark hair was loose and she wore no cap, no jewels. Only a simple gown of ice-blue silk, trimmed with the lace she herself made so beautifully.

"Robbie. You look—terrible." She lifted her hands towards me. "What's happened to you? What have you done?"

"Nothing. I do nothing. You should know that, of all people."

There were no candles lighted inside. She had left the door standing open.

"You're still dressed," I said. "It's very late. Don't you sleep anymore?"

She smiled, but only slightly. "I gave it up. Such a waste of time."

"Where's Gerard?"

"Germany. For the May wine."

"Does— Does he still keep the pigeons at Staple Oaks?" Somehow it helped to think of the orchard grass and the soft whirr of birds' wings.

"The carrier birds?" she said. "Oh. Yes."

"And you—are you well? You look well. Well, you always— look well."

"Robbie, stop this. You are ill. Hurt. Will you not come inside?"

She wanted to tender me and mother me, take her pleasure from my weaknesses as usual, because with her my strengths slipped away from me and I was foolish, lustful smoke. She gave what I could accept—food, fire, kindness, quiet rest.

Instead of her own bedchamber, she led me to a little room

under the eaves where we had never gone before and I slept like the dead with her cool, strong limbs tangled around me and her soft mouth on my breast. I was grateful for her. Proud of her, somehow. If that is love, perhaps I loved her.

In the morning, she brought me strawberries and cream.

twenty

THE VOYAGE

I TELL YOU THE STORY OF GABRIEL'S VOYAGE AS I PIECED IT TOGETHER years later. I was not there in body, but in all the best mouldy tales, time runs backwards and distances are irrelevant. History unravels and refuses to be woven in quite the same pattern again.

I WAS TOO LATE reaching Plymouth. It was a slow ride on the aged but inconspicuous horse I hired, and it took far more than the five days it would've taken by water, had I been able to afford it. When I finally arrived, the ships of the second Roanoke venture had already sailed—almost exactly a month late and barely within Elizabeth's licensed fortnight.

On the eighth of May, 1587, the ship *Lyon* at last weighed anchor and struck south along the coast of France, followed by two smaller ships, the Dutch-built flyboat *Whitethorn* and a little pinnace that carried supplies but no passengers. The route was the same as usual—down Europe to the coast of Africa, then west to the French and Spanish islands in the Caribbean Sea, and finally north along the Floridas to the Outer Banks and the Roanoke. There were no sea-compasses and no charts of the broad seas. It was all done by the stars, by dead reckoning, and by the instincts and experience of the pilot, to whom everything was entrusted. That person was the pirate and spy, the Portugee Simon Fernando.

According to the passenger lists, there were a hundred and seventeen colonists. Those lists were subject to the best interests of the log-keepers, but the hundred and seventeen I can vouch for. Ninety-one men. Seventeen women, several of them with child. Nine boys, some still at the breast, others verging on manhood at eleven or twelve.

And, of course, one Gabriel North.

The wealthier folk had decent quarters in the ships' castles, fore and aft, while the tradesmen's and farmers' wives and children and the old men were quartered between decks, in the leaky ship's belly. The single men slept on the high, open decks of the castles and on what was called the waist of the ship, the flat decking space in the middle. The hatchways and the cookhouse were located on the waist, and the great masts were set into it.

The water butts were there, too, one for drinking and another for washing and shaving, and they soon became a gathering place, always crowded in the mornings. "Been to sea before, have you, friend?" Dick Darige, the blacksmith, asked Gabriel.

"Two or three times."

He did not add that he had been to the Roanoke before. He never spoke of the place or of Naia, not even in his sleep. But he walked the decks with the silent steps she taught him, his toes curled under inside the clumsy boots as though he were walking through sand.

"Don't take to ships m'self," said the blacksmith. "Can't stand being idle, and there's little else to do here but fidget and worry."

"High time somebody did a bit of worryin'," grumbled Will Baird, a farmer from the edge of Dartmoor. "Already too damn late to plant crops by the time we get where we're going. All that shilly-shallying at Cowes, while the Portugee nipped up to London—for a last round of the stews, I wager. What the hell's he up to, that's what I want to know."

"Waitin' for the barleycorn to sprout from the damp, if you ask me," said another man. "Fool ship leaks like a rusty bucket. I was down there for a lookabout yesterday, and there's so much bilge the seed's all starting to sprout—corn, barley, oats, pease."

"*There's* the fellow that ought to be having a lookabout belowdecks," growled Baird, " 'stead of paintin' pictures on the foredeck. Master Governor, sir! A moment, so please you."

John White, who never appeared without his gold chain of office round his neck, came absentmindedly down the forecastle ladder and would've gone straight back up again if he could.

Lily-white John, as thin and sober-faced as a saint at confession. All of him poured into his drawing, and the poor bugger's not that good at it, actually. Flat faces. Little flat people. Don't think an Englishman has ever tried to paint God, but He'd be flat too.

"There's some questions need answers, Master White, sir," said the Yorkshireman Martyn Sutton. "We was told we'd stop at one of them French towns to buy our farm animals, but that lying Portugee has sailed us straight past every market town on the coast of France. We got no breeding stock and we'll have none to butcher if need be. Not a milk cow nor a sheep nor a pig, nor even a goose or a hen. Is that prudence? Or how are we to live?"

White remained on the last step of the ladder in order to be taller than the working folk. "It was decided to stop in the West Indies for the purchase of beasts," he replied primly.

Somebody laughed aloud. "What, drop anchor in them islands and buy from the Spanish? In wartime?"

On the defensive now, White grew even more pompous. "You must trust to the wisdom of your betters," he said with lofty indifference.

"Betters, is it?" Baird pointed his callused forefinger at two men playing draughts near the water butts. "Like them two yonder, eh? They'm branded on their palms with a letter C and that's convicts from Colchester Prison, not betters. Man don't come out of no jail with the chinks to pay passage. If you ask me, they'm somebody's creatures."

Spies, he meant. Spies took bribes, and you never knew who bribed them. Unless you had enough gold to bribe them off you, they accused you of crimes you never dreamed of. Slander. Theft. Conspiracy. Just to get you out of the way of some rich man who found you less than convenient, they slit your lip or they cut off your ear or they branded your forehead, and you were locked out of a decent life for good. Spies peered through knotholes and saw what it paid them to see. And now the spies had come to the Roanoke, too.

B ELOWDECKS, THE women scrubbed and scoured and contrived what privacy they could. "Here, Gabriel What's-Your-Name," Emma Merrimoth commanded him. "Move them boxes over and hang me up this curtain."

Obliging as always, he climbed up on a barrel and began to pound a peg into one of the ship's huge cross-braces, humming a little tune as he worked. She stopped scrubbing a table to observe him and he smiled down at her, thinking of his daughter Judith at that age.

"You'd not be bad looking if you'd scrape off them whiskers," Emma said with a wink.

Couldn't have been more than sixteen, with a pretty round face and a pretty round bum and a pair of nice round breasts peeping out of her bodice. Blond hair tumbling loose of its pins. Joyce Archard's servant, spent half her time on the deck flirting with sailors and the other half washing out pissy baby's napkins and hanging them up to dry.

Gabriel hit his thumb with the hammer and indulged in an oath or two. Emma didn't blush. "What's your second name, anyway?" she demanded. "Or are you some kind of spy, like them two with the convict brands? Spies ain't got second names, do they?"

"Spy? Me?" He laughed. "No, no. Plain Gabriel North. And what kind of a name's Merrimoth, pray?"

"Made-up name, that's what. I was a year with Bittle's Travelling Circus, see, a-selling charms against the evil eye. That was 'fore Cokes took me up and made a foist of me, may he burn for it. Still, it comes useful. Pick your pocket quicker than kiss-your arse, I can. Want to see?"

"Empty, my pet. Waste of talent. Get to the name part."

"Bittle said I was in want of a new one, is all, in case Jandy was to find me."

"Jandy?"

"Said he was my father. Don't know where he got me. Beat me blue and put me to servicing sailors when I was twelve. Didn't take to it and run off with Bittle's circus. Trick-dog lady had a brindle bitch called Merry Moth."

"Ah. Emma Merrimoth."

Suddenly she drew a sharp, crooked breath. "Bugger you and your talk, anyhow. You've gone and made me remember all that. Just you hang up that damned curtain, now, and shut your hairy face."

Tears in her honey-blue eyes. Holiness in those tears. Two hard blinks, and they were gone.

I HAVE THREE WOMENFOLK with child to mind for," said Madge Lawrence the midwife, "and another on the flyboat. Lord knows how many more before we reach Virginia." She scowled at Gabriel as Emma flounced away. "They'll need fresh air and exercise to keep the seasickness from them. And a bit of cleanliness and order wouldn't hurt."

Surgeon Ellis looked about the dark, damp, stinking between-decks and shook his head. "Cleanliness and order? I couldn't properly pull out a splinter down here. For one thing, there's no decent light."

"Lanterns, old chap," Gabriel said. "Need some lanterns. Hang one here and one on that brace there, and another over there."

The surgeon stared. "What lanterns? I don't see a one."

"Plenty up in the forecastle cabins. Take them, can't I?" He grinned at Ellis. "Whatever they do up there, they can do it just as well in the dark."

M ASTER WILDYE, sir?"

"Go hence, Tydway. I am writing my sermon."

Divine service was conducted on deck every morning and for three hours on Sundays in the sublime Oxford cadences of Richard Wildye, published author (*England's Paragon*) and official clergyman to the colony.

"I'm sorry to cause interruption, my dear feller," said John Tydway, the highly unofficial old parson of St. Onesimus, London. "Only some of the ladies lie sick abed from the motion of the ship, and they ask the comfort of prayer. But as I have no deputation—"

"Go and pray over them yourself, man. I am busy. I mean to collect all these sermons and when I go back into England, they shall be printed. It may mean a court pulpit, if it fares well. *God's Light in a New Land*. No, no, sounds like a Puritan tract. Perhaps in Latin . . ."

Gabriel, his hands full of purloined ship's lanterns, stuck his unruly head round the door. "*Florilegium Divinum Virginianae?*"

"Why, that's— *Divine Flowers of Virginia*? Excellent! Who are you, sir? Obviously a keen scholar. At what university . . . ? *Florilegium Divi—*"

"*—num.*"

"Her Majesty's excessively fond of flowers, you know. I might title each meditation for a particular blossom. *The Rose of Repentance. The Pansies of Penitence.*"

"Ahem!" said the parson.

Wildye looked up, annoyed all over again. "What, Tydway? You still there?"

"Er— Only, Mistress Dare has requested—"

The yard-long nose twitched. "Governor White's daughter? Why did you not say so before? Idiot! Where's my testament? Where's my ruff and my cap?"

Gabriel yanked Parson Tydway aside and dived out of the way himself, barely avoiding the ruination of his lanterns as Wildye dashed through the door. "Bluddy piddlejack," he grumbled, setting the old parson upright.

Tydway smoothed his feathers. Something familiar about the fellow. That touseled hair and those grey eyes. "Now, now," the old man told him. "Wildye's very learned. Er—what's a piddlejack, dear boy?"

"Family of cousins. Piddlejacks never know what they want, except that they want more of it. Dozen or so of 'em on the ship here. Admiral Piddlejack. Governor Piddlejack. Captain Piddlejack. The Reverend Piddlejack." Gabriel laid a sober hand on the old gentleman's shoulder. "Put not thy trust in piddlejacks, old heart."

WITH THE FLAG of St. George hauled down from their mainmasts for fear of the Spanish, who now rule Portugal, the little ships ride at anchor in the Bay of Lisbon for two nights. A rich merchant named Prat has brought two players and a musician along to entertain him on the voyage, but he is a generous fellow and that night they perform *The Judgement of Paris* on the foredeck of *Lyon* where the plain folk can see and hear. *Whitethorn* draws near enough for its passengers and crew to watch and listen, too.

Chorus has just finished declaiming the prologue when Emma sees Gabriel unfold his long legs and walk a little way towards the stern. Of course she follows him. "What's afoot, grandsire?" she teases. "Your old bones playing you up that bad you couldn't sit still?"

He is watching two men muddling about amidships, where the small boats are kept. They begin to lower a little skiff over the side, the creaking of gears almost drowned by the noise of the play.

"Them's not sailor-boys," Emma says, peering at them. The sailors are young and lithe on the rope ladders and the rigging, but the two men lowering the skiff are middle-aged, clumsy. "What they up to with that boat? It's them jailbirds, ain't it?"

She and Gabriel stand watching as the two silent men with the branded palms of convicts row the small distance to *Whitethorn*, make fast to the boarding ladder, and climb carefully and quietly aboard.

"Don't mean they're villains, you know," Emma says, her eyes on Gabriel's face. "Any fool can land up in jail. I been there. You?"

"Once or twice. What the devil are those two doing?"

She shades her eyes against the glare from the water. "Fooling about with the capstan, looks like. We best tell old Stripey Socks. I think he's—"

Gabriel suddenly takes her by the elbows and frog-marches her to the shadow of the forecastle hatchway. He speaks in a low, urgent murmur. "Emma, don't tell Fernando anything. Stay away from him. And don't ask so many christly questions. Whatever you may see, keep it to yourself. Then come and tell me."

She shakes free of him. "Do what I like, won't I? Think you can own me?"

"Now, Emma. Old heart—"

"Oh, yes. 'Emma old heart' and next thing I know you'll be creeping into my bed like the rest of them, groaning and grunting and shoving, and you'll leave me a belly and nothing to live on. I've been done like that and I won't be again. Get away."

He looks at her for a long minute. "I wouldn't, you know."

"Liar. Spy. I bet you're a spy, or what're you sneaking around here for, watching them two?" Gabriel just turns and begins to walk away, but the strange ache in her voice stops him. "Why?" she says. "Why wouldn't you bed me? Bet you had your way with Jane Pierce, I seen you on the foredeck, kissing that slit lip of hers, the old baggage. Why not *me*, then? Ain't I good enough for you?"

"Oh, Mistress Emma," he says. She is sweet and sour, fire and ice, always on the edge of herself. Both his twins in one small body. "You're good enough to make a pope renounce his vows, old heart. You are also a pippin. And a half."

N EXT MORNING SHE is on deck washing more of Tomkin's dirty nappies when the ship suddenly lurches forward. Madge, having just come up the ladder from the between-decks, sprawls on the deck of the apron with her farthingale upended and almost everything escaping her whalebone stays.

"Up anchor away," shout the sailors. "Sway the sheets and haul them braces to the yards!"

"Why, we were not to weigh anchor before noon!" Madge says, pulling her busk straight again. "I still have women to tend on the flyboat."

"Look there!" cries the little Welsh physician, Dr. Jones. "*Whitethorn* can't lift her anchor, and *Lyon* stints no sail to help her. My son Gruffyn and his wife are aboard—and the bay full of Spanish warships! That wretched Fernando has abandoned them to the enemy!"

"And a good part of our men and supplies with them." Will Baird's deep voice overwhelms the others.

"Treachery, plain and simple," somebody else shouts, and they all make for the captain's quarters to demand that Fernando turn back.

They have, of course, no success. The Portugee refuses to drop anchor and wait for the *Whitethorn*. Any resistance to his orders at sea would be mutiny.

Emma is back at her washing by the time Gabriel appears. "Seen that clever old trick, did you, grandsire?" she says. "Reckon them two jailbirds fiddled the capstan last night so *Whitethorn* couldn't lift anchor."

They are well out of Lisbon harbor now, the helpless flyboat disappearing in the distance as *Lyon* strikes south for Gibraltar and the African coast. Families separated. Supplies already cut in half.

Emma rinses out a napkin and shakes it with a snap, sending water all over Gabriel. "You could've put a stop to it. If you ask me, you're a useless old gander." Then, quite without warning, she lays a cool, wet palm on his cheek. "But I'd fight by your side, you know. If ever you was scared."

P ARSON JOHN TYDWAY sits fishing off *Lyon*'s stern one twilight, speaking to his wife, Dorothy, who has been dead some nine years:

"Well now, Doll. What have I to tell thee tonight? Niece Janet weathers well, and is not a bit seasick. But this fellow Gabriel troubles me. Certain I've seen him before, yet—" The fishing line

jerks itself tight. "Heigh-ho, we've got a fish, Doll! A big one, too!
Play her out a bit now, keep her head up!"

Taunting him, the fish leaps once out of the water and then
swims away, a glimmer of silver in the darkening waves. The last
light is going, the sun raging into streaks of crimson fire. To the
east, the African shore looms up, vast and harborless.

"Dolly, my dear," the old man says softly, "I'm afraid I've lost
all sight of God. Keeps swimming away from me, just like that
fish. I'm too old for simple answers, that's the trouble. I have only
questions these days."

Up on the foredeck there is torchlight and music. Tom Colman
has his lute, and there is a recorder and a flageolet. They play
"The Queen's Treble" and "The Shaking of the Sheets," and the
sailor boys sing to the wind and the water, their high voices echoing back and forth from mizzen to main.

> *Lie aback, lie aback*
> *Long swack, long swack,*
> *Yellow hair, yellow hair*
> *Hips bare, hips bare*

"It was those children, Doll," whispers the parson. "In the
street, that terrible last day of Shrovetide when the queen was set
upon. *I* brought them to greet her. *I* led them into the Valley of
the Shadow. None were killed, but they *were* hurt, they were
sorely frightened and that fear will never leave them. Doesn't, you
know. Not with children. Bends and twists in them. Comes out as
plagues and fevers and poxes, or else more poisoners and assassins.
I took 'em into harm's path, and they *were* harmed. And I trusted
my Lord God to guide me, just as they trusted me. So now I've
come to question His purposes, you see. Wildye says it's wicked.
Says I'm damned for it. But when towers fall and poisons drift
and wars breed, how can we *not* question? To ask only which

hymn is suitable for Septuagesima or how many angels may sit on a bedpost—is it not to diminish His confounding and terrible Majesty, that permitteth rats and bedbugs and assassins to thrive? *That's* why I've come here. Seven years in the wilderness. Look fear in the face and see if God's there, looking back at me. If He's still in control."

The musicians strike up the old song called "Heartsease" and the parson closes his eyes for a moment to listen. *Heartsease. Pansies. A nosegay of pansies.*

The ship sails quietly onward as Ambrose Viccars and his wife, Audrey, begin to dance to the old tune. Tydway's niece, Janet Mannering, stands watching. Lonely child, she was. Always the last to be chosen for games. And that fellow Gabriel, too. *Lanterns. Wildye. Queen fancies flowers. Pansies of Penitence. Nosegays of pansies.*

G ABRIEL GOES TO Janet. Makes her a nice, civil bow. Nothing flashy. Nothing lascivious. Naia would not disapprove of what he does. That is all he wants now—to claim her in a kind of restored innocence. To be proper, for her sake.

So he offers the Widow Mannering his hand to the dance. Lifts the black mourning hood from her hair. *No sorrow tonight. Enough time for it later. Come and dance now. Flout sorrow and fear. Be alive.*

A T LAST, AFTER six more weeks, they reached the Spanish islands. But Fernando did not put in to buy farm animals. At Mosquitoes Bay, Puerto Rico, he dropped anchor for no reason and two sailors jumped ship, with nowhere to go except to the Spanish fort. One of them was Lizzie Glane's Irish husband.

It frightened them all. Had Glane and his friend worked for the

Spanish all along? Had Fernando sent them, was he in the pay of Spain, too? And there were other things, fearful things. Nights they were left ashore with only poisoned water to drink, water that blistered their throats and left them blinded for days. Islands where the ship threatened to leave them behind to the mercy of fierce native tribes. And Lizzie's sobs from Fernando's cabin every night.

She was Dare's servant, but he lost her to Fernando at dice. Every bed she fell into, she gathered a few crumbs of information and sold them. That's how she met Glane, selling him secrets. Steal anything for him, actually. Including Fernando's Roanoke maps.

A face like a spent rose. Ah, Lizzie. What have you done?

twenty-one

WHAT THE TAPESTRIES HEARD:
REPORTS AND INTERCEPTIONS

Copy of a Coded Letter Intercepted at Madrid.

Transcribed by Robert Mowbray.

17 July 1587. To His Most Serene Majesty, Philip II, from Juan-Manuel Menéndez de Valdés, Governor of San Juan de Puerto Rico. En el nombre de Jesucristo y Su Madre Santísima, etc., etc.

Greetings to Your Illustrious Majesty.

Five days since, on the twelfth of July of this year, two men were discovered making their way along the coast from Mosquetal, which the English call Mosquitoes Bay, to the new Fort at Guayamilla. They gave their names as Dennis Carrol and Dermot Glane. They claimed to be Irishmen impressed by Lord Ralegh to colonize at Madre de Diós del Jacán, which the English call Virginia. They carried maps to the location, but this may be an English trick. The men claim to have been put aboard the English vessel *Lyon*, under command of the well-known Portuguese pirate Simón Fernandes, who they say commands twelve other vessels of the heretics, carrying seven hundred colonists and one thousand soldiers, with supplies for two years. The two spies were taken to Guayamilla and interrogated by Your Majesty's Inquisitor, who applied the advisable methods. The prisoner Carrol died of a seizure during questioning. The prisoner Glane was sentenced to seven years at the oars in our galleys. I await Your Majesty's orders regarding an expedition to search out the location of the English settlement indicated on the maps. Copies enclosed.

Your Humble Servant has had the honor to reply to Your Majesty's letters of 15 November and 21 December 1586, and of 14 March, 28 May, and 10 June of this year 1587 with dispatches regarding our previous efforts to locate the English fort in Virginia. If more is learned, I will of course send another letter to augment this letter and the six letters preceding.

May I venture to wish for Your Majesty's better health, and the restoration of strength to His royal Knees and the purging of His inestimable Bowels, and to implore for Him the protection and blessings of God and His Holy Mother? We pray constantly for the success of that great Enterprise of England, the Grand Armada.

With all obedience and grateful service.
Juan-Manuel Menéndez de Valdés, at San Juan de Puerto Rico

P.S. Don Juan de Cuevas has informed me that Your Majesty takes much delight in the parrot I had the infinite joy of sending You last year. I take the liberty to send two more parrots, a scarlet and a blue. May they live many years in Your Majesty's abundant care.

twenty-two

How the English Returned to America

O N THE MORNING THE SHIPS MADE LAND, THE SOUND BEYOND THE
Secota village was white with swans, and heat shimmered
over the marsh. It was the fifth dry summer in a row, and the corn
plants were firing, drying up from the roots. It was only just daylight, but already the women were forming a line from the stream
to the cornfield, filling their clay jugs and handing them forward,
taking what water they could to the crops.

Because of the heat, Naia got the children up early. Masu
rubbed his eyes. "I don't want to carry water," he said with his lip
in a pout. "I'm a warrior. Warriors don't do women's work."

"When they're not quite eight years old, they do what their
Nama tells them."

She had begun to teach Masu the English way of counting
everything, as Gabriel had taught her. But *was* it eight that came
after seven? How could she have forgotten so soon?

For a long while Masu had kept asking why Gabriel no longer
came to play bears with him, but Tesik spent too much time with
the boy now, filling his head with warrior nonsense and teaching
him to talk back.

"He's trying to win the child away from you," Airstalker had told her. "He thinks if he gains Masu's heart, you'll finally have to marry him, just to keep hold of your boy."

She tilted her chin up. "Then he's wrong. He only wants me because I'm queen. He doesn't even trust me, he still spies on me. The other night in bed—"

"You must end this, Naia. You don't care about power. Why not marry him?"

Her voice was a whisper. "Because he would swallow me whole."

"Then break with him."

"There would be war. He's a Turtle. After Sea, it's the most powerful clan. He has contacts among the Powhatan now. Even the Mandoag listen to him. Oh, I hate him! I hate how he loves killing. Those English soldiers they left behind at the fort—he hunts them like deer and they're too weak to run, they're all starving. What revenge is that? And those friends of his—Thunder-Fist, Black Fox. He's appointed them to guard me, but they spy on me and tell him everything I do. Bed or no bed, I'm not his property!"

"My dear child, Tesik's one of the new men, he can only think in terms of who owns what and how much it's worth. When imagination assaults them, they reject visions and turn them into suspicions. Suspicion is the mother of war and war is the mother of profit. It all goes in a circle, and I don't mean the circle of blessing. I tell you, little darling, we'll pay a hard price if you don't put a stop to this soon."

B UT SHE HAD not. She needed time, needed to feel in control of herself again.

"See," she told Masu that morning. "I've wrapped up some of the roast fish we had last night, and there are berries we can pick on the sand island. It'll be cooler there, where the sea is. We can go swimming and play on the shore. Go and get your father's little boat ready and I'll bring Kia. And stop pouting. It'll be a lovely day."

"Can I row?"

"We'll take turns," Naia said, and tickled him until he was doubled over with laughter. "We'll row all the way to where Sun lives and steal the peaches from his tree."

The three of them were too much for the little boy to row, but he wouldn't surrender the oar until his arms were aching. The reed boat bobbed slowly across the inward sound and past the marshes on the edge of Roanoke. The English soldiers were all dead now, Tesik and his men had killed the last one only a week ago. But the cruel black nose of their cannon still thrust out from the rampart of the fort on the north end of the island.

The gun had a life of its own. Naia looked out to sea before it had time to curse her, and urged the little wicker boat around the last cove.

"Help me pull it up into the marsh," she told Masu when they reached the sand island.

"What do we have to hide it for? There aren't any more English."

She had to fool Tesik's spies. But she didn't want to think of them now, didn't want to talk of them. "The reeds will keep it from drifting," she said, "so it won't come untied." She splashed them with water and laughed.

The marsh was a tangled labyrinth, rich with frogs and turtles and dragonflies and blue herons diving for the quick, bright little fishes. "Up, Nama!" said Kia. She never liked the mud between her toes.

"You're too big to carry. You ought to learn to wade."

"She's scared of snakes," Masu said scornfully. "I'm not afraid of them. Men don't mind snakes."

"That's all right, Kia." Naia lifted the little girl up to ride on her shoulders. "I don't like snakes either."

Slowly the marsh yielded to solid ground and the path disappeared into the maritime forest. Naia set Tanokia down and they padded steadily along, looking for landmarks. "There's the parrot tree!" cried Masu. "I'm going to make them fly away!"

"Don't," she said, but he went running and waving his arms, and the tiny, bright-colored parakeets chattered with fear, the warning travelling from branch to branch, until they all lifted their wings at the same time and flew off in a brilliant cloud.

A few hundred yards farther on, in the long grass under a small grove of black walnut trees, a kit fox was teaching her young ones to hunt mice. "Can I pet them?" Kia said.

"You might scare them and they'd run away. This is their island, not ours. Be very still, now, and watch."

Tails held aloft, the little foxes jumped high in the air and pounced—on the grass, on each other. Arguments broke out and they nipped and squealed and barked in high childish voices. The mother fox glanced at Naia and her children, unafraid.

Skirting the walnut grove, Naia led Masu and Kia deeper among the moss-hung trees. A small stream ran through the place and they stopped to wash faces and breasts and arms in it. "Let's hunt for pearls," begged the boy.

"No. It's too sandy. Mussels need stones to hold on to while they make a pearl."

They turned southwest through the forest, following the stream. There was a clearing in a thicket of gum trees and pines, and in early spring she had chopped off the lowest branches with Ena's stone ax so the sunlight could reach the wild strawberry plants that carpeted the ground.

The clearing was shaped like a bean, the longest curve overlapping itself where it widened, to create a kind of dimple. The

trees at that spot grew in a double clump, forming a natural doorway. She had not trimmed up the branches there, and beyond the
double curve the forest was so dense and dark that it appeared no
one had ever penetrated it.

She crouched down, pulling the children behind her, and they
crawled on all fours through the tiny doorway, heads down to
keep their hair from being caught in the branches. "I don't like
it," Kia whimpered.

"She's whining again," Masu said. "Girls are always whining."

Naia laughed. "That's because boys are always bragging. Come
on, Kia, don't worry. Only a few more yards and you'll have a
lovely surprise."

On elbows and knees, they crawled another three or four yards,
to come out at last into a small natural clearing of uncommon
beauty. The little stream formed a wide curve around the belly of
the woods there, then split itself and sent a narrow brook into the
place, to disappear in a deep clear pond.

"You see?" Naia said. "I told you it was beautiful."

"Can we swim in the pond?" Masu demanded.

Kia, always contrary: "I'd rather pick berries."

AROUND THE POND there are marsh marigolds and elderberry
bushes, fragrant in spring and now heavy with blackish-
purple berries. In the clearing are thickets of wild raspberry,
drooping with fruit and a delight to the squirrels, rabbits, opos-
sums, and foxes. The large trees, with wild grapevines cloaking
their trunks and growing up into their branches, are white oaks,
gums, and pines, with one or two hazelnut trees and a delicate
fringe of dogwoods.

Naia has dug herself a small patch of garden, smuggling the
precious stone tools from the village and then smuggling them
back again, hoping nobody will notice. She has planted corn,

beans, squash, and transplanted some wild onions and artichokes. She comes almost every day and carries water from the stream or the pond in a clay jug. While she works, she invents conversations with Gabriel, smiling at the awkward Secota words he would use. Answering in her own fumbling English, to keep him alive on her tongue.

Do you ever plant carrots?

What is this—car-rots?

Something to eat. A kind of root. Orange-colored root. You know orange? No? Oh! I know! Remember that picture of the English queen I showed you?

Skinny. Too much clothes.

Her hair's orange-colored. Well, her wig.

Wig? I think you make up these stupid words to tease me, so you can laugh at me.

Oh, never mind wigs. Never mind carrots. Never mind queens.

Kneeling alone in the sandy dirt of her garden, Naia laughs to herself. The tide turns on the hook of the world, bringing with it a small wind that touches her with Gabriel's hands.

B EYOND THE GARDEN is the storage pit she has made—a square almost eight feet deep, the sides shored up with strong branches and the bottom spread with clean sand, dry leaves, and pine needles. There is a clay jar of lily roots, one of smoked fish, and another of smoked venison—all taken from the village.

The hut she has built is not very comfortable, but having it makes her feel safer, freer of Tesik and his spies. It is constructed much like Ena's little boat—a frame of willow withes woven with cedar roots and stuffed with moss and mud to hold it together. Over this low skeleton, she drapes reed mats, then well-cured skins which she ties down with vines, leaving a hole in the roof for smoke to escape.

It isn't possible for a grown woman to stand up inside the place, but it is more than large enough for the children, and there is a neatly made pallet bed covered with soft, pale deerskins and a buffalo robe she traded for last autumn when the runners came down from the north. There is a cattail lamp. Some cooking jars and a few wooden dishes. A carved ladle with the head of a duck.

She has needed this small, safe place where the world is still predictable and free. How has all this come to her, this craziness with Tesik and the burden of her people's survival? She cannot remember having done anything wrong. She wants only the simple things most women want—a peaceful life with her children beside her and nothing owing to anyone. Sometimes she sits in the shadows of the Great House, hugging herself and rocking back and forth on her heels. Once, when Tesik was out hunting, she took Masu and Kia and ran with them into the woods. Ran and ran, so far from the village that she no longer recognized the landmarks.

You can't do this to them, old heart. Kia's crying. You have to go back now.

Back? Back to what? Where, back? I'm lost.

Bollocks. You're never lost. Not you.

A T SUCH TIMES, it is only Gabriel's steady voice in her mind that saves her. Only the wicker boat, the hut, the patch of corn, the parakeets and foxes, the wild raspberries, and the children.

"Come here," she says, gathering them against her. "Listen to what I say. You must not tell anyone about this place. It's our place. It's a secret and secrets are precious. If we need somewhere to go where nobody will find us, we'll come here. Do you understand?"

Kia nods soberly, but Masu frowns. "Why can't I tell?"

"Because if you tell, it won't be ours anymore."

"I'll tell Tesik."

"No! Especially not Tesik, nor any of his friends."

Masu looks at her strangely, but he says nothing more.

They pick a basket of raspberries and eat the cold roast fish they have brought with them. Then she leads them beside the stream and among more dense woods, slips through a narrow break in the sand dunes, and comes suddenly onto the beach.

The children squeal with joy, running out onto the wet, packed sand and scaring the tiny sandpipers. The tide is coming in peacefully, slow rolling waves leaving swash lines of foam, bits of sea plants and dead fish and shells. While the children play tag with the waves, Naia slips into the water and swims out a bit, into the tide.

As it comes up higher, she returns to the beach and when she stands up something enters the far range of her vision. The children are fine, Masu is digging for clams in the sand and Kia is gathering shells. Naia climbs to the top of a dune and stands tiptoe, shading her eyes with her hand to see better. A dark shape farther south, near the breach that leads into the inner sound. No—two shapes, one larger than the other.

Her heart begins to pound and her legs almost give way. She is looking at two ships. Their sails have been struck and they ride at anchor just beyond the breach.

The sand island is narrow, but very long, stretching a good distance down the coast. It is too far to tell whether the ships are English, Spanish, or something else. Gasping for breath and with cold fear flooding over her, Naia calls to her children.

"Time to go! The men have been hunting. If they've gotten any deer, we'll have to help smoke the meat."

"I don't like smoke," whines Kia.

"Come on," Naia insists. "I'll race you!"

"I'm too little to run!" cries Kia, toddling as fast as she can. "I'll get a sideache. Nama, don't go so fast!"

As they race back along the way they have come, Naia's brain races, too. The ships are almost a whole day's foot travel away, and the tide is already too high for them to cross the treacherous breach into the sound. There is a little time left her. But if it turns out to be another colony of English, they will go to their fort on Roanoke. They will find the dead bodies Tesik's death squad has left rotting there. War will surely follow, and it won't take long.

Are you there? Are you with them? Help me. Tell me what to do.

No answer. Her mind cannot find any words for Gabriel now.

THE LITTLE WOVEN boat has never crossed the two sounds so quickly. Most of the men are still off hunting and the village is quiet. There are only the crow-boys on the platform over the cornfield, waving their arms and shaking their bone rattles to scare off the birds. Naia takes the children to the Great House and tells old Lady Heartberry to mind them. Then she goes straight to the priest's house. If anyone can help her now, it is Airstalker.

"Old friend," she says, kneeling before him. "The English are back. Or it might be the Spanish, I can't be sure yet."

"English. I've been having visions for a week."

"And you said nothing?"

"Visions only distill the future, they don't invent it. Or *prevent* it, either."

"Advise me, then. Shall we fight them?"

"With what? They have swords. Guns. Cannon. We have sharp sticks and arrowheads made out of seashells."

"God, I knew it. We're lost." Tears roll down her cheeks and she scrapes her fingernails along her arm till the blood comes.

"Stop that," he says sharply. "I taught you better, and so did your uncle. Use your head, not your nerves. Be a queen."

She gets up from her knees and begins to pace back and forth in front of the altar. "That fool Tesik! I tried to tell him not to leave the bones of the last soldier lying out in the open."

"I said think, not blame. It's a waste of energy. Besides, Tesik's not a fool. He believes he has God in his pocket, and that makes him dangerous. In the end, God will be forced to prove him wrong."

"But if it's more English in those ships, they'll find the bones the minute they land on the island. They'll come looking for vengeance."

"Then as I see it you have three choices. Fight and die and don't deceive yourself, sometimes it's best to die fighting. Or we could pack up what we can carry, and hide in the forest. You know the place—where we wait out the great storms."

"Yes! We can empty our storage pits and take the supplies with us. But the fields . . . We need this corn harvest to last through the winter. If we leave, it won't get any water. What's the third choice?"

"Capitulate. Submit yourself to their power. Become a toy of the English. Like that prince from Croatoan who went back to England with them. What was it the English used to call him? The Prince of Prick-Arse Island? The Piss-Ant Prince?"

He means she will be shamed and humiliated. What does that matter? She ignores him. "I could send a runner. Invite them to a feast. Give them presents. Hospitality can do a great deal."

"That's only a bribe, not a submission."

Tesik strides into the temple and bows cursorily to the holy statue. He's been listening outside the doorway. He has a right, of course. She should have called a council, or at least asked him to come with her to the priest. Tesik is the war chief, after all.

Another of her stupid mistakes. She turns back to the old man. "What do you mean by *submission,* exactly?"

He scratches his shaven head judiciously. "Accept that silly queen of theirs. Pay them taxes. Dress in clothes like theirs. Ha! Wait till you see their women. You'd think God hadn't given them skin. In my visions—"

"I won't surrender," says Tesik. He has been in the woods for days and he looks as though he hasn't slept at all. His voice is low and smashed, and something in it is broken. "You can do what you want. But I won't be their tame dog. I'll kill as many as I can before they kill me."

She claps her hands together, furious. "Kill, kill. I know what they did to us was wrong, it was wicked. But more killing won't help."

He grabs her and shakes her, over and over. "Don't be a fool! When your uncle couldn't deal with them, he had us abandon the home we'd lived in since the world was made and move over here to the middle of this swamp. He thought running away would prevent trouble. Look how that turned out."

"But if you just start killing before you even talk to them—"

Tesik lets go of her and begins to pace back and forth, back and forth. Sometimes he bumps into things—the altar where God sits watching, the offering jars of cornmeal and fish. He doesn't notice. Once he trips and falls and doesn't notice that either, just picks himself up and goes on.

"Say you decide to submit to them instead of running," he says. "They'll burn our village again, kill our men. Don't you understand? They want to cleanse the earth of us. All of us. We won't recover from what they do to us, not for a thousand winters."

His face is lighted by a kind of passion Naia has never seen in him before, not even in bed.

"I'll need fifty or sixty men," he says. "I've trained more than that in the other towns up the coast, all we have to do is send a runner for them. They're tough and they can think on their feet. We'll wait till the English have settled in, till they start to get careless. Then we'll attack."

"You don't even know it's the English yet. The visions have been wrong before. Let's at least wait until—"

"Who they are doesn't matter. They're not us. They have to be removed, taught a lesson. We'll cross over at night while they're sleeping. If they've brought women and children, we'll kill them, too."

Naia stares at him. "You can't. Not children. You always say you love Masu and Kia."

"Our children, yes. Not theirs."

"*My* children," she says blankly. "They're my children. Ena's children. They're not yours." She closes her eyes for a moment, then turns back to Airstalker. "You advise submission, old friend?"

"It will gain you time. Nothing else. I don't advise it. No."

"At last the old fool begins to sound like a man," says Tesik. "Men fight when they have to."

"You don't *know* if you have to," Naia screams at him. "You just want to go and kill them, and when I ask you why, you say, 'because they're not us.' What will you do when the Europeans are all dead? Will you start killing Secota, because the rest of us aren't *you*?"

His body tenses, a huge paroxysm of rage passing through him. "My brother and his oldest boy were both killed. Your uncle's head was cut off. And where were you? Hiding with that fucking Englishman. I saw you! I saw how you looked at him, how you let him touch you!"

She rounds on him. "Get out. Keep away from me. Keep away from my children. I hate killing, but to be rid of you, I swear I'll learn how it's done."

His face turns to stone and his eyes have no light in them. Without kneeling to God's blackened statue, he storms out.

"That was a serious blunder," says the priest.

"I— kn——ow." Suddenly she cannot stop shaking. "Oh please, what shall I do now? He'll turn the clans against me and make himself king. He'll make war on everything and most of us will die."

Airstalker puts his arm around her and tickles the tattoo of Mother Sea on her back, just as he had when she was Kia's age. "Dearest Naia," he says gently. "We'll all die one day anyhow. We have only two options in this life—torn out or worn out." He plants a kiss on her forehead. "I'm still waiting for a vision to let me know which is preferable. Or did you think you could save us from both?"

twenty-three

How He Found Her Again

NAIA HAD HOPED FOR A DAY TO TAKE HER PEOPLE TO SAFETY, BUT it had to be done within hours. The Englishmen from the *Lyon* did not wait for the tide in the breach to go down. Instead, they took the smaller transport pinnace and landed safely on Roanoke about sunset that same July evening, to come ashore at the mouth of a small creek that flowed into the outward sound.

"Let us pray, brothers." Wildye fussed with his wilted ruff. "Most Puissant and Unfathomable God the Father Almighty . . ."

Dick Darige the blacksmith couldn't keep himself still through the fiddling business. Instead, he studied the landscape—how the low, sandy hills rose up gradually from the beach, with here and there a steep ridge as the forest took over. Something metal gleamed bright at the edge of the trees. He shaded his eyes and looked again. Remembering the stories of silver and gold, he left Wildye droning on and climbed up to investigate what he'd seen.

Gabriel saw him kneel down in the sand and dig about with his two hands. Then Darige beckoned to George Howe and his boy, and to some of the others.

The metal the blacksmith had seen was not gold and it was not silver. It was an English helm, partly rusted. Beneath it, half-buried in sand, lay a soldier's rotting corpse, still in its steel cuirass. Even in the open air, the stench was overpowering.

"We must give him proper Christian burial," said George at last. "Been battered to pieces, poor sod. Head bashed right in."

"Spanish got him?"

"Nay. Civilized folk don't kill like that. Use a gun or a sword."

"He was struck from behind," said Surgeon Ellis.

"Nasty cowards," somebody muttered.

Wildye's sermon broke off, and John White, in crimson velvet doublet, gold chain of office, and plumed hat, came blustering up the hill with Captain Edmund English, who commanded the soldiers. "It is not permitted to avoid public worship," said the governor angrily. "Whatever you have found here cannot be reason for—"

Then he caught sight of the dead body. Without another word, he turned aside and began to chuck up his dinner all over his stockings.

"Anyone bring a mattock or a shovel?" asked George. "Run, Georgie-lad, and see."

"No good making a grave in this sand," Baird said. "There must be solid earth round here someplace to put him in."

"These savages shall be p-p-punished." White wiped the sick off his face and tried to sound like a governor. "A whole garrison was left here. A fortress. Cannon."

"Garrison, eh? How many, all told?"

"Why—fifteen or twenty."

"Hah! Call that a garrison?"

Gabriel left them to wrangle and climbed onto one of the higher dunes. *Only one thought in my brain. Had to find Naia, get a look at her, see if she was safe. I didn't expect any more than that. Be nearby. Keep my eye on things. Ask her pardon somehow.*

But there was no sign of her. No little reed boat in the marshes. No giggling maidens. Not even a trail of smoke from the cooking fires.

Baird and Viccars and some of the others went looking for the

English village and found another rack of bones on the beach about a quarter mile north. They brought them back and laid them out in their order not far from the first soldier's corpse.

"Nobody to be seen," said Will Baird. "Cottages still standing, but grown full of weeds and such."

"We found three or four proper graves," Viccars said. "Half caved in. It's all sand hereabouts. Dry as dust, too, no rain in a long time."

Those who had been farmers at home looked at one another and shook their heads, but Sutton finally put voice to it. "We can't farm in such a place. Even if we still had decent seed, you can't grow English crops in dust and sand."

"Fernando must take us elsewhere. He can't just put us down here like a bag of weeviled meal."

"Done it, though, ain't he? Says he won't haul us no farther."

"I say we go back out to *Lyon* and take her. Sail her back home."

"Mutiny, that is. Get our necks stretched, if the Spanish don't get us."

"Can't sail a ship anyhow. You, George?"

"By myself? Don't be daft."

"Nothing left to go back home for, anyway. It's all sold up and gone."

"There's still them savage gold mines," somebody said quietly.

"That's right. We must put our hopes in that."

"Aye, you'm right, Thomas. Gold."

It was a chance, it was something. A mirage in a desert. *Gold,* whispered the sea wind. *Gold. Gold. Gold.*

No one has the heart for conversation that night. Guards are set and the men lie down nose to toe under the gaping holes in the reed thatch of the abandoned cottages, to get what sleep they can.

Gabriel and Will Baird take the first watch, with a serjeant called Lacy and young Johnny Chapman, Alis's husband. The night is vibrant with strangeness, as though they have landed on the far side of Styx. The four men walk back and forth, meeting at the corners of the broken-down stockade to speak a word or two, then shifting directions and walking again. The sea in the outward sound laps at the beach. A bird calls in the woods and Johnny Chapman gives a soft cry of fear.

Gabriel's long legs measure the steps. Thirty-eight, thirty-nine, forty, forty-one . . . Turn. Change. One, two, three, four . . .

"Halt!" cries Serjeant Lacy's voice from the other side of the stockade. "Declare yourself!"

"Next watch, come to relieve you!"

"Give the word, then!"

"*Gloriana Regina.*"

"Aye, God save the queen."

*D*IDN'T GO BACK *to the others. Been making plans all through my watch. Knew I couldn't swim to the mainland, but there was a little dory on the pinnace, actually, so I took that. Swing if they caught me. Didn't care.*

He rows around the northern end of the island, past the cove where Naia's husband lies buried. "Where is she, Ena?" he whispers. "Does she still come to see you? Where's she gone?"

The marshes on the mainland are dense with reeds and it is hard to row a boat through them in daylight, let alone darkness. He ties up the dory to a fallen tree near the shore of the sound and wades to the path he remembers. For a few hundred yards, it is partly submerged by swamp lilies, cattails, and reeds. Then the ground lifts, rising to the northwest and following a stream, to intersect the narrow track that leads into the Secota village.

There is a palisade of saplings and a broad gateway, but nobody is guarding it. No cattail lamps burn in the houses. The ghostly carved faces on the spirit posts gaze wide-eyed into the darkness.

Gabriel keeps to the shadows, avoiding the open central meadow. Years of slipping about the London streets have given him a sixth sense for watchers and he can feel eyes on him now. At the gate, he eases himself cautiously into the woods again.

"Come on, my dear," he mumbles. "Where are you? Come on, come on, come on. Show me where you are."

Suddenly he hears bare feet running through the pine needles, the slap of branches. Then a soft, rhythmic splashing, an oar in the water of the stream. A light wind moving the trees, and then silence again.

He makes his way back to the dory and it is then that he catches sight of it—the little reed boat with its oiled-leather cover, turned upside down on the strip of sand between marsh and sound. It was not there when he arrived. It is still dripping, only just lifted out of the water.

Ena's love gift. No one else could've used it, Naia wouldn't have stood for it. Unless it has been taken from her. Unless she is dead.

There is lightning out beyond Roanoke, far out at sea. He stands for a moment in the shine of the inward sound. Then, very softly, he begins to sing, a song he often sang as he worked in the village or prowled through the woods, watching for her:

> *Heigh-ho, nobody home*
> *Meat nor drink nor money have I none.*
> *And still I will be merry.*

A woman's soft laughter comes from under the reed boat. There is a huge excitement in the sound, only barely suppressed. A relief in Gabriel that relaxes the clench of his fists, and the great muscles at the backs of his thighs, and the tensed cords of his throat.

"Why are you hiding from me?" he says quietly. "Come out. I want to see you."

She pushes the boat over and stands up. The storm out at sea has sent clouds to darken the moon, but she is close enough for him to see her clearly. The soft dark hair has grown long again, carefully knotted at the nape of her neck, the little fringe over her forehead drifting a bit in the wind. Her silky shoulders with the faint damask of tattoo marks and body paint he has come to love. Her arm with the faded scars of her mourning.

She pauses, and he can feel her eyes feeding upon the outline of him—the arms that are always too long for his clothes, the head held a little to one side. The chiselled slope of his nose. The steady, pulsing line of his throat.

"What is this singing?" she says, tipping her chin up in the way he remembers. " 'Money have I none'? This is not proper English talk. I have not money—this is proper."

"No money. Have no money." He smiles in the flickering liquid darkness. So near to the inward sound, it is like being with her under the sea. "Still, you shouldn't have laughed at me. Now you owe me a sorry present. I'd settle for your pearls, but you're not wearing them. Chucked you off the throne, have they? Or what's it like, being queen?"

Now her voice is tight, faintly edged with anger. "Pearls can break and spill. Pearls are not for rowing boats and spying on English."

"Ah. You're out spying, then?"

"Of course spying. You are spying, why should I not spy? What else are you doing in our village, poking your long English nose everywhere?"

"Looking for you." His face pale as the lightning. "What I came back for."

"You think I want you here? You think I want you to bring another ship full of English to steal our food and then come and kill us?"

She cannot continue. Why does this anger spill out of her, when she has so longed for him?

"Ena's boat's holding up well," he says. "Must be stronger than it looks." No response. Somehow even Ena has become a difficult subject. He tries again. "How are the sprouts?"

She looks up. "What is sprouts, please?"

"Just a silly expression. I mean Masu and Kia. Are they—"

"They're safe. *You* cannot know where. I saw your English boats come and I sent everyone away where you can't find them." She splashes her bare foot in the water. A sleepy heron flies up. "I may ask you a question. Are these English the same ones as before?"

"No. There are families with us now. They're not soldiers, they just want to make homes here. Plant crops. Have babies."

"Liar. I *saw* soldiers. I saw their tin hats shining."

"Yes, well. A few soldiers. You have fighters, don't you?"

"Did you bring *your* woman?"

"Mine? No."

"What do they look like, these women English? Airstalker says they wear too much clothes and have sour faces."

He laughs. "Come and see for yourself. Come as a queen. You'll amaze them."

"Ha. They'll lock me up like they did Masu and put chains on me."

"They're in a pickle, Naia. Bad trouble. The captain of the ship has betrayed them. They've only half enough food, no animals, nothing. And he won't take them home now. They're just ordinary people and they're scared. They found the dead soldiers."

"Why didn't they stay in their own country and make homes instead of coming to take ours?"

She was sharper than I remembered, quicker to bite. Blaming her-self. That's how it is when things start to slip sidewise. You don't know why you can't stop it. Felt that way the minute I set foot in christly England again. Nothing to do but jump ship.

"Nobody wants a war," he says. "But the governor's already talking reprisals. Punishment, I mean. If anything else happens— I thought I should warn you."

"I knew! I told Tesik, but he wouldn't stop till he had killed them all."

"You're the queen. Who the hell is he? Couldn't you make him stop?"

"In bed, who is queen? You think a woman can tell the man she sleeps with what to do?"

"Oh," he says under his breath. "Oh. God. Oh."

A long silence. "I was a fool to bed with him," she says at last.

"Things happen. God knows they happen to me. Are you married to him?"

"I am not so much fool as that."

"Does he hurt you? Are you afraid of him? You are, aren't you?"

"He spies on me and follows me. That makes me afraid."

"Is he watching us? Now?"

"How do I know? Can I see through a tree?"

It will be hard even to keep an eye on her and the children as he has hoped to do, much harder than he ever thought. Who is this christly Tesik, anyway? "The children," he says, his fists clenched. "Does he hurt them?"

Naia can feel the anger come from him, and it both frightens her and falls upon her like rain that he has not changed, that he loves them so. "Tesik tries to take my boy from me," she says quietly. "It is this that hurts."

Gabriel holds out his hands to her. "How can I help you? Tell me what I should do."

"Nothing." She touches his arm, then retreats. "I have sent him away. But he wants war. Oh, be careful. Set guards when you sleep, and take care of your women."

Naia's scent is heavy and sweet on the air and her skin gleams with oil. The mosquitoes do not bother her, but they buzz eagerly around his own face and hands. He slaps at an especially pesky one, and she laughs her old laugh. So close he can feel the faint drift of her breath.

He has to fight himself to keep from putting his arms around her. The choice must be hers, but somehow he knows she will not make it, perhaps never will. They will travel parallel lines forever, unless he steps over to her side. He sinks wearily onto the sand, the water lapping around him.

"You ruined it for me," he says to her. "You know that."

"I ruined what?"

"Europe. England. Oyster pies. Lute music. Bastard ale. Other women. Hundreds of them."

"Don't be foolish."

She hesitates a moment. Lets her fingers touch his tangled hair, the touch soft and light, distant as the sea-lightning. Then she steps away and rights the wicker boat, pushes it into the stream, and is gone.

twenty-four

THE SILENT DOGS OF WAR

FOR THE SEVENTEEN ENGLISH WOMEN, TOO, THAT NIGHT WAS SHAD-
owed and strange. As soon as the menfolk in the pinnace were safely through the breach and on their way up
Roanoke sound, Fernando had ordered all the women and children and serving boys put ashore on the sandy barrier island.
Their goods and most of their provisions were left behind on
the ship to wait for the return of their husbands. They were allowed to take only a little food and what bedding they could
manage.

As they splashed through the shallows and onto the beach, the
sun was going down in a pale gleam of apricot-gold behind the
dense, mist-hung forest. Even the swooping night birds were
strange, and every sand flea was a savage.

Rose Payne sent the boys to gather driftwood for a fire.
"Thought I'd boil us up a bit of porridge," she said.

"Oh, aye," said Eliza Viccars. "There's always cheer in a fire,
even on such a hot night as this."

But Emma stood shaking her head. "You got no more sense
than a suet pudding, the pair of you. Light a fire, and them woods

full of wild folk? Maybe we should ought to start dancing and invite 'em all in."

So they sat in the dark, eating cold stale food and drinking
what wretched water was left, with only the gleam of the sea out
beyond them for light.

Rose sighed. "I'll wager my Henry's having himself a good hot
English meal in the barracks right now."

"Or the officers' quarters," said Madge. "My third husband was
a captain. They always do themselves proud when they dine."

"Roast swan. I saw swans flying over."

"Bread sauce. Blancmange."

"Oh, yes, with cream. They're sure to have cows. And chickens."

"Ah, real hens' eggs."

"And the menfolk will sleep this night in real beds. Real
beds!"

"Men gets all the comforts in this world, God bless 'em."

"Aye, so they do."

NEXT MORNING, they had a happy surprise. The flyboat
Whitethorn, so long despaired of, came sailing up from the
south, with all the folk on deck waving and weeping and crying
out. After joyous reunions between families who had thought
themselves separated forever by the trickery at Lisbon, they were
all fetched to Roanoke Island by the shoreboats, to arrive just at
fall of dark.

They slept crowded together under the ruinous thatches of the
nine little lime-washed English houses inside the palisade, drank
fine cold water from the shallow stream, and ate for their supper
the huge sweet muscadine grapes whose vines had taken root in
the cracks of the floors.

Just after midnight it began to drizzle and rain. "That thatch is a right sieve," muttered sleepy Jane Pierce, shaking the water off her. "My old petticoat would do more good."

The rain had stopped by morning. They threw shawls and old clothes over themselves to keep off the voracious mosquitoes, then went out to survey the village. "Holy saints, but it's ugly, ain't it?" murmured Emma.

Trees by the dozens had been cut off and the stumps simply left standing, harum-scarum and a dozen different heights. The narrow little houses were set every which way, though they were well enough made. The roofs were the worst of it. They had been thatched with the tough reeds that grew head-high in the marshes, but the bundles weren't properly laid and fastened, leaving gaps for the rain to pour through.

Master Tappan—Tap-the-Thatch, who had learned his craft in the Cotswold villages—puzzled over the problem. "Can't trim them reeds level, see, so the water don't run off as it ought. But we might work in some of that mossy stuff that hangs from the trees to even things up. Let the serving boys and the womenfolk gather it, while some of us goes out to cut fresh reeds."

THE MEN WENT early next morning with a makeshift barrow to carry the bundles home. Tap was there, of course, and Gabriel, that Jack-of-all-trades. Peg-legged George Howe went with them, and half a dozen more.

They found the best thatching reeds about two miles from the village and went their separate ways, cutting and bundling as they moved. It was very hot and humid, the sun pounding down, the reeds higher than their heads, the black flies and mosquitoes a torment. With his stick to help him balance his wooden leg against the current, George Howe waded into a shallow stream and set to work, ducking his face now and then to wash off the bugs.

The sun was almost straight overhead when he realized he had no notion where he was. "Will?" he called out. "You there, William? Gabe? Where you at, old son?"

But there was no answer. No sound of men's voices, no crackle of the reeds, no splashes in the water but his own and the frogs'. He was lost.

Well, well, he'd been lost before, and not on dry land, either. Stick in hand and carrying his last bundle on his shoulder, he crashed through the marsh and emerged at a place where the stream ran deeper and wider and the breeze freshened. No sign of anything to fear. It seemed to him a fine place for a swim. He couldn't *really* swim, not as he used to with two legs. But he stripped off his clothes and waded into the deepest part of the stream, ducking himself again and again till he felt clean and calm and whole.

When he was underwater, he caught sight of a fine big crab in the streambed. Bare-arse naked in the hot sun, his peg leg stuck firmly in the sandy creek bottom, he bent over and swirled the water with a forked stick. "Ah-ha," he shouted, and flipped the crab onto the bank, then another and another, laughing as he worked.

H E'S NOT the right one," whispers Tesik.

For two days and two nights, ever since the English ships arrived, Sharp-Tooth, Twister, Black Fox, and Thunder-Fist have been with him, airing their grudges and smoking pipe after pipe of the strong tobacco that brings courage and war-dreams. Spying as usual, they saw Naia meet Gabriel by the inward sound. They saw him row the little skiff back to Roanoke.

For two nights and two days, they have been watching the English village. Watching the women sweep out the houses and the boys clean the chimneys. Watching the men go out to gather reeds.

George Howe tosses another crab onto the bank and laughs for sheer joy. No lordship to fine him for poaching. No one to cry shame if he's naked. No one to regulate the price of the sunshine and levy a tax on the mud.

Black Fox readies an arrow, but Tesik shakes his head.

"I told you, it's not him. The one I want is taller and his leg isn't made from a tree. You all saw him come to meet her that first night—the English traitor. I knew she was waiting for him to come back, I *always* knew it. We have to take him down first."

"What sense is there in that?" says Sharp-Tooth. "If he betrays them to her, we can make use of him. We can always get rid of him later."

Black Fox nods. "Make her watch while you kill him, that's the way to teach her a lesson. Besides, the one with a tree for a leg will be easier to take."

Tesik has to accept the truth of what they say. Let Gabriel begin to tell Naia the plans and secrets of the English. She will confide in Airstalker, and when the old fool has had too much tobacco, he can be made to tell them everything.

"All right," he says grudgingly. "This one with the wooden leg, then. But no holding back, understand?"

George laughs again, tossing another fine crab onto the bank, and young Twister looks away. It seems perverse to kill a man who can laugh.

But Tesik seats a shell-tipped arrow in his bow. There is no flint on this part of the coast for real arrowheads, and they cost too much to trade for. You dip the shell heads in a poison that makes your enemy helpless. Then you move in with war clubs and shell-bladed knives. "On my signal, we fire."

"Wait!" Twister says.

"What the hell's the matter with you now?" The war chief is tense with rage.

"Can't we at least let him see us before we fire? Maybe wait till he's through catching crabs? It would only be fair. He hasn't got any weapons. He's naked. He hasn't stolen our food or attacked us or anything."

Tesik wears the burnished copper gorget that was his dead brother's. He has deep lines in his face and his eyes dart everywhere, as though he sees a thousand Englishmen instead of one. "His personal innocence is irrelevant. They have to be stopped *before* they do damage. This is the beginning of a resistance that may go on forever."

"You mean a war that goes on forever."

"In the face of great forces, time doesn't matter. Life doesn't matter." His lithe body suddenly turns, the arrow now perfectly aimed at Twister's eye. "If you aren't with us, boy, you're against us. Make up your mind."

The others stare. There is no *us*, there is only Tesik. They all know he is controlling a dangerous part of them, but they can't think fast enough to resist him. And in a strange way, he almost seems to be right.

WHEN THE FIRST ARROW hits him, George Howe thinks one of the crabs has its claw in him. He yelps, then turns, trying to pull his peg leg from the sand. But he cannot move. The wooden leg is stuck fast.

The second shot—Twister's—hits him in the throat. From behind him, Thunder-Fist and Sharp-Tooth fire, their arrows catching him in the small of the back and the shoulder. Then comes Black Fox, who hits him in the groin. Again and again they fire.

Through all this, George is silent. The poison from the arrowheads makes him dream he is running, two-legged and whole, over a long stretch of water, dry-footed, the waves breaking beyond without touching him.

One after another, twelve, fifteen, sixteen arrows strike him. In the legs. In the balls. Once in the right eye. Once in the chest, near the heart.

Fragments attack him. He sees his father's hands laying stones for a pasture wall. Tastes fresh-made currant buns. Hears the hard rattle of coins in the voices of whores.

He feels the sky coming down to meet the water, feels himself smashed between them. He wants to dive, to burrow into the sea. But he cannot move. Both his legs have turned to wood now, and his arms and his shoulders. His sex is the root of a tree. Drunk on the poison, he lolls back and falls sideways, bent nearly double, his right arm and his face in the sandy water. His peg leg still refuses to let go of the sand.

They close in on him. It is, in the end, a lesson in the executioner's trade, each blow of the black oak war club calculated to achieve the optimum result in the shortest time.

At last the death squad disappears into the forest. Somewhere a loon cries, another answers. The smashed bits of George Howe lie in the slow-moving water, very peaceful, the smaller ones drifting away to the sea and the green coasts of home.

Silently, without so much as a shout, the Roanoke is at war.

twenty-five

THE REPRISAL

THE DEAD DO NOT KEEP IN SUMMER, AND IN SUCH A HUMID CLIMATE, delay was out of the question. The battered remains of George Howe and the stray bones of the murdered soldiers were given burial next morning.

At noon John White called the men of the colony together. "Masters," he began, looking over his shoulder at Wildye, English, and the stony-faced members of the Governor's Council. "I am advised—er— In the name of—er—Queen Elizabeth, we must now exact retribution for our dead, lest we be forever—er—forever at hazard in this place. You will, therefore, draw by lot from amongst you two dozen men to attack the savages on their own ground this same midnight."

"I'll go," said a small voice. Georgie Howe. Ten years old and the image of his father. Pale and shaken and angry and tearless.

Captain English nodded his approval. "A good son. It's only right."

"You're all platitudes, you are," said Gabriel angrily. "A mouldy proverb for every occasion. He's a boy. He's just seen his father buried. Let him be."

"These savages are all devils," Wildye said, "and God hates their sins. He fights on our side. He will protect the boy."

"Is there any side God *doesn't* fight on? Or does He consult you before He makes up His mind?"

"Enough blasphemy, Master North!" snapped English. "We attack them tonight. Choose your captains, you men, and do as you're told."

Emma Merrimoth sat on a stump at the edge of the clearing, swinging her bare legs. "If you please, sir," she said, "I'd like to know how us women's meant to live once you've took all the menfolk off and got 'em stuck full of arrows."

Joyce Archard shifted Tomkin's weight on her hip. "Had you never a mother, Captain? Think of her left so unprovided for as we shall be."

"Come, mistresses." White looked as though he might piss himself any minute. "Your—er—womanly fears are to be pardoned, but authority is authority. Draw your lots now, you fellows, and be ready at midnight."

W HETHER BY CHANCE or by design, Gabriel's name is not chosen. He watches the others board the pinnace, with John White in his plumed helmet and steel armor standing in the prow like a plaster statue of Mars.

"Well, grandsire, what's your pleasure? Cup of gruel and a soft bed?" Emma is always where you don't expect her.

The men push the little craft out into the sound and the wind catches the sail. The night is overcast, the moon riding in and out of clouds. Gabriel walks away from the girl, moving towards the little cove where Ena is buried. There are quick, light steps behind him.

"If you was a gentleman, you'd give me your arm," she pants. "And slacken off a bit. Your legs is too bleedin' long."

"Go back to the others and stay there."

"Think I'm a baby? I can come if I want to."

"Oh, bollocks."

He begins to run into the dense woods behind the cove, choosing the most overgrown pathways. Emma cannot keep up with him, but she won't be left behind. When her skirts become caught on the bushes, she unties them and lets them fall. Barelegged in only her shift she moves faster, but he is almost out of sight again, nearing the cove.

When she reaches the edge of the woods, she suddenly stops. The trees have thinned enough for her to glimpse Gabriel's tall shape against the bright water where the moon comes and goes.

Someone else is there. Bare shoulders and bare breasts and shiny earrings in her ears. So, grandsire has himself a doxy, has he? Is it that nasty Lizzie Glane? Sleep with a weasel, that one. Stupid old gander. Who wants him, anyway?

Emma moves closer. It ain't Lizzie and it ain't none of the rest of 'em, neither. Jesu, it's a savage woman. Gabriel says something and the woman starts to walk away. Then she turns back and Emma gets a look at her face. It isn't fearsome, not like she's imagined. Just the face of a woman. Frightened. Needful. I'm needful. Why won't he go slipping through the dark woods looking for *me*?

The savage woman reaches out her two hands and Gabriel takes them. It is a gesture they are used to. A small comfort of the kind husbands and wives have between them after many years. He bends his head over her hands, then, and lifts them to his face and holds them there.

Emma does not believe in love. She understands lust, but what they hold in their hands is not lust, either. There is no name for it that she has ever heard.

There is a funny little boat and the savage woman pushes it out into the shallow water and gets into it. She holds it steady with the oar and Gabriel climbs in behind her. The boat lurches and almost sinks, it sits so deep from the weight of the two of them. But they balance themselves. Gabriel takes the oar and the boat begins to move out into the sound.

Emma follows them as far as she can, running along the beach at the curve of the island, watching the little dark boat with the two silent figures cross to the mainland. The reprisal party are becalmed for a time, while the wind shifts directions. They cannot risk being tangled up in the reeds of the swamp and must sail farther down the coast to find a good landing place.

The two in the reed boat disappear into the marsh and Emma can see nothing more of them. For a long time, she sits watching and slapping mosquitoes. The pinnace makes land on the opposite shore and she can just catch the absurd gleam of John White's armor as the English wade ashore.

There are no cooking fires in the Secota village. Outside the houses a few small lights burn, cattails soaked in grease and stuck into the sand. Two men are at work in the meadow loading a litter of skins and poles with clay jars and bundles, and some women and children are sorting ears of green corn into baskets.

Working in the middle of the night? The strangeness of it means nothing to Captain English. "On my word," he whispers, and the command is carried along from man to man. They are hidden in the trees, nerving themselves for the attack.

"There's no more'n eight or nine of them altogether," says Sutton.

John Cheven is dubious. "They don't look very wicked to me. I don't see no weapons."

"Maybe they ain't the right ones," Peter Little says.

One of the tribesmen finishes his work with the baggage and stands talking to the other. A woman with a baby on her back in a cradleboard comes in from the field carrying a basket of corn.

"For the queen!" cries the captain. "Fire!"

A great volley of shots explodes and the air splinters into shards and crashes down around them. One Indian falls dead, and a second waves his hands in the air, shouting "Croatoan, Croatoan!" The woman with the baby takes a shot in the leg. The tribesmen are shouting the words over and over: "Croatoan, Croatoan."

Gabriel's voice is huge and furious above the noise. "They aren't enemies, you fools, they're Croatoans from the sand islands! *Allies!* You signed a peace treaty with them two days ago. They've only come to steal the Secota corn."

"What?"

Captain English thinks in straight lines and never for himself. His mind lives inside neat little boxes constructed of pieties, patriotic commonplaces, superstitions, and orders from titled gentlemen who've never left England in their lives. The boxes have locks on them. The locks have no keys.

"What are you doing here, North? Eh? You were told to stay behind with the women." He turns back to his command. "Fire, you scoundrels! For the queen, damn you!"

Back in England, they were made to march with the militia once every summer for practice, but they never dreamed of actually shooting anyone. John Cheven throws down his gun and simply walks away. Dyonis Harvie shoots Peter Little in the foot, and one of Harry Johnson's shots grazes Gabriel's side.

It's no use reasoning with the captain. Instead, Gabriel catches sight of Georgie Howe's red hair through the trees, and makes for it. The boy has brought a light bow and five arrows, but none has been fired. "I can't," he says in a stricken voice. "I mean, they're just plain working folk like us."

"Cut away back to the pinnace, boy. Tell Ellis he's got folk here to patch up. Where's the governor got to?"

"Up there."

Georgie points to a small hill, well out of the way of things, and Gabriel takes off again, his mind whirling. Shots are still whizzing pointlessly here and there. Where is Naia? God keep her. Bending low, he runs through the smoky dark, dodging and weaving, fetching up at last by John White's side.

"Is that savage *dead*?" whispers the governor. His eyes are blank and staring. "It was Captain English who insisted we attack them. Subdue the natives to Her Majesty's rule, he said. *I* never wanted it! That woman with the baby—"

"Be quiet and listen. Are you listening? You have to stop it now. Make reparations. Beg those people's forgiveness."

"But the map to the gold mines— We must look for it. The queen must have her legal share of any—"

"If you don't stop this, you'll have two tribes at war with you, and the rest won't be far behind. The gold doesn't exist. Do you hear me? It doesn't exist! It's not real!"

White stares at him as though he is speaking Chinese. But the order is finally given. The English guns fall silent at last.

WHEN THE PINNACE made land again on Roanoke it was nearing morning, and the men trudged shamefacedly off to their beds. Gabriel returned with the others, leaving Naia to comfort the Croatoan women she had hidden in the marsh.

But he did not go with the rest to the cottages and the barracks.

Emma was waiting for him, still in her shift. "Well, grandsire," she said. "What've you done with your savage?"

"Not so loud. Be quiet."

"What's the matter with a woman of your own kind, I'd like to know? I reckon it's them tattoos, eh? Or what's she do for you that us English girls don't? Got some special parts, do they, them savage women?"

"You're not a slut. Why do you talk like one?"

"Yes, I am *too* a slut. Been a slut since I was twelve and proud of it. Bet I can do it in ways she don't even imagine."

"Stop it." Her small hand had found its way inside his shirt and slipped dangerously downward. He untangled himself and stepped back from her.

"You're willing enough with savages." She stamped her foot. "But I ain't good enough for you. Well, you burn in hell, then."

"I will," he said gently. "Just for you, Emma. Just for you."

He caught her up suddenly and wrapped her young body in his long arms. He was thinking of his daughter Judith again, of how often she had run away from her aunt's house. How his sour-faced sister would send an angry message and he would go racing through London till he found the child, hiding always in the same churchyard, sitting on the same huge tombstone. *Standfast Hartwell, Wife of the Above.*

"Mustn't think so small of yourself, pet," he whispered. "It's what they want of us, mostly. Makes 'em happy, the smaller they shrink us down."

"They who?"

"Piddlejacks. Users-up. Fuckers-over. Christ, I hate 'em."

Emma wiped her nose on his shirt. "You really love *her*, though, don't you?"

"Once I'd met her, I seemed to finally grow up, is all."

"I never loved anybody. Don't believe in it. But I don't want to be easy."

"Have to stop putting your hands inside gentlemen's breeches, then."

Strange, it was, how things echoed from one life to another. A thousand years since his girls were little. He kissed Emma's hair and hid his face in her shoulder for a moment.

Standfast Merrimoth. Friend of the above.

twenty-six

HERE'S A NIGHT PITIES NEITHER
WISE MEN NOR FOOLS

*T*HEY PATCHED UP THE WOUNDED CROATOANS AND ARRANGED REPARA-
tions for the wives of the one who was killed, which restored
an uneasy peace. But after that ludicrous reprisal, there was no
doubt that John White would be asked to surrender the governance. The Council met night after night to listen to his half-
hearted whinings and protests.

August droned on, suffocatingly hot and visited with plagues
of flies and mosquitoes. In the marshes, huge flocks of cranes,
swans, and herons began to gather, feeding night and day to prepare for their autumn migrations. The great ships completed the
usual chores—sluicing out the bilge, replacing the fouled ballast,
taking on new supplies of wood and fresh water. They were ready
to return to England, and Fernando was obliged to take back one
man to report to the queen and to Ralegh. One man, and only
one. Everyone prayed it would be John White.

On the seventeenth, his daughter Elinor Dare took to her bed
and, after a long and difficult labor, gave birth to a daughter of
her own, called Virginia. Madge fussed and worried and brewed
herbal tinctures for the childbed fever that seemed to weaken the

new mother day by day. But the birth of his grandchild was the release Master White had been waiting for. A week later, he went aboard the *Whitethorn* bound for England, wearing his plumed hat and his velvet doublet and promising to send relief ships and reinforcements—but leaving his gold chain of office behind.

ONCE THE SHIPS had set sail for home—towing the pinnace, which Fernando planned to fill with Spanish treasure—Naia brought her people out of hiding and returned to the mainland village. "I've decided to visit the English," she announced at morning council. "Sapono, I want you to go to the towns along the coast and invite the other chiefs to come and make peace. It's time to end all this suspicion and resentment. Better to do it before the cold weather comes."

The new herald looked over at Airstalker, but he got no help. The old man spent more time in trances these days than out of them.

"The tribes won't come," said Sapo. "You know Tesik's living with the Pamlico now. He's married Swift Otter's sister. And most of the Turtle clan from the coastal villages have gone with him. There's no use trying to get them to talk peace with anybody, least of all us."

"How many men have they got?"

"The Pamlico? More than two hundred, with Tesik's clan. The others—Tuscarora, Weapeme—maybe two hundred and fifty more, if they hire mercenaries from the Mandoag."

Naia bit her lip. The Mandoag were inlanders from the copper mountains and they had a cruel reputation. "The English don't seem to be getting ready for war," she said.

"Oh, they're not," said Sapono. "They don't even get ready for winter. They came too late to plant crops, just like last time, and their women aren't gathering nuts or wild fruit or digging lily roots. You know what that means."

"More begging," said Slender Eel, Naia's cousin, with a sigh. "More attacks."

But Naia insisted. "We have work to do before winter ourselves, and we may as well let them kill us as sit hiding till we starve. No, no. We must make peace somehow."

Piemacum, the new war chief, considered. He was a Fish, prudent and deliberate. "It's not a bad thought, making friends with them," he said. "We may need the English as allies, if Tesik attacks us."

"They'd never fight by our side," scoffed the Eel.

"It costs nothing to try," Naia said.

"Tesik! Pah!" Airstalker suddenly burst out in a strange, high-pitched voice. He had been sick in his bed for almost a week, and even now that he was better he often seemed feverish and confused. Today he was in some other world altogether. Naia put her hand on his forehead. It felt very hot, and his eyes didn't focus.

"If Tesik does make war, it will be my fault," she told the others. "I'll step down if you think it will stop him."

Piemacum shook his head and the eagle's claw on his braid of hair rattled. "Mustn't blame yourself. You have every right to choose your man, or six if you want them, that's our custom with unmarried women. Most of us were relieved when Tesik left."

"Besides," said the Eel, "they'd have made war on your uncle eventually. We're poor in fighting men just now, but the real power of a leader rests on his wealth, and that's what they want. It sets the prices the traders charge and decides how much tribute-tax the other towns owe you. Your uncle left you a lot of copper hidden away. You control the only paint mines on this stretch of coast. You control the pearl beds."

Piemacum smiled. "And don't forget the famous map to the Gold Mountains."

"Pfu. All we've got is a map that shows how to keep clear of the Mandoag copper mines. Airstalker drew it after one of his visions, you know that."

"They say he also has a map of where he turned the swamp witches into purple fog."

"And made it rain strawberries. Try and explain that to the English."

They all laughed except Naia, but the laugh did not linger. "Have some men waiting with canoes in the morning," she told the Eel. "I'll take Swan's Wing and Heartberry and my maidens. A few guards, but not too many. And my children, of course. We can at least make a start."

"No time, little Naia," the aged priest whispered. They had all thought him asleep, for his eyes had the glaze of oncoming blindness and he stared at the empty air in front of him. "There will be no time for visits tomorrow."

It bruised her heart to see him so. She knelt before him as she used to kneel to her uncle, with her forehead to his foot.

"Tell me, old friend," she said. "What's coming tomorrow?"

Airstalker shook his hands to make his copper bracelets rattle. There were legends about him all up and down the coast—that he could walk on the air, that he could darken the sun. There had been a time when men believed such things utterly, but he was old now and had outlived his reputation. Still, he kept to his ascetic disciplines. Constant prayer. Yaupon tea. Fasting. He read the future clearly, and it was said that he had seen the dark face of God.

"The White Wolves are coming, darling Naia," he said. "The White Wolves that eat up the sand and break the great trees and wash the houses into the sea."

She felt her heart stop, then start again. The White Wolves—it was what they called the hurricane waves.

N EXT MORNING, the water in Parson Tydway's swan-necked weatherglass had dropped sharply. He put on his flat parson's cap and went out to find the lynx kitten called Zebedee that Georgie Howe had brought him for a pet, and to tell his niece Janet not to put the washing out to dry. Madge, struggling back from Governor's House, where she'd been sitting with a dying Elinor Dare, had all she could do to keep her wicker farthingale from turning into a kite.

The hurricane began as a rustle in the stagnant air by the waterside where Gabriel was mending a fish weir. Within minutes, there were whitecaps in the sound. "Jack," Gabriel shouted to one of the boys, "run and tell Emma there's mean weather building. Have her get everybody inside the strongest houses and shutter the windows."

Many were Devoners and Cornish folk, and they didn't fear a gale at the beginning of things. But during the night, part of the thatch blew off Rose Payne's house, and she and her Henry were obliged to take shelter with the Archards. On the morning of the second day, Tap climbed up to fasten a piece of old sail over the hole and was blown off his ladder, while Parson Tydway, on his way to pray at Mistress Dare's deathbed, was buffeted this way and that for the better part of half an hour.

After that came a terrible hollow stillness. The wind fell and the birds were silent. Even the mosquitoes disappeared. Parson Tydway sat at the dying woman's side with his prayer book in his hands and his eyes glazed, like Moses in the presence of God.

Then, as though the very sky had cracked open, the real hurricane struck, and they had known nothing like it. The wind was a huge roar and trees began to fall like kindling sticks. Those with houses near to the forest were forced to take shelter with others or simply ran out into the tempest, too maddened by the great noise of the wind to resist. The others kept to their dark little houses, displaced families crowding together, husbands and wives clinging onto each other. The draught down the chimneys put out the cooking fires, and the children were all wailing and whimpering. Doors and window shutters blew open and had to be tied shut. Rain poured through wind-ripped thatches.

As dark drew in on the most terrible day, the wind seemed to quiet a little. "I'm going to see after Madge and the parson," Emma said.

"Don't you go!" cried Jane Pierce. "No bigger'n you are, you'll be blown back to England."

"I'll go with you," said Alis Chapman. "I want to see if the barracks are standing. John'll be wanting his supper."

They tied themselves together with a piece of stout rope, slipped through the cottage door while those inside kept hold of it, and set out. The wind was still very strong, and they were only halfway across the stump-littered common when the lightning began, great bolts crashing down into the clearing, and rain so heavy it streamed in sheets too dense to see through. They could hear trees cracking and falling as their roots were pulled free of the earth, and once there came a terrible noise and a smell of burning straw. Again and again the thunder crashed and the lightning came down and down and down, until Alis was crying like a baby in huge wailing sobs and Emma was cursing Sir Walter Ralegh.

Waves from the sound had begun to flood the common, but the two women finally reached the door of Governor's House by locking arms, crawling to a tree stump, pulling themselves up, then bracing against the wind and water to make their way to the next tree. At last they stood pounding on the door, shouting with all their might, and Madge and Parson Tydway dragged them inside.

"God's mercy," cried the midwife as they forced the door shut again. "What outpost of hell have we come to?"

The floor was six inches deep in murky water, and more was pouring through the thatch. "How's the sick?" gasped Alis.

"Mistress Dare has gone to her Maker, my dear," said Parson Tydway, glancing through a doorway at the curtained bed. Someone was in the room where the body lay. In the cradle, the baby began to cry and footsteps splashed across the flooded floor. The wailing subsided and a man's voice murmured something that might have been prayers.

Madge tried to wipe her eyes with her wet apron and thought better of it. "She went near two hours ago, and not even her own lout of a brother nor her husband beside her. *He* came to her. What brought him, I know not."

He was helpless, unable to reach Naia. So here he was, needing something to save. His voice was hoarse with shouting over the storm and the words of the lullaby slurred with his weariness.

> *Heigh-ho, nobody home.*
> *Meat nor drink nor money have I none.*
> *But still I will be merry.*

twenty-seven

KINDNESS, NOBLER THAN REVENGE

Nine of the fourteen houses were blown down and most of the buildings in the fort were spoiled. The waves washed the cannon into the sea and four men died trying to save it. Alis's Johnny was one of them, smashed by the heavy black nose of the gun.

The palisade was a pile of splinters. The sea made a breach in the barrier islands and flooded almost everything. They climbed trees and lived in the broken branches like squirrels, or clung onto the rafters of what houses were left, till at last the water began to go down. Mistress Colman was drowned. Reverend Wildye's house was lightning-struck and he died in the fire, along with the others sheltered there. Ananias Dare. Mad Joan. Jack, the serving boy. The thatcher and his wife. John Hemmington, who had left seven children behind him in England. Winnie Powell's husband, Ned. Jack Spendlove, the wastrel who'd failed to marry money.

Many were missing. George Martyn, the wool factor. Christopher Cooper, the recusant Catholic. Thomas Stevens, who owned a ship-yard in Saltaish. Some were found buried in the ruined cottages and the single men's barracks. Some were crushed by falling trees. Some were simply blown away and never heard of again. Henry

Rufoote, a shepherd from Devon. The two actors who had played *The Judgement of Paris*. Morris Allyn, the Colmans' old cowman. Jacky Cotsmur, the dowser. White's drunken son Cuthbert. Lizzie Glane.

It knocked the sense out of many of the living. They sat dull-eyed, unwilling to rouse themselves to work or to planning. They huddled together, talking in undertones, and when you passed them one word buzzed in the air. It was all they had left now. The sweet miracle. The drunkard's dream. *Gold*.

The rest said their prayers, began to pick over the ruins, and went on.

A FEW DAYS LATER, on a clear September morning that made the hurricane seem like a child's bad dream, a long dugout canoe rowed by Piemacum and Slender Eel crossed the inner sound, rounded what was left of the fort, and tied up at the creek's mouth.

"Savages!" called Dick Darige. "A whole boatload of 'em!"

The women gathered the children and serving boys and sent them inside. Some looked round for weapons. Emma snatched up a pitchfork.

"Why, it's a woman," muttered Martyn Sutton as the Eel helped Naia out of the boat. "Sight to behold, though, ain't she?"

She was wearing so many long ropes of pearls that they twisted and tangled when she moved and her women had to lift them and straighten them. There was a wreath of beaten copper and black pearls in her hair, and ropes of white coral and copper wire twined round her ankles. At her breast was the great royal gorget of heavy beaten copper, and she wore a cape of blue heron feathers that went almost to her ankles.

Lady Heartberry and her daughter, the maiden Amagaya, attended upon their queen, along with one or two other women, all of them decked out with swan feathers.

Masumeo walked on one side of his mother and Kia on the other. Both children wore copper and pearls, and short capes of deerskin worked with colored quills. The warriors were unarmed and the women carried gifts—three brace of partridge; handsome baskets of walnuts, hazelnuts, and dried corn; a fine clay jar of smoked venison; and three precious combs of honey.

Gabriel stayed back, content to watch proudly. But little Kia, always irrepressible, ran straight to him, stretching out her small arms.

"Up!" she said. "Up!"

Had a game, actually. Rode her on my shoulders and she pretended I was a tree. Our folk were all gawking, the lubbers. Backing away from me. Would've thought I'd shaved half my head and started doing a war dance.

He hoisted Kia onto his shoulder and began to whirl round and round, faster and faster, weaving in and out among the muttering colonists. Naia's eyes moved from one of the suspicious English to the other and Piemacum put a protective hand on her arm.

But the worst moment passed quickly. The little girl laughed and held on for dear life, until Gabriel tumbled the pair of them, dizzy and joyful, onto the sand. Emma burst out laughing, and one by one so did the others.

"It is good you are still possible to laugh," Naia said in a formal voice Gabriel had not heard before. The queen to the foreign ambassador. "We, too, have our houses to build again. But we had no—wetness?" She looked uncertainly at him.

"Flooding," he said. The water was going down but it was still an inch or so deep inside some of the cottages.

"So. Flodding. You have lost many in these winds?"

He gave Emma a nudge. "Go on. She won't bite you."

"We lost a-plenty," she told Naia somewhat grudgingly. "Ain't buried 'em all yet. Have to dig 'em out first."

"We have lost two men and a child." Amagaya and her mother laid their gifts on the ground. "In such times it is wise to be friends. I will send men to help you find your dead, if you—admit?" She looked at Gabriel again.

"Agree."

"So. If you agree." She waited for an answer.

"Ask her, Madge. What harm can it do?" Joyce Archard shifted Tomkin to her other arm and pushed the midwife forward.

"If you please, ma'am," Madge said, making Naia a nervous curtsy. The maidens giggled at the bobbing farthingale and the busk stiffened with bones. "We've a child here," Madge told them. "Newborn or nearly, and her mother has died. We have two who have nursed her, but their milk begins to fail them and we've no cows to milk. The child's too young to take any other food. I'm at my wits' end. What do your people do in such cases? Have you cows or goats or—"

Naia frowned in Gabriel's direction. "Please, what is cows? You did not teach me cows."

"They're animals that give milk. You can drink it like water. From a cup." He did an impression.

She giggled, her hand over her mouth so as not to offend them. "That is ridiculous. Milk is from women. Milk from a cup is ridiculous."

But before Gabriel or anyone else could explain, Captain English pushed his way through the onlookers. "What is this?" he demanded. "Has this man sold himself to the savages? How does he know this woman? He must be tried and punished. Converse with their women is punished by death."

"Oh, pipe down, sir!" said Madge. "He knows her language and it's plain he's taught her ours. You know he was here with the first expedition, he told us as much, after Lisbon. Why should he not know her to speak to? He's made us a friend, which is more than I can say for *you.*"

"That's right. See how her children are fond of him? What crime is that?"

With Wildye to rage at them and White to shilly-shally, no one would have dared to gainsay Captain English. But the women no longer cared for titles and queen's emissaries. Without realizing it, they had become a new thing that the old ways of home did not control.

The captain could not get his mind round it. He had no idea of the place, of learning to live by its nature. "I will not abandon the queen's commission," he said stiffly. "Nor will I forget the names of any who attempt to impede me."

He marched angrily away, the few remaining soldiers trailing after him. The women looked at one another and the listless men began to drift into small groups, talking in low voices.

"Masu!" Naia called to the boy. "Bring me the doeskin from the boat. Amagaya, carry the basket of walnuts and the dried corn." She turned to the women. "Please, where is this baby?"

They led her into one of the tiny, half-ruined cottages, where Jane Jones was rocking little Virginia Dare. The Secota women looked around disapprovingly at the strange ways of cooking and at the table, walking round and round it and kicking the legs to see if they kicked back. "Have you a grinding jar?" Naia asked Madge.

"Alis, where's the mortar and pestle got to?"

Naia poured some of the walnuts into the stone bowl and began to grind them to a sort of flour. Masu came bounding in with a lovely soft doeskin, tanned until it was almost white. "Now go and get the bread we brought with us," his mother told him, and he was off again, thrilled to be able to show these English how grown-up he was.

The walnut flour was very rich and it gave off a sweet-scented oil. "When the corn crop is bad," she told them, "we make our bread from ground nuts instead. Walnuts or hazelnuts are best, but there are others. You must gather them soon, before the squirrels get them all. Do you know how to keep fish and game for the winter?"

"How can we keep it? We've no salt. They wouldn't stop for it."

Naia looked puzzled. "What is salt, please?"

The women stared at her. "You mean you don't salt your meat and fish?"

"Meat must be smoked to keep for winter. My women will show you."

While they nibbled the bread Masu brought, Naia and her ladies ground and pounded some of the corn, then mixed the two flours together in a bowl. With a little fresh water, it made a sort of milky gruel. Naia tasted it with a fingertip and squeezed in a little honey from one of the combs they had brought. "Like this," she said, cutting and rolling the doeskin around two of her fingers until it formed a cone. She filled the cone with the sweet, milky gruel and cut a tiny bit off the tip to make a nipple. "Now this baby will eat."

The women all held their breaths. Parson Tydway closed his eyes, folded his hands, and murmured a prayer. Virginia opened her mouth to launch a wail, and Jane Jones shoved the deerskin nipple into it. "Make up your mind to it, Mouse," she whispered, "for it's this or nothing."

The surprised baby gulped and burped and began to nurse happily.

P IEMACUM AND the Eel are taken down to view the new fish weir and the Secota women demand a demonstration of the various layers of English female clothing. Kia gets lost and is discovered under Madge's farthingale. Masu and the serving boys run races, slipping and sliding in the sandy mud.

Naia leaves her women to giggle and gossip over the English

ways and walks back to her boat, where Gabriel waits for her. "Madge would eat from your hand, old heart," he says, with a huge grin. "So would the rest of them."

"Today, yes. But it won't last."

"Of course it will. Why shouldn't it?"

"This man with the tin hat. He is a fool and he hates you. You must be careful."

"He's not crazy like Lane was, just stiff-necked and stubborn. Bit thick."

"Now they all know you are friends with me. They won't trust you. They will watch us, like Tesik."

She'd given those women another hope than gold, Robbie. Taught them they could live where they were, not just waste their lives dreaming of gold like their menfolk were doing. And their eyes had brightened, I saw it. But hers were the bottom of the sea.

"What is it, my heart?" he says. Not *old heart*. The familiar term of brotherly affection has undergone metamorphosis. He has stepped over the parallel line.

She pretends not to have noticed. "A runner came to our village from Croatoan this morning. A ship has broken up to the south, off Hatorask. It was Spanish."

He is suddenly as alert as a fox listening for mice in the leaves. "Is the runner still here? Can I talk with him?"

"He went on to the north, to warn the other tribes. There are more Spanish ships out beyond. They were seen before the storm, working their way up the coast. When the weather turned, they disappeared."

"Probably tried to make port at one of their islands. They have forts there, and Spanish towns. Don't worry. Their ships are clumsy, they're apt to go down in a gale."

Thought of Lizzie's husband and the other Irishman who'd jumped ship at Dominica. The stolen maps. Spanish knew more or less where we were. Only had to come and get us. The rest didn't know, didn't have all the pieces. No use to tell Naia, she had enough troubles. Up to me, really, whatever came at us. Lucky as usual. Me.

"Will the Spanish attack us?" Naia's voice is furred with worry. "If it's riches they want, I'll give them whatever I have. I don't care about all this." She stares down at the pearls and the copper. "The tribes war against me because I have these foolish things." She jerks one of the strands and pearls rain down everywhere. "They are what your man with the tin hat wants, too, I could see in his face." She breaks another string. "And now come the Spanish."

"Listen. Please." He snatches her hands and keeps them. "I know you don't want to be English. I know I can't be Secota. Look a damn fool with my head shaved and no breeches on. But there it is. I love you. Proper love. Absolutely proper, inconvenient, mysterious love, the kind even your uncle would approve of. I won't let you get lost. I won't let the sprouts get lost. If you've got a dog or a pet squirrel, I won't let him get lost, either."

She looks up at him, suddenly smiling. Sunshine on water. "Kia has a pet frog," she says, and they hold one another and laugh.

twenty-eight

Overheard in the Villages: Gold, *or* Why It All Fell Apart

Dyonis Harvie

I HAVE A DAUGHTER NOW, BORN IN AMERICA. GLORIANA. WHAT SKIN she's got—soft as satin. Little bubble on her lips when she laughs. It's for her I want the gold. And for my wife, my poor Margery. To make it up to her.

I haven't been much of a husband, God forgive me. Oh, not unfaithful. Well, not often. But mostly I wanted things. Needed them, really. I mean, they were *there*, weren't they, the things? And everyone else had them. If you want to make the right kind of friends, you have to have what the friends have. A set of silver toothpicks. A velvet nightcap. Absolutely necessary to dress in the fashion.

Long and short of it was, I had to borrow some money. And then I had to borrow money to pay the interest on the money I borrowed, and so it went. Bailiffs took Margery's dowry, all the furniture and silver plate. She signed the conveyances without complaining. Knows her duty.

It's a bit better now. Horse came in at the Smithfield races. I managed to borrow enough on the strength of it for a share in the

Venture. I've learned my lesson. No more risky investments. If I can get us a share of the gold that savage queen drapes herself in, we'll go back to London and buy the finest house on the Strand and I'll have something to leave to my son—when we have one. And, of course, a nice dowry for little Gloriana. Buy her the richest husband in London, once she's grown.

Tesik

Things are coming to a head now. It's not just the English who must be erased. Oh no. Airwalker will have to be removed. And Naia, of course. I do not act out of greed or ambition. History demands it. With even the rumor of gold—and with me ruling things—the Secota will be a greater force than any *woman* could make them.

Murder is merely a personal thing, and I have surmounted personality. Killing Naia and the old priest is a political necessity. They're obstructive, they still live in a vanished world. By the time they finally wake up, it'll be too late and all of Europe will be at our throats.

Right now, we still have the advantage. The English are weak and corrupt and outnumbered, so we have to strike now, and strike hard. Wipe them out. Naia thinks she can love them because some of them pretend to be decent. That's her greatest treason, you see. Her capacity for loving the individual and ignoring the historical imperative. The ridiculous doctrine that one human being is as good as another—that's why she must die.

Thomas Harris, Schoolmaster

Gold is more than greed. It is magic, perhaps the last magic. Alchemists summon it from stone, from scarabs, from bats' wings and the blood of black cats. It is an acid that eats away the will to

216 + Margaret Lawrence

create and to make instead of to acquire and command and conquer.

Gold is the greatest weapon of mass destruction ever discovered.

I've made a life's work of studying the ancient histories. The Golden Fleece. The Golden Apples of the Hesperides. The Golden Calf.

Every civilization built upon riches has died stillborn, ebbed away, or fallen of its own weight. Once the inner eye glimpses wealth, the individual life is no longer of interest. The personal on every level becomes insignificant. Wives are abandoned, children discarded. Expendability rules.

Gold erases the past, you see. It erases the mercy of God.

twenty-nine

Into the Wilderness, *or* With What an Ill Grace They Went Looking for Gold

*I*T IS THEIR LAST HOPE, THAT DISTANT GLEAM OF METAL, AND CAPTAIN English misses no chance to encourage them. Parson Tydway's gentle sermons about laying up treasure in heaven fall upon deaf ears.

Even the autumn weather seems made of gold, and in the first week of a blue-and-russet October, Captain English at last makes his move. Gabriel and Georgie are helping the womenfolk build a stone-lined pit for smoking meat and fish according to Naia's instructions, when the soldiers begin going house to house.

"Put that down, you thieving skut!"

It is Emma's voice. Gabriel drops the last of the stones and sets off running, with Georgie a few feet ahead of him. They reach the door of Parson Tydway's house just as Gruffyn Jones comes out with an open barrel of meal in his arms, and Will Baird spills dried pease from a gaping canvas bag.

"Captain's orders," mumbles Gruffyn, and runs off to join the others, who are loading the stolen food onto a handcart.

Inside the house, Janet Mannering is sobbing over the lynx kitten Zebedee, who lies dead in a small pool of his own blood, and

Parson Tydway slumps on the floor with Madge dabbing at a cut on his forehead.

"Oh, Gabriel, my dear feller!" the old man cries. "You must help us! Captain English has persuaded our foolish menfolk to go looking for gold!"

"Kept at 'em for weeks, he has." Emma has a bruise on her cheek from Baird's huge hand. "Gold and their duty and God save the bloody old queen."

"He has pressed those who won't be persuaded," says the parson. "They are taking supplies from every house, leaving their families next to nothing."

"They had no need to kill Zebedee." Georgie is fighting back tears. "He was only little."

"This cannot be God's will. It is some madness." Parson Tydway looks up at Gabriel. "I know you, dear boy. Finally remembered that day at Paul's Cross, what you did there. Beg you help us now. Make the others see reason. Too much of a duffer to do it myself. Broken vessel."

Gabriel's face is grim, the chiseled bones like the veins of a leaf beneath his skin. The grey eyes close for a moment, then open again. "How many are they?"

"Perhaps forty," says Madge, and Emma nods.

Did the sums in a hurry. We'd lost seven and twenty to the hurricane. Take away forty more and it left us barely thirty men and boys. If the Spanish came or if Tesik's alliance attacked us, we didn't have a christly prayer.

H E FINDS CAPTAIN ENGLISH and the others at the old Secota landing. There are three long dugouts waiting—stolen from Naia's people—and English is giving orders right and left.

Gabriel's words rattle the cool morning air. "Brave morning's work, old chap. Broke into a house and attacked a boy, four women, a parson, and a cat."

The captain blinks. "Who is it, pray? The light blinds me."

"Oh, you know me well enough."

"Ah. North. So, you come with us hoping to restore your honor?"

"Bollocks to your bluddy honor. Is it honor to steal? These folk had little enough food and now they've nothing. Expect suet puddings to fall from the sky, do you, so the women and boys and the old men can keep alive through the winter?"

"We shall return long before winter. Long before."

"Yes, and I'm Pharaoh of Egypt. Been stealing boats, too, I see. That'll go down well with our neighbors."

"All this country is the queen's. The boats are ours for the taking. But I would hardly expect a traitor who lies with savage whores to comprehend the law."

Wanted to knock his tin hat off, and his tin head with it. Didn't, though. Had to play grown-up. My God, the restraint. Should've seen me. Proper as hell.

Gabriel speaks quietly, clearly. "You're not a soldier, you're a pirate. A tribal war brewing and the Spanish scouring the coast for us, and you can't think of anything but a hoard of imaginary gold. Working for shares, are you? Or have you sold your famous honor to pay your debts back in London? Shame, sir. Shame. Shame on you all."

"We'll go home rich men when Ralegh's ship comes for us in the spring," shouts Baird. "And no bloody thanks to *you*."

"You'll be rotting in them woods by spring, Will Baird," Emma's voice says. "Or doing slave labor for some savage king. Oh-ho, I'd like to see that, you great cow-turd, you."

"Take that slut away," orders English.

Nobody moves. Nobody obeys him, not even Serjeant Lacy.

"How many of you were press-ganged into this?" Gabriel says, scanning the men's faces.

Dick Darige the smith steps away from the rest, and Joyce Archard's husband with him. Others join them: Peter Little and his brother, Charles Florrie the plasterer. Soon there are ten or fifteen men—all brought by Captain English against their will.

"He can't force you to go anywhere," says Gabriel. "Go on home to your wives."

"But, Gabe, he's the queen's representative."

"Well, it's an odd thing, Dick. I hear a lot of talk of her, but she doesn't seem to be here, actually. And it's too far to swim." The men are still afraid to resist. "Go on, then. It's all right. Go on home."

One by one Darige and the others turn and run. "Serjeant! Arms at the ready! Shoot those deserters!" cries English.

The soldiers are lined up, the petronels primed and fiddled with. It seems to take a long time. "Sorry, sir," says Lacy, his eyes dancing. "They're out of range now."

"This is all *your* doing." English draws his sword and faces Gabriel. "Incitement. Sedition. Treason. I have every right to execute you here and now."

"Go ahead," comes Emma's clear voice. "But you better be ready to stay out in them woods for good, for you'll get lye in your porridge if ever you come back."

Edmund English stares at her for a moment with the sword raised. What does he see? The fraudulence, the shabbiness of all his assumptions? No. He can never admit to that. His mind would fracture and die.

"This naughty trull wastes precious time." He twirls the sword around, then kisses the hilt and holds it aloft. It is unsteady, and he all but drops it. "In the name of God and Queen Elizabeth," he says, and climbs into one of the boats.

Gabriel and Emma stand watching as the oarsmen row across

the sound and turn north, to the mouth of the river that will take them deep inland.

"Won't see 'em again, will we? All them English fools."

"Not all of them."

"Not most of 'em. What's to happen to us here, Gander?"

He turns her to face him. "You weren't meant to hear that bit about the Spanish."

"Fig for 'em. How near are they?"

"Hatorask."

"Judas."

"No landing parties, nothing like that. They just dropped anchor off the Banks for a bit, and then away they went."

"They'll come back, though."

"Not right away. Not till spring, maybe. That'll give us time to get ready. So we mustn't frighten the others. Tell 'em when the time comes."

"Tell 'em when I damn please, won't I?" She is quiet for a long time before the next question comes. "They won't ever send a ship for us from home, will they?"

He slips an arm round her. "You're too clever by half, you. No, I don't think so."

"But why send us here at all? What are they gaining if we die?"

Mice in the attic when the house burned down, that's what we were. Not singled out for it. Nobody forced us aboard ship. Only circumstance, that's what I told myself. The blood mice of history. But I knew it was more.

Emma looks up at him and smiles. "Nobody ever said I was clever before. Let's both of us stay alive just to spite 'em, and a figgo for 'em all."

thirty

THE LONG LOVE THAT IN MY THOUGHT
DOTH HARBOR

HERE WERE NO MORE STORMS. WHILE THE SLOW, MELLOW, RAIN-less autumn moved towards winter and the great flocks of swans left for the south, Tesik circled the marshes behind Naia's village, rowed the sounds at night, and haunted the coverts of the Outer Banks. Twister, Sharp-Tooth, Black Fox, Thunder-Fist, and a few others of the Turtle clan drifted along with him uncertainly, beginning to wonder—like the little mice *they* were—in what huge trap they had been caught.

It was the first quarter of the Flying Goose Moon, the time Naneunt, the famous Occanichi trader, always came on the Great Path. But he had not come. The runners said he was still in the Powhatan country and seemed in no hurry to come south.

His reluctance frightened Naia. Naneunt always heard everything and he never travelled in dangerous country. Rumors came and went through the Secota towns, and the Croatoans—their friends since the rescue in the cornfield—sent several more messages about Spanish ships scouting the coast.

There was no word of the gold-seekers. On both sides of the in-ward sound, the nervousness mounted until you could almost taste it in the air. It made Naia need Gabriel's talking and joking and singing, the way he delighted in life even in the worst situations. They were free to see one another as they pleased now, and she rowed the little reed boat into the inward sound every morning at dawn to meet him. Sometimes she brought the children to play bears with him or learn to spin the wooden top he had made them.

But one day was different. She brought no one with her, only a willow basket with food and a gourd cup for drinking. "Come," she said. "I have something to show you. Get into the boat."

He laughed. "God, you're bossy. Worse than Emma. I'll row. Where are we going?"

"You will not row. This is my boat. I will row."

THEY GO TO the sand island. The storm has changed things, and she cannot take him by exactly the same path she took Masu and Kia. There are shallow marshy spots where they have not been before and the flooding has washed sand into low hills just beginning to sprout dune grass.

The pond is still there, and the clearing. It has taken her weeks to rebuild the little hut and make it a refuge again.

"There is dried fish in the clay jars," she says, pulling back the leaves and interwoven branches that disguise her storage pit. The cured clay and the skins in which she wrapped them have kept most of the jars from damage in the tidal flood, and she has taken out every morsel of food and dried it carefully again. "Here is smoked venison. Dried pumpkin and beans in the baskets, and walnuts and hazelnuts and dried cherries. I brought them only last week."

He says nothing at first, studying the hut and the pond. But it pleases him, she can see the subtle change of light in his eyes. "Can you get to the sea from here?" he says.

"Not by boat. Come."

She leads him through a maze of newly formed dunes until the gleam of the sea washes over them. "The White Wolves have changed it, it is harder to see from the beach than before. That is good."

If Tesik or his spies have discovered this place, they have given no sign and left nothing disturbed. She leads Gabriel back to the pond and begins to spread out the food she has brought. Kneeling there, she takes his hand, her big dark eyes boring into him.

"Remember the way here," she tells him. "If they kill me, bring my children and hide them here. Promise."

"Of course. You know I will."

"Promise in words."

"Right. I promise. I love your sprouts, you know that. Kia wraps me round that little finger of hers. And I'm quite fond of Ena, even though he's not actually visible. But it's all bollocks. You're not getting killed."

"You can't know. My uncle got killed. Got? Is this proper?"

"That's right. Got is all right." He lets her go and begins to pace the outside of the hut. Suddenly too nervous to settle. "It's a good place, this. Hard to find, but not when you know the trick. We could make it a bit bigger, actually."

"There's no time for bigger." She has been waiting to tell him, dreading how he will take it. "Two Spanish ships came up from the south to Croatoan yesterday. The old woman who is their queen sent a runner to me. She thought they would be attacked this time, but one ship tried to cross through the breach and was almost overturned. They sailed away south again. But they'll come back."

Somehow he seems to have known it already. He slips in and out of her mind with ease now, and she welcomes it. "It's late in the autumn," he says, trying to reassure both of them. "They won't risk the cold."

"You do not know this. You always say what you cannot know as if you had some secret virtue."

"I have. I love you. Sleep with me." He returns to her and takes her hand. Something desperate in his voice, in his touch. The last chance. "I don't cheat on a promise unless absolutely necessary. I swear a bit, but I don't snore. Come into your little henhouse and sleep with me. Now."

"In the daytime? This is not proper. It makes no sense."

"Makes perfect sense to me. The Spanish are coming, the tribes are getting ready to make war. Come in this damn poky little house and lie down and be with me."

Already had the plan, you see. Knew what I'd have to do when the time came. Knew how her boat would come into it. Knew the price. Selfish bastard, me, but I wanted to leave myself with her. I'd waited so long for it. All my life, really. Wanted her to have the best of me to save. In case there was nothing else.

IT IS PARTLY the smallness of the place, as if it has grown itself round them. A place out of time, out of space, beyond reach of contention. It is because there is only the bed and the cooking jars, and the ladle with the head of a duck. It is the smell of herbs and the dry sycamore leaves she has spread on the floor. They have a sweet fragrance, like the sap they drain from trees in the springtime. She came yesterday and made the place ready. Made it perfect. She knew it was time.

He has to crawl in on his hands and knees. Bumps his head on the door frame. Scrapes his back. "Bluddy christly henhouse," he mutters.

"See? I told you it was not proper. Now you are hurt."

"Skinned myself, that's all. Nothing to signify."

She does not seem to know what to do with him at first. Sits down on the bed and he sits beside her. He takes off the strand of pearls she wears and discovers underneath a tiny pale tracery where the sun does not reach her skin through the nacre. His fingertip touches the precious faded shape of each pearl on her breast, very slowly, as though he is memorizing them one at a time. When he has finished, he sits becalmed looking at the glow of her skin in the filtered light through the reed matting. Breathes in the scent of her, sweet with hazelnut oil and beeswax and wild honey.

"If Airstalker is living and I am not," she says, "please don't let them hurt him. Bring him here with my children. He is almost my father."

"I'm very fond of Airstalker."

"Fool. You don't even know him."

"At the moment I'm very fond of almost everything."

Kissed her then. "Is it the same as you're used to? Is it how Ena did it?" *Felt her palms slip inside my shirt. Such small hands. Stroking me. Laughing when she began to undress me. Silly clothes these English wear, all hooks and laces. Laid her back on the bed, on the furs and robes she had put there. Kissed her everywhere. Ever so slowly.* "Tell me if I do something wrong. Help me. Tell me if I'm not good enough. I want to be perfect."

"Be still, please," she says. "Oh, stop talking. Be still."

No deceptions. No invisible ink. No secret codes. They already know everything. All around him, the other women of his life are watching him. All his preparations for this moment. Even his failures are smiling. Shaking their heads at him. A few of them crying a little. Setting him free.

Later, as she lies asleep in his arms with his spent sex still warm and foolish inside her, he imagines the soft breathing of the two children across the tiny space of the house. Imagines the wheeze of her old almost-father. Imagines a dog and a pet squirrel. And a frog.

thirty-one

HE TODAY THAT SHEDS
HIS BLOOD WITH ME

HEN THE FIRST ATTACK COMES, OCTOBER IS ENDING. THE nights grow cold and the incalculable flocks of geese begin to depart from the marshes and meadows, their wild chatter filling the air and skein after skein of them blackening the sky. It is a holy moment in the Secota year. For the English, it is Crispin's Day, 1587. Crispin Crispianus.

To wish the wild geese godspeed on their journey, Naia's people hold a festival. The men have worked for days to collect enough oysters, crabs, mussels, and clams for a feast, and for this one day they risk leaving the palisade of the village. The women build cooking fires on the shore of the sound facing Roanoke, steaming the shellfish in huge earthen pots. The remaining English are invited, and several of the larger boats are sent for them.

The celebration begins at daylight, when the first geese rise from the marsh. The Secota carry old Airstalker to the shore on a litter of skins to offer prayers, and the men dance to the flute and the drum, and the women sing the birds on their way. The English women sing for them, too, a song about wrens in a hedge, and Dick Darige tries to dance and makes the Secota maidens laugh.

The children play by the shore of the sound, splashing each other with cold water and shouting, playing leapfrog and tag, as flight after flight of geese rises up chattering. Kia has been sitting at the edge of the marsh playing with her frog, but when Naia looks for her, she is gone.

She grasps Amagaya by the arm. "Where's my daughter? Have you seen her? I asked you to keep an eye on her."

The young woman stares. "Why, she was just over there—"

Then Naia is running, running, running. "Kiaaaaaaa!" she shouts. "Masumeoooooooo!" She races through the cluster of women and the rowdy boys to where she has last seen Masu. But he, too, is gone.

She says nothing to the others. Gabriel is sitting with Airstalker and Parson Tydway, being instructed in the duties of married men, and he does not notice her at first. Silently, her heartbeat heavy as a drum in her ears, she runs back through the woods to the village. There is a guard at the palisade entrance. "Have you seen my children?" she demands.

"Not a sign of them. Is something the matter? Are the English causing trouble?"

"No. Not the English."

She runs among the little reed-matted houses, calling softly. "Kia, darling, where are you? Masumeo, my son, don't frighten me so. Come out and let Nama see you." She goes into the Great House and into the temple where God's statue watches as always, emotionless like all watchers, with the light burning before him. There is no sign of anyone.

Out again, past the guard and into the forest. Along the path to the sound, she meets Gabriel running towards her. His eyes are wide, dark with worry. Amagaya has told him. "You haven't found them?" he says.

"They're gone, they're just gone."

"Christ. Would they go into the forest alone?"

"Masu would, but Kia wouldn't and he wouldn't take her, he thinks he's too big to be saddled with a baby."

"The marsh, then?"

"I don't know! If I knew, would I be looking?"

They break out of the forest and onto the shore, away from the festivalgoers. "What's that smoke?" he says. "It's not from the cooking fires."

"The boats! They're burning our boats!"

"Stay here. I have to go and warn the others."

"No. *I* must warn them. It's proper."

There is already heavy fighting by the time they reach the shore. The attack is three-pronged, with the Pamlico hidden in the marsh, the Weapeme coming in from the sound in their boats, and Tesik and his men swooping down from the forest.

The worst of it is the screaming, the wild cries of the attackers that tangle the air but do not rise like the chattering geese. The war cries strike the mind like the blows of a hammer, and they come on and on.

The Pamlico braves are gathering captured young women and children, tying them together in a long line to march north. The older women are considered worthless and are lined up to be killed, two braves walking down the line and smashing their skulls with war clubs.

Amagaya screams and tears at herself when her mother is killed. Madge would have been next in line but in that moment, her captors distracted, she grabs Agnes Wood by the hand and dives with her into the murky waters of the marsh.

"Can you see the children?" Gabriel shouts.

"Nowhere," Naia cries.

But he can no longer hear her. The attackers on the shore come on and on in huge waves, hurricane waves, screaming their war cries. Gabriel spins like a kite in the wind, eyes burning from the smoke, looking for Naia. They are using fire-arrows now. Across the sound, the English village is burning, sending up a tower of smoke. Behind them, the Secota village, too, is on fire.

He sees Naia pick up somebody's knife and disappear, just as two Pamlico come at him swinging their war clubs. He dodges, rolls, drags himself through small fires and over the bodies of dead men, both English and Secota. Heads split apart, faces of men he knows. He buries himself in the turmoil, crawling on all fours, now and then playing dead. Suddenly he hears Emma's voice, very near him: "Nasty skut, I'll cut 'em off for you!"

In an instant, he is up and running. Picks up a war club that lies beside a dead Secota and begins to swing it right and left, whirling it in the air. Fire-arrows arch over his head, dropping sparks that make a dozen small burns on his arms and his neck.

Emma, Joyce, Rose, Eliza, all together, are being bound neck and wrist with braided leather ropes for the journey to their new masters' villages. Gabriel catches a glimpse of something gleaming and sees copper-haired Georgie Howe with a knife in one hand and Jane Pierce in the other.

Saw Naia stick a fishing spear into somebody. Lost track of how many I killed. Picked up somebody's knife. Strands of blond hair on it. They'd hacked off Emma's long hair for a trophy. I cut her bonds and Naia and Georgie got her away, and the rest with her. Couldn't help them all. Couldn't help Airstalker. Sat there stone dead on his dais, poor old lad. Not a mark on him, eyes wide open. Parson, too, as though they'd simply gone off together. Looking for God.

THE WILLIS BROTHERS from the Isle of Wight lie dead, the same spear stuck through both of them. Dick Berry and his father.

Hugh Taylor, the chandler. John Bridger, William Sole, and Bob Wilkenson, all press-ganged on the same market day in Plymouth. Surgeon Ellis, trained in anatomy and driven out of Portsmouth for knowing too much.

There are eight English women left, two of the three babies and little Tomkin Archard, and some dozen or so of the men and boys. Naia takes them deep into the reed beds and leaves them there with what weapons they can find, while Gabriel tries to find a boat that will get them away.

"They've burnt ours," he tells Naia. "But they won't burn their own. We can steal one of the war canoes."

"Too many guards," she says, and begins to run.

He knows at once where she is going. The reed boat makes no noise and needs only one oarsman, not six like the war canoes.

"Where will we take them?"

"The sand island, for now. In the morning, these enemies will gather their dead to be mourned. Once they are gone we can take the women down to Croatoan. It will need many crossings, but it will do. Take them to the small house. Our house. I will come when I can."

"Hell you will. I'm not leaving you, and that's final. Georgie and Emma can ferry them."

She does not argue. If it had been reversed, she would not have left him.

They run as they may, weaving among the dead, until at last they reach the woods above the village where the small stream leads out into the marsh and then to the sound—the place she keeps the reed boat. They go in silence or else whisper to each other, still unsure Tesik's men are not waiting.

Suddenly Gabriel clutches at Naia's arm. "Hear that?" It is a sort of high whimpering, broken now and then by a sob and a torrent of weeping.

"Kia," her mother whispers. Then she speaks aloud. "Kia! Where are you, darling? Masu, my son?"

There is a breaking of branches and the child's weeping rises to a scream of fear. From a thicket of yaupon, Tesik steps onto the path ahead of them. He knows where the reed boat is, of course he does. He has known all along she will come for it.

He carries Kia under one arm and Masu under the other. The baby is crying but the boy's face is set and tearless. Too grown-up to cry.

Tesik shouts something at Naia, but the words are beyond Gabriel, he has had no instruction in Secota curses. "Give me my children," she says. A calm voice. A strange distance around her. The steadiness in her voice quiets the little girl and her screams pause with a painful hiccup.

Tesik spits on the Queen of America. "You think I want a whore's brats?"

He tosses little Kia away as though she were a clay jar. She crashes down onto the hard-beaten path and this time she does not wail. What does it take to smash a child's skull or break its back?

I looked at the mad bastard's face and saw what I used to see in old Walsingham's. Sometimes even in the queen's, at the worst times. Nothing left inside. Nothing worth losing. Reason I never look in mirrors, me.

Kia suddenly wakes and begins to sob again, and Gabriel draws a long breath of relief. But Tesik cannot bear her endless wailing, his nerves are like knives. She has to be silenced, because he wants silence. That is all he knows. He throws Masumeo into the bushes and raises his war club over the little girl.

"Run, Kia! Run away!" Naia screams.

But there is no time for running, no time for anything. Gabriel dives for the child, his body crashing down on top of her, between her soft dark hair and the heavy war club with the face of a ghost carved on it.

Last thing I saw, actually. That spirit face. Two round eye sockets and a hollow mouth, sucking at the living. The weight of it crashed into me and I felt myself crack open someplace. Pain like a horse kicking you. I heard Masu yelling and I heard Naia scream, and then the bastard hit me again. Think my heart stopped for a minute then. Don't think I was breathing. Death comes and goes, did you know that? For years, sometimes. "Not yet, you fool. Not yet. No rest for you yet." Brain didn't stop, though. Never stopped thinking. Just my luck.

Felt a strange sort of burning, like all the nerves in my body were catching on fire. Little one was somewhere underneath me, wailing and squirming. I couldn't move. Couldn't see what was happening. Lying flat on my face. Naia screaming. How I wanted a last glimpse of her.

Men's voices, then, shouting Tesik's name. Feet, running in moccasins. More Secota cursing. They are fighting, Tesik and Black Fox. Tesik and Twister. Then, as if from a huge distance, an odd sound reaches Gabriel, a sound he knows all too well. It is flesh being struck, flesh resisting something cruel—a knife, a spear, a sword.

Tesik gives a little gasp of surprise and Gabriel feels a body crash down beside him on the path, feels the wetness of blood. Smells it. Smells the bear grease on Tesik's hair.

Naia screams as he has never heard her before. She shrieks his name, keens it. And Masu's name. Kia's. Even her dead uncle's, and Ena's, calling their spirits.

Tesik's men—now Tesik's murderers—ignore her. "Did you see that?" says Black Fox. "The dirty bastard would have killed me! Me!"

Sharp-Tooth: "And me! His mother was my mother's cousin!"

"I told you a month ago he was crazy."

"What about the woman? What'll we do with her?"

"We could sell her. She'd bring a lot."

"She's too dangerous. She's Sea clan and that's still a power on this coast. Just take the pearls. Take the copper. It must be some-place in the village."

"And the man?"

"Is he alive? Doesn't look like it."

"He's still breathing. Shall I finish him?"

"To hell with him. Put them all in the boat. With any luck, the swamp witches will get them. Or they'll drown."

I T HAD HAPPENED more than once in his time there. Unbidden changes of heart in the universe. Streaks of light, of luck, that suddenly cut open the ruin and kept you alive.

He swore an oath or two of his own when they lifted him into the reed boat, wild curses so loud that even Kia stopped crying. He caught no more than a glimpse of Tesik's body on the ground, a furious husk with a trade-goods knife in its back and blood everywhere.

There were no swamp witches, just the mourning screams of the few Secota left alive. The light little boat almost sank with the four of them, but Naia balanced the children and it finally floated. He couldn't lie down, only slump, trying to hang on to the boat's frame. He felt water seeping in around him. Felt Masu's warmth against his bleeding back, and Kia's damp sobs. Heard Naia's slight groans as she dragged at the oar.

Then he slipped away for a long while, into some other life. Into no life at all.

He woke in the hut on the sand island. Our own country, she called it. Our house. He knew he needed a surgeon, but he knew Ellis was dead, he'd seen it happen. Came to terms with the probabilities. If he managed to live, he would be only part of a man. One usable arm. God knows what else ruined. Might never sire a dynasty of pork butchers. But whatever was left, he would have to make it serve.

Days went by, he had no idea how many. At the edge of the little pond, Dick Darige and Henry Payne and the other Englishmen who had survived began to make a clumsy dugout canoe to take them down to Croatoan. He thought it risky, too easily spotted. But he could do nothing. He was barely able to speak. When he was conscious, his mind was brilliant, endowed with a preternatural clarity. He could have saved the world. Then the pain would overwhelm him again.

In the hut, the women came and went, crawling on all fours through the low doorway—short-haired Emma and quiet Alis, Joyce and Aggie and Rose and Eliza, and Jane Pierce with the cross of God cut onto her lower lip. Madge never left him except to search out plants and mix what medicines she could. Georgie helped her to lift him and turn him and bind up the shoulder in an effort to make it heal, but he knew from the feel of it that it was beyond repair. He could hear the bits of bone grating.

"See that stuff draining out of it?" Henry Payne had been helping to lift him. "Kill him, that will. Ought to cut off his arm, let the poison out."

Naia shoved him away. "Go outside. Never touch him anymore."

"Only telling you, woman. Pus like that means it's gone putrid. See how swollen that arm is? You don't cut it off, it'll poison his blood and he'll die."

Her eyes smouldered with holocausts. "Poison blood is ridiculous! Go outside or I will cut off your head!"

They dosed him with poultices, packed him in Spanish moss and spiderwebs soaked with herbal decoctions, brewed horrible potions from whatever they could find. The shoulder kept on draining and draining, a smell so foul he had to ask for something to cover his nose just to stop himself retching. There was pain, and sleep, and fever and chills and more pain, more chills, more fever. The world was in his brain, all of it, all that had happened since that first day at Paul's Cross, wild memories thrust at him. And he talked—to Nico, to his father the pork butcher, to the Russian ambassador's maid. He even talked to Elizabeth. A spy, talking. God only knows what he said.

At last the women had just one thing left to try. They built a small fire and heated one of the broad-bladed English knives until it was glowing red at the heart and almost molten at the edges.

They tied his good arm to a post they drove into the dirt floor, and stuffed a piece of Emma's petticoat into his mouth to stop him biting his tongue off. Henry Payne and Dick Darige and Georgie held him as hard as they could, with his back to the knife.

"God, don't let my hand shake," said Madge, and she laid the searing-hot knife flat upon the place. Gabriel's body rose in a terrible hook, his chest buckled in on itself, his whole spine jerking, jerking, racked with convulsions.

At last he collapsed into a stupor of crystalline pain. They propped him up on rolled buffalo robes, on anything they could find to support him and keep his weight from the shoulder. But it was far from a cure. For days that dragged into weeks, with Madge watching over them, Naia slept beside him, ate by his side, fed him, soothed him through bad dreams, cleaned him. Answered the thousands of questions that spilled out of him when he woke and was able to speak.

"Where are your people?"

"You know, you saw. Any who lived have fled south."

"But you didn't go with them."

"They do not want me. I was a curse to them."

"Bollocks. Who was it killed Tesik anyway?"

"His friends. Thunder-Fist. Twister."

"The ones who spied on us?"

"Yes. I hate spies."

"Oh? Oh God, yes. Me, too. Can't abide 'em. You gave your last pearls for me. Hope I was worth it."

"Fool. I didn't give them. They took them. Besides, it was for my children, not you. You are not so important."

"Too bad. Had a nice ring to it. Put it on my tombstone. 'He was ransomed with pearls.'"

thirty-two

THE LOST COLONY, OR

WHAT THEY KNEW OF IT AT HOME

THE COLONY'S SHIPS HAD LEFT FOR THE ROANOKE IN SPRING AND arrived there in midsummer—that much we were told when Governor White at last returned from America in November. Fernando's ship, the *Lyon,* came back too, but nobody saw hide nor hair of the Portugee. There had been, Ralegh told the queen, "mishaps." The colony needed supplies and reinforcements, and requisitions and contracts and bills-of-sale for oatmeal and salt beef and barley began to circulate around Whitehall.

I knew nothing then, of course, about the real state of things on the Roanoke—the hurricane, the tribal wars, the search for the Indian gold mines, the Crispin's Day battle. By December of 1587, I was half-mad for news.

"I want leave to go and see John White," I told Rowland. "He's in Ireland now."

His narrow mouth tightened. Burghley had refused him a diplomatic appointment and he was still chafing under it. "Sorry," he said sharply. "You're needed here."

"If they're sending relief ships to the colony, I want to go with them."

"My lovely boy, there's a war on. We need every ship to meet the Spanish when they come."

I wanted to smash his pink face in. "Without supplies, they'll all starve on that island. It's common decency. Duty."

He giggled. I shouldn't have used such outdated words.

"Come now, Mowbray," he said. "They're farmers, and so on, yes? Well, then, let them grow themselves something to eat."

I had one last card to play. "I'll have a word with Simon Fernando instead. Where's he living?"

Rowland looked up at me and he wasn't smiling. "Word to the wise, dear boy. Not clever to ask questions in wartime. Next thing you know old Topcliffe's polishing up his thumbscrews and oiling his rack."

But I was not tossed into the Tower or tortured. I was punished as only a spy can punish another spy. Posing as a French merchant, I was sent twice to Spanish-occupied Holland to estimate the strength of the invasion forces. It was the most dangerous job I'd ever been sent on, and to tackle it twice in half a year meant the Spanish officials might remember me and arrest me. I wasn't caught, but it was a near thing, and when I came back I was shaking with more than just the chill I'd caught in the cold wet Dutch summer.

"Where to next, sir?" said Peachum. "Oooh, I hope it ain't the Lowlands again. You're still pale as a pudding."

"Don't fret, auntie. They've stuck me into a room at Whitehall, with a million dispatches to sort through."

"Think they'll really come, Master Robin? This Armada and so on? Got my doubts, I must say. Them Spanish is always full of big talk."

But Peach was wrong. Less than a month later, they came.

The first Spanish ships were spotted off the Lizard at the tip of Cornwall and chased eastward by our fleet. If Philip's army made land, we didn't have a prayer. Bonfires went up, ringing England from Land's End to the Scots border. In London, where I remained at my work of decoding, the church bells rang night and day, till I thought I'd go mad from the clang of them. Lightning struck the Tower of London out of a clear blue sky. By night, comets blazed and stars fell. The wind itself seemed to carry panic.

It was on the third day of our great danger, with that same hot wind rattling the windows of Whitehall, that I found Topcliffe's letter, in a pile of papers meant for the queen. It was not in code. It was a love letter.

Dearest and Most Glorious Majesty, he wrote. *Divine Goddess, as I am parched by the heat of love for Your beauteous Person, so my resolution stiffens and rises of itself and passion claims me to give You sound service. With every scream of the Portugee as he lay upon My Lady Rack, I heard instead Your cries of pleasure in the bed of Your true lover, Your excellent small breasts freckled with a sweat like pearls. . . .*

I tasted bile in my mouth. I could read no more. All I could think of was Nick, how he had screamed in my arms. The letter crumpled in my hand, I stepped into the passage and leaned my face against the cool wood of the panelling.

Was "the Portugee" Simon Fernando? I didn't give a damn, not just then. I had read Topcliffe's reports before, but I had never happened upon one of his letters, and somehow, on that day, with the queen at Tilbury vowing to meet the Spanish army like a soldier among soldiers, it overwhelmed me that Topcliffe should make her his equal in perversion. Elizabeth might flirt with her handsome favorites, but her bedsheets and undergarments had been examined every night and morning from the time she began to bleed until she ceased, in order to be sure she had not been, as old Burghley said, "falsely occupied" by any man, and was still marriage-bait for the princes of Europe. Now that she had passed fifty unmarried, cruel jokes about her made the rounds of the court, started by the spoiled young Maids of Honor. The queen had hair around her nipples. The queen pissed her sheets at night. The queen fancied young girls.

Little wonder if rage sometimes overcame her and she slapped and scratched and cursed. That secret, clear-eyed, unknowable woman—how many such vile letters had she read and forced herself to ignore, and from how many such necessary bastards? Did she bite down on a bit of leather to silence the screams? Or was she like a rare pearl kept too long in a box and the box long since empty, the pearl fallen to dust?

Gabriel knew. His eyes had seen, that first day in Fleet Street. But I could not ask him now.

T HE WIND CHANGED directions that same night and proved to be our salvation from the Armada. The lumbering Spanish ships couldn't tack into it, and so could not turn and attack our smaller, more nimble craft coming at them from behind. With the English ships after them, they became great silent floating coffins in which fever raged and water turned to poison. In a hundred villages all along our coasts, broken, starving, feverish men and boys were washed ashore. In London, the bells went wild again, ringing victory. There were fireworks over the Thames every night for a week and the queen rode through the streets in a white-and-gold chariot covered with flowers.

Because of the trips to Holland, I hadn't seen Annette for almost two months, but on the last night of the victory celebrations, I made my way to Crutched Friars and knocked at her door.

"She's gone off to Florence or Venice or one of them places," the sour-faced servant told me.

"Did your master go with her?"

"No, he sent her in the post-rider's bag. Of course he went with her, you silly get."

"But they won't stay much longer, now the Armada's broken?"

"Oh," she said with a sly laugh. "I reckon it'll be some months yet."

N OR DID THE queen's great victory have much effect upon matters at Whitehall.

"Surely," I said to Harry, "surely now that the Armada's defeated, Her Majesty will let Ralegh send a supply ship to the Roanoke."

"We're still at war," he replied, sipping at a pewter mug of bitter ale. "Philip will almost certainly rearm and come at us again."

"After losing a hundred and twenty ships and thirty thousand men?"

"Oh," he said, "figures are always inexact. And men are expendable. Philip can always get more."

All the next year, reports of Spanish recruitment found their way to my desk. Twice Ralegh fitted up convoys for Virginia, but they were snatched back by the Council or attacked by French privateers. Once or twice Spanish ships actually entered the Channel, and at last—despairing of any rescue for his Roanoke colony—Sir Walter sold his interest to pay some of his astronomical bills.

The colonists were written off and forgotten, but not by everyone. In December of 1589, a small group of family members came to Cecil's office at Whitehall. Tom Colman's brother Robert was among them. Dick Darige's brother-in-law. Margery Harvie's uncle. Roger Prat's son.

Cecil's clerk closed the connecting door, but there was a crack in the old panelling. I put my eye to it.

"We beg you hear us, sir," said Robert Colman. "We've waited in the passageway every day for a fortnight."

Cecil's glance swept over them. "If you cannot be patient, you had better go home."

Colman's anger almost had the best of him. "It's been near three years since our kinsfolk have seen *their* homes."

"They were set down and abandoned," said young Master Prat, "and when we ask the Council's help, we're treated like bumpkins and fools."

"We're fobbed off with excuses about the Spanish war, but there's fishing boats sailing to Newfoundland again, and if *we* choose to chance it, why should Her Majesty care?" Colman brought his fist down on the writing desk. "Sir, we ask nothing more, but we must have the Council's permission to go and search for our families as soon in the spring as may be."

Cecil tapped his quill on the inkwell, wiped the point, and motioned the clerk to sharpen it. When he spoke, his voice was a practiced monotone. "These people determined that their future lay in the Roanoke rather than in the defense of their own country," he said. "They were told of the dangers, but they chose to put their faith in Master Ralegh's promises rather than pay wartime taxes at home. No, sirs. Your friends must lie upon the bed they have made."

The families had exhausted every possibility and could only go on waiting. As for me, I read the reports of John White over and over, but they were obviously contrived to shift any blame from his shoulders. I looked and looked for Simon Fernando, but he was nowhere to be found. If he had been the "Portugee" in Topcliffe's letter—well, men sometimes died on the rack, but I could hardly cross-question Her Majesty, could I?

Besides, she was too occupied with staring into the cow eyes of the young Earl of Essex. Some called it an old woman's passion for a young blade. Some said he was her illegitimate son—perhaps the brother of the madman from Plymouth who announced that his name was Emmanuel and he had been begotten by the Holy Ghost upon the Maiden Queen.

The court would go to the palace at Richmond for Christmas, but I paced London like a brooding ghost with no place to haunt. Annette had not returned and had sent me no message. There was no word of Gabriel, either, of course. After weeks of watching, I had had a brief glimpse of Nico sitting in his father's doorway, wrapped in shawls. I heard he was crippled beyond repair. I heard he was mad from the pain. I heard he was robbed of all memory, that he had forgotten how to read, write, speak, feed himself. I did not go there again. I just wandered, and even Peachum left me to it.

One night, out on my Christmas hauntings, I passed the torch-lit façade of Lord Burghley's modest London house. The queen's coach waited outside, its golden curtains drawn, the Guards standing to attention in the starlit cold.

Then the street doors were flung wide and I heard Elizabeth's voice: "No, old friend, you mustn't come out. That chest of yours is delicate. I shall send you a cordial."

I could hear Burghley's farewells and in a moment the queen came striding out, trailing servants with cushions, servants with silver foot-warmers of hot coal, servants with fur muffs, servants with lanterns. At last she was settled in her coach, and Burghley's footman pulled the curtains more tightly shut against the biting wind.

Once he was gone, Elizabeth drew them open again. In the yard, beside the stableman's fire, a ragamuffin musician was playing the flageolet for pennies, while a girl in a rough blanket cloak sang carols.

The Earl of Essex swaggered out of the bishop's house with another bevy of torch-bearers, and I saw Elizabeth's face clearly. On her forehead dangled a crescent moon set with diamonds.

"Oh the moon shines bright," sang the street girl, "and the stars give a light . . ."

Slowly I realized that the queen was singing with her—a high, clear soprano, cleansing to the ear and all but unconscious of itself. A perfect voice for a simple woman. A lovely and innocent voice. But not the voice of a queen.

"In a little time it will be day," she sang sweetly, "and the Lord our God will call upon us all . . ."

I saw her hand reach up and unfasten the sparkling jewel, the new moon. For a moment it lay there in her hand, a pool of broken light she had caught but could not hold.

Essex, more than half cut on the bishop's wine, lurched up to the coach window. "Shall I g-give the order to d-depart, ma'am?" he stammered.

The queen did not reply. The stars were very bright, the December sky over the dark streets awash with them. But the moon was in its last quarter, not its first.

Essex's feet would not obey him and he folded like a paper fancy. The carol ended. Elizabeth's fingers closed hard upon the diamond crescent and she pulled the coach curtains shut.

Months went by, and there was no more word of Roanoke in the Spanish dispatches.

Then, in early spring of 1590, the reports from Madrid and Lisbon began to be full of wild stories. The English, they said, were reinforcing the Roanoke settlement with eight hundred soldiers. There was a fortified base in Virginia, a great city with a good harbor and many noble mansions, and a shipyard bigger than Portsmouth. A hundred and fifty ships would be launched from it the following year to attack the treasure fleet in the Florida Straits.

It was enough to make a cat laugh, but it made somebody nervous. In late March, I received a letter from Harry with the seal of the Council dangling from it. *A rescue ship will depart from Ply-mouth for the Roanoke in a fortnight. Present yourself at Whitehall for your orders. We want you to go back.*

W E SET SAIL in April and arrived in early August, dropping anchor off Croatoan on the Outer Banks. John White was there, of course, velvet doublet, plumed hat, and all. "Fire a salute," he told the captain. "That will bring folk to the shore."

The small ship's cannon was loaded with grapeshot and fired out over the ebbing tide. I stood watching from the stern, but there was no sign of curious savages, nor of anything else. No smoke from the Croatoan firepits. No scent of venison and wild cherries and boiled crabs. No dogs barking or children laughing.

It was as if we had sailed into a great vacuous tunnel. The tide still rose and fell. Yet everything was changed utterly, somewhere deep in its essence. It was no longer a place that welcomed the human.

White mopped his face with a lace-bordered handkerchief. "Perhaps our friends think us Spanish. Sing some of our fine English songs!"

Standing at the rail like a bunch of helpless idiots, we sang "Tomorrow the Fox Shall Come to Town" and "Fathom the Bowl." There were no shouts of joy ashore. The woods remained silent.

"This is foolish stuff," said Tom Colman's brother. "We must lower a shore boat and go to find them."

"No, no," said White. There was something near to panic in his voice. "It's growing dark and the woods are full of dangers. I won't hear of it."

"Won't hear of it? What have we come for if we never set foot on the land?"

I scanned the place in the gathering twilight, trying to

remember what it had looked like five years earlier when Gabriel and I first arrived. Croatoan was a sandbar, of course, and the sea changed it constantly. But the dunes were drifted up much higher than before, and a new breach had been cut by the sea. The barrier island I remembered was sliced nearly in half.

It meant dangerous weather had struck the coast, very likely a hurricane. I had heard of these terrible tempests from the sailors who hung about the London taverns; they spoke of being maddened by the great roar of the winds and having the skin almost flayed off them by salt water battering their bodies for days on end.

By the look of the sky, we might soon find out for ourselves about hurricanes. The sea began to grow so rough that we were forced to sail farther out to avoid being run around. Thunder rumbled and lightning danced on our rigging. Most of us were sick from the wild pitching and rolling of the ship, and heavy rain fell for two days, then three.

When the sun finally came out, the weather was breathless, muggy, and threatening. To the southwest, over the Florida Straits, huge banks of cloud billowed and surged.

"We shall not go ashore here," White announced. "Our people were never set down in this place."

"But the Croatoans were our allies," I said. "Surely they'd have some word of what's happened."

"How, sir? Nothing has happened."

White's notes had tried to make light of the attack in which he'd killed and wounded those Croatoans raiding Naia's cornfield, and he may have feared retaliation. But it was more. He was terrified of going home with any other report than that, after three long years, our people were miraculously safe. In somebody's interest, the truth had to be concealed.

He bustled us up the coast and soon our longboats passed into the outward sound between Roanoke and the Banks. "No sign of anything," said Tom Colman's brother, shipping his oar.

"Look there!" shouted Master Prat. "That's smoke, that is!"

White stood up and all but capsized us. "Excellent!" he cried. "That smoke is rising from the exact spot where our village was built. Why, even now our good English huswives are making their children's morning porridge. My daughter's daughter will be three years old by now, and no doubt but Elinor has given her dear husband one or two male heirs by this time. Oh, excellent!"

Something in him actually believed it, but his faith was short-lived. We beached our boats at the creek mouth where we'd once had a landing stage, and by the time we'd climbed the sandy path to higher, level ground, it was plain that the smoke didn't come from a chimney. There were no chimneys standing. Aside from a few broken bricks and an iron pothook or doorlatch, there was nothing left of the English village. The fire was in the brush at some distance, probably started by lightning.

The men stared around at the ugly little ruined footings where the cottages and the barracks had been. "Gone," whispered Bailey. "Even the chimney bricks. Gone."

"Don't look like they was set afire, though." Colman kicked at the grapevines that had overgrown the floors again. "Spanish would've burnt the place."

Ashes and blood wash away. Three whole years had passed and it would not have taken three days for the place to be attacked, or demolished by wind or flood.

"It is plain," White announced, trying to sound as though he meant it, "that our good thrifty folk have taken apart their cottages and moved them into the mainland near the Chesapeake, where the soil is very rich for farming. We sent a boat there on the first venture. Master Mowbray can tell you. It is rich, sweet country, with a fine harbor. Indeed, that is where they have gone. I have no doubt at all."

In England, houses and shops were often taken down and moved to new locations. Even though you owned the house, the land it stood upon was usually hired by the year, so it made perfect sense to "move house," for lumber was costly and scarce at home. It made no sense whatsoever in a country all but smothered in trees. And all the heavy timbers and planks and chimney bricks of what appeared to be fifteen cottages—taken all that distance in what? White had left them with only a rickety rowboat.

Widgets. Gabriel's silly word echoed and pounded in my head, and his voice would not leave me. *Seven human widgets and a bag of barleycorn, total price three shillings and ninepence. Replacements requested.*

A hundred and seventeen human widgets. Gone.

"Where's the soldiers from the fort, then?" asked Colman. "You said there was a captain and near fifty fighting men. The settlers might go inland, but there should be soldiers still here."

"Look!" Bailey pointed to the crotch of a big oak that stood near the remains of the palisade. "CRO? What the deuce does that mean?"

I hadn't climbed a tree since I was a boy, but I scrambled up and pulled away the wild grapevines that almost hid the letters. Whoever had scratched them into the wood had barely made a dent in it. A weak arm, perhaps, or someone unsteady at such a height. Or a sick man. A damaged man.

"*Croatoan!*" cried John White joyfully. "The letters mean *Croatoan!* If our folk left here, I told them to carve their destination onto a tree, and so they have done. If they were under threat, I bid them carve a cross of a particular shape, and there is no cross of any sort carved there. I promise you, they have gone safe to Croatoan."

"You can't have it both ways, man," snapped Colman. "First you say they're on the Chesapeake and now you say they're back at Croatoan."

Prat was fit to explode. "Safe, Master White? At that same place where you feared to go ashore yourself?"

"There's another!" cried Bailey.

Part of the palisade was still standing. On one of the posts, the same unsteady hand had carved the whole word: CROATOAN.

A shape drifted through my mind. Gabriel? No. One of Lane's soldiers, the one called Ned. And others, other men from that first bleak year. I remembered voices. Scars. Somebody's branded thumb. Faces growing thinner and thinner as the food ran out. There were few idle hours, but on Sundays after the three-hour sermon, there were games in the woods. Knucklebones. Dice. And sometimes we climbed trees and cut our names in them, or the names of sweethearts, mothers, friends left behind. Places we came from. Places we longed to be . . .

"That palisade is new-made," White was babbling. "They have not been long away from here. And again there is no cross cut into the wood to tell us of danger. They are safe. There is no cause to seek further."

John White wouldn't have known new wood from his old paint stick. But he was frightened, like all of us—of the dry leaves the wind tumbled with a sound like hoarse laughter through the invisible rooms, of the vines that tangled our feet, of the Spanish moss that sighed as it drifted in the branches above us. *Lizzie. Agnes. Elinor. Joan. Madge. Eliza. Janet. George. Dyonis. Peter. William.*

Once again White had found the excuse he needed to turn tail for home. He went bustling off to look for the trunks of personal goods he had buried before his abandonment of the colony three years ago. But he was right about one thing. The sky grew more and more threatening and the wind raised whitecaps out in the sound. If we meant to get back to the ship before the storm hit us, we dared not linger.

I walked away into the woods, my mind still simmering with memory, with images. *Fool*, said Gabriel's voice in my head. *You need lessons, you do. You watch everything but you don't see anything, not even yourself.*

I heard the sound of a bird's wings and looked up. On the trunk of a gum tree the remains of another word was carved— *Emma*. On the bole of a swamp oak—*Alis*. The names were everywhere—bark peeling from the cuts, moss slowly erasing them, scribed in the air itself. But I saw them. *Henry. Nicholas. Hugh. Audrey. Winifred. Joyce.*

"Master Mowbray, sir," said Colman's voice at my elbow.

Bailey, too, had trailed after me. "What do you make of all this? Ought we to go back to Croatoan and make a proper search?"

They stared at me, looking up into the branches. They saw nothing, but those men didn't need to see. They knew.

There are many stories about battlefields, about the sound of a hundred marching feet being heard in the night along Offa's Dyke and Hadrian's Wall. About the cries of the slain echoing at Marathon, at Hastings, at Crécy, at Agincourt. I heard no voices that day at Roanoke. But in London and in the old cottages and churches of rural England, you meet spirits everywhere, and I had grown up with the dead on my shoulder. We all had. Whether we spoke the words or not, we couldn't deny them. The English settlers were lost.

While the other men readied the longboats, I climbed onto a high dune that faced west, overlooking the inward sound and the dense woods that reached, for all I knew, to Cathay and the Indies. It wasn't just the English who were missing. There was no sign of Naia's village, either. No little boys with half-shaven heads. No sign of Gabriel.

Piddlejacks. Users-up. Fuckers-over. Christ, I hate 'em.

I thought of Ralegh. Of Walsingham. Of Fernando. Of Top-cliffe.

"May their children breach and die," I whispered.

That night aboard ship I wrote my resignation to Lord Burghley. It was my last night's work as a spy.

thirty-three

The Third Beginning

A COLD NIGHT IN THE SPRING OF 1593. FOG WRAPS THE CORNISH coast. Three more years have gone by since all hope for the Roanoke was abandoned. We are still at war with Spain.

The fog drifts on the tide, feathering out where it meets the narrow beach of a rocky cove. The sound of an oar in the water, a longboat feeling its way ashore—a smugglers' boat. With only a flickering horn lantern to light them, the crew begin to unload crates, barrels, and canvas bags of contraband.

They pay no attention to the three passengers who make their way cautiously up the cliff path from the cove. Three slight shapes, eager for the darkness. Man, woman, child.

Suddenly the horn lantern is quenched. "Excise!" one of the smugglers says in a hoarse whisper, and the men dive for cover.

Only the slap and creak of the boat against the sand then. The stink of rotting fish and tallow smoke in the wet English dark. At last the rattle of horses' hooves on the coast road just above them. Torchlight like a flail, lashing the darkness.

"Queen's Coast Guard," the man says urgently. "Down, my loves. Hide your faces."

"God save us," murmurs the young woman.

They hunch among the jagged, chalky rocks, waiting, the little girl's fingernails digging tiny perforations into the palm of the man's motionless hand. The torch swings round one last time, and then the hoofbeats move on, beyond hearing. Looking for Catholics. Looking for Spanish spies.

"Right," he says, and they scramble up again. The rocks clatter down in small landslides underfoot. He has almost forgotten the hard, solid noises of England. Rocks. Slates. Horses' hooves. Walking sticks. Shoes.

He's forgotten the damp, aching cold of an English spring, too. They reach the top of the cliff looking down to the wood and stand shivering in an east wind, the little girl tearless and silent, wrapped in her mother's shawl. Down below, the smugglers' shoremen have brought donkey carts to be loaded with kegs of French brandy and barrels of contraband Seville oranges and Spanish olives.

"Where are we?" the woman says.

"Penross Cove." He takes her hand and holds it to his face, letting his warm breath find her. "There's a village beyond. You need a decent fire."

"No, no. We mustn't, for your sake. You know what might happen."

He picks up the child in one arm and they disappear again, into the night and the fog.

EARLY NEXT MORNING, an old gamekeeper called Davy Shand, out tallying his master's deer as he has for thirty years, stands on the brow of a small hill at the edge of the New Wood, sniffing the wind. Wood smoke, and close by, too. Smugglers and gypsies, most likely, come up from the cove for a bit of poaching. Let 'em get a taste of it now and he'll be plagued with them all the summer.

Davy shifts his long, awkward gun into the crook of his right arm and begins to run, a shuffling old man's dogtrot that moves him steadily through the drenched spring green of the wood, his cork-soled felt boots splashing in and out of a narrow little stream. Daffodils in pale drifts here and there. Light falling through barely fledged treetops.

The sharp-sweet smell of the wood smoke is stronger, and now it carries with it the dangerous fragrance of rabbit stew. Some magistrates'll take the skin off your back for poaching a rabbit, or send you to prison for two or three years.

Just beyond a new-leafed clump of alders, he catches sight of the rogues. A fair-faced young woman in a plain cap and a decent stuff gown stands hunched over a cooking pot, stirring it with a peeled stick. The little girl is more gypsylike—small and dark-eyed, with creamy brown skin and soft, wavy dark hair beneath her cap. Foreign blood. Spanish bastards all over the west country these days, since the Armada foundered. But there's a proud sharpness to the Spanish blood, and a dormant anger, and Davy can see none of that in the child.

"Wash your hands in the brook, my love," the woman calls to her. "Then go tell him it's ready."

Two more rabbits lie on the ground, waiting to be skinned. Snared before dawn and their necks neatly wrung, good as Davy himself could've done it. The fear-cry of a caught rabbit is terrible and you want to still it as quick as you can.

"Come on, come on, come on," coaxes the man's voice from the trees. A bit of northern in the accent. "Coom on, coom on."

The little girl runs to him across the clearing and he steps suddenly out of the woods—a tall, scruffy fellow, shadow-thin and sandy-haired, darker-bearded and just beginning to grey. Broad crooked shoulders, one crumpled forward. He has a small bunch of daffs in his hand, and a broken twig of whitebriar. His voice comes out hoarse for the first few words, as though he has to pull it out of him.

"How's my lovely girl, then? Want a flower? Want a ride?"

The child smiles shyly and nods, and he bends down sidewise and swings her onto his good shoulder. The other arm hangs limp at his side.

"Dinner, eh? Oh, hungry as a bear, actually. Rrrroooowwww-rrrrrr!" She squirms away, giggling, to hide in the bracken, and he goes down on his knees, then rears up like an angry beast. "What's this I spy? Who's this tasty young morsel? Rrrrroooowwwwrrrrr!"

"Wicked old bear!" cries the laughing child, popping up from the bracken and then hiding again. "Get away!"

"Rrrrrrrroooooooowwwwwwrrrrrrrr!" He tries to go down on all fours, forgets his bad shoulder, and puts his weight on the useless arm. The bear's roar is suddenly a huge scream of pain in which all else—fear, caution, pride, salvation—is forgotten. Then, in an instant, he smothers it, cuts it off short by sheer force of will.

The ferocity of that instant of enforced silence sends a shiver through the old man. He thinks again of the strangled rabbits.

The woman runs to kneel by her companion. "You always forget yourself when you play with her," she says, slipping her fingers inside his shirt. A stain of watery blood has begun to soak his sleeve.

"Bollocks." He lifts her hand away and struggles to sit up. "Brought you some bluddy flowers. Dropped 'em somewhere." He looks about for the child, who is hiding by an elder bush, silent tears streaming down her face. "Now, now. Come here, young Morsel."

He makes a silly weepy face, and she can't help laughing. She creeps near and he takes her small hand and sticks her fingers in his mouth. "Ggrrrrrrrrrooooowwwwwwrrrrrrrr! Delicious morsel. Let's have another!"

She pulls back her hand with the fingers bent under, as though he has gobbled them up. It's a familiar game and it drowns the last of her fears. "Go and look for the flowers, Leatha my lamb," says the woman. "He's dropped them."

"Nay, give's a kiss first. Coom on."

Leatha spares him a peck on the cheek, then runs off to look for the scattered daffodils. It is time for the old keeper to make his move.

"Afternoon, friends," he says mildly, wading across the stream to them. The woman's whole body jerks with fear when he speaks. "Name's Shand. Keeper of these here woods. See you got some of master's rabbits. Fine fat ones, too."

The man with the ruined shoulder maneuvers himself into position and struggles to his feet, running a hand through his shaggy hair. He glances at the old man's gun. At the canny little eyes in their veil of fine wrinkles.

"What's your name, then?" Davy asks him.

"Me? Ben. Benjamin Tregelles." Tregelles is an old respected name in Cornwall, but the family died out in King Henry's time. Has he read it on a tombstone? "This lady's Alison. Alis. Widow. Knew her husband, so I'm just—seeing her safe home. And her daughter."

A nice quiet smile and mannerly ways, for all his clothes look to be stolen from half the wash lines this side of Truro. But Davy Shand pushes his probe one inch deeper.

" 'Fraid I must take you to the village," he says. "See you locked up proper till Sir Edward can hear your charge. Justice of the Peace. They'm his rabbits, see."

The poacher's grey eyes retreat. The straight, full lips part a little. The back stiffens, making the crooked shoulder thrust raggedly forward. There is a tiny click when he moves, bone grinding on bone.

"I won't be locked up, old heart," he says simply. "Couldn't stick it. Rather be shot, if you'll favor me."

He looks at Alis standing by the fire and at the little girl still collecting the scattered daffodils. Gathers into him the pale green of the newly leafed trees, the sound of the brook running over stones, the chatter of a squirrel in an oak tree.

"No harm must come to them afterwards," he says to the old man. His voice is still quiet and polite, but urgent now. Utterly serious, if not commanding. "No questions. No constables. *You* must see to them."

Davy's small blue eyes blink. To be trusted so suddenly with these unknown lives? Surely the man isn't serious.

"I'll just go a bit into the woods, then," says the stranger calmly, "and you follow me. In the back, as though I was running away, do you see? No blame to you. My choice entirely. Only try not to miss."

He simply turns and walks, soft-footed, into the woods. The woman watches, wide-eyed and scarcely breathing. A woodpecker rattles its beak on a beech tree and the old man's body sways slightly, as though the world has slipped a bit underfoot.

"Nay," he suddenly calls out. "Shrew all that! What kind of a Christian do you take me for, anyways?" Gingerly, he lays the clumsy gun on the ground and bends over to sniff at the steaming pot, looking up at them with a toothless grin. "Wood's teeming with bloody ol' rabbits, blast 'em, and I'm damned if I'll waste a good stew. Smells a treat, don't it?"

✦

T HERE WAS SOMETHING about the way Alis had looked at the man who called himself Ben Tregelles, about how deep she had trusted him and how the little girl had laughed. Something about those few words: *You must see to them.*

So Davy made them an offer. Alis could keep his house and Ben could have work for a bit, helping out with the deer tally. He took them back to his snug little stone cottage at the edge of the wood, and the two men had a pint of home brew after supper. Be glad to stop roaming for a bit, Ben said. Good for the Morsel. Suit us down to the ground. Thanks, old heart.

Davy never asked him how they came to be on the tramp. Never asked what Ben feared so, enough to die sooner than be locked away. Reckoned to leave those questions to the morning. But by morning, "Ben Tregelles" had gone, without so much as a farewell to his friends.

N EXT DAY a wheelwright from the village, come out to mend the broken wheel of a farmer's cart, caught sight of a man's foot not quite hidden by bracken at the edge of a barley-field.

The foxes and field mice had been at him some—a stubby fellow with a coarse, brutal face. Something in him that even in death would not stop conniving, battering, snatching.

No one admitted to knowing him. It was in no way un-usual to find a traveller murdered, for the roads teemed with gangs of robbers and thieves, and men with no work and no bread. But those who never shuddered at the sight of the dead dreamed bad dreams once they'd seen the man's body. In two days they had buried him, stripped of clothes, shoes, and the rings whose marks could still be seen on his swollen fingers.

"Killed like a rabbit, he were," Davy told the stern-featured fellow from London who came round to the cottage asking questions a fortnight later. "Had his nasty old neck broke, just as neat as you please."

thirty-four

THE DARK WORK

ASIDE FROM A FEW DIRTY JOKES AT THE PLAYHOUSES ABOUT THE
hot lust of savage women and a tribe of blue-eyed children running naked through the woods of Virginia, I had heard nothing of the Roanoke for three years. Nothing of Gabriel or Naia or the lost settlers.

It all sprang to life again on the day I found a message from Harry pushed under my door at Dame Phoebe's: *Come to Whitehall on Friday. We need to talk about Roanoke.*

"Will you go, sir?" Peachum asked me.

I crumpled the note and pitched it into the fire. "Bugger 'em. I'm out of the spy business. Let them come to me."

Bold talk, but I *would* have to meet with Toady and Ratsbane. Retired spies were carefully watched and seldom trusted. I knew too much of the Roanoke affair, and if I couldn't satisfy them, it was only a short wherry ride from Whitehall to the Tower. I compromised and met them in a grubby Southwark tavern instead, where my actor friends were just a shout away.

"I've told you," I said to Harry for the tenth time. "The Roanoke colony's been lost for a good six years now. You never gave a fig for them before. At this late date, what's the bother?"

"*They're* the bother, blast them." He tossed a paper onto the table in front of me. "The bloody shareholders. They want an accounting."

There was an official seal. You could buy fake official seals for a shilling at the Thieves' Market at Moorfields and pick your own official. But I recognized the list of signatures scrawled on the paper—one or two members of the Queen's Council, an earl's stepson, a baron's cousin, several rich merchants. I tossed it back to Harry. "All right, they're Ralegh's investors. And?"

Rowland giggled. "The great fool pissed away two hundred thousand pound of their money without a penny's return. Now everybody's in debt to the eyebrows and they're demanding a royal enquiry. The Virginia Commission. Heard of it?"

I hadn't, but I nodded. "They want to know why the colony failed to make them rich, and whose fault it was." Harry looked at me, eyes narrowed. "I've heard the word *treason* mentioned."

"You can help us clear this business up, Rob," said Rowland.

He meant pin it on somebody. I tried to sound unconcerned.

"Naturally I've heard of the—uh—Virginia Commission. But if they think they'll find a hundred and seventeen English settlers waiting ashore with their knitting—"

Harry glared up at the greasy rafters. Poor Harry, cursed with blockheaded inferiors. "Blast the settlers, man! We need numbers. Pounds and pence. Facts."

In the playhouse next door, the clowns were performing their opening jig, tripping over their pointed shoes and doing pratfalls. Sparse laughter spattered outward, and I felt it like gravel on my skin, every nerve screaming. I knew how men like Rowland and Harry thought. If they feared you might talk out of turn, they trumped up a charge and cut your tongue out. If you knew how to write, they would cut off your hands.

"In your report on the first voyage, you spoke of a ship, Rob. Can you describe it a bit better?"

"It wasn't a ship, it was—"

"Nobody else mentions a vessel of any kind. Not even your blessed Gabriel North. Why is that?"

"How should I know?"

"You know his mind if anybody does. You were his proctor. You sent him back there a second time. Made a special request of Lord Burghley. Why did you do that?"

"I didn't. He sent himself. He wanted—"

"Did you split the profits between you?"

"Profits?"

The tip of Rowland's tongue licked the rim of his mouth. "Gold, dear boy. Lovely American gold. What the investors were promised. Somebody's got it. Gabriel claimed to have found nothing, but he knew where it was all along, didn't he? Got it out of the savage woman and told you—his controller. His friend. Were you actually lovers? I've been dying to know."

"Go to hell."

He smiled. "Ah-ha. So it's yes, then. Is that why he's sharing the gold with you? Pillow promises?"

I couldn't help laughing at the idea of my pockets full of gold. I had a tiny annuity from my uncle, who had died the year before. But I hadn't had a real job in months, unless you counted the odd bit of spear-carrying at the playhouses. My best doublet was fraying out at the lacing-holes and my breeches were only just this side of indecency.

"Come along, Rollie," I said. "Do I look as though I'd got a secret supply of American gold? And if Gabriel knew where it is, he won't be spending it now. Whatever happened on that island, he must've got caught in it. I assume he's dead, like all the rest."

Rowland smiled a gap-toothed smile. "*Never* assume. Maybe

he *wants* to be thought dead. Maybe it's *safer* to be thought dead. Maybe he's been *paid* to be thought dead."

"Or maybe," I said, "he'd be better off if he were."

"All the more reason to find him before it's too late to get the story out of him. He could be anywhere, talking to anyone. Find him for us. Prove yourself."

Excitement flooded over me. Something must have happened. They knew something I didn't.

I motioned the potboy to bring me a clay pipe from the rack on the wall, and took my time filling it with tobacco and lighting it. I had been well trained in intelligence tactics. Dance a jig, if you have to. Bore them with dithering. Get them off balance. Then pounce.

"I don't have to prove myself to you, Rollie," I said at last. "I don't even know who you work for these days. And I don't care if Gabriel's talking to the King of the fucking Fairies. Never assume, you said, but you're both assuming he's alive. Now, why is that, I wonder?"

A fine rain had begun to wet the filthy cobbles outside, raising little drifts of malevolent vapor and sending the stray dogs and meat-pie sellers scuttling. Harry got up and threaded his way to the door to look out. Trying to decide how much to tell me, calculating whether I had enough money for bribes.

He stood there for a long moment, then came gingerly back to the table, feet crunching the pig bones and oyster shells on the floor. "We do need to question Gabriel," he said, putting a gloved hand on my shoulder. Ah, kindly Harry, pure as the driven snow. Trustworthy Harry, who understands about friendship. "We need him rather urgently, Robin. And if anyone can find him, you can." A smile. "Might even earn him a sovereign or two."

"Question him on whose behalf?"

Walsingham, Leicester, and Christopher Hatton were all dead now. Burghley was said to be a bit dotty—though I didn't believe it. Robert Cecil was as devious as his father, highly educated, and sharp as a needle, but Cecil had never, to my knowledge, had an investment in Roanoke. There was that epic young idiot, Essex. And Ralegh, of course—but he had impregnated one Maid of Honor too many, had the effrontery to wed her without the queen's permission, done a stint in the Tower, and was currently banished to the rural delights of his estate down in Dorset. Besides, Ralegh was no good as a spymaster. He talked too damned much and he meant every word.

"We want you to trace over all the Roanoke tracks," Harry was saying. "Take us back through the whole business. Chief players. Words and deeds. Mustn't leave anything out of your reports to us. Are we agreed, then? You'll oblige? At Her Majesty's pleasure?"

He was making *that* up, I was almost sure of it. Elizabeth's personal service might contain bastards, but they were clever ones, not middling civil servants. At the moment, though, I couldn't refuse. If the thing was real and official and I said no, I'd be instantly suspect and probably arrested before the week was out.

"All right," I told them. "It's pointless. But I'll do it."

"Good. Excellent." Harry was purring now. "And of course you'll appear before the Virginia Commission and answer any questions the noble gentlemen put to you."

My guts writhed and I prayed God he was bluffing. A hearing they could turn into a trial in the blink of an eye? *My* trial? Or a session on the rack, like Nico? In the meantime, my lodgings would be searched. Annette had finally returned from Italy, and her house in Crutched Friars would be searched, too. In a week, two weeks, they would know every time I had cuckolded her decent husband, every time I had failed her in bed. They would know everything I had done in the twenty years since I was recruited at Cambridge. The enemies, the betrayals, the lost friends, the drink, the debts. The play about Roanoke I was trying and failing to write.

My face was cold and my mouth was dry. Beneath my tatty doublet, sweat soaked my shirt. Getting old, I thought, you're getting too damn old for all this. I knocked out the pipe and re-filled it with stringy tobacco. The pungent stuff now grew in half the gardens of London—Ralegh's only success in America. "How soon will the Commission meet?" I asked Rowland.

"September. October. You have to find North before then."

"*If* he's living. I'll need money."

Harry slid a small calfskin bag across the table, the coins inside chinking warmly. Gold pieces. I knew the sound. Somebody was frightened enough to pay very well.

I pushed a bit harder. "And I'll require access to the relevant papers. The old reports from Burghley's people. Walsingham's. Leicester's. Ralegh's account books, of course. And the Spanish dispatches. Who's the Lord Advocate?"

They were silent. No lawyer for the Crown at a royal enquiry? I should've walked straight out the door, but how could I? They knew something I didn't.

Rowland peered at me over his cup of sherry sack. "Why did Gabriel North insist on going back to the Roanoke?"

My friend's lost voice was whispering in my ear again. *I can't live in England anymore. I have to go back.*

"The point is this," Harry said. "What does North know about the Roanoke business? And if you find him alive, will it be in Her Majesty's interest to leave him that way?"

Her Majesty's interest, indeed. I decided to push them a bit. "Gabriel was never entrusted with important state secrets. How has that changed? Have you heard something?"

Again they didn't reply. Rowland took back the reins.

"What kind of tonnage was this ship you reported? Two masts or three? Was it Spanish-built?"

So that was it. Spin a tale. Make Naia's frail little boat into a ship, and the ship into a *Spanish* ship, then blame Spain for a hundred and seventeen heroically martyred English. And Gabriel? Why, he was to be the scapegoat, the traitor. He had sailed away in that mythical *ship* with his pockets full of gold and pearls that belonged to England and the queen.

They could twist a clutch of straw into an executioner's ax. I'd seen them do it more than once. If Gabriel was dead, they could use him for whatever they had in mind. But they had to be certain. If he was alive and I helped them to find him, then guilty or not, his punishment would be quick, harsh, and public. The whole Roanoke episode would be neatly buried with whatever was left of him. And if they couldn't have him, I would do well enough.

So why didn't I just go along with it, invent some false evidence that would keep me safe? Because Rowland reeked of civet and bit his lips and his fingernails, and even his eccentricities were not real. Because Harry's eyes looked at me and saw nothing worth his notice. But mostly— Mostly because there's a threshold to the tolerance for mediocrity raised just high enough to piss on the rest of us, and that afternoon I had finally crossed it.

"Naia's *boat* wasn't Spanish," I said quietly. "Write it down, Rollie. Not ship. Boat. It wasn't a pilchard boat or a Thames wherry or a tiltboat from Deptford. It was a little woven contraption of willow withes and red cedar roots, covered with deerskin and caulked with pine tar. A love gift from a dying husband. Remember love?"

Harry frowned. "Just a native craft, then?" he said. "Couldn't manage a sail?"

"Not even a kerchief."

"But you lot brought some horses ashore on the first expedition, didn't you? If North got the map out of his Indian whore, he might've ridden inland. Gone looking for their mines."

"There were no horses left, Harry. We ate them."

Grow up, I wanted to say to them. *Stop making invisible ink out of onion juice. Stop playing christly games and grow the fuck up.*

Wну do you punish yourself?" Annette said softly. She took off her bedgown and climbed up to sit naked on the edge of the bed again. "Come and lie down, *ami*. The covers are still warm, and I want you."

"I'll only disappoint you again."

It was the morning after the night that had followed my meeting with Rowland and Harry. I had told her nothing of my summons, nothing of Gabriel or the Roanoke enquiry. So far as she knew, I was still just a writer of bad plays who'd been to Virginia.

"I don't mind the failures, you know," she said, and padded over to the window seat. I had ended the night there, hunched naked, dry-eyed and sickened and ashamed of myself. I had failed her three times, battling that tyrannical few inches of male presumption. "It wouldn't be half so sweet and gentle if it were easy for you," she said, kissing my rumpled hair. "But I can live perfectly well without it. Most women can."

She began to rub my shoulders with the heels of her hands. That morning she had even cooked for me, panperdy and bacon, and brought it to the bare little room under the eaves where Gerard's pigeons strutted about on the roof outside. It had become our room, the one room in the house that had nothing to do with her marriage. She never again took me to the other bedchamber—Gerard's treasure vault, with the Venetian silk bed curtains and the silver and damask and velvet.

She sat beside me, nibbling a snippet of the spicy, eggy toast. "Why don't you go back?" she said.

I thought she meant go back to Dame Phoebe's. "I'll go as soon as I'm washed. You may not see me for some time. After last night, you won't mind that, I'm sure."

Her fingertips stroked my shoulder, then slipped down to my hip. Her hand felt cold, though sun streamed through the mullions. "I didn't mean go home to your lodgings. I meant go back *there*. You were dreaming of it again last night. Whispering 'Roanoke, Roanoke.' As though it were a woman." She laughed and her fingers travelled over my thigh. "Is it so beautiful there?"

"Yes. Yes, it is." I turned to her suddenly and pulled her against me. "Come there with me. Leave Gerard and come to me. Stay with me."

Her fingers stopped moving. I could no longer hear her breathing. Her breast felt cold against mine. "Do you mean it?"

I had thought so. But now my mind raced backwards. If I snatched her away and ran, we would always be running. I would become Harry's scapegoat, and she would pay for it. No home. No future. I couldn't give her anything but myself, and what was I worth? She didn't even know who I was.

"Do you mean it, Robbie?" she said again.

I could have told her the truth then. It would have changed everything. But I didn't reply.

She moved apart from me and put on her bedgown again. Cream-colored silk with her fine hand-knotted lace at the sleeves, the sort of thing I could never have bought for her. She glanced into the polished steel of her looking glass and laughed softly, as though she knew what I was thinking. Then she set about changing the sheets.

"Oh, look," she said, peering out at the pigeons. "See that big one with the green-and-rose breast? It's Sultan, surely. Someone at the farm must have let him go free."

She pulled open the casement and teased the bird with a bit of panperdy. It came waddling in and began to peck at her plate, but she picked it up. "Ah, someone's sent us a message." She unfastened the tiny contraption attached to the pigeon's leg and shook it over the polished tabletop.

A glitter of gold tumbled down and lay there, shining. I knew it in an instant. It was the gold earring shaped like the new moon with which the queen had long ago rewarded Gabriel. *Safe as pigeons' eggs*, he had said of it, and I didn't understand him. He must've hidden it at the farm, in the loose stones of the dovecote, and now he had come back for it. Nobody else could've sent it, nobody could've known. My blood roared in my ears. Gabriel was living. He had come home. He was there now, at Staple Oaks.

Annette picked up the delicate crescent moon and laid it on her smooth palm. "Dear Robbie, how lovely. What a sweet way to send me a present. And a long trip you had to the farm and back."

I didn't deny it. She fastened the earring in her dark hair, kissed me deeply, and led me back to her bed.

thirty-five

THE SPY AND HIS TUTOR

"C OMPANY LAST NIGHT, SIR," SAID PEACHUM.
I stood in my chilly, low-ceilinged little room later that morning, trying to see the imprint of the search. "How many were there, Peach?"

"Only the one. Silent as a footpad he was, too." The cobbler hesitated. "It was your Moorish friend, sir. The poor chap that was racked."

"Jesus Christ," I whispered. "Nico, after all this time. Here?"

I hadn't seen him since before the last voyage to Roanoke—a ruin hunched in a doorway. But in the past few months, I had begun to hear rumors again. Nick was mad, but alive. His hair had turned snow white, but he could finally spell his name aloud. It was nonsense, tavern gossip. Needing the truth, I had gone to his father's door and got a pot of boiling water thrown at me.

Now I was almost afraid to ask for a description. "Did he walk with a stick, Peach? Did he limp? How did he seem?"

"Joints is different from toes, sir—joints'll compensate in time. He took the stairs a bit tender—runs his boots over sidewise. You'll see that now and then in a man with bad ankles or knees, or his hips out of true with his shoulders. They walk on the edges of their feet."

"I was sure he'd retired from the dark work."

"Tough as old boots, he must be." Peachum grinned. "And he ain't forgot his talents, God love 'im. Picked the Clap-Dragon's lock before you could say kiss-my-arse."

I began to dig through the battered sea chest at the end of my bed. Nick had searched it with his usual subtle competence, taking nothing away with him. I took out the few notes I had kept from my year on the Roanoke and put them into my travelling scrip, along with my other shirt and some cleanish stockings.

I had decided to risk going to Staple Oaks. If Gabriel was alive, he was bound to be somewhere nearby, and I had to find him, speak to him, shake his hand. I had felt a deep excitement all the morning, jittering my nerves and making my heart race. And now there was Nico, alive and unruined and come looking for me.

But it might all be a web, spun to catch me. I dared not go straight to the farm. I'd been followed from Crutched Friars by what we called a double-hitch—a carter pulling a barrow full of produce on one side of the street and an old woman selling gingerbread from a tray on the other. I'd have to lose them first, and there were still questions to be asked and people to talk to.

Suddenly I was deep in the game again, the old ghosts coming awake. "I'll be off in the morning, early as I can manage," I said, handing Peachum my scrip. "Put this in your squirrel's hole overnight."

"Won't cost me my head, will it?"

"Of course not. But if good Mother Netley gets wind of my leaving without notice—"

He laughed—a silent, openmouthed chuckle like a fish suffering a fit of mirth. "Old cow. She'll have herself a pleurisy. Oooh, and that niece of hers, Arabelle—if she gets wind where you are, she'll have a tale or two to tell. Ain't seen her of late, though, worse luck to 'er. Warming somebody's bed, no doubt."

I HAD NO TROUBLE finding Matthias Rands, Nick's father; he still plied his wherry from the stairs at Blackfriars. "Where to, then?" he muttered as I stepped into the shallow little craft.

"Manningford stairs."

"Cost you twopence. Way out in the country, fairish bit of rowing."

He was thinner than I remembered and past fifty now, an old man for such work. A marvellous deep voice much like Nico's used to be. When he swore at a boat on the river, you could hear him in Wales.

Finally he turned and saw me plain. "You! What the fuck do you want?"

"I need to find your son."

He stood over me with a heavy oar raised. "Get out of my boat or I'll sink you, swear to Christ I will! Stove your fucking head in!"

"I had no hand in what was done to him, Matthias. Ask him, he'll tell you. To this day, I don't know who ordered it, or why."

"It was your doorstep they left him on! It was you got him mixed up with spies in the first place!"

"For God's sake, man, keep your voice down."

"He *crawled* for going on two years. Did you know that? Damn near tore him to pieces. Christ. A son of mine, crawling like a bug."

That was the worst of it. Not Nico's brush with death nor his pain nor the damage he still had to live with. It was the shame of having a son so brutally humiliated. The oar lifted an inch higher and the vein in his throat jerked visibly. That old man could have smashed my skull open with ease. Yet I liked his stubborn pride. In him, it was a ferocious sort of love.

"Why not row upriver a bit?" I suggested in as neutral a voice as I could manage. "You can always brain me later."

"Ah, you're not worth the trouble to squash." He sat down then, and seated the oars, and the wherry began to move. "Bloody pisspuddle fools!" he boomed as a river taxi full of country folk came within six inches of ramming us. The wherry shot forward, squeezed between a Dutch flyboat and a pinnace, and suddenly we had the Thames almost to ourselves.

Manningford was out in the country a mile or two, a ruined abbey with a huddle of market farms beyond. We were both silent for a time as the prow cut smoothly through the water, impeded by nothing but an occasional family of swans.

"What you want with my Nick?" Matthias said at last.

"Ten minutes' talk."

"He's through with all that. He's married, got a boy of his own."

I couldn't put the pictures together for a moment—a quiet domestic man and that huddle of loose bones in the gutter. "He paid me a visit last night," I said, "but I wasn't at home. Who's he working for?"

"None of your kind! He's journeyman to a glover in Fenchurch. When he gets his papers and joins the guild, it'll pay well. I tell you, he's shut off you and your nasty business. If he came to see you, it was likely to cut your throat."

"Tell him to be at Constable's bookstall in St. Paul's Yard. Four o'clock. I need to see him."

"*Tell?* He don't take orders from you!"

"All right, then. Ask him." We reached Manningford stairs and I paid him the two pennies and climbed out. "Don't forget. Paul's Yard, the bookstall. Four o'clock."

He pushed the wherry back into the current. "I'm telling him nothing! Rotten bastard. Should've sunk you when I had the chance."

B EYOND THE WATER meadows lay the broken ruin of Manning-ford Abbey, and to its right a narrow lane veered sharply south between high, tangled hedges. After a mile or so, you passed a sort of orchard, then a ruinous fruit house and a clutter of other household buildings.

The house itself was half-timbered, the thatch old and in bad repair. Two peacocks pranced contemptuously about the door-yard, and an old ginger tomcat stood his ground as they ran at him. From inside a wattle pen came the dithering of a great many hens.

"If yer a bailiff," said a woman's voice at my elbow, "he ain't got it, see? Ain't paid me a groat this half-year. You got to take it in chickens, that's what I do. Well, go on in, dear. He'll have done with his dinner."

Indeed, he had. The house door creaked open and a small boy all but dragged my old Cambridge tutor James Pembroke-Gibbons into the yard. "Get away, you little plague rat!" he said, slapping at the boy.

Aside from Lord Burghley himself, Gibbie was the one man who might help me understand what sort of nasty stew was brewing over the Roanoke business. He was retired from both his professions now—spying and the teaching of Greek—but he still kept his ear to the political keyhole.

Twenty years ago, before my father lost his fortune and I was recruited for Burghley's service, Pembroke-Gibbons had been one of those alabaster Englishmen—pale and lithe as a Phidian statue, with a bewitching manner and a mind polished by the fine grit of an elegant cynicism. Behind the sea-blue eyes, there was more darkness these days than ever; he seemed to see me at a distance, vaguely. Then, slowly, his mouth formed a mischievous smile, and the smile turned to one of his wicked cackles.

"I'm having my airing," he said. "Twice a day, the brat drags me outside where the wind can get at me. I stink, it's my one remaining freedom."

"They say thought is free."

"Don't you believe it." He paused to rub the ginger cat with a delicate toe. "I've been expecting you. Nico says you're scribbling theatre plays now, like that ass Marlowe. Bet they're rotten."

"So it *was* you who sent Nick to search my rooms. In whose interest do you both strive? Ralegh? Essex?"

"Jesu, I'd rather work for a Barbary ape." He turned round in a circle, looking for listeners. But there were only the peacocks. "Well, come inside, then. Have some brandywine."

The house was dank and chilly and smelled chokingly of cat piss and cabbage. I raked up the embers in the grate and added a few coals from the bucket, while Gibbons poured two beakers of brandy.

The place was medieval, the foundations sunk beneath the dark little interior chamber to which he ushered me. The floor was littered with tottering heaps of books and papers, stringless lutes, broken clocks, hobbyhorses, maps. But he moved among them, graceful and certain.

"It's to do with the Roanoke," I said. "But you know that, of course."

"Lunacy to dig up old bones." He downed his brandy and poured another. "Who's running you? Who's your proctor?"

"Rowland and Harry. But they've only told me the half of it."

"Probably sold the other half to the competition."

"But who *is* the competition? And for whom do they strive?"

Gibbie only shrugged. I had no intention of telling him about the golden charm or about Staple Oaks. I still respected his talents, but trust him? Hardly. "They keep harping on Gabriel," I said. "Has he been seen alive? Heard from in some way?"

His blue eyes sparkled with delicious temptation. He still lived for the racing pulse of the work. "If you say who's told you this, I'll deny it."

"Naturally."

"Right. Well, there've been rumors. But they begin to add up."

I should've brought him something—candied quinces, spiced almonds. He doled out his secrets like a jealous lover gives kisses, and he expected to be spoiled. But today he seemed almost eager to talk.

"A little more than a week ago," he began, "a man named Full-wood was found stripped and strangled in a barley field down in Cornwall. Windpipe smashed and neck snapped like a stick. One of Burghley's postmen picked up the story soon after, asked some questions, had the body dug up, and recognized it. My lord sent for me. I sent for Nico."

His delicate bones etched the shadows and he laughed softly. The sheer pleasure of being himself, and not old and shunted out to grass.

"Who was this Fullwood?" I asked him. "I don't remember him."

"Then your wits are rusty. When you get back to that hovel of yours, have a look at the list of investors in the second colony, the one that got lost. Oh, that's lit the candle, has it? Willie Fullwood was an extortioner. It was said he'd cut a few throats in his time, but no charges were ever brought."

"One of us, then?" Charges against spiders had a way of disappearing into the fog of Elizabeth's courts of justice. "Is that why Burghley's in this?"

"No, no. Fullwood was Walsingham's man. That old wolf used all the dregs." He gulped his brandy like cold water, then went on. "Willie turned fairly respectable as he got older. Went into the Russian fur trade and travelled a good deal. He picked up some tidbits of treason and tried to worm his way into a place at court. He wanted a knighthood, can you believe it?"

"I think I remember him now. Dressed like a lord, dripped jewels?"

"Even wore them on a ribbon round his prick, I was told. Of course the old nobility snubbed him, so naturally Wat Ralegh liked him. Same revolting taste. 'Oho, Willie,' says Sir Walter, 'how'd you like your own coat of arms? That'll make 'em sit up and take notice at the palace.'"

"And the price?"

"A little investment of ten thousand pounds in Virginia. Willie had his traps and his serving boy sent down to Portsmouth that April. Never boarded the *Lyon*. Never even left London, so far as we could discover. But he doubled his income within the year."

"Bribes?"

"Who can say? He might have sold his place to somebody's spy. Or perhaps he just heard something and was paid to keep his mouth shut."

"What was he doing down in Cornwall two weeks ago? Going back on his bargain and threatening to talk? Or demanding more money? And how does Gabriel come into it? For that matter, how do I?"

Pembroke-Gibbons sank down on some moth-eaten cushions. He had told me more than he intended and he was frightened. "Really, I don't feel well, Robin. My head aches. Go away now. Come play spy some other time."

Suddenly furious, I kicked aside piles of clutter, sending books and curiosities flying. I took him by the shoulders and shook him, hard. "All your life you've climbed over other men's bones! Mine,

Nico's, Gabriel's—God knows how many others. You've lived on our risks and fed on our damage and left us—"

"Left you what? Numb at the crotch?" Gibbie's voice was jagged as broken ice. "Carry it yourself, boy. What you are, *you* created."

"And you pushed and you prodded and you wheedled and seduced. I was sixteen when I went up to Cambridge and met you. *Sixteen!* You owe me for those days. You owe Gabriel. Now pay your debts, damn you." I let go of him and poured us another brandy. "Rumors, you said. Rumors of what?"

He poured a brandy, gulped it down. "The bloody women, you ungrateful bastard. Roanoke women."

"Yes. Go on."

"They're coming back from the dead."

The sky beyond the window flipped over and split in two. I had no breath, and sweat ran down my beard. "Which ones? How many?"

Elinor Dare. Joyce Archard. Janet Mannering. Aggie Wood. Winnie Powell.

"A woman calling herself Mary Stokes," Gibbie said, "turned up three months ago in the same part of Dorset where a certain Jane Pierce used to live. Helped with the cheesemaking in somebody's dairy for a few days, but she walked in her sleep and they began to think she was possessed by the Devil. Her lower lip had been slit."

Jane Pierce, a sturdy widow of this parish, charged this day with the crime of slander, is sentenced to have her bottom lip slit in the Sign of the Cross of Our Lord on the fifth day of September, the Year 1584, twenty-sixth of the Reign of Her Gracious Majesty Elizabeth.

A kindly constable, Jane had had, with a steady hand, according to Gabriel's notes. The cross like a tiny dark-red shadow, once it healed.

Jane Pierce. Susanna Colman. Rose Payne. Margery Harvie. Margaret Lawrence. Jane Jones.

"Who else?"

"A new cook turned up during the winter at an old estate out on the Fens. Stokesby Abbey. Young woman, fair-haired. There was a child with her, a boy of three or four. Dark-skinned, black-haired. Set the tongues clacking."

"What did she call herself?"

"Avisa Holmes. She hasn't run off, the mistress is fond of her. But Stokesby—one of the Roanoke women once had a place there for a while. Emma-something."

Emma Merrimoth. Lizzie Glane. Audrey Tappan. Elizabeth Viccars. Joan Warren. Alis Chapman.

"The last was called Alis. She had a dark-skinned child with her as well, but a girl this time. Old gamekeeper down in Cornwall swears she's his niece. Backs up everything she says—which is almost nothing. Village near Penross, little steep pile of stone cottages, a jail, and a church."

Jane. Emma. Alis. "Who else? How many others?"

"Only the three, so far as I know. Robin, take some more brandy."

"Screw brandy. You said Willie Fullwood was murdered in Cornwall."

"May he rot in peace."

"Could he have threatened this Alis? Why did they all come back under false names? They're not criminals." *Alis. Emma. Jane.* "Did anyone come with them? Besides their children, I mean?" *Half-Secota children. Half-Croatoan or -Chowanok or -Powhatan. Half-Spanish?* "Has anyone seen a dark-skinned woman, an American savage? She'd have two children, a boy and a girl. Well, she *might* have, if they're living. Has any man been seen round that village in Cornwall? Besides Fullwood, I mean?"

"Oh yes. A bearded clean-shaven tall short thin man with a fat belly and bald curly sandy black hair. He could snap an extortioner's neck with two fingers. Or else he had a useless arm and couldn't have killed one of Granny Plague Rat's chickens." He looked at me and laughed. "If you could see your face. You seriously think it's our Gabriel, don't you? Come back from the dead with a gaggle of women just to murder Uncle Willie and then disappear?"

"As for disappearing, he knows how to erase himself. You taught him well. But he was never any good at killing. He hated it."

"People change," Gibbie said softly. "Where he's been."

"No, no. He thinks too damn much, and it makes an impediment. But Walsingham's people were all taught to kill with their hands, and now he's dead they must be working for somebody else. Could Robert Pooley have done it? Or Ingraham Frizer?"

He shuddered. "That pair of vengeful whores? No strangling for them. They like knives best."

"Give me a name, then. Come on."

Gibbie's beautiful hands hung limp at his sides. "It might be anyone," he said. "Walsingham died three years ago, while you were off in Virginia with the search party."

"So deep in debt they had to bury him in the middle of the night to keep his creditors from prying open the coffin. Go on."

"He also *died* in the middle of the night. By dawn, every scrap of his records—letters, lists of his spiders, damaging information on half the population of England—had been taken from his workroom. After three years' searching and spidering, nobody even knows yet who has those papers or what may be done with them."

"Jesus. No wonder they're all shaking in their boots."

His face had taken on the coldness that meant *Bully me if you like, you won't get another word out of me.*

"Just one more question," I said, "and then I'll go. What's become of Simon Fernando? Was he racked?"

"Not by me."

"Could the queen have ordered it?"

"She hates torture, she always has."

"People change," I said softly. "Where she's been."

thirty-six

NICO

I STILL HAD MORE QUESTIONS THAN ANSWERS, BUT I LEFT GIBBIE TO luxuriate in his personal doom and fixed my mind on Nico Rands. I was at the bookstall on time that afternoon, leafing through the latest collections of merry tales, travel books, pious meditations, and anti-feminist ravings for almost an hour. But Nick didn't turn up.

At last I decided Matthias had done as he threatened and refused to pass on my message. I was weary and I wanted food and beer and time to think. My body longed for Annette and my mind longed for the elegance of her slender fingers on the keys of her virginals, for the sleek curve of her bare back in the candlelight. Adultery or not, lies or not, she occupied what was perhaps the only clean and perfect space in my mind.

But I did not dare go to Crutched Friars again. I had brought risk enough upon her already. I walked back towards my lodgings, up Ludgate Hill and then down the other side, past a gaggle of hucksters.

"Oysters, oysters, fourpence a bushel! Hot oyster-patties and smoking-hot pies!"

"Gingerbread, gilded gingerbread! Currants and citron! Gingerbread of the best!"

Oh yes, there was the gingerbread woman, still keeping me in sight. Across the street, the carter was there, too, hauling baskets of cabbages down the gradual slope of the road.

I knew I must shake them off. If Nick were anywhere about, he wouldn't risk coming near me till they were out of the way. Munching a hot oyster pie that was more grease and gravy than oyster, I dived into the crowd around an astrologer casting horoscopes for tuppence.

A ND THEN, suddenly, I am out of the orbit of time again, pinned to the present like a bug to a board.

At the turning into St. Bride's Lane, a woman with a dancing dog is performing for pennies, while her foist picks the pockets of the crowd. I push past them and make for an alley that cuts between a cookshop and a chandlery, when out of nowhere a great black horse comes galloping, hooves cutting chasms in the muck. In the dim, narrow alley, the animal is huge, monstrous. It is flecked with foam and its eyes are wild and its nostrils flare, the long bones of its skull naked and spectral. The rider is almost invisible, clinging low over the animal's neck and riding more with the pressure of knees and thighs than with bridle and bit. Is it man or woman, short or tall, old or young?

Suddenly I am running, full out, feet slapping the uneven cobbles. Fear-sweat blinds me. The alley is closing in upon me, the brick walls of the buildings seem to inch nearer, until my breath is so tight it stabs me. The horse is almost on top of me. Once a hoof comes within an inch of my thigh and I swerve to one side and nearly fall, but somehow I right myself and keep running, dodging the sharp hooves, tacking back and forth and back again among the scattering street folk.

Then I come up short, hands slapping the blank face of a stone garden wall. It is too high to jump or climb. My side cramps and my breath is gone. I can't run any farther. I can feel the horse's huge heat on my neck as it rears up at the wall. I am somewhere among the flailing hooves, somewhere between the gigantic animal body and the stones.

I am trapped, smashed. I try to crouch, to cover my face, but it will be only a matter of seconds until those hooves find me. "*Dive,* you fool!" roars a deep voice from somewhere, and I do. I throw myself aside, strike the ground hard, flip over, roll a few feet along the base of the wall, and lie still.

I am stunned and stupid, but I know I must fight it off. I have only a split second to get myself out of the way, before the rider turns and brings those hooves down on top of me.

Then my luck changes. The great horse is too much for his rider, he is out of control, rearing and screaming. I hear shouts and the yelps of the dancing dog, as horse and rider plunge out the other end of the alley and into the crowd. Someone else screams, some random casualty. The astrologer. Death in the stars. Death in the streets. Modern London. Modern times.

I collapse rather than roll onto my back, strained tendons screaming. There are footsteps and then a shadow falls across me. I look up at the face of Nico Rands.

"Can you walk?" What a question, from such a man. I thought Nick would never stand upon his feet again.

I scramble up. "Where's the rider? Did you get a look at him?"

"Small, slight. Flat cap. Dark blue, I think. He left the horse behind and made a run for it."

It doesn't make sense to me, this attempt on my life. I've only just begun the task Rowland and Harry have set me and I ought not to be dispensable until I actually find Gabriel for them. Unless, of course, I have by some means become dangerous since yesterday.

"I owe you my neck," I say to Nico. "Will you not come and raise a glass with me?"

He shakes his head. It's plain he doesn't trust me any more than his father does. "Let's wander a bit," he says. "Talk as we go."

We turn back in the direction of St. Bride's Lane. He walks just as Peachum said—on the sides of his feet, but with a light, rolling step, like a sailor on an unsteady deck. "Matthias told me you're wed," I say to him. "And she's given you a son. Good for you."

He looks down at his feet as though they are not really part of him, and smiles. "Yes. Very good for me. You still with your Huguenot beauty?"

"I'm not sure I've ever been *with* her, exactly."

"Bedgames," he says with a brief smile. "I remember them well."

We sit down on a splintery bench in front of a cookshop. "Did you ever find out who gave the order?" I ask him quietly. "The rack, I mean."

He turns to look at me, his face a wilderness. "Gibbie says you put them onto me. That you were doubling, working for somebody else as well as Burghley."

"That's rich. *One* master was getting too much for me. I think Roanoke finished me for the dark work, really. If Gabriel hadn't wanted my help getting back there, I'd have left service a lot sooner."

"But you didn't give it up for three years."

"The Armada was on the way. They'd have put a dagger in me some night to be sure I didn't sell my secrets to the Spanish. And then—"

"Then there was the second Roanoke. The lost one. An excellent puzzle to solve, and you couldn't resist it. I know."

"You don't." I hardly recognize the words as my own. "You don't bloody know. They weren't a puzzle, they were *people*. They were real. They still are."

Nick's deep voice, suddenly kinder, more familiar. "Is this

Robin talking? The perfect spy, detached from the world of needy mortals? You've changed, my old son."

"Not enough. Ask the Huguenot beauty."

Silence. Then: "You think no one at all survived the Roanoke?"

"I was sure of it. But now— Has Gibbie told you?"

"The three women. Yes. Could it be Gabriel with them? Alive? I can hardly believe it."

"If he is alive, I'd like him to stay that way. But I have to find him first."

Nick gets up and walks a few paces, then returns to the bench. "I may as well tell you. My wife, Judith—she's his daughter."

"You clever old rogue. She's not much more than a girl, surely. However did you—?"

"It's been coming on slowly. Most of her life, really. The twins' mother ran off with a wool brogger and left them to Gabriel to raise. Well, he couldn't give them a proper home, so his sister in Bishopsgate took 'em. Next square down from our place. Sour old dose of Puritan bile. Wouldn't have Gabriel in her house, said God had cursed him. My mother was still living then, and sometimes he'd bring the little girls to our house. Always a lute or a viol around, and he'd teach 'em songs. Dances. Play hide-and-go-seek. Bears. He loves children's games, it's the grown-up ones he can't stand. Sarah takes after her aunt, she wants naught to do with him. But Judith has always adored him."

It makes Nick smile even to speak of her. I try to summon the faces on the miniatures Gabriel carried. Not identical twins. One dark-haired and sallow, the other with a tangle of light red-gold curls. *Judith.*

"She just came sailing into the house one day," he goes on. "Threw my physician out the door with her boot up his arse and dosed me herself. Valerian, I think. Horrible stuff. But her kisses sweetened it nicely."

"I need to talk to her. About Gabriel. Anything she can tell me."

"No, Rob. She's pregnant again. Better not."

"Think what it'll do to her if he *has* come home, and they trump up some charge against him and put him in the Tower. It's what they want, I can feel it in my thumbs. A nice public execution to put paid to the whole Roanoke business."

I can hear Nico's light breathing. "All right. I'll let that cobbler of yours know where and when. But if you upset her—or if I find out you're lying—"

"I was your friend once. And Gabriel's. I'm with him in this, if I'm with anyone."

It is getting dark, the streets in that strange leaden fissure between afternoon and evening, and the river air damp and chill. The stink of burnt onions and mutton grease from the cookshop. The distant cry of an herb-woman—"Rosemary! Sweet rosemary for remembrance!"

Nick's back straightens a little more. "The racking," he says. Three equal syllables, spat out like broken teeth.

"Don't. Have some pity on yourself, Nick. There's no need to tell me."

"There is." The deep rumble of his voice, held by sheer will to a steady monotone. "Because it all had to do with the second colony. They had a list of the passengers."

"Men? Women?"

"Both. They kept reading the names out to me. Was this one a spider, was that one, who worked for Walsingham, who worked for the Spanish. What were the codes, where were the dark drops for messages, who was the postman, what houses were safe and which ships' captains could be bribed. I knew nothing. I told them, but they didn't believe me. Didn't even hear me."

His deep voice is compressed to a monotone rumble, his back slammed hard against the wall of the shop. His hands try to grip the edge of the bench, but he cannot quite manage it. His fingers shake and shake.

"Gold," he says. "They kept asking what I knew of the American gold. Was it real? Did Ralegh have a map to it? Did Gabriel? Of course I couldn't tell them. He'd only spoken about the woman, the savage woman."

"Naia."

"I always knew he'd go back to her. That it had nothing to do with gold and pearls and maps and lies, not for him. But I knew *they'd* never believe such a thing. It was beyond them. Do you see? Love like that."

"What brought you to my lodgings that night, Nick? Were they following you?"

He looks up at me. "I came because you sent me that message, of course. 'We're wanted at Greenwich. Come and fetch me.' They were waiting. They met me halfway down your stairs."

"'Wanted at Greenwich'? I never sent any such message."

No wonder he believes I betrayed him. No wonder Matthias wants to stove in my skull, scald me to death with hot water, send me to hell.

"Nick, I swear to you on the soul of my father. I didn't lure you there. Please." I have a dagger inside my doublet. Modern times. I hand it to him, hilt first. "Cut my throat if you want to. If you still believe—what you've thought of me all these years."

His eyes search mine for a long moment. Then he laughs, deeply. "Christ, I can see why you never get any good parts in the theatres. You lay it on with a trowel, you do. Naked daggers and 'on the soul of my father'?"

The weapon rattles down into the gutter and I start to breathe again.

"How did you get that damned message? Who brought it?"

"A girl. Blowsy. Fair hair, if she'd ever washed it. Eye like a gimlet. Stank of pisspots and wig dye. Know her?"

Arabelle. Arabelle listens at keyholes, and what she don't hear she makes up.

"She works at my lodgings, the little bitch. I'll kill her."

"Don't be an ass. Watch her, that's what you're good at. She might lead you somewhere."

"Where did they take you that night? Were there sounds? Other prisoners?"

"If you mean was it Bridewell or the Fleet, no. It wasn't official, of that much I'm certain. I'd been knocked about a bit and the noise of the gears woke me, when they—began. I was naked as a plucked capon, upside down on a bed of open lath. Feet strapped to one roller and arms to another. I saw a stone floor underneath. My own piss on the straw. There was a torch that smelled of rancid fat. A door that opened and closed again. Somebody's cellar, I think."

"Topcliffe's house?" The place was infamous. Blackened windows. Bars and chains. In the kitchen, his wife cooking supper.

"No. Not Topcliffe." Nico gets up and walks a few steps, mops his face with his sleeve. "They'd turn the gears a bit, and then they'd ask more questions. When my vision cleared, I saw and heard things. Feet, mostly. Heard a servant come in. Livery. A coat of arms on his shoes."

"Did you recognize it?"

"It looked new, I know that. Bright colors."

"Can you remember what they were?"

"It blurs, Rob. I can see it sometimes, but others, not. I can only tell you what's there now, in my mind. Somebody mutters something and then more feet come. Yes. Red-and-black-striped stockings, like a bloody mummer. I remember them well enough."

I swallow hard, but keep silent, trying not to jump to conclusions. Simon Fernando wore such stockings, but they are the fashion. I've seen Rowland wear them, too.

"One of them had a pair of purple linen shoes with high heels and something bright on the laces," Nico goes on. "Jewels or gold—you know. Court laces. And the third—he came without a servant. Very cautious. Didn't make a sound. Long feet, terribly narrow. Satin slippers, black satin, plain but expensive. Wooden heels, for dancing. One foot pointed almost straight outward, splayfooted. But it may be my memory. Things are misshapen, sometimes. My eyes, when they tightened the gears—" He is shaking violently now. The memory is too clear, too close. "After he came into the room, I smelt oil of clove. I can't— Can't stand the smell of cloves now. Ah, Christ, it's cold. Isn't it cold here?"

I cannot predict what his voice may pull out of me. I take a step nearer and my arms hoop themselves round his shoulders, hold him hard. Slowly his shaking stops. Mine takes a bit longer. Then we let go.

"It rages sometimes," he says, "when I let the monster loose." He steps back from me, still unsteady. "What will you do now? How will you sort it on your own?"

"I'd do better with your help. You're still the best sifter in England."

"No. I wish you well. But my young master wouldn't like it." He looks over at me and smiles, and suddenly the air is warmer. "He's called Lucas, my boy is. It's his birthday today, and he's two."

thirty-seven

GABRIEL

I F ARABELLE HAD BEEN AT DAME PHOEBE'S THAT NIGHT, I'D HAVE SET Peachum to follow her. But a new servant came to fill my pitcher of water. "Where's the other one?" I asked her. "I haven't seen her in a while."

"Arabelle, you mean? Run off, ain't she? Nasty slut."

"And what's your name?"

"Deborah, sir."

I tossed her a penny. "If you hear anything of her, come and tell me. She stole my best lace ruff."

G ERARD WAS IN France and it would be safe enough at Staple Oaks. I sent Deborah with a message to Annette, asking for the farmhouse keys, then lay down to sleep. But my thoughts danced and wove patterns, then unravelled them again, till at last it was daylight. I retrieved my scrip full of notes, pictures, log-books, and depositions from Peach's squirrel hole on the landing and handed him one of Harry's gold crowns. "Change clothes with me," I told him. "I want to look like a cobbler."

His breeches were of a style twenty years out of date and he wore a long leather jerkin in addition to his cobbler's apron with its sagging pockets for his threads and cutters and awls. His shirt was rough grey linsey, and the brim of his old hat flopped down almost to my shoulders.

It proved an excellent disguise. My two watchers of the previous day had been replaced by a seller of ballad sheets and a baker's cart, but they paid no attention to a down-at-heel cobbler. No black horses tried to ride me down, and I made my way safely through the city, rented a swaybacked mare that would sort with my costume, and took the Oxford road.

I went on without stopping for food or drink, but the mare was a bad-tempered plodder and it was almost sunset when I neared the farm. At a crossroads by a rickety old gibbet three women were hunched over a bit of kindling, struggling to light a small fire. One was buxom and nearing sixty, the second thin as a rake, the third faded but still handsome in her bones. There was a boy of fifteen or sixteen with them, his red hair catching the last of the daylight.

"I have a good flint and steel, mistress," I said to the eldest. "You seem to have little success with that fire."

She looked me over, eyes narrowed. "The flint's still damp, I fear. When we forded a stream, this one dropped it in the water." She ruffled the boy's hair and laughed. "He drops everything, and then treads on it, after."

I swung down off my horse and set to work striking sparks onto the bits of sticks they had gathered. The thin woman began to cough and could not stop—a dangerous sound, hollow and empty.

"Your friend needs a roof over her," I said. "Will you not come along with me? The place isn't far."

"No, Madge," said the sickly woman in a hoarse whisper. "We daren't."

The third woman—Eliza, they called her—stood with her arm shielding the boy. "I thank you, friend," she said to me. "But we are stayed-for elsewhere tonight. We'll warm ourselves and then go on. It's only a mile or two more."

I left them and rode toward the farm. *Madge.* If they were stayed-for a mile away, why stop to build a fire and take a meal? *Eliza.* Within a mile or two, there were no villages and no other freehold farms that I knew of.

Madge. Margaret Lawrence. *Eliza.* Elizabeth Viccars. And copper-haired Georgie Howe.

I F THEY *ARE* some of the Roanoke women, Gabriel must be close by. I turn the stubborn mare back again towards the crossroads, keeping to the wooded streambed that follows the road. The four of them are still there, the little fire burning low. I dismount and hunch at the edge of the stream, watching.

"Georgie," says Madge. "I begin to worry. He's never left us so long alone on the road before."

"I'll wait till Aggie's asleep, and then I'll go looking."

"Oh, she'll do well enough. I've put a pinch of anise in her broth. That's sovereign for coughs, and it'll make her sleep. Best go now, my dear."

Suddenly Eliza stands up, very straight and still in the dim fire-light. "Is it him?" says Madge. "Can you see him?"

Georgie gives a barn owl's cry and a moment later, on the ridge that runs above the road, a dark figure appears. Tall. Slender. One shoulder hunched and the arm hanging useless. Where the light of a rising moon touches him, his sandy hair is like an aureole in the evening wind.

I'd know the shape of him anywhere, ruined arm and all.

The boy snatches up a burning stick from the fire and makes circles with it in the dark for a signal, and I see Gabriel lift up his good arm and wave back, then start to make his way down to the road. In another minute or two, he will be here and I can get the lot of them safely to Staple Oaks.

But it all comes to nothing. My old fool of a nag decides to whinny, not once but again and again, rearing and stamping in a fit of bad temper. "Run, my dears!" cries Madge.

"Gabriel!" screams Eliza. "Away! Away!"

There is a fall of pebbles from the ridge, and when I look for him next, he has gone. I can still hear the women and the boy running into the woods, into the fields, even the sick woman running. I can hear her harsh cough in the darkness, but she runs as they all do, headlong and wordless. They are running for their lives.

"I won't hurt you," I call out over the dark fields. "Why should I want to hurt you?"

But they do not come back.

T HERE ARE ONLY two old servants at Staple Oaks, Mrs. Trott and her husband. They treat me as a sort of likable poor relation and are used to my solitary comings and goings. They have a kindly chuckle at my tatty clothes and my cobbler's apron, feed me and my confounded horse, and consign the pair of us to our stalls.

For the second night in a row, I am too unsettled to sleep. Two days of resurrection have taken their toll of my nerves, but I still hope that if Gabriel sees my candle burning, he will make his way to me somehow.

I fill a beaker with Gerard's best French brandy and drift into his library—a rich, dark-panelled room with many shelves of handsomely bound books and more of the Arras tapestries that all but overwhelm the London house. I spread out my papers on a long polished table and pull up the high-backed chair, determined to break apart the boxes of foolish fact surrounding the Roanoke story, and seize upon possibility instead.

I begin with the murder of Fullwood, but I can get nowhere with it. If someone fears his betrayal, why not dispose of him sooner? And why down in Cornwall? Had he known Gabriel and Alis would come ashore at Penross Cove?

Fullwood was the sort of fellow who might have had informers anywhere, and there are plenty of smugglers along that coast, men of reputation and position whom an old extortioner could work upon. Perhaps one of them killed him to be rid of blackmail. Or perhaps it was someone whose name I would never be told.

Then there are the shoes Nico remembers seeing. And the stockings. Black-and-red-striped stockings. Behind my closed eyes, I summon what little I remember of Simon Fernando. His dark oily hair combed into a lovelock and his stocky shape bent over his charts. His voice singing Portuguese *planhas* whenever he got drunk enough. "A fine voice," I remember saying to the old alchemist, Ganz, who sat mending his own stockings on deck one night just after the ships of that first expedition turned west from the coast of Africa.

The pirate's deep voice rose to a passionate wail and Ganz tipped his head back, listening. "A death song," he said.

"Come, Joachim, you don't speak Portugee."

"You think the words matter? Listen."

Fernando's voice rose another three or four notes, and a sob broke it. Then he suddenly laughed.

"What does it mean?" I asked Ganz. "Why is he laughing?"

"Ah. He thinks the death will not be his own."

THE BRANDY IS finally making me sleepy. I am about to take my candle up the stairs to my bed when the library door creaks open. My heart almost stops. "Gabriel?" I say softly.

"Oh, sir!" says the old housekeeper. "I declare, I thought you was a ghost, sitting there in your shirt. Shall I make you up a fire? You'll go cold in this dampness."

"Thank you, Mrs. Trott. There's no need of a fire. I'll be off to bed as soon as I put away all these papers."

" 'Tis terrible late to be at your writing. Cold veal pie in the larder, if you're hungry."

"Sounds a treat. But tomorrow. Er—Mrs. Trott? Has anyone let the master's pigeons loose in the last week? Have you seen anyone in the garden?"

"Now, it's odd you should ask, sir. Somebody come when me and Trott was gone to market at Little Pagford and let out the big fellow, Sultan—remember him? None of the other birds, just that one. We reckoned it was them snotty-nosed young rascals of Esdras Kettle's."

"And Sultan hasn't returned?"

"Why, he come back not an hour before you arrived, just this evening. Safe in his own dovecote now, ain't he? He's that clever, he must've got away from them boys and flew home."

Annette has sent him, of course. Sent her love to welcome me. It is the sort of unpredictable and trusting sweetness that draws me to her. "Did he carry a message?" I ask the housekeeper, my voice a bit too warm and eager.

Mrs. Trott opens a small inlaid box on one of the shelves and produces a snippet of paper. "Neither me nor Trott can read, but I thought it might be something to use against them Kettle brats."

I take the bit of paper and unroll it.

Bastard, Annette has written. *If you ever come back here, I will kill you. They searched the house today. They searched me.*

For hours, in the sheer country darkness, I watch and watch what must have been done to Annette under cover of that awful word *searched.* All my failures in bed were preparations for this, all my lies and half-truths and deceptions are compliant in it. They have done to her what they should have been doing to me.

Standing at the foot of the stair, I smash my forehead against the railing, over and over, over and over. There is blood on the carved phoenix that watches the hallway. I wipe it clean. Leave no traces. Tell nobody. Keep in the shadows. Use only invisible ink. Secrets serve best when lies will not suffice. Modern love. Modern hearts. Modern times.

I stumble up to my bed and fall down upon it fully dressed. I do not intend to sleep nor do I remember doing so. It simply happens, and I wake to what seems part of the same fragmented dream.

The casement is half-open and the window overlooks the back garden, by daylight a colorful spill of purple and yellow and blue and white—early pansies, primroses, pied violets, snowdrops. The moon is still up, shedding its light at an oblique angle now, turning the new leaves of hawthorns and elder bushes to silver.

At first, I see no more than a flicker of shadow. I hear not the slightest creak of the iron gates of the dovecote. There is a sudden beating of wings against the air and then I see him, bent in a ragged confusion of darkness and bones. With his good arm, he lifts the last bird up and throws it aloft. The little flock circles low, then rises, gathers, and flies away, dark pewter against the fading moon.

"Gabriel," I call softly, standing there at my casement. "Don't run from me. Help me."

He looks up at the window for a moment, his face open as a child's in the moonlight. The freed birds disappear in the distance.

"I'm coming down," I call to him. "Wait for me!"

But when I reach the back garden, I find only the empty cage.

thirty-eight

O Mistress Mine

I TRIFLED MRS. TROTT'S KITCHEN FOR A BREAKFAST OF BEER AND COLD veal pie and set off for London, returning my foul nag and going straight to Crutched Friars on foot. It was some danger to go there. The place would be constantly watched in case I turned up—though I still didn't know by whom.

For almost two hours, I kept my own survey of the house from a shadowed doorway across the square, but I could identify no known spiders amongst the butchers' boys and pickled onion sellers and kitchen maids bound for the market stalls. At last I slipped through the passersby, crossed the cobbles, and knocked at the door.

It opened only a crack. "Here," said the maid's voice. "What you think you're about, cobbler? Tradesmen round the back."

I'd forgotten I was still wearing Peachum's clothes. "Esther, I must see your mistress," I said.

"Oh. You, is it?" She opened the door another inch, and I could hear the virginals. Annette was playing "Shall I Come Sweet Love to Thee." The maid smirked. "I'm to say she ain't home. And if it's you, I'm to kick you in the privates."

I gave the door a quick, nasty shove. It smacked into her belly and she fell backwards with a yelp, upsetting an Italian table. "Here!" she screeched. "You get away!"

The music stopped. A man's voice from the next room, a French accent. Gerard, home so soon? I didn't care. I could hear his boots crossing the dark polished wood. Then he peered around the open door, smiling. "What is it, Esther?"

I'd never seen him in person before, only his portrait hanging in the gallery hall. Thin grey hair. Hooded blue eyes, set deep in his skull. A wide mouth that maintained the same polite half-smile as in the portrait. I wondered if it remained there when he slept with her, like making love with a picture. Still, it was an intelligent, civilized, kindly face.

"This lewd fellow," gasped the maid. "He pushed his way past me, sir, or I'd not have let him in!"

"Never mind. You may go now." He turned to me. "What is this, cobbler? Has my wife neglected to pay your account?"

"No, sir," I said, a little too loudly. I wanted Annette to hear my voice. "That's all right about the bill," I told Gerard. "Only your good lady wanted her foot measuring for a new pair of slippers, and I promised to wait upon her."

YOU'RE LATE," says her voice from the doorway. "You should have been here yesterday."

I make her a clumsy, cobblerish bow and steal a quick glance. Beautiful as ever. Wearing the ice-blue gown. But her face is too pale under the faint blushing of rouge and cosmetic she never wears otherwise, and her eyes are swollen and red, shadowed with blue-black smudges the face-paint does not hide. When the lace falls back from her wrist, I can see a deep bruise there.

"Pardon," I murmur. "It'll take just a minute or two to do the measuring."

"No, *ma petite*," says Gerard. Does he know? Surely he has seen the bruises, all of them. Seen her body as they have left her. "You're ill. You have need of a physician, not another pair of shoes. Come another day, cobbler, eh?"

The maid turns and gives me a triumphant stare, and Annette draws a ragged breath. "Never mind, *mari*," she tells Gerard. "I'm well enough. Come along, fellow."

She turns and marches up the stairs, and I make a bow to her husband and follow her.

"What have you come for?" she demands, closing the bedchamber door with a thud. It is the treasure chamber, the one she and I do not use anymore. The maid has done a creditable job restoring order downstairs, but up here it is different. The painted silk curtains hang in shreds and the tapestries have been pulled down and trampled. Rugs are torn from tables and pictures slashed.

Annette's delicate features are drained of expression and her voice is dull. "What do you want? Haven't you brought enough trouble on me? For the love of God. You might have warned me."

"I thought— I thought, if you didn't know—" But I cannot even try to explain. "I'm sorry. Sorry. Your message. Sultan. You said they—"

"Yes. Well? What of it? That is what men do with women."

"But you've seen a physician?"

"Of course not. Physicians blab."

"A midwife, then. They've hurt you."

"What did you think? That it was pleasant? Fool. Oh, never mind. It's not usually fatal, unless they had the pox."

She is not so hard as she pretends. Sometimes she cries in her sleep.

"Who were they?" I whisper.

Her slim hands cling to the heavy, dark bedpost. "How should I know? They didn't present me with letters of credit. Four men, that's all. Four leopards."

"Christ. Did— Christ. What—did they come for?"

"You, of course. They looked everywhere for something you might've left here. I was all they could find." She tilts her head back and her eyes close for a moment. "If I'd known where you were, I'd have told them. Set them onto you. I swear before God."

"You *did* know where I'd gone, you gave me the keys. I put you in danger, I failed you. But you protected me. You even sent Sultan to warn me."

"To curse you."

I cannot look at her. "I'll do anything."

"Go away. We're finished. I won't die of it, I told you that. If they've left me a brat, I'll get rid of it. There are plenty of ways, and I've done it before. Didn't you realize?"

She means mine. A child of mine. The sudden trip to Italy that took months. The sly gleam in the maidservant's eye.

"If— If Gerard finds out, if he puts you away from him—" In her world, it is what husbands do with soiled wives. "If you need help—"

"He won't find out. He doesn't want to know."

"But surely, in bed— You can't disguise everything."

"Idiot. He doesn't sleep with me. He never has."

"What, never?"

"He goes with boys."

It is a huge desert between us. A sky of empty brass.

"Oh, Annette."

"I don't want your pity. He's kind. He gives me everything I want. And he's never lied to me. You—you're nothing but a dirty spy, peering through keyholes. God. Why didn't you tell me? Why didn't you trust me that much? Ah, Robbie. Did you really think I'd betray you? Or were you all the time only spying on me?"

She is right, of course. Part of me has watched her as I watch everything—with interest, with sympathy, with passion, even with need. But without the last dangerous inch of connection that might keep me from walking away scot-free.

It is why Gabriel does not trust me. Why Nick's honest father despises me.

"I'm sorry," I tell Annette in a raw whisper. "Insofar as I can love anyone, I did love you. I still do."

"I wonder why I don't believe you." She goes to her velvet jewel box and opens it. "Here, Robbie." She puts the gold charm into my hand. The virgin moon. "Look at it every evening and think of me. It's as near as you will ever come to love."

thirty-nine

How God's Eye Sometimes Blinks

YOU WEREN'T FOLLOWED, WERE YOU?" SAID NICO AS HE LET PEACHUM and me into the kitchen that night. For a moment, he peered nervously out at the shadowy back garden of his father's narrow house. Then he shut the door and barred it.

"Don't worry," I said. "We've doubled back four times. There's nobody."

"If you please, sir," put in Peach, "I don't mind keeping a watch outside, just to make sure. I'll stay the night, if you fancy."

I nodded and he slipped out again into the darkness. The worry lines on Nick's forehead didn't relax. "What's happened?" he said in a low voice his wife wouldn't hear. "You look like hell."

I shook my head. "A little too much truth for one day, that's all."

"Let me get you some of Judith's *aqua vitae*. And a mug for your friend, as well. There's a chill on the night."

Two grey-and-white cats jumped off a bench and went to hide under the table, and I took their place. In the cupboard bed against the far wall, Matthias lay tossing and grumbling, and Judith sat at her spinning wheel by the fire, the little boy Lucas curled asleep by her side.

She was so much like Gabriel that I could hardly take my eyes off her—the same fine, sandy hair that fell softly around her face; the same tall, lithe body; the same habit of looking with intense concentration at something invisible. She glanced up at me nervously.

"Mistress Judith," I said quietly. "I've seen your father."

She said nothing at first, only stood up with the child in her arms and carried him to his cot in the next room. Then she returned to her wheel.

"You spoke to him?" she said, her voice full of suppressed excitement.

"I tried. He ran from me, I don't know why."

"Was he well? How did he look?"

I thought it best to say nothing of his crooked shoulder. "He seems well enough." I shook my head. "I only wish I understood what they're so afraid of, he and the womenfolk. All of England should rejoice that they've survived."

Nico's arm slipped around Judith's softly swelling waist. "It may be," he said, "that having survived Roanoke is a danger in itself."

"My husband believes the colony was intended to fail," she said. "Subverted by someone even before the ships left Plymouth. And now, fearing the discovery of his past treachery, the monster doubles the wrong."

I could see that Nick had kept nothing from her. She knew everything of his old life. Every danger. Every sin. Every harm he'd done or had had done to him. Everything he thought and felt and worried over. They were rich with one another, and they would never come apart.

Nick got up to put more coals on the fire. "Since we spoke of the—" In this place, in her presence, he could not speak the word. *Racking.* "I haven't been able to get it out of my mind," he went on. "The questions about whether there were spies aboard, whether any meetings had been arranged for with the queen's agents in the islands or at Lisbon. As though they already knew the answers and wanted to find out what *I* knew. And there was a thing one of them said when they thought I'd passed out. 'How much longer can you hold off sailing?' Those winds at Portsmouth that delayed them a month. You remember? And then Cowes. And I laughed at you for fussing over it."

I nodded. "To keep a ship from sailing on time you'd have to be in command. That means Simon Fernando."

Judith stared. "The pilot? The admiral of the voyage?"

"A pirate and a spy," I said. "Not much he wouldn't do if the price was right."

"Including a bit of doubling on King Philip's payroll," Nick said.

"And Ralegh trusted such a fellow?"

"My love, if you eliminated all the pirates and spies from the merchant ships of England, nothing would ever leave port."

"But what could they gain from a mere delay in sailing?"

"Failure," I told her. "A broad-sea voyage means months at sea. With enough delays, supplies would begin spoiling. Others would run out. If the water and the beer went bad, there might be fever aboard before ever they made land."

"How *could* they send all those poor creatures out to be lost? There were women and children. Babies. Who could possibly have gained from their destruction? And gain *what*?"

"I don't know yet," I said. "But your father does. Why else is he running and hiding?"

J UDITH CALLED PEACHUM inside, then, and poured us more of her homemade liquor, while Nick described the shoes he remembered seeing during his racking. If we could identify those three faceless brutes, we would have, at the least, a place to begin.

"First off," Peach said, "as to your court laces. Unless it was an earl or the like, them jewels was most likely glass. Half of them that wants court laces ain't the real article themselves, if you take my meaning. In my best days, I made it a practice never to deal with 'em. Almost never had the chinks, see. All flash."

"Was our man a peer of the realm, Nick, would you say?"

"That one? Oh ho."

"Common as dirt, eh?" said Peach with a chuckle. "Second off, as to the black satin slippers. Plain, was they? Not needleworked? Because I know all the best needlewomen that works shoe tops and the master embroiderers that employs 'em."

"They were plain black. But the stuff looked expensive. A fine luster."

"A long, narrow foot, and turned out sidewise? And dancing heels?" A hiss of air through the teeth. "Wooden heels is a plague to handle. Warp in the wet weather, see. Could you make me a picture, sir, of how them feet was as he stood there?"

This was practical stuff and it seemed to calm Nick's horrors, not prod them alive again. He fished out a bit of burnt coal from the fire and sketched on the back of a penny songsheet.

Peachum studied it. "Even allowing for the state you was in when you saw him, that foot almost points to the wall, don't it? Can't be too many like that about, not in the range of paying for fine satin slippers." He sat for a moment staring into the fire. Then he folded the drawing and hid it away inside his shirt. "Somebody made them shoes special to fit such a foot. I'll ask about at the Cordwainers' Guild, see if anyone can put a name to the buyer."

"What about the servant, Nick?" I said. "Anything about that coat of arms come back to you?"

"Only colors. Green and blue. And the quartering in red. Common enough."

But Peachum lit up like the fireworks on Accession Day.

"Coat of arms, you say? Now, that's something your embroiderers keeps careful track of. I've got a friend in that line, name of Ducket. I could take you to see him, sir."

"No, Nick," I said, thinking of Annette. "It's one thing talking to us here. It's another, this business of shoemakers' guilds and master embroiderers. It's too open, too public. Keep close, and don't leave Judith and the boy alone. And stay clear of Gibbie, whatever you do."

Between the time I had spoken to Rowland and Harry and the time the black horse tried to ride me into the mud, I had seen only Annette, Matthias Rands, Peachum. And James Pembroke-Gibbons, who knew much too much about Roanoke and about me.

P EACH IS DETERMINED to watch over Nico and his lady till morning, and Judith sends him off to the garden swathed in blankets and provided with bread, cheese, and a jug of *aqua vitae*. I take my leave and begin the long journey through the back alleys to Fleet Street. But after such a day, I do not want to go home to Dame Phoebe's. Instead I wander, in and out of wherries, up and down narrow lanes, hardly conscious of the Night Watch. For a while I walk the riverbank, watching the poor folk who come out in the darkness to sift the sand at low tide looking for salvage. At last I find myself outside a church Gabriel and I sometimes used for our meetings. We often left messages for one another in a dark corner beneath a choir stall, where the light never penetrates. In a candlelit world, there are such corners everywhere, but this one was ours.

St. Walburga's is an old church dating back to Saxon times. The Papist frescoes of the Last Judgement have been whitewashed over, creating a stark and chilly atmosphere in which the shadows loom huge. Two large racks of candles stand at the heads of the outer aisles, but at such a late hour only one candle in each rack is lighted. Between nave and chancel are the choir stalls.

I see no one at worship. Except for the skittering claws of a family of mice making a meal of the sleeping verger's supper crumbs, I hear no sound but my own boots as I make my way up the aisle and climb the three steps to the back row of the choir. Seven places along, then sit down. Reach under the bench.

Something is there—a paper message tightly rolled in a piece of fine black linen and tied with bits of heavy black thread that will disappear in the dark corner. Dark drops, we call them. Fingers clumsy as paws, I break the threads and unroll the paper, then am forced to return to the chancel where the candles give enough light to read by.

The black linen is clean and the paper is new, not brittle and six years old. *Stay out of the Hornets' Nest*, Gabriel has written. *Pirates rampant.*

The Hornets' Nest is Whitehall, one of our silly private codes. *Pirates* is his word for unknown spies who might be working for anyone. He was always left-handed, but his left hand must be useless, from what I have seen. He writes with the other now, and it is amazingly the same—careful and precise, bearing down on the paper as little as possible. I think of the labor it has cost him to retain this visible sign of himself. Of the iron control inside that shabby, tousled shell.

Then my nerves catch sharply. A heavy door closes somewhere in the ancient church and in a moment there are footsteps at the altar. I stuff the message into the top of my boot, then turn to see who is there.

In the days of the Papists, a priest attended the altar every hour during the night when Mass was not being sung. In old churches like this one, the custom is still somewhat adhered to, a vicar or verger appointed to be certain the great altar candle burns safely, and to offer a prayer for the souls of those abroad in the dark.

Tonight it is a tall, slender, middle-aged vicar. A plain cassock and the small square cap worn by Protestant clergy. Where he kneels at the altar, he is too deep in shadow to see much more of him. But his left shoulder juts painfully forward.

He is so near that I can hear the slight drift of the long cassock when he breathes. Still, I fear he may run again. I kneel at the communion rail and say an Our Father for Annette.

"Didn't know you'd got religion, old heart," Gabriel says from the shadows. "Must be a comfort. Can't seem to manage it, myself."

I remain on my knees. "You don't believe His eye is on the sparrow?"

"Well, but He blinks, doesn't He? Anyway, it's not His eye the sparrow needs. It's His fist."

"Lord, but you've led me a chase. Does this appearance mean you've decided to trust me?"

"Wouldn't count on it. Tired, though. Had to stop running."

"Are your friends safe? The womenfolk and the redheaded boy?"

He doesn't reply, only takes off the priest's cap and rumples his shaggy hair. "You do know you've got watchers trailing after you? Greasy lot, look more like bullyboys. Private hire. Don't know who runs 'em."

I have to fight to keep from staring at his shoulder. It is painful to see it, the arm thin and the bones shunting forward, unsupported by tendons. His fingers still work a bit, but they move stiffly, like those of a very old man. He could never have strangled Willie Fullwood beside that Cornish farm field, whatever they might try to charge him with.

"Will you come with me now," I ask him, "and at least let me feed you? Give you someplace to sleep tonight?"

"Dame Phoebe's rubbish heap?"

I dare not risk it, in case the treacherous Arabelle has returned. "Not there, no. But we'll find a place."

"Better alone just now," he says. "There's a play at the Rose to-morrow. *Henry the Sixth*. Bluddy bore, but there'll be plenty of people. At the back of the pit where the whores go, we can talk there."

He turns to leave. "Wait," I say. "Where's Naia?" Her absence is a huge part of him missing, adrift somewhere. "Is she in England?" Again he doesn't answer. The candle is guttering and I get to my feet and light another. "She's not dead?"

"No. I can't talk about her now. It's wrong to talk of her."

"To me, you mean. Wrong to talk to me."

"Oh, leave it! It's too soon, that's all."

"Was she taken, Gabriel? Sold?"

He had told me long ago. Capture was the one thing she truly feared. The worst thing.

"Not sold. Tell you one day. When this is over." In the candle-light, his whole body seems transparent. "If you've turned pirate, Robbie, if you're working for one of the bastards, then you're for it. Understand? Drawn and fucking quartered, that's a promise. Do it myself."

"Damn you! I'm only here because I don't want your head on the block."

He draws a deep breath. "Sorry, old heart. Told you. Tired."

"So it's vengeance you've come for, is it? Like a bad theatre-play?"

"Screw vengeance. It's justice. The bastard threw us away."

"Which bastard? Who was it?"

"Know soon. Weeks. Days, maybe. Have to be certain."

"And when you find him?"

"What do you think?" His grey eyes search for me. "If you're in this, you're in it, Rob. No sitting in doorways and watching it happen. You have to stand for something now. Take sides."

"I'm with you. I'm on your side. I'll be your postman. I'll be your advocate. Whatever you need."

I speak with great feeling, and I mean it. But I wonder if I'm telling the truth.

forty

FLUNG AWAY

GABRIEL TOLD ME SOME OF HIS ROANOKE HISTORY THAT NEXT afternoon at the Rose, and afterwards, through many nights talking, I drew from him what more I could—joking him, teasing him, sometimes prodding him with what I knew was real pain.

We sat hunched beside the Thames as a cold spring mist fell over London. It had been a dark few days for him. He had just left the last of the Roanoke women—Joyce Archard and Rose Payne—in separate villages on the northeast coast, near Jarrow, and whatever they had cost him, they had also brought him comfort and a sort of home.

"Don't tell me you bedded all of them," I teased. Playing the lustful lout, like the old days. Trying for a flare of temper, a laugh, anything.

But he was scarcely in London at all—slipping from place to place, sleeping in doorways and under river stairs. With Peach standing guard, Nico had brought Judith and the child to a book-stall outside St. Paul's so Gabriel could see them. Stood browsing over a book. Risked a look at her, and she at him. Risked a smile at her little boy, his grandson. Grandsire he was now, indeed. Old Gander. How Emma would have laughed, he said.

He looked bereft now, and was showing his age, the ruined shoulder dragging him down and down.

"Bedded them? Oh. No. After Alis's husband was killed in the storm, I slept by her a night or two. Touched her a little, that's all. Stroked her breast." There was no trace of lust in the word. He might've been speaking of a bird. "And Madge. Healed everybody else's troubles. Busy every hour of the day, she was, but the nights in that place—"

"Madge? Why, she's nearly sixty, she must be."

"Must she? We danced sometimes. No music by then, of course. Mostly we just sat at a table reaching hands across. Sat there till it got light outside."

He stood up, a scribble written dark against the torchlit Thames. It was very late, even the packs of wild dogs gone to bed. There is something about London at that hour, especially in the rain. It precludes all self-interest, all self-deception. My friend's face gleamed with mist and innocence.

"If you took me to your Virginia Commission or whatever it is," he said. "If you fed me to them. 'Here's the guilty bastard who took down Roanoke.' Would they be satisfied? Stop baying the trail and let the women alone, let them live?"

"I thought you wanted justice. We'll untangle it. We'll find out who—"

"Who was pulling the strings that pulled the strings of the one who was pulling the strings of the string-puller?" He stood poised there, the rain dripping off him. "Oh, Rob. What if it all just went to hell in a handcart? It did, you know, in the end. I saw it. Six directions at once. Storms. Gold-fever. Indian wars. Comfort to believe in some great ironhearted bastard who made it all happen. God knows, it's kept me alive these years, hating the bugger. But Christ,

Robbie." He turned to fix me with those terrible eyes. "What if the world just caves in on you? What if there are no strings at all?"

"So she's dead, then," I said suddenly. "Naia's dead."

"No! What? No!"

"But she must be. You wouldn't talk of throwing yourself to that pack of wolves if she weren't. You'd keep fighting."

"Alive or dead." His voice cracked. The crack ran deep, through his chest, through his belly, all the way to his balls. "I betrayed her."

"You don't mean with the women."

"Worse. Much worse."

"How, then? Why?"

He shook his head, trying to pull back. "It's late now. You lose sight of things late at night. Say mad things."

"But this betrayal—"

"She'll forgive me. I know her. Shuffle the pieces about till it all comes clear to her. Draw one of her God-circles round me and scour my soul."

O UR NEXT MEETING took place during the festivities to welcome the dowdy little Duke of Aufmahlen-Koblenz to Elizabeth's court. It was at Greenwich, one of the many nights of fireworks that spangled the Thames that April. We were, of course, not within the palace grounds, but the liveried guilds and companies took the opportunity to hold lavish dinners of their own, with musicians to play for dancing afterwards, a company of players— I played the Third Servant—and the royal fireworks for a huge, fiery sweetmeat at the end.

I was stabbed to death in the second act and when I had transformed myself back to what served me as normal, I found Gabriel waiting.

We moved through the crowd to a dark corner in the court-yard. Cooks minded the roasting fires where three whole pigs and twenty-five swans turned on the spits, and servants raced in and out with huge chargers of roast larks, poached salmon and turbot, cabbage stuffed with spiced meat, new asparagus, strawberries and clotted cream, eight kinds of bread, and twelve kinds of wine.

The music of lutes and gitterns and recorders drifted out from the windows, and we could hear, now and then, the soft whoosh of three dozen or more silken skirts as the men took the girls by their waists and lifted them high off the floor, swirled them round, then handed them to a new partner. From a barge on the river, the fireworks began, a huge spiral of fire like a golden dragon's tail.

"I have to meet Rowland and Harry tomorrow," I said.

"Sooner you than me. What'll you tell them?"

"That I can't get hold of you. That you're dead. Or have you definitely decided to turn yourself over to them and be flayed alive?"

"Nay, why give 'em a half-day's free entertainment? I'll see it through."

More fireworks. Comets shooting blindly out into the darkness. A Catherine wheel was lighted on the barge, then another and another and another, leaving great swirls of pale smoke on the sky. Trumpets sounded from all the palace gates and guards with torches stood to attention on the towers. It was the Queen's Goodnight, Her Majesty leaving the festivities for her private apartments.

"I want to talk to Kit," I said. "He's gotten drunk with almost everybody in London at least once. He's sure to know something useful."

Like Simon Fernando, the poet Christopher Marlowe was one of Walsingham's spiders. Gabriel and I had known him since

Cambridge, and when he made friends—which was seldom—he made them forever. But he could be a risky fellow to be seen with.

"Robbie," said Gabriel with a sudden urgency. "Don't meet Kit tomorrow. Don't meet anybody. Find a hole and crawl into it."

"Your nerves are gone, my friend. It's no risk for me to see Marlowe. I've got an official excuse. I'm an actor."

"Bollocks. Couldn't act your way out of a sack. At least promise to stay clear of Toady and Ratsbane. Send them a message in onion juice. Say you've got the pox."

The music inside the hall ended and a stream of guests began to leave. We attached ourselves to them, but as we passed from the yard into the street, I felt something tug at my sleeve. It was a ragged little boy of eight or nine.

"If you please, master," he said, "there's an old gentleman wants a word with you."

"What old gentleman?"

"Oooh, a rich one with a furred gown and a fine velvet cap and a gold chain. Long white beard. Walks with a stick, he does."

It sounded for all the world like Lord Burghley. "Don't," said Gabriel sharply. Then the crowd separated us, and I lost sight and sound of him.

If it really was Burghley, braving his gout and a trip on the river, he must have something of great importance to tell me, something too dangerous to entrust to a messenger. The boy kept tugging at me and I couldn't resist; I followed him to the nearest river stairs, where a small boat without a lantern was bobbing. I dug into my purse for a coin, but when I turned to find him, the boy had disappeared.

I got into the boat and the oarsman pulled out into the current. He was short and stocky and he kept muttering to himself in what might've been Polish for all I could make of it. We bumped the shore by a river stair at the bottom of somebody's garden and he pointed in the direction of a bower covered with leafless vines. "Who lives here?" I asked him, but he said nothing.

I GET OUT and wait for a moment or two by the steps while he pushes the boat out again. The river is busy, wherry lanterns bobbing in the smoky darkness. Fireworks still going off.

The garden rises steeply from the riverbank, and a broad flag-stone path leads through yew bushes clipped into the shapes of elephants, camels, and lions. I see no one at first, but as I approach the bower I hear something—a light tapping sound. Wood on stone. A walking stick. The heel of a shoe. A foot stamping? Once. Twice. Three times.

Otherwise, it is all done in silence. As though by furious ghosts, I am seized from behind and my arms pinned. I try to kick, to bite, to butt with my head—all useless. I count four pairs of feet—the four leopards who came to Annette's house? No slippers and no coats of arms, only old scuffed boots. I manage to kick one man and he doubles over, yowling. Something leaden crashes into the back of my head, and for a little while, I die.

When I come alive again, it is to a hell of methodical blows that are slowly caving in my rib cage and filling my mouth with blood. Two men hold me while a second pair beat me, great crashing punches to the face, the chest, the belly, the groin, the kidneys. I am helpless. I am nothing. I am being ground away.

They begin to kick me, rolling me from side to side. I fight to remain conscious on some level. If I can see something, hear something, smell something, that will let me find them again, and if by some miracle I survive, I will kill those men. Stick my dagger in their backs if I get the chance, strangle them by a roadside, sink them in the Thames, tear them to pieces, rack them, pull out their fingernails, feed them lye. Cruelty like a warm light floods all through me. I have become Topcliffe.

The blows go on and on, and all the while the leopards never utter a word, never demand information, never speak my name. Then it all stops, so suddenly that I wonder for a flicker of a second if I am on some stage somewhere, if I ought to get up and wipe off the sheep's-liver blood from my face. Wait for the applause and take a bow.

I can only lie still, my mouth full of real blood and grass and broken teeth, my head jerked to one side. Vaguely, through battered senses, I seem to hear the tapping sound again. One, two, three, four. Footsteps on the flagstones. Wooden heels, a little unsteady, the foot coming down hard as a hoof. Am I in another plot now, a different play?

Then he is there, looking down at me, Gabriel's ironhearted bastard is real. I can feel him standing over me and I want to see him. I try to open my eyes, but they are swollen shut, the lashes matted with blood. Do I smell oil of clove, or do I dream it?

The leopards pick me up by my wrists and ankles and carry me down to the river stair. The pain is worse than before and I cannot even scream; my mouth and throat are clamped tight, thick with blood. I feel the four men begin to swing me out and back, out and back, until they let go and I soar free of them. My mind is suddenly clear as glass and I know I am being thrown into the river to drown.

I feel a strange surge of relief just before I hit the water, as though I have been waiting all my life for this ultimate freedom. I am out of my sealed box at last. I have absolutely nothing to lose.

My body curls around itself, knees pulled up and head tucked under. The water is cold for April, and perhaps it is that cold that strengthens me. I fight my way up through water weeds and schools of tiny baitfish and break the surface downstream a bit from the landing stair. I try to float on the current, but my arms and legs won't obey me and I keep going under and having to struggle back up again. But I do struggle. God knows why.

The cold water washes my eyelids open temporarily. From the barge downriver comes the last great glorious burst of fireworks, like hundreds of candles being tossed up into the sky and raining down on the water. All those wherries and I cannot make a sound to attract them. My tongue is huge and my throat only gurgles.

"Try over here," says a voice. Then, by the light of the fireworks, I see a blur moving slowly towards me on the water. A boat. I thrash with my hands and make ridiculous wordless noises, rest a moment, then try again.

My eyes are swelling shut once more, but dimly I see the wherryman take his lantern from the standard and swing it out over the river, searching for something. Not for me, surely. Who in God's name would be searching for me?

"There! Row closer. Be careful."

There is a soft splash in the water and the sound of somebody swimming a few yards, dog-paddling awkwardly, his feet seeking the shallow, sandy bottom. An arm grabs me around the waist and the swimmer flails wildly with his feet. Once or twice we both go under.

"I can't," Gabriel sputters, fighting to hold on to me with his one usable arm. "For God's sake, man, lend a hand here."

Another arm seizes mine, a huge strength, and between them the two men heave me into the boat. A hard hand pushes my wet hair from my face. "Christ almighty, these bastards," growls the voice of Matthias Rands. "Well, get him settled, then. You tip her over, swear to God I'll let the pair of you sink."

forty-one

O Gentle Faustus,
Leave Thy Damnèd Art

WHEN I WOKE, I WAS IN THE BACK OF A CART ON THE ROAD TO
somewhere. I had no idea who was driving or where I
was going. I could hear the creak of the wooden wheels and my
bruises felt every rut in the road.

My eyes were swollen shut again and I couldn't speak or ask
questions. My old habit of watching without involvement had
been turned into a vengeance upon me.

I fell asleep to the creaking of the cart wheels and when next I
woke, it was to a sense of morning, with sun on my face and a
goosefeather mattress beneath me. The swelling around my ears
and my nose had declined enough to let in the distant twittering
of sparrows and the fragrance of newly mown grass. I lay on my
side, naked, carefully propped up with blankets and draped with
a linen sheet. My ribs had been tightly bound and there was a
poultice that smelled of camphor and herbs tied with cloth bands
to the small of my back.

I heard footsteps. A woman's, light and mouselike. She approached the bed and I could sense her eyes upon me though I
couldn't see her. I tried to reach out a hand to her but my arms felt

as though they had lead weights fastened onto them. Instead I moved my fingers.

Her feet trotted quickly away. "Madge!" she called softly. "He's waking."

A heavier tread and a swoosh of skirts. A fragrance of mint, camphor, rosemary, and new-baked bread. Madge Lawrence put a warm, plump hand to my forehead. "Can you speak?" she said. I tried, but couldn't manage. "Never mind. You've bitten that tongue of yours. It needs time, is all."

And Madge. Busy every hour of the day, she was, but the nights in that place—

I could do nothing but take her hand when she gave it. A broad, capable hand, calloused, the thick knuckles starting to show her age. Yet the touch was subtle, tender. A good hand to hold across a table in the dark.

"Gabriel sent you to us," she said. "By means of some fellow called Beachum or Teachum or Peachum? He was eager to stay and help, but it was not wise. We dare not draw attention to ourselves. It's only a small village."

I heard the sound of water poured into a bowl and she laid a cool cloth on my throbbing face. "Agnes will come in with her sewing," she said, "and sit by you to rinse out the cloth now and then. Try to sleep for a bit. I've prepared a soporific, and something for the pain."

The drug made me sleep a long while, borne back into the little world of the cottage only now and then. When at last I woke fully, I found I could open my eyes. My vision was still blurred, but I could make out Agnes's shape against the light from the small, deep-silled window where she bent over her stitching. *Agnes Wood, spinster. No fortune. No living relations. All nerves, really. Like a grass in the wind.*

Her cough was not so harsh now. A danger-cough, I thought, that worsens when the world tightens its screws. She looked up from her sewing to find me watching her. "Oh, praise God," she murmured. "Madge? Oh, Madge, he's better at last!"

Better? I could not have said so. I was alive, that was all I knew.

Something had gone from me in that garden lit by the fireworks of hell, or perhaps it had come to me, rather than gone. Once I studied my own face for nearly an hour in Madge's steel looking glass, as though I were confronted by a page written in some unknown language, long ago fallen into disuse.

I remained with the two women for almost a month. May Day came and went again. June approached, and still Gabriel put in no appearance and sent me no word. Had he gone to find Naia? Had he been arrested? Was he dead?

There was no sign of leopards or black horses. Perhaps they were convinced they were rid of me and thought themselves free to concentrate on Gabriel and the others. I was safe in Madge's clean little kingdom, but if I stayed any longer, I might become a danger to her and to Aggie. So I made a spiderish exit. Without a good-bye, I tiptoed out of the cottage at daybreak and cadged a ride in a brogger's cart bound for London, trying to lay plans as I went.

I had hoped to worm something out of Rowland and Harry, but as the Scripture says, the truth was not in them. Kit Marlowe had once had great truth in him, whether he made free of it or not. I decided to find him, but I stopped at a Holborn cookshop first for a breakfast of bread, bacon, and beer. As I left I was delighted to catch sight of Peachum limping along with his bag of tools and his little cobbler's bench.

"I'm that glad to see you!" he said, wringing my hand. "Heard you was dead. Then Master Nick comes and says would I haul you to some village or other, and keep close about it." He tapped the side of his nose with a knobbly forefinger. "Oooh, you did look like an old pair of broke boots."

"And you didn't miss a bump on the road, you old fright. Have there been any more visitors at Dame Phoebe's?"

He frowned. "They come while I was out and about, sir. Fair tore your room to splinters. Took your pile of scribblings clean away, I'm sorry to tell you. Ooh, and Arabelle's dead."

"How? When?"

"Fished her out of the Thames the day I come home from the country. Washed up against the pilings of London Bridge."

"Drowned?"

"Throat cut before she was sunk. Been some while in the water, that's what Deborah said."

It was often the fate of informers. But Arabelle had been young, not very clever, hard-used, and thus easily tempted. After what she'd done to Nick, I had thought I would rejoice if her treachery caught up to her. I found I could not.

"I've a bit of other news," Peachum said. "Remember them shoes with the coat of arms on 'em that Master Nick spoke of? He went round with me to the Embroiderers' Guild after all, and old Ducket give us a look at their books of stitching patterns."

"Devil take embroidery! I told Nick to keep out of this."

"I wouldn't worry, sir. Ducket's a safe hand. Took us two days to get through all them livery patterns, but we finally found one that fit the reckoning. Quartered in red, with two quarters bosky and green, and the other two bearing jugs overflowing with water, painted in blue."

"Bosky? You mean trees?"

"Aye, sir. Grove. Forest."

"Or wood. And the jars— Full! Fullwood. Naturally."

"One William Fullwood, Gent. Fine house out at Richmond. Recently deceased. They was about to move the pattern to the Unlikelies, there being no heirs and no title."

"Ah, but he had hopes, Peach. He once had hopes. Proud of his new Roanoke coat of arms and plastering it onto everything, including his servant's shoes. And very likely decking himself out in high heels and court laces." I clapped Peachum on the back. "Blackmail. Extortion. Fullwood knew how to squeeze and in the end, he squeezed himself to death. Well done, old friend."

So I knew who two of the three men at Nico's racking had been—Fullwood and Fernando, one dead and the other missing, very likely at the bottom of the Thames. That left only the cold, silent bastard who commanded the leopards and made the earth cave in, the man with the strange foot and the black satin slippers. Did he command Rowland and Harry, too? Or was he himself under someone's orders?

The old game, you see, still pounced on me at the most unpredictable moments. Decipher the coded message. Read the invisible writing. Then add up the pieces, a neat syllogism of which Aristotle himself would be proud.

But logic was a myth for smug university boys. In that split second between life and death, as my battered body sailed out over the Thames, I had finally looked into the matrix that determines which human fragment strikes which, and when, and how hard, and to what purpose. If I knew nothing more, I knew it defied every rule of our game.

I TOOK A WHERRY across the Thames to Southwark and the Rose Theatre, where the Admiral's Men were preparing a performance of Marlowe's *Faustus,* to open on the last day of May.

The playwright was nowhere in sight, but Kit had always preferred taking his friends by surprise. If he *was* here, he'd be lurking in the gallery stalls or under the stage where Mephistopheles kept track of the prompt book and rose through the trapdoor to torment Faust.

Philip Henslowe, who owned and managed the Rose, was doing what he usually did—loaning money at illegal interest to whichever players and poets were short of the chinks. "Ah, pretty Robin," he said, giving me a toothless grin. "How much will it be? Good rate this week. Shall we say ten shillings? In six months, at forty per cent, calculated daily—"

"I haven't come to borrow money, you old thief. I need a place to sleep. Can you find me a spare corner in the tiring-rooms?"

Henslowe clicked his tongue. "Horned another husband, have you? Ow, and he's had his licks on your face already. Nothing better than a poultice of grated raw apple for that. On the table there. Ten pence each."

I threw a shilling down. "May I sleep here or not?"

"You may, you may. But if I might suggest—I have a fine house of pleasure not half a mile from here, where that coin and another like it would buy you not only a bed but the tender embrace of—"

"The embrace of a poxy old madam who will labor over you like a fat jockey on a thin horse and leave you breeding contagion for the rest of your life." It was Kit Marlowe, entering on cue as usual. "My dear Robin, do come in back and have a glass of canary." He turned to Henslowe. "He can sleep under the stage, you tightfisted old ponce. No one will find him there but the Devil, and I'm sure *he* won't mind."

Kit was just as I remembered him—slight as a girl and barely five feet tall, with a narrow face, a head of dark crinkly hair that stood out like a lion's mane, and huge luminous eyes.

"How's the Roanoke play?" he said. He spoke with a slight Cambridge lisp—which, thank God, I had never acquired. "Still not beyond the prologue? I thought you might have discovered a proper ending at last. From what I hear."

He knew. Kit always knew everything. Gibbie had told him or perhaps Wat Ralegh had told him. They were friends, they spent days and weeks together at Ralegh's place down in Dorset—talking philosophy, blasphemy, mathematics, politics, or one of the new sciences nobody else approved of. Reading their poems aloud and getting drunk on contraband Spanish wine.

Marlowe led me to a small room behind the stage with its own door onto the alley where the tradesmen and stage carpenters came and went. There was a table heaped with manuscript pages held down by two human skulls. By the table, a chair, its back draped with black velvet embroidered in silver. On the opposite wall, a narrow bed covered with a fine piece of French tapestry. Kit lounged on the bed as usual, and left the chair to me.

"Like it?" he said, stroking the bedcover. "I do things up. Can't bear grubby places. You could sleep here, but you can never tell when the Queen's Council may decide to arrest me and you wouldn't like to be nabbed by mistake. They forged some idiotic account of my blasphemous opinions and Her Pissing Majesty believed every word of it. Credulous cow. So now I have to report to the palace every day and sign my name, just to be sure they can get their hands on me in a hurry and hang my insides out to dry."

"You don't seem very worried."

"Which of them ought to concern me? That old ewe Burghley? Or his son, Crooked Nancy?"

He meant Robert Cecil. "I'm told he's very clever," I said.

"I had an uncle taught a pig to count to ten. Now, *that's* intelligence. Cecil's a clockwork. When he farts, there's a ticking sound." He looked at me over a silver goblet of wine. "He hates me because Ralegh likes me. Thinks we're laughing at him. Quite right, too. They were friends once, did you know that?"

"But no longer?"

Marlowe laughed. "Oh, Ralegh still thinks so. I've tried to disabuse him, but it's no use. He can't imagine why anybody wouldn't take advantage of the opportunity to adore him."

"And serve his interests. He trusted Simon Fernando to do that."

"Very little choice. The Council insisted on Fernando, Walsingham recommended him. Ralegh owed most of them money. *Ergo*."

"Was Fernando ever set to the rack, Kit? By Topcliffe, I mean?"

"What year?"

"The autumn of 'eighty-seven. When the empty ships came back from Roanoke."

He shrugged. "Walsingham didn't order it, I'm sure of that. Still keeping his head down after the Scots queen lost hers. Out of favor just then, didn't dare risk much. None of them did, not even old Burghley."

"And now? Is Fernando living?"

"You won't find him in a grave, darling. But there are women and little boys from here to the Azores who've breathed a sigh of relief." His huge eyes stroked me. "You're meant to be dead yourself, you know. If you don't oblige them on the first try, they take on increased zeal."

"It wasn't the first try. The first time they sent a boy on a horse to ride me down."

"No, no, that wasn't a boy. Somebody's slut. I forget whose. Arabella Somebody. I heard of it in a tavern the day after."

Arabelle. And now she was dead and safely beyond my questions, or anyone else's. Fullwood was dead. Fernando. How many more still unknown?

"There were four bullies this last time," I told Kit. "And it was meant to be permanent, I promise you. Who controls them? Whose toes have I trodden on?"

Marlowe's fingers played with a sheet of manuscript, pushed it aside. Played with another. "Have you found Gabriel?" he said at last.

"Suppose I do. What does your master have in mind for him?"

"No man on this earth is my master," he said in a low, furious voice. Then he smiled. "Such fellows as you speak of are dross, Robin. Forget them. The universe shits. Now and then it makes pearls. But we dare not live in gorgeous expectation."

I took another tack. "Of all the men in England, who hates Ralegh enough to ruin him?"

"Oh, they all do. They were all hoping the old vixen would keep him in the Tower for good, but she's let him out again. She needs him. He'll be back at court in a year."

"So they hated him enough to arrange for Roanoke to fail and ruin him. But who had power enough to make sure of it? Walsingham? He had at least three spies on board those ships."

Kit smiled. "He had money in the colony, so he spied on his money."

"What about Leicester?"

"Couldn't afford the bribes."

"Hatton?"

"Thought much too well of himself."

I was ready to scream. "It's hopeless. I just keep chasing my own tail."

"You've forgotten someone. Who was spying for Elizabeth before Walsingham ever set foot in Whitehall? Whose influence at court hasn't faltered in forty years? Who has had to look for a decade now at his own bunched-up muddle of an offspring standing next to the handsomest man in England and pretending to love him? Clockwork Nan even asked Her Majesty to dance once, can you believe it? The poor fool, with those splayed feet of his? It was Ralegh's idea, that ridiculous dance."

I wouldn't have called Robert Cecil splayfooted, exactly. His weight was out of balance and he came down too hard on his heels. But his feet *did* turn out a bit. Off his guard and with no one to impress, he might give more rein to his imperfections. Certainly it was he who had persuaded Elizabeth to allow the

Roanoke ships out of port, and he'd been adamant about refusing special license to the search party.

But I didn't believe it. Cecil, in league with the likes of Willie Fullwood? Never. And the idea of Burghley himself being involved was ridiculous.

"Whatever motives his son may have had," I said, "the success of that venture was in the queen's interests, and Burghley's almost a father to her, you know that. He may have cared nothing for the colonists, but he would never countenance such a plot, let alone take part in it."

"Perhaps not. But whatever Nan's doing, whatever he's already done, Burghley will protect him. By any means necessary."

"Then why hasn't Gabriel been arrested?"

He laughed. "So you *have* found him, then."

"I didn't say that!"

"Of course you did. I knew nothing, and now I know everything you don't know and almost everything you do. Game, set, match. The universe shits, darling. Sometimes it shits poets. Sometimes it shits crookbacks and spies."

forty-two

THIS NETTLE, DANGER

GABRIEL WAS SIMPLY GONE. I WALKED AND WAITED AND KEPT TO THE shadows, hoping he would find me. I haunted every river stair where we'd ever met. I watched the entrance to St. Walburga's for days. I even risked sending a message to Madge, with Peach's help. But there was no word, no sign of the man anywhere.

At last, I couldn't bear waiting any longer. Hoping to find him with some of the other womenfolk he'd brought home, I determined to go looking. I stole a false beard and some cast-off nobleman's clothes from the costume basket at the Rose—claret velvet doublet, pleated ruff and fine cambric shirt, grey woollen breeches and high kidskin riding boots. I had to hire a really good horse to match the clothes, but I passed through London and took the road for Cornwall without a moment's disturbance.

So far as I could tell, I was not followed, and just as Gibbie had said, I found Alis Chapman carding wool by the kitchen hearth of Davy Shand's snug cottage. She was hardly forthcoming at first: I told her all I dared, but it took hours before she would trust me. She and her child were at peace with the old man, and she meant to keep it so—and I could hardly blame her. In that room with its

bunches of dried herbs hanging from the rafters, its pewter chargers and copper pots gleaming, and its oaken floor scoured and
scattered with clean rushes, she told me of her life on the
Roanoke. It was like hearing about the daily life of some ancient,
ravaged world—Persia, Lydia, Egypt. Even her voice when she
spoke of it was old.

"You've seen nothing of Gabriel?" I said when she fell silent.

"No, sir. Not since he left us here. Middle of March, that was.
Just before Lent."

"Where's Naia? Gabriel thinks he's betrayed her. What's happened to her, to her children? Was she captured by the Spanish?
By one of the tribes?"

"The tribes? No. Nor killed."

"But you were captured."

"By the tribes, yes. Emma and I. A few others. We were easy
pickings by that time."

"So Leatha's father . . . ?"

"He was Chowanok, I think. We ran away after a few months."

"We?"

"Emma and me. Winnie had been sold to the Powhatan, they were
far away to the north. A runner came from the Mandoag to buy slaves
for their copper mines, men and women. They work many to death,
and we knew we could not live long, and me with the child in me. So
we took our chance, we two. When we reached the Roanoke, we
found a sign Georgie carved on a post for us, in case any of us got free.
We made our way to Croatoan, where the others were then. Emma
married a man of their people. Manteo, they called him, but she
called him Matthew. He was killed just before—"

"Before what?"

Silence.

"I mean Gabriel no harm," I assured her, "nor any of you. But
I've learned things he ought to know, for his own safety. And
yours. If he's still in England, where would he go?"

"Oh," she said, "it would always be Emma he'd go to. He fathers her, brothers her. She'd claw the eyes out of a panther to keep him from any more harm." She laughed. "It's how Emma registers love."

Next day I bought a place on a boat out of Truro bound for that dip in the east coast called The Wash, where the rich soil of the Fens washes out to the North Sea with the annual floods.

Stokesby Abbey, where Emma and her little half-Croatoan son lived, lay on a narrow strip of land between the sea and a water-locked village called Market Sweffling. In King Henry's time, before the break with Rome, Stokesby had been a foundation of the Grey Friars and part of the house retained its monastic character, with a long arched porch fronting the gardens where the monks had once paced at their beads. I paid for a ride on a cart coming up from Long Sutton and arrived just as it was getting dark.

"Who's there?" said a rickety voice from the other side of the heavy door that gave onto the stables and the kitchen garden.

"A traveller," I said. "The dark's caught me and I won't risk these roads in the nighttime. I'd like to buy a meal and a bed in the straw, if your master doesn't object."

The door slowly creaked open. The old footman shuffled away through the scullery and into the kitchen, and I could hear him talking to someone. I caught a glimpse of a small dark-skinned boy with big brown eyes and thick, dark hair in a fringe over his forehead. He was a bit younger than Alis's Leatha, but not much.

"Matthew!" a woman's voice called to him. "Get yourself in here and scour them hands before supper."

"Yes, Nama," he said, and skittered away.

"What did I tell you about calling me that?"

"I'm sorry."

"No, you're not, you plaguey little rabbit."

Giggling and the sounds of a brief rough-and-tumble, then a swat on his bottom and a noisy kiss. In another moment, his mother appeared, wiping her hands on her apron.

"I'm told you want to buy supper," she said. She was just as Gabriel had described her—round in all the right places, fair-haired and bold-eyed. "Ten pence'll buy you fresh-baked bread and cabbage boiled with mutton. You can sleep in the stables, but make sure you're gone by daybreak."

"Thank you, Mistress Emma," I said.

She gazed at me, the tip of her tongue peeping out between her teeth. "There was a cook here called Emma Soams once," she said. "But she's gone now. I ain't her. You can eat in the scullery. Don't want you making eyes at the maids."

"Your boy's handsome. I knew a Croatoan prince once. His name was Manteo, but the English called *him* Matthew."

The full lips closed tight. The blue eyes narrowed. "Wash your hands. Be a few minutes yet."

"You're a fine cook," I said, when I'd finished my supper. "Excellent mutton. What's the seasoning? Dried lily root?"

It was too much. She swirled around. "Who the devil are you? What do you want?"

"Gabriel. I need to find him, Emma. Things in London are coming to a head. It would help if you'd trust me."

"Think I'm a mug? Don't trust nobody."

"Except your Gander."

"How do you know that name? Who told you?"

"He did. Gabriel. And Madge spoke of it, and Alis Chapman."

"You've seen them? Are they settled? Are they well? Oh, and how's Alis's limp?"

"Either it's disappeared," I said with a grin, "or she never had one and you're trying to catch me out."

She risked a smile. "Well, all right. Come into the kitchen.

There's strawberry tarts for pudding. But you can't have more than the one."

I asked no more questions until the maids had finished in the scullery and the old footman had creaked off to his bed. Emma motioned me to a place on the fireside settle while she sorted some raisins and put them to soak. "Will you tell me where Gabriel's gone?" I said.

"Oh, he'll be back soon. Went tearing to London on Monday. Friend of his got himself murdered. Some famous player or the like."

"Not Marlowe? Christopher Marlowe?"

"Kit, he said. Yes, that was it."

For a moment I couldn't compass it. But it was almost a fortnight since I left London, and anything might've happened. Emma studied my stricken face, then rummaged in a cupboard and brought out a jug of *aqua vitae*. She poured each of us a mugful and sat down by my side.

"You told me you had questions," she said. "I've answered but one of 'em so far. And now I've told you what you didn't want to hear."

"Kit Marlowe was a friend. We'd both known him a long time. How did Gabriel learn of it?"

"Went up to Peterborough on market day to fetch me a loaf of sugar. Players at the inn there talked of it. Didn't talk very loud, though."

We both sat in silence for a while, sipping the strong caraway-flavored liquor. "As to the questions," I said at last. "What about Naia?"

She smiled. "Come up trumps, she did."

I managed a smile in return. "So you don't hold her tattoos against her anymore?"

"Hah. Got some myself now. Want to see?"

"Is she safe? Alis says she's still living."

Her open features seemed to close and then to lock. "Can't say, can I? Death comes slipping in when you least expect him. Breathe him in the air. Eat him in a bowl of cabbage. Sleep with him in your arms at night." She poured us another mug of drink. "They was living when I seen 'em last, that's all I can tell you. Her and the sprouts."

"But where is she? Why hasn't she come with you?"

"Lord, you're a worse plague than Matthew. Told you all I can."

"Just one more question. The men who went looking for gold—were they all lost?"

"One or two come back with the marsh fever and died after. Mad as loons, they was. Some was took far inland by the tribes, slaving to dig copper. Most died in the Indian wars." She sat staring into the mug of liquor.

I liked her. I could have cared for her, but I didn't want to. I didn't want any more women. "Your Indian husband," I murmured. "Matthew. Did he love you?"

She flared up. "Think because he was a savage he had no feelings? None of your damn business anyway. He's dead."

"I shouldn't have asked it. I'll go. Shall I go?"

I went out into the gravelled yard, bound for my bed in the stable. But Emma's voice followed me from the scullery door, echoing out across the foggy Essex darkness.

"I never took no stock in love," she said. "Lot of sugar-tit mush, to smear over the poking and grunting, that's what I thought. But I see now. Love is strong as hate, and it's cruel-heavy. Not much odds, is it? If you ain't up to the load."

forty-three

HOW HE BETRAYED HER

"POOR OLD KIT," GABRIEL SAID.

He returned to Stokesby two days later, looking weary but all in one piece.

"How did he die?" I asked him. "Another street brawl? One of his jealous gentleman-lovers?"

"Worse. He met Frizer and Pooley at one of Walsingham's safe houses in Deptford."

"Dear God. *Those* two?"

"He got a message that afternoon, telling him to go to Deptford and sign in instead of going to the palace. You know about his having to report to the agent of the Queen's Council every day? All bollocks. They'd fixed up the whole thing and he walked straight into it. Frizer put a dagger in Kit's eye. Coroner came at dead of night and declared it self-defense. Papers all neatly signed and sealed and filed away. Kit was six feet under before the next sunrise. Greatest poet since Chaucer. He was, you know. Theatres don't even dare mourn him. Business as bluddy usual."

"Christ." Another name to add to the mounting list of the Roanoke dead.

Gabriel looked over at me, his eyes endless tunnels that had ceased to lead anywhere. "Ingraham Frizer was one of your leopards, Robbie. Now that Walsingham's dead, he works for Cecil."

Cecil had the queen's seal at his command, he could use his father's spiders without raising suspicion. But not Walsingham's, not unless he had stolen those papers on the night of the old fox's death. And we didn't know he'd stolen them. We didn't know how Harry and Rowland came into it. Besides, maybe it made too *much* sense to blame Cecil. Maybe it was part of some other game entirely.

"We're making too many assumptions," I said. "Whatever happened to Kit, it still doesn't prove Robert Cecil was behind what happened to the Roanoke venture. There may have been no connection."

I feared my visit that day had brought Kit's death upon him. I didn't want to see a connection.

"All those people on the ships," Gabriel whispered. "Archard, dreaming of the inn he would build. The parson. Harris the schoolmaster. Gentle Janet. Why, Robbie? If it *was* Cecil—why the hell punish *them?*"

"I don't think they mattered, whoever was behind it. They made it plausible, that's all. That many people, willing to go out and settle."

"The bigger the venture, the harder the fall."

"Ralegh staked everything, including his standing at court and his friendship with Elizabeth. And according to Kit, Cecil hates him. Ralegh teased him and made him look foolish. Ralegh's handsome and Cecil's not. Ralegh can dance and Cecil limps. But we still have no proof—"

Gabriel swept his good arm across Emma's table, sending her wooden spoons flying. "I'm not taking the fucking bastard to court! I don't need proof!"

"Well, why not just execute all of them? Walsingham and

Leicester are dead, but there are always their wives and children. And Ralegh, of course. And Elizabeth—you can't excuse her. God knows how much she knew and what she didn't bother to put a stop to. Because— Because she trusted him. Ralegh. Because she *wanted* his dreams. Anybody's dreams. He has courage, brains. A heart, I think. I think so. And she loved him, for a while. At least she tried to. Needed to. She did, and he wasn't good enough, or he was past loving by that time, or— No. He *did* love her. He *did*."

I was not really speaking of Ralegh and Elizabeth. "Go and get your French girl," Gabriel said quietly. "Take her out of this mess."

"It's no use. She wants nothing to do with me now." I stood up to face him. "But I'll go anywhere you like, if you'll give up this hopeless vengeance. You can't possibly win."

"I can't just stop. They were *people*, not mice! If Cecil's responsible, then he must pay, and if not him, then someone else. It needs justice, Rob, and not only for the English who died. If I don't see to it, who will? The queen's bluddy Council?"

"All right, then. What about Tesik and his death squad? And who ordered the hurricane? Or will you kill the wind and the sea?"

His good fist slammed the table. "You don't punish a sword, you punish the bastard who used it!"

"So. You'll be Rafe Lane, then, and kill God."

Just then Emma's Matthew came rollicking through the room with his hobbyhorse and stopped in his tracks. Gabriel looked over at him and the anger suddenly withdrew.

"Hello, sprout," he said. "Want a game of knucklebones? Beat me last time, bet you can't do it again." He reached into his pocket and drew out something wrapped in a twist of cheap cloth. "Here now, who put this in my pocket? Sweetmeats? Sugared almonds? Nobody here wants sugared almonds, do they?"

It wasn't possible, I thought, that the same Gabriel who played bears and knucklebones with three-year-olds could walk into Robert Cecil's mansion and kill him in cold blood, or kill anyone else. But if he'd really betrayed his Naia, he was capable of anything. Perhaps I no longer knew him, any more than I knew myself.

T ELL ME the rest of it."

"Hell with you. Sick of your piddling."

"If I'm likely to be pulled apart from four directions and have my guts stretched, I've got a right to know all of it. Was it the Spanish? Is that how it ended, a Spanish invasion?"

We burrow into the straw in the Stokesby stables that night. It is a good place for truth-telling, a warm, sapient darkness smelling of ox and cow and nanny goat, of what is undeniable and real.

In that dense darkness, he seems shaken as I have not seen him before, almost afraid of his own mind, of what he will have to remember. He needs help with this last part of it, and I give what I can—cueing him when he falters, trying to calm him when his voice falters.

"Alis said you went to Croatoan."

"The English went there. Not me."

"Ass. You *are* English."

"I am who I am. People don't have countries. Countries have them."

"What year was it?"

"Christ, how do I know? Winter came and then spring came. I think winter came again. A year, maybe two."

We both fall silent then, and I almost think he has gone to sleep. The ox lows mournfully. The nanny goat watches us with a philosophical smirk.

"The Spanish ship," I finally prompt. "There *was* a ship, was there?"

"That's enough, now. When we've found the bastard and faced him down. When it's finished. Then I'll tell you the rest."

But Naia is waiting for him somewhere, she must be. It should have been Masu and Kia eating those sugared almonds. And I have left Annette staring into an empty future for which I must somehow atone.

"I'm better at court politics than you are," I tell him. "You'll just put your great foot in it. Let me find a safe way to finish it and then you can come home and settle down."

"You poor fool!" He sits up too suddenly, the bad shoulder yanking at him. "I can't ever come home. Oh, don't you see? I'm a bluddy traitor. Why did you think I kept running? We're still at war and I've been these four years in a Spanish prison, betraying every secret I could think of, and making a good many up."

THE ANSWER TO saving the others had first come to him, he said, during that long-ago night he spent locked up in Lane's tiny prison house, rocking Masumeo to sleep while I watched from outside. Not the method, but the reason. The luminous sense of the rightness of things.

In that smothering darkness, knowing Lane might hang him for comforting the enemy, he had scraped out of himself everything but the ultimate motives. Killing had never been one of them. Profit had never concerned him. He had never been loyal to governments, religions, public fictions of any kind. How could they define right and wrong when they were so often broken and dangerous themselves? All his life he had failed those who valued the fictions above everything else—his father, his girls' mother, his Puritan sister. He had never understood why they called him a silly fool and a wastrel. They didn't know, he told me, but to him it had all become suddenly clear.

The right thing, the human thing, was merely the one thing that you could not *not* do, even if you died for it.

AFTER THE FIRST cataclysm, the ruin of Roanoke unfolded an inch at a time. Instead of going with the others to Croatoan, he and Naia and the sprouts remained in the little hut on the sand island. A year of tribal warfare went by, and then another. The fighting ebbed in the cold months and then rose like a spring flood when the weather warmed; whenever the war parties came too near, the family would hide in the forest, then come back again, repair things, replace what they could. Once or twice Spanish ships were wrecked somewhere at sea, and bits of Spanish lives washed ashore on the islands. A bottle containing a printed page of Castilian verses. A woman's tortoise-shell comb once set with pearls that the ocean had reclaimed.

His shoulder healed slowly and he began trying himself, teaching himself to do things in the unconventional ways his battered body now made necessary. "Help me with the boat," he told Masu one afternoon. "And don't tell your mother."

The boy frowned. "All right. But if this shoulder gets worse, you must not let her blame me. Where do you want this boat? In this stream or on this pond?"

"On the shore, old chap. The sea."

They pulled the reed boat out of its covert and dragged it through the gap in the dunes and down to the beach. Light as it was, it needed only one paddle, but he managed no more than a few awakward strokes before a strong wave overturned him.

"You cannot row smoothly with this only one arm," said Masu, wading into the surf. "The paddle slips back and forth." He thought for a moment, then went running back to the house and returned with a length of braided hide. He lashed the paddle to Gabriel's usable arm. "Now try."

It was better, but not perfect. He worked at it for months. Sometimes he pushed himself too hard and his shoulder broke open and began to drain again, but he kept at it. They made new paddles, trying different lengths, different shapes. Three or four times the boat had to be repaired.

All through the readying, Masu would not leave him. He ran along the shore like a long-legged brown bird and when the boat faltered, he would swim out to help. Twelve was the age of manhood among the Secota and he was almost ten, growing tall and lean and swift-footed.

"He'll be taller than I am," Gabriel said. He sat cross-legged that last afternoon, helping Naia stretch a rabbit skin on a willow hoop to cure.

Couldn't make myself leave her side that day, actually. Followed her about. Tasted her cooking. Watered her bit of a garden. Made her a new hairbrush from a stickleback shell.

The children were picking wild strawberries at the edge of the woods. Their voices rose and fell, squabbling and then making friends again.

"Masu is shaped like his father," she said proudly. "Ena had long legs."

"You never told me that. Was he a runner? Did he like swimming?"

She smiled. "You want to know everything."

"I do. Yes. I do." He put his hand on her thin arm where the old tattoo marks lay like a bracelet. "I'm going to take the boat down to Croatoan tomorrow, my heart," he told her.

"Is Emma's baby born?"

"There's no news," he lied.

"I'll go with you. I can help with the rowing."

"No. Better stay here till— Better stay."

He had never before made a choice for her. Never refused her company. Now he spoke too sharply, almost angrily, hiding something away. Her breath began to rattle inside her ribs. "Will you at least take Masu?" she asked.

He bent and kissed her breast. Kissed the tattoo of her clan, the wavy lines on her back. Let his cheek lie against her skin where the sun warmed it. *Take the sun in her with me. Not likely to see it for a while.*

"Better not let the boy come along this time," he told her. "I want to try rowing alone."

The tribal wars had grown worse and worse since the new alliance between the Powhatan and the Mandoag, and Gabriel had simply run out of choices. He'd known for some time that it would come to it, that the Spanish might be their only means of survival. If they'd had a proper little ship, he'd have tried going north instead, up to Newfoundland, where the fishing fleet spent every summer. In wartime, the English boats might not be there, but there were plenty of Germans and Danes and Swedes who'd have given them passage home.

Trouble was, they had no boat that would handle a sail and he couldn't possibly build one. Heading north, you couldn't hug the shoreline either, the tribes up there were too fierce. No, going north they wouldn't last more than two or three days. North was out of the question. Nor could he sail or row all the way to St. Augustine or Havana.

So he waited. Knew Fernando and the other spies had smuggled out those maps to the Spanish. Knew the ships would come looking eventually.

Georgie Howe came running up the sandbars to warn us that morning. Caught me out alone checking my rabbit snares. Said Croatoan had been raided two days earlier. The Mandoag killed Emma's husband and some of the others and took the few Englishmen prisoner, slave labor in the copper mines. Henry Payne. Dick Darige. The women and children hid on one of the smaller sandbars. Spotted two Spanish ships working their way along the coast.

Gabriel didn't sleep all that last night. Just lay beside Naia thinking about how he ought to do things, how best to approach the Spanish commander, how to make his offer. He had always been a creature of intuition, not of logic, but that night he discovered new practical powers as he lay there staring up at the low rafters of the rabbit hutch.

Reasoned out the whole business. Made a mental list of every nasty trick history could play on us. Surely the war had begun by now. God knows, the Armada might've taken London and the whole thing would be academic. Queen burned at the stake. Spanish grandees larking about Whitehall.

If luck was with him, though, the war would make him a valuable property to be questioned, perhaps traded or sold to the French, or to the Spanish government in Holland or Portugal.

Didn't mind whose subject I was. Didn't mind whose God I was expected to pray to. Knew enough Church Latin to pass as a Catholic. Knew French well, and quite a lot of Spanish. Torture I was prepared for. Didn't relish being roasted by the Inquisition, but it had to be added to the list, along with serving ten years or so in the galleys.

Everything depended upon the Spanish commander. Most of them prattled on about their honor, but you could pervert that nine ways from Sunday and still lay claim to it, as Captain English had done, and Rafe Lane, and all the rest.

No, honor wouldn't do the job. If the other women and little ones were to be saved, Emma and Madge and the rest, it would have to go deeper, into far more dangerous country. The human taproot, or nothing at all.

The last night with Naia was the longest of his life. No question of telling her. She'd never have agreed to it. He ached to make love to her one last time, but feared coming too near. Feared he might not be able to go through with his plan, might not be able to tear himself away in the morning. Instead, he kissed the children. Told the boy to keep an eye on things, not to let his little sister wander. Not to leave his mother alone.

"Tell her to remember the little parrots," he said. "How they always come back again. Tell her not to forget."

forty-four

SEPARATION

SLOWLY, SLOWLY, THE LITTLE WICKER BOAT CREPT ALONG THE OUTER Banks towards Hatorask and Croatoan. There was no breach deep enough for the big Spanish ships to enter the inner sound. Once they passed the Cape of Feare where the Gulf Stream and the southerly crosscurrents were at their most deadly, they would, he reckoned, keep a few leagues out to sea and ply northward slowly, watching the Outer Banks for English ships. When they were satisfied, they would drop anchor and send out shoreboats to look for the English colony.

Where they touched the Atlantic, the Banks were an endless empty shore, sloping and curving, bent out towards the sea like a bow and then springing back again near to the mainland. He passed Croatoan in darkness, so Georgie and the women would not catch sight of him. He could not have deceived them about his plans, he was beyond that now.

He rowed, then drifted, rowed and drifted. Sometimes the shoulder ached so much that he slipped into the sun-warmed water and floated. A day went by, and a night, and another. The sun was dropping westward on the fourth day when he caught sight of the Spanish. Two ships, not galleons but caravels, bigger than an English ship but not overwhelming, riding at anchor no more than a mile out to sea.

They fired a round over his head when they saw him approaching—four sailors with hackbuts. He tried to remember his Spanish. *"¿Quién es?"* they shouted. *Who are you?*

"¡Amigo!" he cried. *A friend.*

He was hustled up the rope ladder and over the side, his feet barely able to manage it. He'd been folded up in the little boat for three days, and his shoulder was draining again from the constant rowing. The Spanish sailors looked at each other, half-terrified of him.

Weren't sure what I was, poor sods. Skin almost as brown as a native's. Beard hacked off helter-skelter, hair to my arse and wrapped with leather. I crossed myself and gave them the Pater Noster in Latin. Thought it couldn't do any harm.

THE COMMANDER'S QUARTERS are large and handsome. There are murals of suffering martyrs painted on the bulkheads, but some heretic has hung a woman's portrait over the bloodiest of them. There is a long table of dark polished wood. A curving row of leaded windows. A scent mingled of spices and wine and soap and ripe pears and brown bread and oiled leather.

Commander sat at the table. Diego Mendoza-Reyes, just packing in the last of his dinner. Silver chargers, real glasses for wine. His sword hanging from the bedpost, gold braid and all the trimmings. Not wearing a doublet. Shirt unlaced at the throat. Wide-set dark eyes with a past locked inside them. Living eyes.

Mendoza motions the Moorish servant to pour some wine from a silver-gilt carafe. He fills a glass and sets it in front of his master, but the commander shakes his head and the wine is given to Gabriel instead.

A look is exchanged with the Moor and he glides away, his long robe of striped linen scarcely moving when he walks. In a few moments he returns with a small, dark, grumbling surgeon. Arab. Perhaps Egyptian. The shoulder is examined, cautiously probed. "If you're planning to kill him anyway," the surgeon growls, "I'm not going to the trouble."

Mendoza's eyes flash. "You will do what needs doing. Now."

Gabriel is taken below, to what passes for an infirmary. The ship has only left port in Havana a week before, and the place is empty. The surgeon makes a drain to get the pus out from among the smashed bits of bone inside the shoulder, and the Moor holds Gabriel down while it is inserted.

He is given more wine with some drug in it that makes him sleep, and when he wakes, he has been washed and shaved and his hair and beard have been trimmed. The Moor stands like an ebony statue at the foot of his bed.

It is beginning to get dark when Mendoza finally comes. An orderly follows with clean clothes and some food. Mendoza watches in silence while Gabriel devours it. Then he moves his chair nearer.

"So," he says. "You are an English spy?"

"Used to be."

"But not now? You don't come to my ship to learn secrets?"

"Need your help, that's the thing. Know we're at war. Spain and England, I mean. Invasion and so on. Might be some use to your people. Worked for old Burghley—know of him? One of his most trusted agents, I was, actually. What I know might be of great use to your Armada. If you help me."

Helluva gamble. Didn't really know much, never been that important. Thought I could fake it. Been faking for most of my life.

Mendoza strokes his spade-shaped beard. "If you know anything useful, I could simply have it tortured out of you."

"Wouldn't get as much, though. And you'd never be certain I wasn't lying to save my sweet neck."

The Spaniard smiles. "It is, to be sure, a tempting proposition—these most valuable secrets of yours. But I fear you have miscalculated. The Armada was destroyed in a great storm. Two— Almost three years ago. It never reached England."

"So— So we're not at war now?"

"Oh, yes. A silly business. I sometimes think there's only one war. It began when the world was made and it simply moves from place to place."

It is a terrible setback—to be prisoner of a war that no longer matters. But Gabriel has no choice except to forge on. It is as he knew it would be. It is down to the two of them.

He tells Mendoza about how the colony was set down and abandoned and the people left helpless on the island. Tells him anything he can think of. The names of the eight English women still living, and the names and ages of the children, what they look like, what games they play. Tells him about Naia and the sprouts. About the broken strands of pearls. The quillwork embroidery. About Kia, how she is still frightened of snakes. How she still has bad dreams about Tesik. Tells him about the tribal wars. The dirty politics. The carefully planted spies. The countless losses. The self-created illusions. The mythical gold.

Inch by inch, he refines himself, pares himself to the bone and lays that open as well. He speaks of his father the pork butcher, of his furious Puritan sister. Of his lost twins. Of their mother, wandering the roads of England with her wool merchant. Of his useless hopes of scholarship, his years of aimless drifting. Somehow it comes together on that day at Paul's Cross. On the child called Rosie. On the queen he saved quite by accident. On the young assassin who dreamed the throne of God.

He says very little of Naia, but everything else is defined by her. Even some of the words are hers. *It is too small, this boat. You must do this because it is proper.*

He speaks with a calm he has not known he still has in him, while Diego Mendoza-Reyes sits quietly beside him, letting it all spill out, listening intently to the soft, contained voice speaking scraps of Spanish, bits of Latin and French and Secota and Greek. Everything that has ever been civilized in the world sits there between them. Does he read a thousand years of the past and a thousand more of the still-possible future in the clearness of the Englishman's gaze and the complete absence of cunning in his face?

"This Secota woman and her children," Mendoza says at last. "If you betray her to us, she will hate you."

"No."

"Do you realize what will happen? They will take her children from her. They will sell them—and her—in St. Augustine, in Havana. Many people keep Indian slaves there."

"That won't happen."

"Why?"

A moment's stillness. The grey eyes probing. The quiet voice then.

"Because you won't let it. Old heart."

NEXT MORNING, CHAINS were put on him. Philip's spies were everywhere and Mendoza's career was not unblemished by a tendency for independence of mind. So the rituals of capture had to be adhered to. A locked space in the bilges where the foul water washed over the English spy's feet. A pint of watery gruel and a few bones with some mutton clinging onto them. And the chains.

Just after daylight, the heavy studded door creaked open and he was led up to Mendoza's cabin again. "Eight English women and four children," said the Spaniard, as though he had been all night adding them up. "A Secota woman and two children that are hers. Are they also yours, these two children?"

"No." Gabriel seemed not to bother about the chains on his ankles. But his good wrist was chained to an iron collar locked around his neck and his voice choked, now and then, on the sheer weight of it. "Wish they were mine. But no."

"And there are no other English towns on the mainland?"

"None."

"And no gold? You're certain?"

"As good as."

"So. No English treasure to send back to Spain and win me a promotion. Even the priests would be disappointed with so few heretics to burn. I suppose I could sell these women." He laughed. "But if my wife heard of it, she'd abandon my bed for the rest of her days."

Gabriel looked across the table at him. "Nothing I can offer will convince you. Haven't got the keys to the queen's private apartment or anything. But I believe you are—proper. Inside yourself. So you must find a decent place for these women. You mustn't shame them. You must keep them from harm. *You* must do it. For your own sake."

Mendoza's gaze did not waver. "I repeat. In return, what?"

"I'll answer your questions. About England. Who's spying on whom. Who's in favor and who's out."

"Your information is long out of date. And we have our own court spies."

"About Roanoke, then, and the country beyond it, what it contains, what the dangers are. How the native people think, what their words mean. Which tribes are treacherous bastards. When you run out of questions, send to Spain for some more. I'll tell them the absolute truth. Or at least, I won't embroider till the truth starts to bore them. Save our necks, you see. Yours and mine."

It was more than complicity he was asking, and he knew it. It was partnership in a strange human conspiracy. It was also treason.

There was a long silence then. The ship's timbers creaking. Bell striking the hour. At last Mendoza looked up, his dark eyes shadowed with lack of sleep and a concern that went beyond promotions and priests. He knew exactly what he was doing, and he knew why.

"A fair bargain," he said. "I accept."

"Oh, Christ. Oh. Thank you."

"But I'm afraid you must go with the boat I send for your *indina*. You must face her. We'll never find her otherwise."

S AFELY HIDDEN IN her clearing, Naia is cooking fish stew in a fine clay jar, stirring it with the duck's-head ladle. She holds the polished handle with delicate fingertips, letting the grain of the wood stroke her palm. Alone at her work, she disciplines her mind to summon in intense detail the touch of owl feathers or sand on her skin. The fragrance of sweet oil, or the bite of raw honey in the throat. It is her way of keeping a balance inside herself, of growing her soul.

She has begun to exercise this same regimen with Gabriel, now that his place in her bed is empty. He has been away too long, almost ten days. In the dark of the small hut, she lets her own finger drift across her lip before she sleeps, remembering the eight tiny parallel lines at the bend of his knuckles. The smooth, hard oval of his fingernail. The faint smell that only she can isolate, the scent of whatever he has done that day—fish scales, the stems of reeds and grasses, the sweet juice of wild grapes.

Ten days. Ten nights.

"We need clams," she tells Masu. "Go and dig some. Look out for raiding parties. Be careful."

The boy frowns. "We don't need clams. That stew's already too much for only three of us."

"I had a dream. He will come home today. All that rowing will make him hungry. I want to have plenty."

Kia giggles. "He eats like a horse."

"And how many horses have you known? Be respectful. Get the roasting pit ready for the clams."

"I'd rather pick raspberries."

Something changes then. The color of the light or the sound of the sea. The shape of the wind. Air caving in upon itself from the weight of spirits. Naia puts down the ladle and straightens her back.

"I need some lemon grass for the stew," she says to Kia. "I'll get it. Don't let the food burn."

But she does not go for lemon grass. Something is coming, dragging her towards it. Something is ending or beginning.

Look very steadily and far out to sea, Airstalker used to say, and the wind becomes visible—not its effects on wave and dune and dust mite, but the thing itself, the changeful spirit clenching and gathering, thickening the light. Naia selects a high dune and climbs, bare toes digging into the hard-packed sand. At the top, she stands very straight, looking out at the sea. Waiting for the wind to decide.

The Spanish longboat has been following the coastline far enough from shore to avoid the shoals, the oarsmen moving it rapidly up from the south. Someone stands in the stern—a tall man, but hunched from heavy weight upon him.

He lifts one arm. Sways in the boat and almost falls overboard. Points at the shoreline with a thin hand. *There is the place. Go there and take her.*

The boat turns a wide half-circle and makes for the beach, skimming the rising tide. Naia sees it, but she does not move from the top of her sand dune. Now the sharp sudden fall of things must be ridden as a fish rides the heart of a wave.

Masu is digging clams on the beach, plunging his stick into the sand, then pushing it skilfully downward. He does not notice the approaching boat until its wooden prow scrapes the shallow sand. At the sound, he looks up. "Nama!" he shouts, his boyish voice all but drowned by the tide. "Run, Nama!"

He drops the basket of clams and tears off across the sand, but still Naia stands watching. Time's circle closes itself, tilting side-wise. Once again she hears the terrifying rattle of steel helmets and cuirasses as the soldiers jump out of the boat and run after the boy.

Then they catch him, pin his arms behind him. One of them slaps him across the face, and suddenly his mother wakens from the circle of her dream. "Kia!" she screams. "Run!"

She slides down from the dune, falls, rolling over and over through the sand. But when she gets to her feet, Mendoza's men are already there, in the clearing. Kia is wailing as they tie her wrists with a bit of hawser-line.

Naia crouches in a clump of sassafras, trying to think. Better to be dead and yourself than to live smeared with someone else's idea of you. Be a queen. Be a whore. Be a servant. Be a fool.

From deep inside her, the truth slashes outward. The boat knew exactly where to come. The soldiers knew just where the labyrinth of the dunes opened into the clearing. Knew the chil-dren would be nearby. There can be only one source of this knowledge. Gabriel. She can still feel his mouth on her skin. In her mind, his foolish songs sing themselves over and over. *And still I will be merry still I will be still I will be.*

The soldiers have taken the children to the beach and now they are beginning to search the woods for her. There is a knife in the hut, if she can only reach it, and she breaks from her covert, running like a shadow along the shore of the pond. Dives through the low doorway, clawing among the cooking jars and baskets for the broad, grey steel blade.

The men don't bother with doorways. They smash the frail reed walls with the butts of their guns. Her hand is on the knife when they snatch her up, and she slashes one of them in the thigh. Then they hit her and she falls forward, her face in the dirt, blood streaming from her nose.

It takes three of them to drag her to the beach. The children, bound with ropes, kneel in the sand, Kia's face streaming with tears. Masu silent, blank-faced. "Ayyyiiiieeeee!" Naia screams. "Ayyyiiiieee-yah!"

For a moment she struggles free of the soldiers. Her cries cease, quite suddenly she is dry-eyed and ceremonious. It is the grief ritual. Methodically, she begins to flay the skin from her forearms with her fingernails.

"Naia! Na'iya! Don't!"

She looks up. Gabriel is standing in the boat. She hardly knows him with his hair and beard cut short. His body curves dangerously downwards and his eyes see through her, beyond her.

"Please," he says. His voice is barely audible. He tries to speak louder, but his words break in two. *Puh. Leez.*

She straightens her body. Pushes her hair back from her face. Out at sea, the wind becomes visible.

Didn't rage at me. Would've been easier if she had. But she did what was proper. God, the dignity. That calm, terrible voice.

"If you meant to betray me, why did you not slit my throat as I slept?"

"I only want— I want you to live. My— Heart."

"I am not your heart! I am my own heart! You cannot *make* me live! I will die if it suits me! Coward! Coward! You think you are God?"

He tries to lift his arm but the chains prevent him. Some wall in her mind will not let her see them, but the boy touches her.

"Look at him, Nama," says Masu. "Don't turn from him, look at him! He's not such a coward. They have made him a slave."

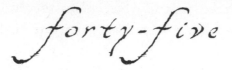

forty-five

CAGES

HE WAS NOT ALLOWED NEAR HER DURING THE JOURNEY BACK TO Mendoza's ship. All day he sat useless with Naia opposite him, at the other end of the longboat but so close he could smell the hazelnut oil on her skin.

Kept looking at her. Couldn't deny myself that. Kia cried and cried, till finally Naia clapped her hands twice. Hadn't seen her do that in the longest time. Some way or other, in her mind she'd become queen again.

"Did you see the English women?" I asked him.

"No. Heard them, though, aboard ship. Emma's voice, mostly."

"Swearing."

"What else? And Madge, lecturing that snake of a ship's surgeon."

He himself was kept, he said, in his small, dark, sodden cell in the bilges. Didn't see daylight again until the ship reached Havana.

Turned out Mendoza was more than a ship's captain. Just been given command of the garrison—ships, soldiers, arsenal, barracks. Military prison. In exile from Spain for conduct-unbecoming. Which means he thought too bluddy much.

Not a nice place, the prison, he told me, but when his moccasins wore through they let him have enough old cracked leather to mend them. Gave him work to do, making adobe bricks. With only one arm, he was slow at it and the lash bit him a few times. But at least they took off the iron collar, replacing it only when he was taken to be questioned. At night, he was chained to the wall of his cell.

Traitor, you see. Enemy agent. No other prisoners allowed near me. Heretic. Hell, they didn't know the half of it.

He spent two or three hours a day with Mendoza, answering questions, pulling from his mind whatever he could invent or remember, while three sober-faced clerks took everything down as if it were holy writ.

What impressed them most was that I seduced a lady-in-waiting in the gardens at Greenwich. Silly woman. Years ago. Couldn't think of her name. Well, actually I could, but I don't blabber that sort of thing about.

It took the best part of a year for the first consignment of his dubious information to reach Spain and be evaluated, and for a list of questions regarding the English secret service to be sent out to Havana. He was pronounced valuable enough to be worth keeping alive for a while, and Mendoza rewarded him with a copy of Ovid's *Metamorphoses* translated into terrible English and a job weeding some officer's garden one afternoon a week.

As they marched him back and forth from the prison, head down and chains everywhere, his eyes could not keep from wandering. Now and then there were women, but none of them was familiar. Some were Indian house slaves who cooked and cleaned for the officers' wives. They were dressed in plain, ill-fitting European bodices and skirts, almost always black or brown, their heads covered with dark-colored kerchiefs that hid their hair.

Whenever he met one of them, he would look at her forehead in case she had tattoo marks there. Sometimes there were marks, but never the right ones, the pale blue traceries that had formed a sort of crown among the fringe of Naia's hair. Once he saw an Indian woman with a basket on her head and a young girl of about Kia's age walking beside her.

But it wasn't Naia. Her eyes did not lift at the sight of him, not even in rage.

The ENGLISH WOMEN AND children are taken to the convent of Santa Reverencia. Children with stunted, inappropriate bodies. Babies with distended bellies. Ragged women with wild, thinning, almost colorless hair, and huge eyes that bulge, and fleshless bones that seem to pierce the sunburnt skin.

Still, they are Europeans and their souls may be reclaimed. Naia must be kept away from them. She is a heathen, tainted with horrid secret sins.

The nuns take Masu and Kia away, too, and put Naia in a small breathless white room with a lock on the door. I will die now, she thinks. White is the color of death. *He has taken the White Road,* they said when Ena died.

Screams slice the air. Kia, screaming. The lock clatters and two nuns come in, their black robes billowing. One has a nose like a parrot's beak. The other has anger bleeding into her eyes.

"Come along," says the angry one in Spanish. "Be obedient, quick, and don't dare to lie to me."

"I do not know these words," Naia says in English. "Where is my daughter? Why is she screaming? Where is my son?"

Her English is as incomprehensible to them as Secota, and the angry one slaps her across the mouth. "You will not speak in that heathen tongue of yours again, do you hear me?" She pokes at the tattoos on Naia's wrist. "The Devil has claimed you, but we shall scrub you clean of his marks, that I promise you!"

It means nothing. None of the Spanish words reaches her. They drag her to another room and strip off her painted cloak and her doeskin apron. Naked in the white light from the window, she stands waiting. There is a trough in the floor. That is where they will kill her and gather her blood.

"Oh," says the Parrot. "She's got those colored marks all over her. I wonder what they mean?"

"Evil," says the angry nun. "Just look at her face. We'll have to set guards tonight, or we'll all be murdered in our beds."

A young nun brings jar after jar of water, until the stone trough in the floor is almost full. Then they all begin to scrub Naia with brushes, trying to get off the marks of her honor and the clan mark on her back. Without it, she will not be found by her rightful dead in the next world, by her uncle and her mother and Ena. Even her children will not know her. She will be surrounded by strangers and enemies forever.

She makes no sound, but tears run down her face. "Harder. The Devil is very strong." They scrub until the soft skin of her throat and breasts is so raw that it bleeds. Her face is blotched and her back is full of scrape marks. They have taken lye soap to the tattoos, but they do not come off. She still has her clan mark. She is safe for her dead.

Then they put clothes on her of the same kind the English women wear. They bind her raw breasts tight in a terrible frame of bones covered with cloth and tie a skirt around her waist, and then another and another. Then they put a coat over the bones and long stockings on her legs and hard clumsy shoes on her feet. The cloth is rough against her scoured body, cruel as torture. In the shoes, with her toes pinched together, she does not know how to walk and she falls over and over again.

For days, death hovers above her in the whiteness of the small half-empty rooms. Her children are gone. She cannot even hear

Kia's crying now. At certain hours there is singing, the high voices of the nuns climbing and weaving together, full of private sorrow. In the dark nights, she talks to Gabriel.

I want to curse you. What is the worst English name I can call you? Don't know. Bastard. Son of a whore.

This is an insult to your mother. I do not know your mother. You are not her fault.

All right. Toad. Pig. Snake. Liar. Cheat. Spy.

Slave *is bad enough. You carry the chains of a slave now. You deserve them. You are shameful.*

Always was, you know. Right from the start.

In a week, perhaps three weeks, Mendoza's black servant comes. The angry nun will not keep Naia any longer, and she is taken to the house of a priest in black robes. An old man, sad-faced, who prays and prays over her. Once he lays his hand on her head, and it is steady, warm. Not unkind. She scrubs his floors and empties the night jars and gathers dried dung in the street for the fires. When she goes to the small room he has given her, the priest does not lock her inside.

More time slips away. One night the Moor brings Kia. Another night, Masu is returned to her. The old priest still prays and prays, but his mouth is not so sad.

The house is made of thick adobe, a pale gold in the hot hours of sunshine and at night a glistening silver-blue. There are many unused rooms and once Masu is finally sleeping and the worst of Kia's dreams have released her, Naia wanders the house, listening to the old man's mumbled prayers stroke the darkness. One room is full of books, another has nothing but birds in wire cages. In still another there are fragrant plants in stone jars. Dragging her blanket-bed like a train behind her, she pads barefoot from room to room, sleeping where she chooses, sampling other lives.

She is looking for Gabriel, growing herself towards him again.

Then pulling back, enclosing herself. Then moving closer. Teaching herself to forgive him.

In the sheer, tropic darkness she summons the colors of Roanoke sky, of sea-glazed sand, of water plants. Turning her bare foot at a precise angle on the flat slates of the walled garden, she fits it to the hollow of a certain tidemark she remembers. Cups her hands to the shape of a shell. Of a squash blossom. Of Gabriel's face, his grey eyes looking back through her fingers.

In the priest's garden, a tangle of tiny gold and silver fishes swim in a tiled fountain. She dips both hands into the water and catches one. Lets it flicker against her palms for a moment, fighting, nibbling, kissing.

"What do you think, Fish?" she says. Holding her hands above her head, she lets the water splash over her throat and her breasts in their cage of European bones.

The fish does not advise her. It jitters down to her waist and flips soundlessly away.

F OR ANOTHER YEAR, he heard nothing of her. He was moved to San Juan, where the prison was worse and the weather was hotter. Got fever once or twice. Shook it off. Busied himself cleaning filthy straw from the cells and putting down fresh. Taught the guards how to play knucklebones. Made more bricks.

Again, they kept the ordinary prisoners from him. Again, they put him in a tiny cage where he paced the length of the chain along the wall at night. Sometimes he thought he heard her laughter or tasted her skin in the air. Sometimes he would walk to the end of his chain and step into the embrace of her shadow.

Then back to Havana. Mendoza's position was tenuous and he dared not write to a prisoner-spy. After a month he was replaced and sent back to Spain. The new man proved to be a bully who cut the prisoners to half-rations and doubled their work. The soldiers mutinied and the slaves in the town began burning the Spanish villas. Gabriel fretted himself sick, trying everything he could think of to find out if Naia was still in the city, if she and the children were safe. He wasn't able to sleep, sometimes for four or five nights at a stretch.

Then Mendoza was reinstated, he was suddenly back in command. Gabriel was given a job in the prison infirmary, helping the same surly doctor who had worked on his shoulder.

There was a window in the surgery. A real glass window, makes it light enough for tooth-pulling. Amputations. All that. I would scrub up the blood afterwards. Wash the window. My fourth year, and still no word of her. One day a procession of nuns walked by, coming from the convent.

They stopped at the prison to pray for us and I saw them, disguised in the long robes and white wimples of postulants. Saw their faces looking back at me. Jane. Emma. Madge. Alis. Aggie.

At the back, a small woman in a dark gown, a shawl covering her hair. A servant, surely. Her hands braced against the glass wall of the world.

She looked up then. Let me see her eyes. Her parted lips. Took the shawl from her hair to let me see the tattoo marks. My face pushed against the hot window glass, trying to reach her. Her shadow pressing my face.

forty-six

SPIES AND THEIR MASTERS

H<small>E HAD SEEN HER ALIVE, AND THAT WAS ENOUGH TO GO ON WITH.</small> He still clung to the belief that his grand conspiracy with Mendoza would hold firm to the end and that he and Naia would somehow pick up their lives again. But I knew that the Roanoke was like a wire underneath his skin, turning and turning, causing more subtle harm every day, as much guilt as anger. He had betrayed one-half of Naia to save the other, preserved the living woman he couldn't do without, no matter what it had cost her. And he didn't simply want justice—I realized that now. He wanted the forgiveness of sins.

"You're to keep out of sight during the day and meet me at the Rose after sunset," I told him as we rode across London Bridge three days later. "The actors rehearse most of the night, so nobody will notice you."

"Why all the bluddy delay? Let's just have it over with."

We had decided to confront Robert Cecil. If we were mistaken, we would get no second chance.

"I don't want to rush this," I told Gabriel. "I want to know how his day works, when he comes and goes, who's around him and at what hour."

"I can tell you most of that now. He has rooms at Whitehall, does everything there except sleep. He leaves home every morning precisely at six o'clock, even in winter. Big house on the river, but there are too many servants. He doesn't take a public wherry to Whitehall, he has one of his own fitted out with cushions to ease his spine. Crimson cushions, gold tassels. French damask. Two oarsmen in his father's livery. One rows, other one toadies. Doesn't have livery of his own. Too pinchpenny. Apartment at the palace has its own river stairs. Two fireplaces. Blue-and-white Dutch tiles, very handsome."

"You actually got inside?"

"Flirted with one of the kitchen girls who takes his meals up to him. She says he never eats in the Great Hall with the rest of the locusts. Hard for him to walk and the passageways go for miles. Could take him while he's eating, but the boat sounds best."

"Nick's still got some of old Burghley's livery badges, Peach can get them for me. Yes, the river's much the safest. We have to get him alone, or neither one of us will live through this in one piece."

His quiet laugh then. "What makes you think I expect to live through it at all?"

I LEFT HIM IN the middle of a mob of cheering citizens waiting for the queen to pass along Thames Street on her way to Richmond, then rode out along the river toward Manningford. I had to satisfy myself that our suspicions of Cecil were real enough to proceed with, and if anyone could tell me what ran the clockwork of his brain, it was Gibbie. He'd resist me, but I'd have to get it out of him somehow.

The ramshackle house was silent as I rode up to it. There were no hens cackling, no peacocks stepping arrogantly about. The old woman was nowhere in sight, nor was the Plague Rat. A cart stood in the yard and a saddle horse grazed under a tree.

When I pushed open the creaking door and stepped inside, the stench almost overcame me. With my hand over my nose and mouth, I navigated the odd levels and turns to the cluttered room where Gibbie had plied me with brandy three months before. A fair-haired young man with a deceptive air of bumbling innocence sat on the window seat going through an untidy heap of papers. He wore one of Lord Burghley's velvet badges on his doublet.

"Oh!" he said. "Are you called Robert Mowbray, by any chance?"

"I am."

"Thank God. The smell's making me gag, but I wasn't to leave till you arrived. Name's Byceford. First name Athelstan, but I wish you'd overlook it."

"Where's Master Pembroke-Gibbons?" I asked him angrily. "Why are you going through his things?"

"My lord wants it all bundled up and sent to him, just in case there's anything—well, *you* know."

"No, I don't know. I haven't been in London."

"Oh yes. Visiting the Fen country, I believe?"

So they'd been following me all the time, even after Gabriel joined me. They might've laid hands on us in an instant. But they had not. "Where is Master Gibbons?" I said again. "Has he been arrested?"

Byceford peered at me. "Oh, I *am* sorry. Didn't you know? He's dead, poor old fellow."

"Murdered?" After Marlowe, after everything else, it would hardly have been surprising.

But young Byceford shook his head. "Not murder, sir, no. Choked to death on a chicken bone. What an irony, eh, for so subtle a fellow? Gone in a twink. Buried in the village church yesterday. Fine bronze marker. My lord Burghley wept, sir, when we told him about it. I assure you, he wept."

A most convenient chicken bone, I thought. There are poisons that choke before they kill.

"I thank you for giving me the sad news, sir," I said. "Godspeed to you, and to your master." I prepared to leave, throwing my cloak over my shoulder.

"Oh, dear," he said. "Thought I'd told you. I'm to bring you to him." His bumbling innocence dropped away from him like a mask at a carnival. "My lord Burghley wants you most particularly, sir. Today, if you please. In fact—now."

LORD SECRETARY BURGHLEY'S great estate of Theobalds is in Hertfordshire, but we do not go there. Although his working life on the Council has declined due to his age, he still makes it his rule to be present at whichever of her palaces Elizabeth is in residence. Today, she has chosen Richmond, taking almost none of her court with her.

Greenwich and Whitehall and Westminster are huge public places, always mobbed with dignitaries. But Richmond is designed for personal comfort. It is more elegant and less gaudy than the houses that are constantly on public show, and she has decorated it to her own taste. There are no tapestries here, and few invited guests.

We arrive at early evening, the wherries on the river just lighting their lanterns. A groom takes our horses and leads them away, and somewhere between the stableyard and the yew alley, Athelstan Byceford vanishes into thin air. Servants are kindling torches in the gardens and on the terraces, and there is virginal music from somewhere inside. I pause, trying to get my bearings, when a page in Elizabeth's personal livery touches my arm.

"My lord of Burghley's in the orchard, sir," he says, pointing to a shadowy bridle path between rows of blooming apple trees. My former master, clad in his plain grey gown and black velvet skullcap, is riding a white mule up one aisle of trees and down the next. When he reaches me, he does not dismount, and I make him a perfunctory bow.

"Well, Mowbray." His voice is very soft at first, almost inaudible. Then it suddenly turns to a shout. "WELL?" Next, he changes to a mumbling monotone in which words suddenly jump out for no reason and assail you. "Looks a good YEAR for apples these are ORANGE pippins MAKE excellent cider."

"My lord grows very deaf, sir," says the groom at my elbow. "Can't hear his own voice anymore. No way of telling how loud it is, y'see, when you can't hear. Folk think he's in his dotage, but don't you believe it."

A servant plants a torch in the ground in an iron bracket, then another and another. With a wave of his hand, Elizabeth's oldest spymaster rides meekly on, with me walking beside him. When we reach the kitchen garden, the old man struggles to dismount from the mule and I assist him. I could lift him, almost, with one hand.

"Nearly as thin as SHE is, eh?" He smiles from behind his long white beard. "Time and care drain the body of humours. When SHE rides, her bones rattle so her PHYSICIANS fear she will break a rib. Is she playing the virginals now?"

"Someone is playing. A delicate touch."

"Don't shout, boy. Dangerous. What song?"

"I don't recognize it, my lord."

"One of HERS, I wager. Composes music. Verses. Could have been anything. Done anything. Wasn't a man, though. Lack of scope, like her poor mother. Is it a sad tune?"

"A minor key, my lord, I believe."

"Ah. Yes. It scalds HER heart, too, you know. Time. Time. Time."

A second groom appears from nowhere and takes the mule, and Burghley walks a few paces. In spite of his gout, he uses no walking stick and does not ask for my arm. His deafness comes and goes as it serves him. "Now, then. Make me your report."

"It seems I have very little to tell you that you do not know by other means, sir. Since you've been having me followed."

"Don't sulk, Mowbray. Always have people followed. Formed the habit in my youth. SHE wouldn't be on the throne now if I hadn't had people followed. Go on."

"I'm sure you know there were spies on the Roanoke ships. Hired to make certain the colony didn't succeed."

"'Course there were spies, man. Only natural. Israelites sent spies into the Promised Land, didn't they? Well, there you are. What does Pembroke-Gibbons say?"

The question takes me off guard. "Why, nothing, sir. He's dead."

"Ah, yes. Forgot for a moment." Burghley stares into the torch-lit dark and I almost think he has entered that middle distance of Gabriel's in which spies disappear and decent men take their place. "Poor old Gibbie. Knew everything. Quote you the Scriptures in three or four tongues and didn't believe a syllable of it." He wipes his eyes, which seem to weep almost continually. "I loved him. Vile old heretic. Chicken bone. Did you know? God's justice is harsh." He looks at me shrewdly. "Some of us pay the price of hell before we die, you know."

"Certainly the lost folk Her Majesty abandoned on Roanoke must have found a hell on earth."

"Don't be an ass. Not HER fault. Ralegh's. Silly fool. Ridiculous idea in the first place, I told 'em so."

"No one bothered to search for them for three years, my lord. Surely that amounts to abandonment."

"Tush, tush. Couldn't go and get 'em. Spanish WAR, man. Poured every farthing into defense. SHE pawned her jewels, sold half of 'em. Sempstresses took the pearls off one dress and sewed 'em onto another at night. Politics of ornament. Government is sleight of hand, Mowbray. Never forget."

But I won't be drawn aside. "It was your son who implemented the queen's orders regarding the ports. And by the time the Armada was defeated, it wouldn't have been safe to bring those settlers home, would it, even if they were yet living? They were sure to make accusations. They'd have realized that almost everything had been done to assure they'd *never* return to England. That no supply ship would ever come. A spy sailed them there and a spy left them to die."

"That prancing pirate of Walsingham's, you mean?"

"Simon Fernando's real master was neither Ralegh nor Walsingham, my lord. He was in league with a brute called Fullwood, and there were others. At least one other. Was it your son?"

"What? MY son?"

He knew it all. Why else would he have brought Gibbie into it and sent Nico to search my room? He knew, but perhaps not all of it. "Your son hates Ralegh and he wants him down," I said. "If the war had not dragged on so long, the failure of Roanoke would've given him means."

"Down? Ralegh? Wish he was, by God. Wish he *was* down. Wretched heretical coxcomb. Necromancer, that's what the Archbishop says."

The old man seems not in the least disturbed by what I have dared to say of his son, nor does he contend with me. He merely stands for a moment, considering a whitewashed bench near a bed of pansies. He calculates the exact center and lowers himself cautiously onto it, as though a miscalculation will send him off the edge of the earth.

"SHE'S fond of pansies, you know," he says, looking down at the carpet of purple and yellow blooms. "Likes the simple country flowers. Lady's-smocks. Purples. Pied violets. Grew up in the country. Father denied her. Said she was the bastard of her own uncle. Nobody believed it, but nobody stopped it. Jesu, what a world." He wipes his eyes again. "Who else knows?" he says suddenly. "Who knows what you suspect of my son's part in the Roanoke nonsense?"

"Most of them are dead. Including Master Gibbons. I would be dead myself, if someone hadn't fished me out of the river."

"Ah. Yes. That fellow North, eh? Slippery rogue. No respect for the chain of command."

"He'll be next, then, will he? Master Cecil's foot will tap out its orders and those four bullies of his will be set loose again, and somebody else will die or be racked. The two fellows you sent me will very likely be next, or—"

"Fellows? What fellows?"

"Why, Harry and Rowland. I thought perhaps you—"

"Those two? Wouldn't trust 'em to count the fleas on a brindle bitch. Cast them off long ago."

"But your son might have used them, knowing such men are easily disposed of. If they aren't dead already, they soon will be. Put a stop to it, my lord. You can't protect Master Cecil forever. Let him answer for himself."

Burghley stares into the torchlight. "I am not a sentimental man, Mowbray. I taught my son to seek power and devote himself to serving those who possess it. Robert is not beautiful, but he works all the hours God made and there's not a trickier fellow in England. If HE can't sniff out a treason, he'll invent one to serve, and he serves HER well. Oh, he's a crocodile, not a man. I made him. Wish to God I could like him. But it isn't requisite. It doesn't convict him. And as I say, I'm not a sentimental man."

"The Roanoke women, sir. And Gabriel North. Will they be harmed?"

"Not by me. What have I to do with them?"

"But you've had them watched. You know their whereabouts—everything."

"It has been the business of my life to know everything. It's not so much what you know. What you do with it, you see. Besides, my everything and HIS everything are different breeds of cat, sir. On the night Walsingham died, Robert crept into the house and stole all the old jackal's papers, did you know that? Might have been me lying stretched out in the next room. Wouldn't have hindered HIM. What we've made of the world, you know. Cutthroats and plunderers grow from our balls, and when we get old, they eat us."

There are footfalls in the shrubbery, and shadows move beyond the torchlight. The virginal music has stopped now, and from a terrace at the end of the garden I hear the sound of a lute and the peculiar hysteric laugh I know is Elizabeth's. Burghley hears it and looks up.

"Never have sons," he says. "I had a daughter that loved me, but I married her to a brute and he broke her. Dead now. I have nothing about me but the monsters I've made. No, no, Mowbray. Don't have any sons."

"If Master Cecil is guilty, he ought to be punished. You must know that."

"He will be," the old man says softly. "But if HE pays, SHE will pay. So if you make one word of this public, I shall smash you. For HER sake. I owe her that. I'm responsible. I don't like him, you see. But he's mine."

forty-seven

The Course of Justice

*I*F YOU TOUCH CECIL," I TOLD GABRIEL THAT NIGHT, "THEY'LL KILL you and then go after the women. Burghley will trump up some charge—witchcraft, sedition, blasphemy. You must think of Emma's safety, and Madge and the others. I know you don't care anymore what becomes of you. If that's because you think Naia's dead by now, or that she'll never forgive you—"

"Don't say that again. Not ever."

"Then you can't possibly go through with this. Forget Cecil and think of her."

He was silent for a long while, looking out over the rooftops of London. We sat in the tiny upper turret of the Rose, the little space from which trumpets were blown whenever a play was about to begin. Next door at the baiting pit, the bears roared in their cages, while below us the players rehearsed a comedy about lovers divided. They were always reunited at the end of the story, came into a grand inheritance, got married in half a page, and the clowns launched a joyous celebration of singing and dancing that sent the audience home purring and ready to come back and pay their penny for another play tomorrow afternoon.

Even I wanted it to be so. But it was a dream, and I knew it. In some theatres, nobody wins at the end of Act Five.

"What'll you do to Cecil if he admits to it?" I said. "Sink him in the Thames? Poison him and say he choked on a bone? Or just smash his head in with your war club?"

It was past the hour when the Night Watch went round quenching torches and silencing drunks. The stews and the taverns still had lights, and a few churches gave dim indications that a candle or two kept vigil. On the river, the lanterns of wherries bobbed and danced. Otherwise, London was very dark. Europe was dark.

Gabriel's voice was a low growl. "You're still afraid. Still just watching."

"I think about consequences, damn you! Is that cowardice?"

"Are you in this, or aren't you?"

"You go to hell! Go and stage your little performance. A one-armed cripple executing a hunchback—now there's the stuff of comedy!"

For a moment I thought he would kill me, push me off the roof and stand watching till I smashed.

"Cecil leaves his house at six in the morning," he said. "Be at the river stairs below his garden a half hour before daylight. I'll be there. Whether you come or not."

THERE ARE RAIDS all over London that night, Her Majesty's men battering down house doors and taking people away. I watch out the remaining hours of darkness among the thieves and the illicit lovers who claim the gardens of Blackfriars at night, the sounds of rutting and the rattle of coins all but overwhelmed by the thump of marching feet and the sharp crack of halberds on the cobbles outside the garden gates.

There is still no light in the sky as I make my way down to

where the wherries tie up. The river is blanketed with fog, but I wake a sleepy boatman and pay my fare up as far as Queenshithe. From there, I backtrack on foot along the river's edge. Ralegh's huge empty mansion is there, and Essex has a house not far away. Cecil's is modest as such places go.

The fog and the darkness make it impossible to see how the garden is laid out and where the best hiding places are. The private wherry that takes him back and forth from Whitehall is tied up to an iron ring fixed in the stone stairs, but I see no sign of the oarsmen, nor of Gabriel.

"Here," says his voice from out of the fog. He grabs the neck of my shirt and pulls me back into the shelter of a yew arbor. "You're late."

He is wearing a flat workingman's cap and a woolsey shirt and leather jerkin, and his hair is slicked down and parted in the middle in the manner of bumpkins the world over. "You look ridiculous," I tell him.

It is a lie. He looks as tall as a tree. Perfectly contained. Patient. Polite. Last night's harsh words are forgotten. There is a muscularity in his control of himself I have not noticed before. He will do this with dignity, or not at all.

I am anything but contained. I am on the edge of panic, I can hear it in my own voice. "Did you see the Queen's Guard last night? Were they after you? My God, what a night."

"Hush!"

Heavy footsteps make their way down the garden. "Fog won't lift before noon," says one man. Cheapside accent. No teeth, from the sound of his *f*'s.

"For Gawd's sake, Gaffer," says the other, "don't bump the bleeding boat into anything today or he'll have your head. The pikemen was out and about, so he'll have been up all night signing warrants."

Cecil's two oarsmen, coming to work. As the man called Gaffer puts his foot on the stone of the river stairs, Gabriel snatches him. One-armed he may be, but he is still very strong, very agile. We get the pair of them firmly bound and their mouths stuffed with rags. Next we strip them naked and drag our shivering captives into a shed at the bottom of the garden. Shame is a great silencer, in case they get the rags from their mouths.

The sky is already trying to grow light above the fog. Five o'clock, or thereabouts. A little less than an hour to wait before Cecil appears. We hunch down by the landing in silence, till at last I hear St. Paul's great bell strike six times.

Robert Cecil is as punctilious as his reputation. "Get your head down," Gabriel whispers. "He knows you."

I climb into the boat and crouch over the oars. As the footsteps draw nearer, all my suspicions come together. I can hear the uneven clop of wooden heels, exactly as I remember them from that night in the garden, except that this morning Cecil carries an elegant walking stick, barely touching it to the ground now and then for balance.

"Who the devil are you?" he demands, stopping at the top of the river stairs. His monotone voice is thinner than I remember, and weedier. Something moves under its plausible surface like blood under the skin of a bruise. "Where's the regular oarsman?"

"Gaffer's down with the plague, master," says Gabriel.

"I've heard nothing of plague."

"Bankside, sir. Only a case or two. Gaffer's a tough nut, he'll weather."

"What do I care for that? It grows late. Help me into the boat and keep your mouth shut." He suddenly pauses, staring. "Are you mocking me, you turd?" He gives Gabriel's bad shoulder a sharp whack with the walking stick. "Stop hunching yourself and stand up straight!"

I can see Gabriel's body fighting the pain and the fury. His head lowers a bit and his breathing grows shallow and hoarse. Then it deepens. Comes steady again, and he doffs his cap and bows. I have never seen such control.

"Sorry, sir," he says. "Can't straighten 'er. Made that way."

"What the hell did you come for? You can't row with one arm." Cecil turns to me, but I am a servant and more or less invisible. "You do the rowing by yourself. I don't trust him. He can attend me. Half the regular pay."

Gabriel settles him in the cushioned passenger's seat and takes his own place opposite. The smell of clove oil assails me and I think I will surely puke. Suddenly I want Cecil dead, almost as much as I had on that awful night of the beating. Justice doesn't come into it. I don't care what it costs me, I want to make nothing of him. To erase him from the face of the earth.

I pull the boat out into the current as quickly as I can and move into the central channel where the fog lies heaviest. It holds off the morning and we still travel in thick darkness. None of the large merchant ships can move and the wherries have their night-lanterns lighted, but until they are almost on top of us even the lantern light cannot be seen.

In the middle of the river, with the fog like shifting grey walls all around us, I suddenly turn the shallow boat sharply into the current. It heels over dangerously and Cecil's body lurches. I ship the oars and the boat rocks, steadies, and lies there adrift. It is almost high tide, and bits of river flotsam strike the sides of the boat now and then. Once I glimpse a man's corpse just under the surface. It bumps the hull and glides away towards the shore.

We have shipped water and Cecil's fine black satin pumps are awash in it. "I'll have your ears for this," he cries, "both of you!"

"Stand up." The calm firmness in Gabriel's voice demands absolute obedience. "Do as you're told. Be quiet and stand up."

"What?"

"You heard. Stand up. Do it now."

"I—I am the queen's secretary, I can have you quartered for treason!"

His hand reaches into his doublet. He carries a dagger—finely worked steel, the hilt jewelled with a large ruby—but it is not hard to overpower him. We wrest the dagger away and Gabriel keeps it. I see someone's arm float past. Then a severed head.

Cecil forces the panic out of his voice. He speaks softly, with that mannered intelligence the queen values in him. "What do you want of me? Are you going to kill me? Whose are you?"

"No one's," says Gabriel. "I told you to stand up."

"You're Ralegh's, aren't you? Yes, of course you are. What's he paying you?" A quiet laugh. "He can't afford much. I'll give you three times the amount."

"We don't work for anyone," I tell him. "You can't buy us."

People say that a crooked body betokens a crooked soul, and the gross injustice of that prejudice serves Robert Cecil. It is hard to distrust him without accusing oneself, impossible to watch him closely without seeming to stare. I suddenly realize that although I have often been in his presence, I have never really looked him in the face before.

Now he turns to glance over his shoulder at me and I see a pale, nervous countenance with small black eyes half hidden by lids that never open quite fully and never quite close. The hunch on his back turns his whole body sidewise, so that he seems to see the world from a precipitous angle. His hair and beard are very dark and they shine with the unnatural sleekness of a frightened animal that grooms itself constantly. A small man. A man who has never forgiven himself for being born.

"A thousand pounds," he says calmly, his eyes tossed like a tennis ball from one of us to the other. "Five thousand. Take me back to the shore and I'll give you five thousand pounds to divide between you."

A young girl's naked body floats past us, her long hair streaming behind her. Around her a swarm of small fishes flicker and shine.

"I want you to stand up now," Gabriel repeats.

"Ten. Ten thousand."

"I want you to stand up and step out of the boat."

Cecil almost laughs. "Are you mad? Who are you?"

"Roanoke."

There is a silence. A hollow hole in time. Then Gabriel again. "Get into the water now. Get out of the boat."

"But I can't swim."

"Did you ask if *they* could swim? In what waters did you leave them? You saw that their food was destroyed. You made certain the Spanish could find them. You saw to it no supply ship was sent. You pissed on their lives. You drowned them in dangers. You threw them away."

"I didn't make the wind blow contrarywise in the Channel. I didn't invent the Spanish war. The spies were my father's and Walsingham's, not mine."

"But you gave them their orders," I said. "You shuffled the papers and selected the players. Fullwood. Fernando. When they grew troublesome, you killed them. Oh, you had Fernando racked first, just to be sure you were safe. Did he die that night? Or did he survive Topcliffe and cost you the price of an assassin?"

"I, use Topcliffe? Put the royal seal on an order for private torture? It could have cost me my head, you fool. Besides, I thought the pirate died of fever, like most of his crew."

Elizabeth, I think, and her hysteric laugh echoes in my ears. Elizabeth got the truth of Roanoke, she used Topcliffe to get it. Years before the end, she knew. And still the relief ships did not sail.

But knowledge is not guilt. The Spanish war is real enough. It still drags on. Whatever she knew, we dare not accuse and she cannot defend herself, innocent or not.

"Forget the damn pirates," Gabriel says. "You maneuvered everyone. Ralegh. The Council. The queen. Me. The colonists meant nothing. Lizzie. George. The old parson and his niece. Harris the schoolmaster. Surgeon Ellis. Nico Rands meant nothing. Kit Marlowe and old Pembroke-Gibbons. Piemacum. Lady Heartberry. Slender Eel. Airstalker. You made us all pieces in a game of bluddy draughts."

"It was Ralegh's idea from the beginning, an English colony in that godforsaken place! His ridiculous stories of gold and pearls and silk growing on bushes! Those common fools trusted him because he was Ralegh, because he's handsome, because the queen adores him."

"They trusted him because he offered them half a chance when they had none. And you took it away!"

Cecil stares into the fog. "Pygmy, that's what she calls me. Little Man. Elf. But I'm loyal to her. I am. I serve her well, and she'll keep me because I know how the game's played, it'll be my only protection once Father's dead. I've read all his papers and I stole Walsingham's and I read them, too. I know things and I know how to use them and against whom, and *she* knows I will, so she needs me. What do you think would become of me otherwise? It was Ralegh she loved. Now he's disgraced, it's young Essex. She only wants to look at pretty people, you know. Did you know that? No plain, homely ladies-in-waiting. She's so afraid of it. No warts. No scabs. No crossed eyes. No twisted feet."

His mouth opens, but nothing more comes out of it. The soundless pain cracks apart and falls down through the fog to the river.

"It's not good enough." Gabriel's eyes are clear and pale in the smothered light. "A whole world torn to pieces. And all because nobody loved you in spite of your hump?"

"All right, then." Cecil wipes his mouth with his sleeve. "Ralegh's adventures would've drained the treasury. The investors were putting money into it that might've been loaned to the Crown for defense. We had to take huge loans from the German banks at ridiculous interest. I did it for Her Majesty. For England's survival."

"England died in America," says Gabriel quietly. Then suddenly his voice is a roar. "Stand up! Get out of the christly boat!"

"It's just how things are, don't you see that? Some people matter and some don't. It's always been that way. You think I invented it?"

With his good hand, Gabriel begins to rock the shallow wherry back and forth, back and forth in the current. Faces just below the surface. Just beyond the fog. Arms. Legs. Heads.

"I told you, I can't swim!" shouts Cecil, hanging on for his life.

Gabriel keeps on rocking the boat from side to side. Cecil stands up, sits down, stands up again, trying to keep his balance. In the slosh underfoot, his court pumps slip and slide, and his walking stick is useless. Beyond the fog a reckless boat passes us, setting up a backwash. He flails at the air for a moment in silence. Then there is a splash as he simply steps over the side.

Gabriel still holds the fancy dagger in his two hands. "Row, damn you," he says in a terrible whisper. "Get us away from here. Let him sink. Let him go."

I row us a little distance from what we have done. I want to be rid of Cecil and everyone like him, every leaden shaft of power that is slowly overbalancing the world. But I don't want to watch.

He breaks the surface, water streaming from him, from his sleek animal hair and from his ringed hands and from his crooked back. I saw a man hanged in the rain once, and it was something like this. He fights the water and he fights the air but he doesn't cry out.

"If he dies, he still wins," I tell Gabriel. "You may be alive, but you'll be gone. What you are now."

He looks over at me and I can see little more than the shine of his eyes in the foggy half-dark. "Christ, Robbie. At the pleasure of their games? All of us? Our whole lives?"

I have no answer. Cecil is under the water again. Down, then up, thrashing and fighting. Terrible choking sounds from deep in his belly. He doesn't have much time left.

Gabriel draws a long, slow, awful breath. It is released in uneven jolts, like arrows being pulled from his body, like the choking of the iron collar.

"I—c—can't," he says. "I thought— God. *She* never asked for justice. My dear heart. Not once."

He is sobbing, broken deep like a ship on a shoal. It is bitter, brutal, raw weeping such as I have never heard, weeping that tears his throat and clenches his body into a crooked fist. It is all his life pouring out of him. All the selves he has given away.

Most of all, it is a little hut in an empty clearing beside a pond. It is a clean beach, scoured even of footprints. A woman's dark, steady eyes. A spirit-pearl.

"Go back for him," he says in a hoarse, dry whisper. "God help us. God keep us. Go back."

forty-eight

How It Ended and How It Began

THE FOG HAD LIFTED BY THE TIME WE DEPOSITED ROBERT CECIL, half-drowned and silent, as far from where he wanted to be as possible. In his terms, he had won. He still had power and we had none, and no one would ever know the truth of Roanoke. If Elizabeth knew, we could not ask her. Cecil would shuffle his papers and that would be that.

Burghley would keep his word about protecting the women, but we had no such certainty where we ourselves were concerned. Gabriel went off by himself, instructing me to meet him at Moorfields that night. You could buy false travel papers at the Thieves' Market there, and we'd need them to get out of the country. And disguises, too. If Cecil alerted the Coast Guard, the ports would all be supplied with our likenesses. Walsingham had kept a secret file of such pen-and-ink sketches, and they would all be the Little Man's now.

I bought a false beard and wig from one of the theatre suppliers in Cockle Lane, and a blanket cloak and a Puritan hat at a second-hand clothier's. I should have hidden myself away in some corner and waited. But I couldn't leave London without risking a last trip to Crutched Friars.

Wrapped in the old cloak, I crouched in a doorway across the square and waited. I'd forgotten it was Whitsuntide, the Pentecost holiday, when half of England got married. There would be bride-ales in tents and pavilions, and St. George plays and morris dancers all over London. A mummer in a hobbyhorse costume and a Maid Marian in a straw wig and bells on his stockings stopped to drink from the well. The maid Esther came out to fetch water and stood flirting with them for what felt like hours.

Then at last the house door opened again, and I caught sight of Annette.

She wore a gown of quilted grey satin, almost the color of the fog the sun was burning away. Esther came running, fetched a cushion, wiped the fog-damp from the bench beside the door. Finally Annette waved her inside and sat down to work lace on a cushion, her graceful hands moving the bobbins over and under in invisible patterns. Above her, Gerard's pigeons fluttered round their cages on the rooftop. I could see him there with them, stroking their feathers and treating them to bits of food.

He was kind. She was safe. But I couldn't make myself leave her. I stood across the square while brides were walked to church and morris men in wicker masks streamed past in a blur. The church bells began to ring all along the Thames—Elizabeth coming back from Richmond to preside over the crowning of the Summer King and Queen, as she always did.

It had nothing to do with me anymore. London had nothing to do with me. I had ceased to be English, or anything else.

A ballad singer passed, caroling away, and Annette looked up from her lacework. I knew she had seen me. I stood up and risked a step towards her.

Her two hands lifted from the lace-pillow and hovered like wings in the air for a moment. My failures could not be forgiven. It would not have been proper. It would not have been just.

With the street still between us, my own hands reached out for her. She looked one last time at me. Then she got up and went into the house.

I WAS MAKING MY way along Cheapside towards St. Paul's, when a mummer in a wicker mask and a lion's mane ran up to me. He began to dance in a circle, shaking the bells on his stockings.

"Gabriel's taken," said Nick's voice from under the mask. "An hour since, at Lincoln's Inn Fields." He shoved an owl mask into my hands. "They'll bring him this way."

"To the Tower? Dear God."

"It'll kill Judith. Put on the damn mask. There isn't much time. Once he's locked up, he's lost. We can catch him at Paul's Yard."

WHAT IS HER MAJESTY'S name, Master Cecil?" says Elizabeth, smiling.

They have built her a platform in the yard of the great old church and draped it with crimson cloth, and someone has painted a Tudor rose on a placard and hung it above her chair. It is the armchair from somebody's dining room, gilded and twined with flowers.

The Summer Queen has just been crowned with a gilt-paper crown. She is a buxom, goggle-eyed girl with the look of a barmaid about her, and the Summer King is an old lad of seventy, if a day. They carry sceptres of gilded lath wound with blush roses.

"Kneel to your Sovereign Lady," murmurs Cecil pleasantly, making a sort of bow. He seems little the worse for his morning's swim in the Thames. Like Elizabeth, he wears black velvet. A white lace ruff and bands. A heavy gold chain of office, set tastefully with rubies.

The real queen is enjoying herself, smiling, laughing, waving to the people. She is still handsome in her sixtieth year, dressed in a rich black silk-velvet iced with silver lace and pearls, her ladies ranged behind her in pale, unremarkable dresses. They are almost all young girls now. Kat Ashley is long gone, and blind Blanche Parry. Good Mary Sidney, who suffered the scars of smallpox to watch by the queen's sickbed.

With deft politeness edged with just the right benevolent condescension, Cecil motions the Royal Couple to kneel at Elizabeth's feet. He smiles. "Our Summer Queen is lately married, my lady. Even this morning, I believe."

"Yes, yes, but her name, sir?"

"I'm called Dorcas, Your Majesty," says the girl. She is missing a tooth and her breath is far from sweet.

But Elizabeth pats her and smiles. "I observe you answer for yourself, my lady," she says, laughing. "You do not give precedence to any man to speak for you, and that is the mark of a true queen, indeed. But I doubt it will make you much prized as a wife!"

A roar of applause and laughter. Cecil smiles and mutters some remark and Elizabeth gives him her hand.

In our animal masks, Nick and I thread our way through the crowd, attaching ourselves where we can to groups of mummers. There is music, constant chatter, laughter, the rumble of barrels being hauled into a bride-ale pavilion just inside the Yard.

"What?" cries Elizabeth. "Have we no maypole for dancing?" Holding up her heavy skirts, she steps down from the platform. "Come, my lord king. You and your queen must dance a country measure for your loyal subjects. Gentlemen! Let us have 'Sellenger's Round.'"

The Summer King and Queen and their court form a circle for the roundel, and the musicians strike up merrily.

✦

A T THE FIRST chord, I suddenly see Gabriel, as though the music has conjured him. He is tied by four ropes to the saddles of four horsemen of the Queen's Guard, moving slowly down Fleet Street. He cannot keep pace with them and when he falls he is dragged between them, rolled back and forth on the sharp-edged cobbles. Every time, every time, he fights his way up again, pulling with his good arm. Four Yeomen run behind him, their pikes smashing down in perfect rhythm at every third step. He doesn't seem to notice or care.

When they reach the gates of the Yard, the dreaded crash of the halberds drowns the music. The frightened crowd parts and Nick's hand clamps my arm.

"What is this?" Elizabeth peers through the muddle of people. "Bid the Guard halt!"

A messenger in a cloak of Tudor green runs past us and the horsemen stop. The Yeomen set their pikes at heel.

"What is this intrusion, Pygmy? What fellow is this? I seem to know him. Is he under our warrant?"

"Indeed, so, ma'am. He is a notable traitor."

"And where is this warrant? Have we signed such a document? I remember being presented with no traitor's warrant. Only a paper concerning the weight of barley flour and another regarding the patent on starch." She smiles sweetly. "But perhaps I did not rightly attend. And then, your hands are so swift and so clever with those papers of yours."

Robert Cecil bows low. "I thank Your Majesty."

The sweet voice darkens, rises, swells. "They are *my papers,* little man. They are *not* yours. Do you think the queen knows not what she signs, when she signs away a life? Do you think she pays not the cost of it?"

"Certainly not, madam. That is, certainly Your Majesty is aware— But our agents—"

"Little man, little man. I know more than you imagine. I know of certain cellars in which private torture is a game of greater delight than the baiting of a bear. I know of little men found dripping wet on foggy riverbanks. Oh, I know of such deeds, such strivings in secret, as cost decent folk too dear for compass. A queen, you see, may have spies of her own. For such little good as they do her."

She leaves him speechless and ashen-faced, and walks quickly through the crowd to where the Yeomen are waiting with Gabriel. "Dismiss these guards," she says. "Take off these bounds and bring the fellow into this pavilion here. You, Master Lion, and Sir Owl, you—go fetch dressings. Well, make haste, then. The man bleeds."

I NSIDE THE BRIDE-ALE tent, Nick and I tend Gabriel's shoulder and the queen does not dismiss us when we finish. "Have some ale, my good fellows," she says. "A bridegroom is long stayed-for, I fear. But he will not come today."

She sits on a rough bench, her nervous fingers stroking the velvet of her skirt. Her voice is quieter now, the anger drained away. But the amber eyes are sunk deep in their sockets and the face-paint only thickens the lines about her mouth.

"Well, Ragpicker," she says. "You saved our life once. Cecil tells me you come now to take it."

"No. No."

"This is a miserly reply. Come, something more."

He looks up. Smiles a ghost of his old smile. "How's the tooth? Did you ever try the remedy?"

"Oh, I'm a good housewife, I never waste a decent cure. I keep a book of receipts for them." She takes stock of him. "You're a ruin, Ragpicker."

"Proof of innocence. Couldn't assassinate a fly."

"What a fellow! You offer no flattery. You don't even call me Your Majesty."

"See right through it, wouldn't you? Despise me for trying, and so you should. I could start saying Your Majesty, actually, if you like it. Must get tiresome, though. Doesn't anybody call you by name?"

"There was a man once who accorded me that—privilege. But he is long dead. Besides, old women are strangers in the world. We go nameless, if only to be safe. What a strange creature you are. To make me talk so open." She looks down at her fingers, alabaster white against the black dress. "My mother had six fingers on one hand. People said it was a sign of her witchery. There, you see! I never speak of her, but you pull her from me. I think you have some witch-power of your own."

His dirty, battered face is wide open, his mind reaching into her. What does he see? A child in the arms of her condemned mother, held up to the palace window where her father is signing the order of execution? A young girl with a prayer book and a secret fire between her legs? Or only what I see through my owl's eyes—an aging woman abandoned by love, left with vanity, flattery, treachery, and orange wigs?

"Go now," she says. "Make your way to the coast and leave England. I will give order of safe conduct, but waste no time and do not come back. My control of these fellows has its limits, and they have grasping arms everywhere. It's all intrigue and plotting these days, and swordfights in the passageways. Young queens may be mastered, so they think, and milked of great fortunes. But old queens are empty dugs. They want to be rid of me now."

His good hand lies open on the table. Hers opposite, a few inches of wilderness between them.

"This cunning fellow would not have spared *your* life," she says suddenly.

"What will you do with him?"

"Watch him. Use him as I can. As I must. It is sometimes expedient to know a man's sins. Besides, there is little that can be proven against him in any court, he's seen to that. My skirts are soiled by his meddlings and I must clean them as best I can. But I cannot shame him openly, I cannot. His father is old and sick and I—still care for him. There are few enough of whom that may be said." She looks up. "Well, go, then. Take your menagerie with you."

Gabriel manages to get to his feet without help. Bends his face to her open hand on the table. Not quite touching. Her fingers very pale, very still.

"You have a talent for unlocking hearts, sir," she says quietly. "Take care you do not leave them to the mercy of thieves."

ONE COLD, WET night less than a week later, Gabriel and I sat huddled on the deck of a smuggler's ship bound for a certain cove on the coast of Brittany.

"Why Brittany?" I said. "What's in Brittany?"

"Good a place as any to go to ground."

Three little fog-bound islands, he said, and some old Druid stories. A pile of prehistoric stones looking out to the westward Half a dozen fishermen and their superstitious wives.

I didn't breathe properly till we'd crossed the Channel and dropped anchor off the Breton mainland. The smugglers lowered a dory full of contraband English beer, Dutch gin, and half a dozen rolls of fine English woollen cloth, and we made for a tiny, tree-covered island in the neck of the bay.

"What's it called?" I said as the dory bumped ashore.

"Don't know. Don't think it's got a name, actually."

A kind of steep stair had been carved into the granite cliff and we began to climb it, feet slipping on the wet rock. At the top, we reached a small clearing. There was a low farmhouse of whitewashed stone, a well-sweep in the yard, and a stable. Beyond were the woods, tendrils of thinning fog drifting between wind-bent pines and oaks. All around, the sea mumbled and hissed. An ancient place. A place that had seen everything and forgiven it.

"Not much to look at," he said. "Thought I might plant us an orchard. You know, like Staple Oaks. The biddy on the other side of the cove says you can't grow fruit here, too much salt in the soil. Daft old bat. Do what I want to."

Inside, the house was dark and cold. I'd been hoping he would lead me to the end of a fairy tale, but it was plain that nobody lived here. He built a fire and lighted some candles, set out a bottle of contraband gin and two wooden cups.

"Place needs brightening up a bit," he said. "Let her do that when she gets here. Likes that sort of thing. Well, women do."

"Mendoza brought you here? After they let you out of prison, I mean?"

"Christ, no. Much as his life was worth. His Moor brought me. Turned up with the women and children a few at a time."

"But not Naia."

The English women were one thing, and Naia and the sprouts were another. They were savages. In our world, in Mendoza's world, too, they were nothing but freaks. Once unprotected, anything might become of them.

"She'll come," he said. "One day the old Moor will lead her up from the cove. Won't be long now."

Deluding himself, I thought. He had paid a high price to come round in a circle. He was stuck again on another small island, hoping for a ship that would never arrive.

"What will you do if she doesn't come? If she never comes?"

"Wait" was all he said.

W E DRANK MOST of that night. Talked only sporadically. Something about him made confession unnecessary, but I told him I wouldn't go back to England, not ever, not even if it was safe.

We slept off the gin for much of the next day, and the following morning I handed him the gold crescent moon earring. "You might need money," I said. "You could sell it."

He looked at it, gleaming there in his palm. Then he turned his hand slightly and let the charm tumble down the stone stairway and into the sea that was breaking on the rocks below. I watched the tiny spark of golden light until it drowned.

"Is there anything you need?" I said. "Can I help you in any way?"

He smiled. "Bring me back a decent Greek copy of Ovid. Funny how Greek stays with you. One thing to thank old Gibbie for."

I didn't plan what I said next. "If Naia does come here, if she tries to become European—you know what happens to them over here, and she won't be the first. They get angry. They mourn themselves empty. And they die."

I hadn't really meant to punish him, but somehow, back on his island, he didn't seem hurt by what I'd said. He smiled at me and embraced me as I stepped aboard the smugglers' boat. His long metamorphosis was finished, and he had come home.

I COULD HAVE CHANGED my mind and gone back to England, lived quietly somewhere. Five men were hanged after that night of searches and raids. Rowland and Harry were among them, and from what I could learn, the others were three of the four leopards. Elizabeth, cleaning her skirts.

But I didn't go back. I drifted from one city and country to another—Greece, Egypt, Italy, Germany. I learned how to bargain like an Arab in the bazaars of Cairo. In the Greek islands, I learned to make love with the subtlety and skill of Odysseus. I went to Poland, then to Prague and Vienna, and then south again, to Naples and Florence and Rome.

At last, unable to hold myself back any longer, I travelled up the coast of France from Lisbon and found my way to the small Breton cove and the tree-covered island, clutching Gabriel's Greek copy of Ovid under my arm.

He had planted two spindly apple trees and a cherry in the dooryard, and built an arbor for grapes. There was a path of gravel and ground shells laid out from the house to the woods, and a cow grazed in a small fenced pasture. A stone oven was being built in the yard.

As I watched, a long-legged boy of thirteen or fourteen with black hair and big dark eyes dashed out of the woods and ran around to the side of the farmhouse. It was late autumn, but midday, and the sun was hot. He stripped off his shirt and I could see between his shoulders the double wavy lines of the Sea clan tattoo.

And then, in the shadowed doorway of the house, the figure of a woman appeared. An open face turned up to the ragged patterns of cloud. A plain gown and bare feet and no kerchief on her fine dark hair. A calm, secret woman neither happy nor unhappy. A woman with skin like brown silk and eyes that could not be evaded.

Not a fairy tale, then, with clowns and a song. Merely the bewildering survival of the personal. The only justice there is.

From the woods a little girl of ten came running, dark hair flying, awkward skirts held up to her bare knees. Kia, tossing her laughter into the air as though it could fly.

Behind her, Gabriel's tall, loose-limbed shape broke suddenly through the darkness of the trees and into the clear light as he must have done on the day when he took off the cage of Europe's bones from Naia's body. When she forgave him the last of his chains.

But just now he was pulling with his good arm a light sledge of cut firewood strewn improbably with flowers—deep blue autumn gentians and russet and green ferns and white laceflowers and crimson asters.

"How's my lovely girl, then?" he called to the child. "Want a flower, my love? Want a ride?"

Author's Notes and Acknowledgments

The historical material surrounding Roanoke is rich in some areas and scanty in others. The names of the colonists and their family groups are real (including the single woman named Margaret Lawrence, who made it more or less inevitable that I would write this book). With a very few exceptions, we do not know their occupations or what brought them to Roanoke, though the rampant poverty and decline of the English middle class at the time is well enough recorded. There was a Gabriel North on the first expedition, and someone listed only as Robert, from whom I made Robert Mowbray, the narrator. The coastal tribes were matrilineal, though no one really knows who succeeded the murdered Wingina. The customs of Native American life at that time are as accurate as I have been able to make them, using John White's paintings and Thomas Hariot's journals and his list of words. Since history doesn't happen in plots, I have had to telescope a number of tribes under the name Secota and use various incidents that occurred between English and Native Americans at several places and times. There was a woman ruling on Croatoan, but Naia is a fictional character, along with all the other Secota except for Wingina.

Assigning the guilt for the loss of the colony is a problem faced as much by historians as by novelists. The remnants of evidence are so few and so worn by time and remote location that a case might be made for the guilt of a number of personages. Walsingham did save Simon Fernando from the gallows and turn him to spying. There were two convicts on board *Lyon* who had been released from Colchester Prison; one of Walsingham's favorite means of recruitment was to promise release if you signed on as a spy. John White's journal of the voyage is full of inexplicable decisions, such as the delayed sailing, the abandonment of the flyboat in enemy waters, the refusal to take aboard farm animals or salt, and a dozen other things that doomed the settlers to dependence on the tribes. Two Irishmen did jump ship in the islands and were found by the Spanish. Lizzie Glane was the common-law wife of one of the men. Spanish ships did move up and down the coast frequently from Florida, which then included what are now Georgia and South Carolina.

After White left the island in the autumn of 1587, there are no other written records of what happened. The English ports were sealed against the Armada, and even if they had not been, Elizabeth could spare neither ships nor experienced sailors to go looking for colonists. The Exchequer was all but bankrupt, and the queen was brought to pawn or sell most of Henry VIII's ceremonial gold and jewels. Her pearl-women actually did take the pearls and jewels off one gown and stitch them onto the other at night. Private sources like Ralegh and Drake provided her with most of the warships that chased the Spanish, and many sailors were pressed who had never been to sea before.

The report of what was found on Roanoke when a supply ship was finally sent in 1590 is baffling, but no more so than the fact that John White—in command again—seemed more concerned with the ruined contents of the trunk he had buried than with the fate of his family. In three days, the "rescue" expedition turned around and sailed home.

There is no evidence that any of the Roanoke women returned to England, nor is there proof they did not. Women in general were taken little account of, especially if they were not rich and had the sense to conform and keep quiet. There were smugglers' boats from France and fishing boats of many countries that plied the Atlantic and sometimes picked up stranded people. There was even one man who claimed to have walked from somewhere on the Gulf Coast to Newfoundland after escaping the Spanish prisons.

The spy networks of Elizabethan England are well documented and in spite of the howls of literary scholars, there seems plenty of evidence that Christopher Marlowe was recruited from Cambridge—like many spies from that day to this—and remained a part-time intelligencer until he was killed. Both Frizer and Pooley, who killed him, were known and dangerous spies.

Robert Cecil may or may not have borne some of the guilt of Roanoke. He was a sly and cagey fellow, raised in the business of spying, and though she gave him power, Elizabeth seems never to have trusted him enough to make him a permanent member of her Privy Council. He turned on Ralegh after years of friendship, and after Ralegh's beheading his papers disappeared just as Walsingham's had, and were found in Cecil's house after Cecil died. He did steal all of Walsingham's private papers on the night of the spymaster's death. As Elizabeth grew old, Cecil ingratiated himself with James of Scotland, who wanted the English throne. What Cecil did to make that happen is not known, but it was under James that he rose to great power and wealth, and was named a marquis. But whatever maneuvering he may have done to make Ralegh's failure more likely, he did *not* send the Armada and close the ports, cause a hurricane to break one of the worst documented droughts in history, nor initiate tribal wars and Native American politics.

What it comes down to is that making a novel based on history requires us to leap beyond fact. It is unlikely that we will ever have conclusive proof of what happened on Roanoke and why. But the province of fiction is possibility, and the prying open of factual boxes. What we *don't* know about Roanoke is still, I think, where the real story lies.

    I should like to acknowledge particularly the invaluable works of the great Roanoke scholar David Beers Quinn, and those of David Stick, Alan Haynes, Carolly Erickson, Alison Weir, Lee Miller, Karen Ordahl Kupperman, Christopher Hibbert, Samuel Eliot Morison, Geoffrey Parker, David Howarth, Keith Thomas, and Michael R. Best. Thanks also to Ann and Charles Wilhite and Gwen Timmons for patience and support, to B. J. Frederiksen for keeping me more or less sane, to Tom Boyle and the staff of the Midland Lutheran College library for ferreting out all those interlibrary loans. To Alex, for babysitters and kitty litter and warm fires on bitter nights. And most especially, thanks to Jane Chelius.

about the author

MARGARET LAWRENCE is the author of *Hearts and Bones*, which was nominated for the Edgar, Agatha, Anthony, and Macavity awards for best novel, and three other novels. She has also written for film and theater.